VOICES

Adapted from a screenplay written by Award-Winning Screenwriter, Jason McCulloch.

J.M. Spratner

Copyright © 2020 Michael Johnson and Jason McCulloch

All rights reserved

The characters and events portrayed in this book are fictitious. Any similarity to real persons, living or dead, is coincidental and not intended by the author.

No part of this book may be reproduced, or stored in a retrieval system, or transmitted in any form or by any means, electronic, mechanical, photocopying, recording, or otherwise, without express written permission of the publisher.

ISBN-13: 9798569209453

Cover design by: Art Painter
Library of Congress Control Number: 2018675309
Printed in the United States of America

CONTENTS

Title Page	1
Copyright	2
Dedication	7
Voices	9
Christmas Morning.	11
Early Morning. December 18.	12
2	16
Morning. December 18.	21
4	28
5	34
6	37
7	45
Afternoon. December 18.	56
9	66
10	77
Evening. December 18.	84
Morning. December 19.	95
13	106
14	112
15	116
Afternoon. December 19.	118
17	121
18	126
19	128

20	136
21	143
22	145
23	149
Evening. December 19	155
25	165
26	168
After Midnight. December 20.	171
28	183
Morning. December 20.	188
30	193
31	198
32	207
33	212
34	217
35	220
36	227
37	236
38	246
After Midnight. December 21.	253
Early Morning. December 21.	258
41	261
Morning. December 23.	266
43	272
44	276
45	281
46	288
47	296

48	303
49	308
After Midnight. December 24.	314
51	316
52	324
53	327
54	331
55	333
56	335
57	336
58	338
Christmas Eve	347
60	352
61	357
62	361
63	363
64	366
After Midnight. Christmas Morning.	371
66	374
New Year's Day	375
Christmas Eve. Sixteen Years Later	376
Acknowledgement	385
Books By This Author	387
Caution! Huge spoilers ahead!	389
And now for something completely different.	391
About The Author	393
About The Author	395

Dedicated to every author who has poured their heart and soul into a novel, somehow managed to complete it, then, warts and all, dared send it out into the universe.

And, of course, to our wives, children, friends, and anyone else who didn't say: "You? Write a novel? Are you nuts?"

VOICES

Adapted from a screenplay written by
Award-Winning Screenwriter, Jason McCulloch.

CHRISTMAS MORNING.

The bulb hanging from a ceiling joist in the backyard shop had steadied; its anemic, yellow glow barely acknowledged by the darkness. He found her in the back corner, hidden among boxes of Christmas decorations. She was seated, shoulders pressed against the wall, knees bent, legs spread so wide he wondered if she had dislocated her hips jumping from the window. She was naked from the waist down, steam from the amniotic fluid rising off the frigid concrete, the air polluted by the coppery smell of blood.

"*NO!*" she cried, her chest heaving—every short, shallow breath freezing as it exited her mouth. She crossed her forearms in front of her swollen belly as if flesh and bone could stop a bullet. Light knifing through a gap between two stacks of boxes spotlighted the space between her legs.

He could see a tiny, protruding head.

Shoot! echoed in his skull, his trembling hand barely able to support the Luger's weight. Her crossed arms mirrored his movements as he moved the gun erratically between her head and belly.

"*Stop!*" she wailed, lips stretched and twisted, sweat-soaked hair clinging to her face, eyes wild with pain and anger and helplessness and fear.

Shoot!

Tears stained his cheeks as his finger reluctantly found the trigger. "Forgive me," he whispered, surrendering. He had no choice. He knew that.

EARLY MORNING. DECEMBER 18.

Seven Days until Christmas.

Despite a third Ambien, Allan Abrams was wide awake. A psychiatrist, he had never written himself a prescription—a slippery slope with an unforgiving rock-hard bottom. But an ongoing feud with the Sandman had him re-evaluating the policy. Too frequently over the last six months, he had performed the same maddening ritual: down an Ambien—stare at the ceiling; down a second Ambien—stare at the ceiling some more; rinse and repeat. And once per month, usually on the seventeenth, he would require a third Ambien.

He turned to his pregnant wife, Clara, asleep beside him, shadows concealing her delicate features. He closed his eyes; her image painted on the backs of his eyelids: silky, olive-colored skin that refused to reveal her age, thin lips, high cheekbones, hazel eyes, and a thread of freckles dotting her jawline like flecks of melted chocolate.

His hand found her belly.

The twins were due in two months.

Two months, he thought, dread hardening his insides. How the hell am I going to make it two more months?

Hiccup, their middle-aged Oreo-colored Shih Tzu, chirped. Puppy dreams. Allan slid his hand between Clara's legs, located Hic in "his" spot, and scratched the top of his head. Hic was their only child. And for fourteen years before

Hic, that role had been played by Zeus—a six-pound, brindle chihuahua with a bigger personality than Liberace.

Three times over those twenty-one years, the promise of a *real* family had ended in misery. First with Michael, their stillborn son, then with one-day-old Khloe, and finally with Isaac, whose heart pumped strong and steady for twenty days, filling him with life and his parents with hope as frail as his brittle bones. When his heart sputtered on day twenty-one, they feigned strength. *He'll be fine*, they reassured themselves and each other. Sixteen minutes after midnight on day twenty-two, those reassurances proved worthless.

Allan knew the prospects for couples who lost a child; excluding false alarms and countless starts and stops along the way, they had lost three. The fact they were still together was a testament to the strength of their love. But like a spent gold mine, only traces of that love remained, sparkling in rare moments when a fleeting ray of sunlight found a shaft and hit the right spot at the perfect angle.

Even the strongest spirit could be robbed of its ability to shine.

Talk of adoption had always ended with Clara suggesting they "Wait and see." Shortly after one such talk, Allan—deep into a bottle of Lagavulin—thought: Screw it. I'll just come home with a baby. Clara hadn't wanted a dog, he had drunkenly reasoned, but holding eight-week-old Zeus had instantly changed her mind. A little deeper into the bottle of sixteen-year-old scotch, he'd laughed at how ridiculous the idea had been. He laughed again when he imagined himself back at the adoption agency, sliding the poorly repackaged but unused child across the agent's desk and saying, "I should have cleared this with my wife first."

Clara shifted positions, the stubble on her leg scraping against his calf. *I'm too fat to shave my legs*, she had groaned hours earlier. He'd laughed, thinking she was joking. She'd cried. Her emotions regularly got the better of her now. And her OBGYN's COVID-related stay-at-home order was not helping her emotional well-being, nor were the "discussions" they would have when she disregarded the order. And constant news reports of escalating political and social unrest provided even more fuel for her unpredictable emotional fire.

The future was not supposed to be a dark and scary place.

He tossed back the covers and padded toward the door. If he couldn't sleep, he may as well pluck away at his unfinished manuscript. Five years and still no ending—not a good one, anyway. Beginnings and endings, he thought. That's all that matters.

As he passed the window, movement in the backyard turned his head. The storm had passed, and an acre of fresh, foot-high snow and a crisp moon were conspiring to cast an eerie blue-white glow. Treetops acknowledged his presence with a gentle, synchronized wave.

An owl, he thought, seeing nothing. His gaze slid past the backyard shop and stopped on the playground. Over the years, he had never found the time to tear it down. Monkey bars, a cyclone slide, and a six-foot climbing wall topped by a fortress from which all manner of attacks (water balloon, snowball, toy gun) could be launched or defended. Two swings hanging from the main crossbeam swayed, nudged by a breeze on its way south for the winter. The movement sent his mind forward five years to a perfect summer day, the twins shrieking as they scrambled off the swings, Frankenstein's monster catching then tickling them until one couldn't breathe and the other cried: "Daddy...STOP! I'm gonna...pee!"

Daddy, he thought. He let the word settle in his mind. Held it there. Caressed it.

He turned to Clara. In a few hours, she would be at her monthly ultrasound appointment. Most expectant parents couldn't wait for ultrasound appointments, anxious to slip copies of the sonogram into Christmas cards, or use them in new and imaginative gender-revealing ways.

Not Allan.

He had developed an irrational fear of ultrasounds. After an appointment ended with good news, he would hear a rumble of distant thunder: *What if?* The storm would build, its thunderheads growing larger and darker and its winds stronger and stronger. Then, the night before the next appointment, the storm would spawn an F5 tornado of *What ifs?* In a recurring vision, a doctor would hand him a blank sonogram, the twins gone. Not dead, gone. Never there. A cruel hoax.

He watched Clara's chest rise and fall, each breath filling three sets of lungs. Don't we deserve a family? he asked, quite certain no one would answer. Have we not suffered enough?

By Christmas, a single bullet fired from Allan's Luger would answer both questions.

2

Precinct Sergeant Al Murphy ignored the sound. On a typical night, the distinct *bang! bang!* would have snapped him to attention, sent his hand to his holstered weapon, and his eyes in every direction at once. But tonight, he remained seated at his desk with his eyes closed, his chin on his chest, and his forearms balanced atop his stomach.

Bang! Bang!

Not my job, Murphy thought, refusing to budge. He was beyond exhausted. He had spent most of the graveyard shift crime-fighting (crime *processing,* if truth mattered), micromanaging power outages caused by the snowstorm, and negotiating with a belligerent, malfunctioning escape alarm. He was done. The suddenly unsecured lobby door and howling wind would have to settle their differences *sans* police intervention.

BANG! BANG!

"Murph!" a distant, annoyed voice growled.

"Jesus H. Christ." Murphy snapped his eyes open and surveyed the front end of Witten, Colorado's downtown police station. About a dozen or so sleepy-eyed night-shifters were ignoring the disgruntled lobby door. Some, he knew, simply did not care, while others were busy interrogating gangs of Angry Birds or crushing contraband dropped by fleeing candy traffickers. Lazy bastards, he thought, disgusted by the lack of initiative. He stood and hiked his khaki pants up several inches. But even they refused to cut him a break, sliding back to their preferred position almost immediately. An unwrapped meatball sub sat deathly still on Murphy's desk—the hot, late dinner turned cold, early breakfast hoping not to be noticed. "Don't you move," he warned the sandwich.

At the lobby door, he extended a hand only to squeak out a mouse-sized *"Eeek!"* and slap his hand back against his chest as a walking cane crashed against the open door. A sympathy shiver rippled through every one of Murphy's 300-plus pounds when a frail old man, swamped by a long-sleeved white shirt and unwashed jeans, stepped inside.

Murphy pulled the door closed. "It's twenty below with the wind chill." Assuming the old man had come for a reason and would follow, he headed to his desk.

In his seat, Murphy tried to ignore a niggling voice. The kind of niggler that urged people to give up bus seats to blue-haired old ladies and jump into swollen rivers to save drowning puppies. He nodded reluctantly in the direction of his meatball with marinara sub. "Hungry?" The skeletal old man ignored the offer and completed a deliberate sweep of the front end as though searching for someone. "Are you cold?" Murphy added, suppressing his enthusiasm that the sandwich issue had been settled in his favor. "Our Goodwill bin might have one or two ugly Christmas sweaters."

The old man, devoid of expression, hooked his cane over the chair's arm. "I am here to turn myself in."

To be held in high esteem, Witten PD officers required talent in at least one of three disciplines: police work, the department's never-ending game of *Insult Your Fellow Officer,* or practical jokes—the latter having reached Olympic event status eight years earlier when a janitor crafted a "gold medal" from melted bullet casings. Every year since, five duly elected and unimpeachable judges determined the year's best "gotcha." This year, courtesy of a fake heart attack, Murphy became the station's only two-time champion. His gold-medal performance featured Oscar-worthy acting (flailing on the floor like a landed fish) and state-of-the-art special effects (foaming at the mouth thanks to an Alka-Seltzer tablet and a mouthful of

Sprite).

A bored cop's mind was a dangerous weapon.

"Turn yourself in for what?" Murphy asked skeptically.

"I killed Sedrick Palette."

Mother fuckers, Murphy thought, his gaze sharpening and sliding to his night-shifters, this time searching for a group of knee-slapping, gut-clutching jokers. "Ha! We *gotcha* good, Murph!"

He spotted no such group, but Murphy knew his status as a two-time champion made him a target. And as the old man posed no threat to a serial killer on death row, he decided to play along and look for an opportunity to turn the tables on his fellow officers.

"Sedrick liked little girls. Did you kill him because he had a little fun with your granddaughter?"

The question floated past the dead-eyed old man. When Murphy noticed his hearing aid, he held back a chuckle. Was the old man silent because he hadn't heard the question or because he was waiting for an unseen interpreter to translate English into Crazy Old Man?

"In 1938," the old man said, "representatives from the United States and thirty-one other nations gathered to discuss changes to their immigration policies. All expressed sympathy for the plight of German Jews but refused to open their borders to Jewish refugees."

Okaaay, Murphy thought. Entirely unqualified to play a psychiatrist, he decided he had no choice. If instead of part of a prank, the old man was actually mentally ill and Murphy let him leave, he would die from exposure within an hour.

"Those were horrible times," he consoled. "Thankfully, we learned our lesson."

"We ignored the signs then," the old man stated cryptically. "And we are ignoring them now."

Murphy watched sadness penetrate all seven layers of the

old man's skin. Wanting to help him but with no idea as to the correct psychological response, he went with the logical one. "What signs?"

The old man completed another scan of the front end, then asked, "Where is your mask?"

Despite pushing paper for seven years, Murphy had retained enough of his beat cop instincts to recognize the old man's sly tone. "The virus is one of the signs we are missing?"

"The signs were clear then, and they are clear now. What is coming can be stopped."

Murphy's heart broke a little. Since the virus began killing people and clashes between protesters from the left and right began to escalate, lost and vulnerable street people had started wandering into the precinct claiming the world was about to end. He was no shrink, but he knew people needed explanations for things they did not understand. It was not that long ago that people believed tornadoes and volcanoes were the work of angry gods. Today, some believed the world's greatest country ripping itself apart was the start of End Times. By the look of the old man, he likely spent his days on street corners preaching that very thing. Murphy would never admit it, but, at times, he felt just as confused and scared.

Murphy swallowed the lump that had formed in his throat. "With everything going on in the world, I'm like you; I wish we had a silver bullet that could make everything better." He checked his watch. "How about I fix you a bed in one of our guest rooms. In the morning, I'll arrange for you to talk to —"

"You *need* to arrest me," the old man insisted, his eyes wide, and his wrinkled skin stretched tighter by hard edges not present moments earlier.

Murphy tried to console the man with a broad smile. "I'm not going to arrest you for killing Sedrick Palette. I might give you a medal, though. He was a real piece—"

"*Arrest me*, goddamnit!"

Every set of previously sleepy eyes were now locked on Murphy and his guest. Murphy stood and extended a scolding finger, his compassion and patience wearing thin. "Look, I realize—"

On his feet in a flash, the old man locked a hand around Murphy's wrist and yanked him forward. Unable to break the surprisingly tight grip, Murphy slapped his free hand onto his desk to brace himself. As he did, he caught movement in his peripheral vision. The blur of action meant help was on the way, or his fellow officers were scrambling like paparazzi for the best cell phone camera angle from which to shoot the soon-to-be-viral YouTube video: Obese Cop *Wrastles* Grandfather for Meatball Sub!

Murphy grunted, his wrist already aching. "You're heading down a road you don't—"

He yowled, intense pain sending his huge heart into overdrive and his eyes to his hand. The old man had driven the tip of a pair of scissors through the flesh between Murphy's thumb and index finger, *nailing* his hand to the desk. A flood of adrenaline gave Murphy the strength to break free from the old man's grip and lunge for the scissors. The old man intercepted Murphy's stretching hand and, using his momentum against him, pulled Murphy across the desk, the scissors tearing his flesh as he slid over the desk and crashed hard to the floor. By the time Murphy was back on his feet, officers had cuffed the old man.

He clutched his wounded hand against his chest—his tan-colored uniform stained with blood and the guts of his meatball and marinara sandwich. He studied the old man, wondering: What the hell just happened?

The suddenly calm and compliant old man's expression lightened, and he raised his hands in front of his chest and jiggled the handcuffs. "That wasn't so difficult, now was it?"

MORNING. DECEMBER 18.

If you don't acknowledge it, it doesn't exist. Detective Liam Huffy repeated the thought often. Despite the silent mantra, December eighteenth remained hard-wired into his internal clock, a permanent entry with 365 all-day reminders and no snooze button to slap, batteries to remove, or cord to rip from the outlet. December eighteenth was his Great Red Spot; its blustery rage felt every hour of every day. On good days, he buried it in a part of his mind he knew little about —a part he feared and cherished. On bad days, and there were many, it clung to him like a shadow, bombarding his senses with sounds, smells, and images. Pallid, dead skin against cold, stainless steel; chemical preservatives stinging his eyes and nose; and worst of all, silence. The absence of sound that accompanied death was unbearable.

Less than six hours into this December eighteenth, Huffy's sleepless night had been interrupted by his buzzing cell phone —an electronic summons from his boss that read: Bachman ASAP. Sedrick Palette. Early Christmas present.

His day significantly worsened when he arrived and met Bachman Correctional Facility's warden—a balding pug of a man wearing an off-the-rack suit and infested with unearned arrogance. As the warden droned on about the do's and don'ts of "my" prison—*do's* that included wearing a mask, *don'ts* that included refusing to wear a mask—Huffy pined for the Glock he had surrendered to security upon arrival.

Stuck behind an enormous DOC officer whose walking speed topped out at *mosey,* Huffy was rummaging through a recently acquired mental toolbox. The toolbox was one of three birthday gifts he had received in May, the other two being a red-bowed bottle of scotch and a heart attack. The scotch was from the father of a thirteen-year-old rape victim whose rapist Huffy put away for twenty-seven years. The father had spared no expense. The scotch was the *good stuff;* the kind people savored on special occasions like birthdays on which they did *not* have heart attacks. The heart attack was a gift because it had tapped the soon-to-be-divorced father of none on the shoulder and whispered, "Wait 'til you get a load of my big brother." Enough of a scare for him to seek help in his never-ending battle with anger and stress. Two and a half sessions with a mental health professional later, he had his mental toolbox.

He shifted his gaze from the heels of his slow-moving escort to the prison cells on his right, a number stenciled onto the white concrete beside each eight-inch thick, steel door. Having settled on the tool of distraction, he started counting at *C-14*—an unusual vacancy sign popping into his head.

GUARDED/GATED, RENTFREE COMMUNITY. RAPISTS/MURDERERS/PEDO PHILES WELCOME. SORRY, NO PETS.

Huffy pulled a pen and small notepad from the breast pocket of his wrinkled, ash-gray suit and entered cell *C-56*, where Witten's diminutive Medical Examiner, Dan Button, was at work beside the cell's recently deceased tenant. Sedrick Palette was naked, coated in dried blood, and stuffed headfirst into the stainless-steel toilet. "Nice of you to stop by Horatio." The half-moon lines around Button's eyes gave away the grin beneath his blue medical mask.

During an eight-year back and forth that had covered an array of insults from physical size to who was losing hair faster, the CSI Miami character comparison had become Button's go-to dig. Huffy thought it absurd but preferred it to others he had heard. "You look like a stop sign draped in a wrinkled, gray suit," his ex-partner-turned-boss had once claimed. Huffy considered neither comparison accurate. Like most men, he'd snapped a mental image of himself during his physical prime and never bothered to update the photo. Time, stress, gravity, and a premature battle with Alopecia areata could kiss his ass; he would *always* be a six-foot-six, emerald-eyed, abrasively handsome Adonis with a head of *thick* red hair.

Button lowered his mask and motioned at the crinkled rectangle of polypropylene tucked under Huffy's chin. "Let me guess, that's the same mask I gave you in July."

A sarcastic grin. "I have it on good authority that excessive cocaine use protects against COVID, so…"

"Less than twenty thousand people die each year from HIV/AIDS," Button stated, grabbing a box of disposable masks off the top of his crime scene kit. "People go to jail for exposing someone to HIV." He shook his head and slapped a handful of masks into Huffy's hand. "If these protected against cancer, we'd never see anyone's face again." Huffy, his grin widening ever so slightly, stuffed the masks into his pants pocket as Button turned to Palette. "Over thirty slash wounds and a severed carotid artery." He aimed a finger at the toilet's base. "And *that* my lanky anti-masker might look like a Weight Watchers' portion of sausage and tortellini in congealed tomato sauce, but it's a chunk of our boy's tongue and both of his ears." Perhaps feeling a twinge of sympathy pain, he tugged at an earlobe. "On the lighter side of the news, his testicles are missing."

Huffy continued making notes. "Those'll look nasty on a milk carton."

"Best I can tell, TOD is between 3:00 a.m. and 4:03 a.m. If you need that narrowed, call me tonight."

"COD?"

A sigh. "For now, I'll go with most of his blood being outside his body." Button slipped on his mask. "He was a few hours from execution; why bother?"

Huffy shrugged a *Don't care,* said, "One less steaming pile of shit in the world," and pointed to a small straight razor on the floor beside Palette's hand. "Maybe the guilt was too much."

"Suicide by micro-razor?" Button laughed. "That would have taken balls."

The sound of hard-soled shoes clopping on concrete turned Huffy's head. He watched the warden march past the open door, slipped on his mask, and exited the cell. His escort and the warden were outside cell C-58—a location chosen, he assumed, to avoid the unpleasant odor escaping from cell C-56. Wait twelve hours, he thought, the smell of decayed victim's bodies rushing back like memories from a regrettable night with tequila.

"You found him?" Huffy asked his DOC escort.

"Yes," the large, Mexican officer answered.

"At 4:03 a.m.?"

"Yes."

"Do you normally come here at 4:03 a.m.?"

A head shake.

"What changed?"

The officer hooked his meaty thumbs over his belt. "After the power went out, I heard some fussin' and—"

"Fussing?"

"Talkin'."

"Screaming?"

A head shake. "Just talkin'."

"Then what?"

"Power came back on, and I checked each cell." A head-tilt toward cell 56. "Found that."

"What caused the outage?"

"The storm caused outages all over the city," the warden said, somehow managing to make a simple statement of fact sound pompous. "We had one. It only affected C Block. As of now, we are unsure of the cause."

"A tad convenient, no?"

The warden clasped his hands behind his back, his medicine-ball belly testing the strength of both straining buttons on his black suit jacket. "When one runs a zoo, it is poor design for the lion cages to open because of a power failure in the gazelle paddock."

Well, snooty-fucking-snoot to you, too, Huffy thought. I would rather be home not sleeping than pretending to give a shit about who carved up a pedophile while your guards jerked each other off in the guard station. Prick.

Huffy asked more questions and added more notes whenever he felt the information was relevant.

```
TOD3-4:03a.m.CODTBDlikely blood loss. Tongue/ears/balls cut offSending message? Storm caused outages all over. Only one hereC Block. Unsure of cause. Backup power failed to kick in. Warden looking into why. Cell doors remained locked during outage. Every staff member/cell/inmate searched  no bloody clothes.
```

"Why the delay in giving us access to Palette's cell?" Huffy asked the warden, who was clearly tired of answering questions. A fact that only made Huffy more eager to ask them.

"Even without COVID protocols," the warden said, "moving sixty-three dangerous inmates is a time-consuming endeavor."

"Why not move the adjacent inmates and let us into Palette's cell while you moved everyone else?"

"Without knowing what caused the outage or why the back-up system failed, it would have been unwise to allow your people onto C Block with sixty-three of our most dangerous inmates."

"But you told me the cell doors remained locked the entire time." Noticing contradictions was one of Huffy's finely-tuned investigative skills. Contradictions, he liked to say, were cracks in need of a jackhammer.

"We have no reason to believe the cell doors were unlocked," the warden said, each word sharper than the last.

Huffy noted the contradiction while asking, "Is it possible the back-up system didn't kick in because someone *turned* the power off?"

The warden scowled, offended. "The back-up system is designed to work *regardless* of why the power goes out. And as only my staff have the knowledge and access required to turn C-Block's power off, I assure you, the storm caused the outage."

Huffy read a note out loud. "Storm caused outages all over. Only one here. C Block. Unsure of cause." He watched the warden's face morph from corpse white to *How-Dare-You* red, then (perhaps after digging into a mental toolbox of his own) ease into a blotchy mix of both. His day getting better by the second, Huffy was now grateful for his wrinkled mask. Not because he feared COVID, but because it hid his wide grin.

"Detective, do you not find it odd for someone to kill Palette the morning of his execution?"

Most criminals weren't the brightest bulbs on even the dimmest Christmas tree, so Huffy never considered *Why would I do something so stupid?* exculpatory. "I guess *odd* is a subjective term," he answered.

Despite the top of his comb-over falling several inches below Huffy's broad shoulders, the warden managed to look down on him. "Sedrick Palette was a coward and took a coward's way out. If—"

"You think he cut off his ears and tongue, slashed himself more than thirty times, then severed his carotid artery?" Before the warden could answer, Huffy added, "Isn't cutting off someone's tongue symbolic in places like *your* prison?"

"Inmates are resourceful," the warden responded, "particularly when it comes to importing all-manner of contraband. With the right drug, I am sure Palette could have done *all* of that while tap dancing and singing God Bless America."

Huffy pocketed his pad and pen. "Before I leave, I'll need the contact information for every on- and off-duty guard and a copy of your surveillance footage from six last night until I arrived."

The warden retrieved a folded sheet of paper and flash drive from his breast pocket and handed both to Huffy. "The flash drive contains the guard roster and Palette's file. The paper is a list of his recent visitors." Pocketing the flash drive, Huffy scanned the paper as the warden continued. "We are a private facility, detective, and a third party, Triton Security, handles our electronic surveillance." A grin too small to register. "But I will be sure to pass on your request."

Huffy looked up from the paper. "Allan Abrams met with Palette last night?"

A nod. "The log shows he was Palette's last visitor."

"Why was he here?"

"You will have to ask him."

Curious why Allan Abrams would meet with an inmate hours before his scheduled execution, Huffy watched the warden stroll toward the guard station until Button called out from cell 56. "Hey, Huff. Come look what I found."

4

The muscular interrogator slid both toaster-sized hands over his shiny scalp. "You expect me to believe that bullshit?"

Allan Abrams, his wiry six-foot frame slumped in a chair on the opposite side of the table, was not intimidated by the bluster. In fact, the entire interrogation had only proved how new the "interrogator" was to the game. Allan decided to have some fun. He ran a mocking, latex-gloved hand through his full head of thick, dark hair and slid his eyes up the bald interrogator's white T-shirt to his denim-blue eyes. "Believe whatever you want, *Mr. Clean.* Everything I told you is true."

The frustrated interrogator took his seat. "Your story sounds like the plot from a Stephen King novel." Unmoved, Allan thumbed over the initials carved into the table. Who is A.R.J? he wondered. Murderer? Car thief? Tax evader? Cheated on his SAT? "You know Colorado has the death penalty, right?" the interrogator added.

Hearing that, Allan glanced at the nearby tripod-mounted video camera and smirked at those he knew were watching.

"Wait," the interrogator yelped, flashing both palms. "I get it now. Instead of the needle, you want a suite at Rodin Psychiatric Hospital where a shrink can dig inside that freak show head of yours and figure out how to stop the next Bundy or Dahmer...or Donald—"

Allan lunged forward, his hands stretching across the table, reaching for the interrogator's throat. The interrogator instinctively lurched backward, his folding chair rearing up onto its hindquarters. Allan watched in stunned horror as the behemoth's face flushed, his eyes bulged, and his massive arms flailed like a wounded bird trying to fly. When the chair collapsed under the interrogator's immense weight, an eruption of laughter ended the tension.

Allan, standing over his red-faced cadet, offered his hand. "Not what I had planned. Sorry, J.J.."

Witten PD cadet Jimmy Johnson pulled himself to his feet and smiled sheepishly. "No worries, Doc."

Tormenting one's fellow officers was a subject in which none of Allan's cadets ever required training, so *Mr. Clean* did not make it back to his seat unscathed.

The mock interrogation room restored to its natural state, Allan used a remote to click off the video camera and projection screen at the front of the auditorium-style lecture hall. "I'll delete that recording before J.J. files his lawsuit." A rumble of laughter followed him to the center of the room, where he grabbed his black-framed reading glasses off the podium, slipped them on, and warned, "Don't laugh too hard." He crossed his arms across his chest. "Law enforcement is a noble calling, but it is also under fire. Nowadays, *little* brother is always watching, so you need to assume someone is recording your every word and action. That said, I know you are all good people and will be good police officers." Sounding a lot like a college football coach at half-time, he added, "What do you need to be?"

"Guardians, not warriors," his twenty-three physically-distanced cadets chanted. Allan smiled half-heartedly. Not long ago, his claim that "You are all good people" would not have been true.

Thirty-six applicants had qualified for this training class, and before the horrific murder of George Floyd, thirty-six cadets would be here now. But a revamped screening program had reduced the class size by thirteen. The recruiting department had rejected two would-be cadets because they had links to a white supremacist organization and the remaining eleven for reasons including inappropriate social media posts. Common themes among those posts were: "Floyd shouldn't have resisted!" "Floyd got what he deserved!" One person going as far as: "If I were the arresting officer, it wouldn't have taken nine minutes!"

He had met with each of the rejected cadets and tried to educate them, to open their eyes to truths that should have been obvious. He had asked if their opinion would be different if *their* brother or father or best friend had been choked to death over *allegedly* passing a counterfeit twenty-dollar bill? And what if George Floyd had received that counterfeit twenty-dollar bill as change for a *real* fifty-dollar bill he'd used to buy gas? He wasn't sure he'd changed any minds.

Since revamping the screening process six months ago, the city had disqualified nineteen applicants over two training classes. Allan had been training Witten's police officers for fifteen years; he shuddered every time he wondered how many lions he had inadvertently sent out to guard the lambs.

He tucked his N-95 mask under his chin and stuffed his latex-gloved hands into the front pockets of his Lucky brand jeans. Securing his hyperactive limbs while he lectured had become as automatic as breathing ever since a cadet's funny but painful *Wacky Waving Inflatable Tube Man* joke.

"Other than it is far too early to be here doing mock interrogations," he said. "What did we learn?"

"J.J. doesn't know Colorado abolished the death penalty," someone called out. After some laughter, someone else said, "Expect the unexpected."

Allan nodded. "I was having fun with J.J. to try and illustrate that point, but—"

He waited for a burst of jeering directed at J.J. to subside.

"But, yes. No matter the circumstances, criminals are unpredictable, and you—"

The sound of an opening door turned all heads. Allan and his cadets watched Detective Liam Huffy enter through a door at the top of the lecture hall. Despite his red hair being visibly thinner and cut military-short, Allan immediately recognized his old cadet.

Although Huffy's first name had momentarily escaped him, Allan remembered him as a bright-eyed recruit with a great outlook, an even better sense of humor, and highly intelligent, making detective two years faster than anyone before or since.

Allan had no way to properly prepare his cadets for what they would experience on the job. For fifteen years, he had encouraged them to seek him should they need to. Many did; the first few years on the job were often difficult. Huffy had stayed in touch for about a year, disguising informal counseling sessions as beer and wing night at a local cop bar, The Blind Pig. In the years since, their paths had rarely crossed. When they did, the interaction generally consisted of a friendly nod or wave and a "Hey."

"Where did J.J. blow it?" Allan asked, still trying to remember Huffy's first name. Ian? he wondered.

"You were delusional," a female cadet correctly answered. "I think your wink-wink-nudge-nudge look into the camera was your way of letting us know J.J. had fucked up."

More laughs.

"Good catch, Maddy. And how did J.J. *mess* up?"

"He shouldn't have tried to scare you or attack your story," Maddy continued. "A delusional individual is not lying or making things up, so trying to *scare* them into telling the truth or challenging their story won't work. You would have more luck convincing the Pope there is no God."

"Bingo," he said over a bit of laughter. "And—"

"I thought you were faking," J.J. called out.

Allan smiled and watched Huffy start down the stairs.

"Can a person fake mental illness?" someone asked.

"It depends on the person, the illness, and who they are trying to fool." Out of habit, not necessity, he checked his watch and resuscitated its temperamental second hand with a tapping finger. The money he had spent keeping the ten-dollar watch functional could have put him in a Rolex. "But as a general rule, no."

"I can spot crazy a mile away," J.J. bellowed.

He eyed J.J.—as close to a glare as he ever came with one of his cadets. "As I have told all of you many times, a distorted reality is still a reality. A street corner preacher warning about Armageddon believes he knows something we don't. *Crazy* is an ugly, meaningless word; *complicated* is more accurate."

Huffy was now striding toward the podium, oblivious to the fact Allan was teaching a class. Curious why Huffy had come, Allan decided to wrap early and dismissed the class.

"Doc." Huffy extended his hand.

"Hello again." Allan slipped on his N-95 mask and offered Huffy a COVID fist-bump. Huffy eyed the gloved fist, his face bent into a *Seriously?* look Allan had grown accustomed to. Since the second wave hit hard in the fall, masks had become more common, as had fist and elbow bumps. But not many people wore latex gloves.

Huffy reluctantly obliged the fist bump and eyed Allan's watch. "Still can't afford a Casio?"

He wasn't surprised by Huffy's recall power. He was a brilliant cadet, and fourteen years on the job would only have sharpened his mind.

"It has been a while," he replied, ignoring the jab.

"Two years ago. City Christmas party."

A beat.

"*Right,*" Allan drawled, wondering which was more obvious, his clueless stare or his *I have no idea what you are talking about* tone.

A cadet joined them.

"Hey, Maddy," Allan said. Maddy said hello, nodded at Huffy, and he at her. Both turned to Allan. A few awkward seconds ticked away. By her expression, Maddy was waiting for an introduction, while Huffy's sly look seemed to indicate he knew Allan had forgotten his name and was happy to let his old professor squirm.

"Maddy," Allan finally said, deciding to trust his memory. "This is Ian Huffy. He is a detective with the SIU."

"Special Investigative Unit," Maddy said, extending a hand. "Nice."

Huffy shook her hand while glancing slyly at Allan. "*Liam.*"

Allan cringed playfully.

Huffy winked at Maddy. "I've called him worse."

Allan chuckled, and, reacting to Maddy's inquisitive expression, made a "so-so" hand gesture. "I used to be a *tad* animated when I lectured. Liam cured me by comparing me to a Wacky Waving Inflatable Tube Man."

They all laughed and chatted until Maddy wished them a Merry Christmas and left.

"So," Allan grabbed his briefcase off a shelf inside the podium, "what brings you back to class?"

Huffy lifted the red file folder. "I need to ask you a few questions about Sedrick—"

"Sorry." Allan checked his buzzing phone and was instantly concerned. Why is Clara calling me? She should be at her ultrasound appointment.

An irrational fear sent his heart into his throat.

5

Having melted the shadows cast by the Rocky Mountain Foothills, the waking sun had started spotlighting Witten's vast natural beauty; if God ever needed a postcard, Witten would do nicely. But even the purest ray of sunlight could not alter the nature of what it illuminated.

A mile beyond the city's western boundary, an abandoned church—its stained-glass only a memory, and its steeple bowed slightly as if in prayer—stood meekly against the sharpening horizon. DaMarcus Kennedy despised churches, almost as much as their keepers. Some were merely false prophets using hollow words to feed empty souls and fill bottomless collection plates. But others were sheep-skinned wolves inflicting burdens far greater than those they eased.

Kennedy despised churches. But this visit was business.

At a rear entrance, Kennedy slipped past the rusted, deformed door clinging to the frame with a single, twisted hinge. The crisp morning air turned heavy and damp as he passed through a long corridor under the church—the darkness interrupted by random dust-filled rays of sunlight that seemed to appear from nowhere. In what was once the church's vestibule, he stopped—a man had just cried out. Howled, really. Begging. Spiritless. He knew the voice was that of his close friend, Mark Cooke.

Kennedy eased into the nave. His black skin, Royal blue overcoat, and the low light making him more shadow than man. He stayed tight to the wall, gliding silently past dozens of toppled and broken cob-webbed pews.

Cooke was at the front of the church, naked and slumped in a chair, his wrists bound behind his back, his ankles secured with bulky chain-gang-style restraints. His captors were Chris Tam—a stocky, heavily tattooed Vietnamese man—and Benny Carpenter—a linebacker-sized concrete block with a buzz cut mohawk. Tam was standing behind Cooke, a hand on each of his shoulders. Carpenter, on a knee in front of Cooke, had a forged-steel sledgehammer held next to his ear.

"This won't hurt a bit, Mark." Carpenter's enthusiastic grin was visible despite the low light. "It'll hurt *a lot.*" He brought the handheld sledgehammer down, the powerful strike flattening several of Cooke's toes against the floor. Cooke's cries rose sharply but faded quickly. His mind and body were shutting down. They had been at this for a while.

Kennedy emerged from the shadows roughly ten feet from the three men. Carpenter saw him first, Tam a half-second later. Tam did not move, but Carpenter rose to his feet, the muscles in his massive forearm popping and rolling as he tightened his grip on the sledgehammer. Kennedy eyed Carpenter, nodded at Tam, and pulled a cell phone from his overcoat pocket. He dropped to a knee in front of Cooke and lifted his head with a fistful of blood-soaked hair. Cooke tried to speak, but the damage to his face and jaw made his words inaudible. Blood formed a bubble in one of his nostrils and popped.

"We all make mistakes, Mark." Kennedy released his handful of hair and watched Cooke's pendulous head flop back to his chest. "And forgiveness is in my nature." He stood and started to record events with his cell phone. "But an eight-year-old kid?" He shook his head. "Even I have my limits, brother."

Before melting December's burner phone and replacing it with January's, Kennedy would download the video, mask all voices, faces, and identifying features—except for Cooke's—and upload the short film to the Dark Web. Those who mattered would recognize the stars of the poorly lit documentary. More importantly, they would know who wrote, directed, and produced it. Memorializing the final moments of men like Mark Cooke served as rare but vital reminders that in Kennedy's band of merry men, the boss's loyalty and friendship were conditional.

Using a series of connected chains and pulleys, Carpenter raised Cooke by his ankle restraints as Tam maneuvered a large metal drum into place. Carpenter lowered Cooke until his head and shoulders were inside the drum. Tam, repeatedly dipping a paintbrush into a paint can full of pink gel, coated Cooke from his knees to his genitals.

"Build a man a fire," Kennedy said, taking a butane barbeque lighter from Carpenter. "And he'll be warm for a day." He leaned forward and spoke into the drum's open top. "*Set* a man on fire, and he'll be warm for the rest of his life."

Kennedy flicked on the lighter, touched the flame to Cooke's thigh, and completed a pan of the inverted, flaming body. Screaming and a warm glow followed him as he left.

6

Allan, fingering through file folders in the middle drawer of the cabinet behind his office desk, glanced over his shoulder. Huffy was seated opposite him, still studying the picture of Clara he'd pulled off the desk. Her earlier call had tripled Allan's heart rate, but it settled as soon as he learned she'd called, not to break horrible news, but to inform him that because her ultrasound appointment had been rescheduled, their Christmas-tree hunt could be moved up an hour. As the yearly "hunt" occurred in the woods just beyond their acreage's property line, he had no objection to her breaking her stay-at-home order.

On the short walk to his office—nowhere near long enough to fill in thirteen years of backstory—they'd stuck to current events, both expressing surprise that so much had changed so quickly. And both equally amazed that, rather than ease tensions, the election had heightened them, solidifying the left and right's hatred of each other to the point the country felt less like one Republic and more like two tribes. He'd suggested "Blue versus red," to which Huffy had responded, "Bloods versus Crips." Sadly, Huffy's comparison felt closer to the truth.

They'd also agreed that Witten had been lucky compared to other cities, a shared grimace reflecting mutual concern over what passed as "lucky" in the *new normal*. And Allan had cringed when Huffy reminded him that it could have been worse had an anonymous tip not stopped a group of White Supremacists from bombing two primarily black elementary schools.

Allan closed the cabinet drawer, swiveled his chair, and

slid Sedrick Palette's file across the desk. "Thanks," Huffy said, his gaze lingering on Clara's image as he set her picture back on the desk. "How long have you been married now? Twenty-two years?"

"Twenty-three in August."

"Is she still a nurse at Saint Pete's?"

"Yes, but she has been on leave since June. The twins are due in February, but with COVID and her asthma, her doctor wanted her as far from the hospital as possible."

"Speaking of the zombie apocalypse, any issues?"

He flashed his latex-gloved hands and pointed at his N-95 mask. "I'm extra cautious, and Clara only leaves the house for ultrasounds and doctor appointments. We are both tested weekly."

Huffy had pulled a different picture off the desk, his face now contorted like a Korowai Warrior from Papua New Guinea studying a Jackson Pollock painting. Don't laugh, Allan silently joked. He has a gun.

"It was fourteen years ago," Huffy said, still confused by the picture, "but I recall you being excited to be a dad. You must have a baseball team by now."

Allan started to answer but stopped himself. Should I tell him the truth? Does he want to know the truth? Do *I* want him to know the truth?

Allan pointed at the picture. "That is an in-utero photograph of our twins at four weeks." Huffy's confusion disappeared, his face suddenly blank and pale. Allan wondered if the abrupt change meant anything.

"Girls? Boys?" Huffy set the frame back on the desk. "One of each?"

"We are having MCDA twins," Allan stated. When the Korowai warrior returned, he added, "I won't bore you with the details, but they occur in roughly one percent of twin births. They are exact replicas of each other, from sex to birthmarks.

So," holding up two fingers, "*two* boys or *two* girls."

"I thought you agreed not to bore me with the details?"

Used to similar reactions, he chuckled. For him, conception activated an otherwise dormant mutation that caused him to ramble about his pending offspring regardless of his audience's level of interest. *Sorry, Liam, you didn't ask why MCDA twins are always the same sex? Let me go ahead and tell you anyway.*

"Ballerinas or ballers?"

A shrug. "Clara likes surprises."

"You?"

"If only for practical reasons, I would prefer to know." A playful grin. "But we compromised."

"A surprise, then," Huffy deadpanned.

Allan belched a laugh. "You're *obviously* married. Any kids?"

The sudden reappearance of Huffy's blank expression had Allan paying closer attention. Like the gambler from Kenny Roger's classic song of the same name, he had "made a life out of readin' people's faces" and had long ago lost the ability to turn the skill off. He noticed Huffy's burdened brow and how he'd lowered his chin fractionally, his eyes moving down and to the left. More importantly, he saw how quickly Huffy had caught himself, wiped the expression from his face, and re-established eye contact. Everything about the short-lived expression had been heavy, weighed down by something immense—something he was both fighting and trying to hide. It took a moment, but he realized that *something* was sadness. And not your everyday run-of-the-mill sadness; Huffy's pain had depth—depth only time could produce. His pain had been fermenting over a significant period, possibly several years.

Huffy wiggled the naked ring finger on his left hand. "Compromise was never my thing."

A failed marriage, Allan thought. Good reason to be sad.

"Any names?" Huffy continued, removing a notepad and pen from his jacket pocket as if the question were relevant to his visit.

He pointed over Huffy's shoulder at a brown-leather couch set against the small office's back wall. Spread across the middle cushion was a baby-sized Denver Bronco's jersey —MANNING stitched across the shoulders. "Peyton and Eli if they are boys. Peyton and *Elise* if they are girls."

Huffy made a weak effort to turn and look at the jersey. "And Clara?"

"She'll come around." A wink. "Or we'll compromise."

"You were Sedrick Palette's psychiatrist, correct?" Huffy asked, dispensing with the small talk.

"He has access to several physicians and mental health professionals, but I am his primary."

"Was he the type to commit suicide?"

"Suicide?" Allan frowned. "He's dead?"

"Earlier today."

"Suicide? The morning of his execution?" He shook his head. "Psychopaths are consumed by self-preservation, so it is —"

"Which is why they are hard to catch."

A nod. "And why suicide is unlikely."

"If self-preservation was no longer an option, could he have killed himself to deny us the opportunity?"

Allan was not sure if he should be saddened or impressed by Huffy's insight into human nature. A psychiatrist with a Ph.D., he had spent two decades honing his craft. A four-year degree, a residency—during which he had met, fell in love with, and married Clara—and a few financially challenging years in private practice preceded fifteen years with the City of Witten, where he continued his professional development while teaching at the Academy, expert witnessing for the DA, and providing an empathetic ear for depressed, disgruntled, and otherwise curmudgeonly city employees and wards of the state. Sadly, Huffy had gained his insight into human nature by hunting men like Sedrick Palette.

"That would make suicide plausible," Allan answered. "Still unlikely, but plausible." Huffy handed him the red file folder. He flipped through it, stopping after viewing a few of about a dozen gruesome photos. The pictures reinforced a brutal truth; he would never get used to hearing and seeing what people could do to themselves and others. Visibly shaken, he closed the file and dropped it on the desk.

"Assuming suicide," Huffy said, "what drug would have allowed Palette to slash himself more than thirty times, sever his carotid artery, slice off both ears and part of his tongue, and cut off and try to swallow his testicles."

"Swallow his..."

As Allan's brain temporarily severed communication with his mouth, Huffy beamed. "Like he was trying to smuggle them into Hell."

After a long moment, Allan managed to ask, "What would lead you to believe those injuries are consistent with suicide?"

"It is too early to rule anything out. For now, I am simply trying to determine if suicide is even a possibility. To be honest, I would be happy to call it a suicide and close the case. Determining Sedrick Palette's cause of death is not exactly a question with a burning need for an answer."

Had Huffy's comment registered, Allan might have offered his old cadet some advice on how to maintain compassion, even for the worst in society. But he still could not shake loose the lingering images of Palette's mutilated body. As though his mind was an Etch-a-Sketch, he tried to erase them with a forceful shudder.

"Doc?" Huffy said. "You okay?"

"Huh? Yeah. What?"

"Drugs?"

"Oh." A second shudder cleared his mind. "Sorry, yes. I think PCP is a candidate. It is a hallucinogen with anesthetic qualities and can create feelings of invincibility. Send me the tox report. I will give you my opinion once I see it."

A nod. "Bachman's log shows you were Palette's final visitor, arriving around nine last night and staying for thirty-six minutes. Why were you there?"

"Sedrick asked to see me."

"Why?"

"He wouldn't tell me, but when I arrived, he tried to convince me he was incompetent."

"To delay his execution?"

"Yes, which is another strike against suicide."

Huffy sniggered. "But you saw through the charade and certified him competent enough to die?"

Huffy was joking, but there was an underlying sharpness to his tone. A voice emanating from deep in his mind warned him to let the comment go. He almost did.

"I know your job is difficult, Liam, especially now. But I have never found humor in *anyone's* death. It is easy to forget that Sedrick Palette, not unlike someone with Autism or Down Syndrome, had no control over how his brain functioned."

Huffy's expression hardened so quickly he looked like a different person—a Liam Huffy from an alternate dimension where rage was the only emotion. "I've never met a parent who took comfort in the knowledge their child was slaughtered by someone who didn't *choose* to become an animal." His eyes narrowed to slits. "And I don't recall meeting a father or husband who thanked God upon learning his daughter or wife was raped and murdered by a man who'd had a rocky childhood." A beat. "I recently told a mother that her nineteen-year-old daughter and six-month-old grandson wouldn't be home for supper...ever. I recommend you save the nature versus nurture debate for people who think that shit matters."

Allan had counseled hundreds of cops; he knew the toll they paid. Parasitic in nature, the job feasted on their hope-filled cells. He'd heard people say, "Cops take the job home with them." But that was not accurate. Fry cooks, cashiers, teachers, and accountants take their jobs home with them; cops left pieces of themselves with every victim. And in Huffy's case, not much remained of the cadet Allan met fourteen years earlier.

His instinct was to comfort, to let Huffy know the world he lived in—a world filled with monsters and, more recently, people who viewed the police as the enemy—was not reflective of the *real* world. But as unsolicited advice, even from a well-intentioned psychiatrist, could result in missing teeth, he opted for: "I'm sorry. I wasn't trying to mitigate his actions or suggest he shouldn't be held accoun—"

"Do you like dogs?"

Huffy's tone and glare were intense, more applicable had they been mortal enemies with a long history of conflict. He clearly had a switch that could flip without notice as it had on this occasion. Concerned about the consequences of saying the wrong thing—especially if Huffy were a cat person—Allan stayed silent.

"I prefer dogs to people," Huffy continued. "But if my little Scruffy wouldn't stop chewing on my neighbor's kid, I wouldn't care if another dog had molested him, or if nature had fried his wires at birth, or his mom hadn't suckled him enough; I would blow Scruffy's brains out and head back to the pet store."

Allan tried to think of the right words to calm Huffy but couldn't. A long and uncomfortable moment of silence ended when Huffy sighed and said, "Apologies, Doc. That topic is a trigger for me. I'm working on it. According to my doctor, I have no choice." He tapped his chest. "Says the next one might kill me." Then, as though the adversarial portion of their conversation had never occurred, Huffy casually added, "Something else happened this morning. It's a bit bizarre but might be connected to Palette. Can you come to the station, or do you have plans?"

Having just faced a charging grizzly and unsure what might trigger another charge, Allan decided to withhold the truth. He did have plans. As a Jew whose sole day for prayer was Powerball Fridays, he and Clara had always celebrated Christmas. And their annual Christmas-tree hunt kicked-off a tradition of two weeks spent watching classic Christmas movies in the company of Orville Redenbacher, Mrs. Vickie, Ben and Jerry, and an apocalyptic supply of moderately priced wine from the Okanagan Valley in British Columbia, Canada. "Napa North," as Clara referred to the region. The respite always rejuvenated them, individually and as a couple.

But this Christmas was different. An out of control pandemic and the escalating political and social unrest certainly weren't helping, but this Christmas was different for a more personal reason. The deaths of three children had taken a massive toll, and they were now in the final stretch of yet another risky pregnancy; any more heartbreak would end their marriage. And if by some miracle it didn't, they would spend the rest of their lives as strangers roaming shared halls.

That looming calamity was generating extreme and constant anxiety. To cope, he had adopted a forced enthusiasm for all things twin related. A positive attitude would not alter the result, but *Fake it till you make it* felt better than *Bah, humbug!* Conversely, and significantly out of character, Clara had given in to her dark side, convincing herself the twins' approaching due date was an unstoppable countdown to more pain. The conflicting coping strategies had led them to master the art of filling time with everything but each other.

"No," Allan said, passing the red file folder back to Huffy. "I have no plans."

7

Allan used an elbow to jab the call button of the downtown precinct's parking garage elevator—a habit developed before the pandemic was a week old. Shit, he thought, watching the floor indicator light head up, not down. He tapped his watch—another habit, this one ingrained over nearly forty years. As he waited, his thoughts drifted to the man who'd gifted him the unreliable timepiece.

Allan Abrams's father had bravely faced a moment that all parents dread. But with a stiff upper lip, William Haggard Abrams severed the figurative cord. *I've done all I can for you, boy. It's up to you now.* Granted, he may have jumped the gun as most parents wait a little longer than their child's ninth birthday to exercise that right of passage. Still, through some form of parental reverse-osmosis, father managed to pass on two tidbits of wisdom to his son: *Nothing is more important than family,* and *You get what you pay for.* Allan's malfunctioning watch was a constant reminder of the latter.

During Allan's first nine years and one week, sightings of his father were as rare as those of Sasquatch. But after school ended on the last day of Fourth Grade, he returned home to find his old man leaning against the hood of a shimmering black Trans-Am. Almost immediately, shock turned to excitement when he wondered if the car might be a belated birthday present. Based on an overheard conversation between his mom and Bubby, he knew his old man was into him for *ten large!* And despite knowing nothing about cars or what they cost, a Trans-Am seemed about right.

During that same conversation, he had also heard words

like "court-ordered" and "overdue child maintenance." But he had not stuck around to find out what sort of "maintenance" he was overdue for or why his dad owed him ten grand. Unsure what it meant, and unwilling to find out, the moment he heard the word "dead*beet*" he raced across the street to Davey Berkman's house and begged to stay for supper. A *deadbeet* sounded about a thousand times worse than a regular beet. And as an avid beet hater, he wanted no part of either.

But the car was no birthday present, belated or otherwise. A fatherly, "How you been, boy?" was followed by the story of how he had come to own "The same *got*damn car Burt Reynolds drove in Smokey and the Bandit." Before driving away, William Haggard Abrams tossed his son a watch he'd not bothered to wrap. Even to a nine-year-old, the watch looked more used than new.

Allan had no way to know it then, but the watch would end up doubling as a souvenir of their time together.

You get what you pay for, and *Nothing is more important than family.* Valuable life lessons, indeed.

As the elevator doors opened, he thanked his father for the lessons that helped ensure the next generation of Abramses would have no reason to cling to a shitty, ten-dollar watch.

–

FIFTEEN YEARS ON the job, and Allan had still met only a fraction of the city's nearly ten thousand employees, some via counseling sessions, and others, like Sergeant Al Murphy, during brief on-the-job interactions. After following Murphy through the station's front end and hearing the taunting he had endured, Allan was confident the sergeant would soon be a member of both groups. Two of the taunts had every cop within earshot busting a gut. Ridiculing Murphy's bandaged hand and tomato-sauce-stained uniform, a female officer praised him for heroically breaking up a domestic dispute between a plate of lasagna and a bowl of spaghetti. That knee-slapper was followed by a male officer, bellowing through cupped hands, for all units to respond to a "51-50 in progress." According to that officer, a 51-50 was code for an assault on a desk sergeant by a troop of Girl Scouts.

Nearing the end of a long hall, Murphy stopped and held the door to Observation Room Four open so Allan could step inside.

Huffy, standing in front of a large panel of one-way glass, greeted Allan with a nod and Murphy with a mischievous, "Rolo."

Murphy looked ready to crawl under a desk. Allan dropped a sympathetic hand on his shoulder. "Tough day at the office?"

Murphy perused his soiled uniform, shook his head, and moaned, "You have *no* idea."

"Rolo?" Allan queried after Murphy left.

"Based on Murph's name, size, and love of chocolate," Huffy responded, "someone turned RoboCop into *Rolo*Cop."

"Ahh," Allan said, finding the nickname more cruel than funny. But most police officers used humor and ball-busting as a coping mechanism, so Murphy probably gave as good as he got.

Standing beside Huffy at the one-way glass, he saw an elderly man in handcuffs seated at a small stainless-steel table. His wrinkled skin hung loosely over what might once have been a handsome face, his expression frozen somewhere between exhausted and empty.

"Old guy tossed Murphy around like a rag doll."

"*Rolo* Murphy?" Allan exclaimed, doing a double-take at the rail-thin old man.

Huffy, enjoying every word, quickly summarized the events that had motivated Murphy's tormentors, ending the story with, "Rolo claims he lost his balance and that the old guy was high. Makes sense. Gramps looks like he might stroke out if he farted too hard." Huffy went on to say nothing surprised him anymore and relayed a story of a crack-addicted mother who thought it would be funny to spike her fourteen-year-old daughter's beer with the powerful street drug, bath salts. Instead of the Thanksgiving turkey, the daughter carved up her mother, jumped off their third-floor balcony, and, oblivious to her fractured ankle, ended up at McDonald's, where it took three responding officers to pry the box of french fries from her hand and cuff her.

"Gramps claims he killed Palette," Huffy continued. "Normally, I would chalk it up to a case of the crazies." Huffy appeared to notice but disregard Allan's *complicated-is-a-better-word-than-crazy* scowl. "But he confessed a few minutes after Palette's heart stopped beating *and* knew about his last meal."

He grimaced, recalling the location of Sedrick's severed scrotum. "And you want me to find out who gave him that information."

"Yep."

Allan watched the old man inhale the coffee fumes rising out of a Styrofoam cup, then spotted a reddish-brown stain on his soiled white shirt. "Is that blood on his sleeve?"

Huffy answered with a *Don't know* or *Don't care* shrug. "More than likely, he knows an inmate or employee at Bachman."

"What has he told you?"

"Not much." Huffy planted a hand on each hip. "Why does he smell his coffee?"

"Probably a form of self-comforting." He stepped to the door. "Has anyone offer him food? He looks like he hasn't eaten in a month."

Huffy shook his head. "All he wanted was coffee, half a teaspoon of sugar, *not* sweetener."

"Does he have a name?"

"I'm sure he does. Boys up front are going with Grapplin' Gramps."

Seconds later, Allan entered Interview Room Four, rubbed in the hand sanitizer pumped from a wall-mounted dispenser, and sat across the table from the old man, who was watching Allan's every move with an odd intensity.

"Nice to finally meet you."

"Pleasure's all mine, *Mister...*"

"Vilhelm."

"Mr. Vilhelm, I am—"

"First name," the old man corrected. "And *Wi*lhelm is easier on the tongue."

He pulled a new mask from his pocket and offered it to the old man, who seemed genuinely amused by the gesture and returned to his coffee. "A virus is the least of our worries."

Allan slid his chair back a few feet and left the mask on the table in case Wilhelm changed his mind. "I'm sure your coffee is cool enough to drink by now."

Wilhelm pushed the cup away, his handcuffs scraping the table's metal top. "Hate the stuff."

Allan's grin never materialized. Instead, he studied the thick, vertical scar running from the base of Wilhelm's left palm up underneath his stained shirtsleeve. On the opposite side of the same arm was a six-digit number in faded blue ink.

Aware of Allan's curiosity, Wilhelm pulled his sleeve over the tattoo and scar and said, "Things are not always as they appear."

If Wilhelm was suffering from a mental illness, there would be no benefit to challenging odd or cryptic comments he might make, so Allan moved on. "Wilhelm, I'm Allan. I am a psychiatrist, and I want to help you. Can you tell me why you are here?"

"How much time do you have?"

This time, a grin formed under his N-95 mask. "All the time in the world." Wilhelm's soft chuckle had Allan wondering if he had missed an inside joke. "Detective Huffy mentioned you had confessed to killing a man inside a maximum-security prison. How did you manage that?"

"I had help."

That was easy, he thought. "Who helped you?"

Wilhelm did not respond.

Always seeking the path of least resistance, he changed direction. "It might be helpful for me to speak with people close to you. Do you have any siblings or children? Grandchildren?"

Wilhelm's head shot up. He briefly locked eyes with Allan before returning his attention to the Styrofoam cup. Curious about the reaction, Allan decided to probe.

"Do you have family in Witten?"

"What does that have to do with me going to jail?"

"I wouldn't worry about jail," he reassured. "I am sure the officer you assaulted won't be pressing—"

"I am not talking about that." Wilhelm's tone had shifted toward annoyance. "I killed Sedrick Palette. And others."

Needing to build trust and sensing friction, Allan decided to simply follow Wilhelm's lead. "People can be *directly* responsible for a death, or they can *feel* responsible. Which applies to you?"

"Both."

"How many deaths are you *directly* responsible for?"

"308."

Allan noted the number. "You had help killing Sedrick Palette. Did you have help with the others?"

"You could say that."

The terrible nature of Sedrick Palette's crimes and Wilhelm's high kill count made it easy to anticipate where he was headed. "Were the other 307 people like Sedrick Palette?"

"Much worse."

He thought for a moment. "Is it your job to stop bad people

from doing bad things?"

Wilhelm's eyes deadened as though his soul had just left his body. "Something like that."

"How do you know who to stop?"

Wilhelm took some time to think. "Most people ignore or misunderstand the world around them. They are blind to what they should see, and deaf to what they should hear." A shrug. "I am not one of those people."

Allan made a note. "If you are directly responsible for 308 deaths, how many deaths do you *feel* responsible for?"

Wilhelm looked toward the ceiling as if doing the math in his head. "Depending on which history book you read, somewhere between seven and eleven million."

He studied Wilhelm, searching for signs of deception but finding none. Wilhelm believed every word.

"How could one man be responsible for so many deaths?"

"Hitler was one man."

"You are not Hitler."

The first sign of emotion flushed Wilhelm's face. "No." His chin fell toward his chest. "But I could have stopped him."

—

ALLAN AND HUFFY watched Wilhelm through the one-way glass.

"I don't know about you, Doc." Huffy stuffed his hands into his pockets. "But I'll sleep better tonight knowing the sonofabitch responsible for the Holocaust is finally in custody."

Allan ignored the joke, pulled a pill case from his pants pocket, lowered his mask, and dry-swallowed two pills.

"Migraines?" Huffy asked, again showcasing his impressive recall power.

"Yeah, and they're getting worse. I just had an MRI. I'm kinda hoping they find a tumor." A sour grin. "At least they can cut a tumor out." He pocketed the pill case and turned to

Wilhelm. "He may be suffering from Grandiose Delusions. It is common with a variety of psychiatric diseases, as well as a few substance-abuse disorders. Wilhelm taking a drug like PCP and Sergeant Murphy being off-balance could explain the surprising result of their altercation."

"Uh-huh," Huffy said, sounding disinterested. "How old do you think he is?"

"Mid-seventies. Give or take."

"You saw his tattoo?"

"Yeah."

Huffy folded his arms across his chest. "Even if he is in his early eighties, he would have been a toddler at the end of the Second World War." He turned to Allan, eyeing him as though he'd offered a riddle to solve and was waiting for a guess.

"And?" Allan asked.

"Nazis didn't tattoo kids."

"They didn't?"

The meaning of Huffy's cockeyed expression was clear: You're Jewish. Shouldn't you know that? "Not unless he was a twin," Huffy added. "In any event, if he was a toddler at the end of the Second World War, why not just show him the math?"

"Trying to convince him his delusion is not real would be as easy as convincing you that we aren't talking right now. He will have well-researched details that support his delusion, and he will have filled in any flaws and gaps with quasi-facts, science fiction, or the supernatural."

Huffy looked unconvinced.

"Palette died inside a locked cell on the most secure block of a maximum-security prison," Allan added. "Dollars to donuts, the 'help' he mentioned will be of the science fiction or supernatural variety."

"He *actually* believes he has killed 308 people?"

"Yep."

"And as a toddler locked in a concentration camp, he could

have stopped the Holocaust?"

"People who suffer from Grandiose Delusions often believe they've played significant roles in important historical events. Auditory and visual hallucinations can strengthen the delusion. Trauma he experienced during the war, probably in the camp, could have triggered his mental illness. If he has gone untreated, he may have been building on and strengthening his delusion for decades."

Huffy shook his head. "Our only lead is crazy. Fantastic."

Charging grizzly, Allan thought, deciding to ignore Huffy's choice of words. "To varying degrees, beliefs shape our reality, not the reverse. What is *real* often depends more on what we believe than on facts. The more powerful our belief, the harder our minds work to interpret what we see and hear in ways that support it. Just like statistics, we can use information to prove anything. Even sane people interpret information in ways that support what they believe. And sane people can behave in ways that might cause others to question their state of mind. My mother once drove almost two hundred miles to my summer camp because she *knew* I was hurt. About an hour into her drive, I fell out of a tree and broke my leg." A beat. "Even so-called *sane* people can act irrationally."

Huffy *humphed*. "At a High School dance, my dad pointed to a girl he'd never met and told his buddies he was going to marry her. They laughed. My mom and dad were married a year later. They'll celebrate their forty-fifth anniversary in January."

"I rest my case." Allan turned to Wilhelm, who seemed to be having a hard time staying awake. "Elder abuse is always a possibility in these situations, which is why I asked about his family. The mention of a child or a grandchild got his attention. Might be something there."

"Did you learn anything *useful*?" Huffy asked. "Like how he knew Palette was dead before we did?"

"No, but it isn't a huge leap to go from abusing the elderly to murder. If someone is abusing Wilhelm, they could work at Bachman or know someone who does. Wilhelm could have overheard the planning of Palette's murder and used the details in his confession to—"

"Escape his abuser," Huffy finished.

A nod. "Wilhelm's abuser and Palette's killer could be connected, or they could be the same person. Makes a lot more sense than suicide. Palette's wounds would be difficult to self-inflict, and that scenario does not fit his pathology."

Huffy shook his head. "Never get in front of an investigation."

"Wilhelm confessed minutes after Palette died. Either that was a massive coincidence, or he knew when Palette planned to kill himself."

"An investigation is just a series of closed doors." A shrug. "If he didn't kill himself, sooner or later, I will find someone hiding behind one of those doors." A sharp grin. "Someone I can hang."

Allan nodded. "That's fair. No point ruling anything out. On that note, if someone *is* abusing Wilhelm, and they are involved in Palette's death, you are probably looking at a relative. It could be a son, but my guess is a grandson."

"How can you possibly know that?"

"I don't. But a male grandchild is a reasonable assumption based on Wilhelm's age and the physical nature of Palette's death. It may take a day or two, but I'll figure out how he knows what he does."

"A day or two?" Huffy croaked. "He's delusional. Why would it take more than five minutes?"

"Earning trust takes time. Even after I have it, I still have to work around his delusion to get to the information you want."

Huffy sighed disappointedly and looked to Wilhelm, who was sleeping now—his gaping mouth and the steep angle of his neck making it look like he dozed off while catching M&Ms in his mouth.

"Is the counseling office on the fifth floor available?" Allan asked.

"Why not talk to him here? The counseling office isn't wired."

"I'll have more success in a place where he can relax."

Huffy glanced back at the sleeping Wilhelm. "He looks pretty relaxed to me."

AFTERNOON. DECEMBER 18.

Huffy checked the time on his phone, propped his feet on the corner of his boss's desk, closed his eyes, and lost himself in the sweet sounds of "police work." Phones ringing in a chaotic, indictable melody, fingers tickling keyboards, shuffled papers "whooshing" like brush sticks on a snare drum, and a choir of muffled voices generating vapid verbal static that lingered like an eighties power ballad. He loved those sounds; he needed those sounds. He had no idea how or when the aftermath of human depravity had become comforting, but it had, and he wasn't about to ruin a good thing by delving into why.

Minutes later, he laughed out loud after reading a text from his boss. In a world gone mad with political correctness, she would have had to resign if anyone else had seen the text.

> Running late. B there soon. Btw this text accidentally came to me. *Liam, u forgot ur anal beads again. What should I do with them? Chief Dickson.*

Her partner for a little over six years, he knew Frankie Bryant better than anyone in the department. At age six, she had woken up to find her mom asleep on the couch. Five hours later—a teary-eyed Frankie still trying to wake her mommy up—daddy came home, removed the needle from his dead wife's arm, scooped Frankie into a hug, and called 911. The day before Frankie's eighth birthday, her father was killed in the line of duty responding to a break-in at a liquor store.

Raised by her grandmother, Frankie followed in her father's footsteps. A Massachusetts Statie by twenty, a captain by thirty, she swapped her captain's hat and half her pay for a detective's badge when her wife, Beth, was offered the Head of Pediatrics at Witten's Saint Pete's Hospital.

Despite a few higher-ups believing Frankie had the wrong skin color (and gender and lifestyle), she swiftly moved through the ranks. Six months ago, she was promoted to Commander of the Special Investigative Unit. Those same higher-ups criticized the move, but Frankie had not become Witten PD's highest-ranking female member because of her skin color (and gender and lifestyle); she had earned her position with a tireless work ethic, fierce intelligence, and unshakable confidence. It was her confidence Huffy admired most. Frankie was the Jekyll to all the Hydes raging against political incorrectness. She felt no duty to "educate" those who felt that gay, black, and female were genetic flaws. And when confronted with descriptive narratives like *Nigger* or *Dyke,* she was confident enough to walk away, citing "sticks and stones" if questioned about her retreat.

Five years ago, after a long and stressful shift, he and Frankie stopped for a quick bite at a favorite Italian restaurant. During dinner, a man, there with his wife and three young children, made sure to express his opinion on interracial couples loudly enough for everyone to hear. When his wife *shhh'd* him and he suggested she shut the fuck up and eat her spaghetti, Huffy started to wriggle out of the booth. Frankie stopped him. *Just words,* she had said. *He has been taught to hate. More hate won't erase those lessons.*

On the way out, Frankie stopped at the man's table, her badge looped over her belt and visible. She asked the woman how old her children were. "Three, five, and seven," the woman answered, her eyes bouncing nervously between her husband and Frankie. "My wife and I are thinking of having children," Frankie said to the woman. "If we do, I hope they are as adorable and well-behaved as your kids." The woman, smiling awkwardly, thanked Frankie for the compliment. Frankie handed her a business card and encouraged her to call "day or night" if she ever needed anything.

Frankie never once looked at the man.

On the other hand, Huffy had watched the prick the entire time, hoping he would do something to justify a broken jaw. He remembered watching Frankie approach the table, the man smiling arrogantly in anticipation of a confrontation that never came. Without a word, Frankie had made it clear that he possessed no power. He was irrelevant.

The woman called Frankie less than three hours later, after the man had taken out his anger on his wife and oldest child. Huffy asked for the honor of arresting him. Frankie obliged. According to the official report, the man broke his jaw after walking into a door—clumsy oaf.

"Apologies." Frankie closed her office door. "Dickson held me back after class." She used a glare to order Huffy's feet off her busy but organized desk.

"Stray bullet stuff?"

Frankie nodded and took her seat. "He also wanted me to know how unimpressed the warden was with you."

Huffy grunted his disapproval; the chief and the warden were loathsome creatures who worked with, not in, law enforcement.

"Palette was RUV," she continued, "and you are the lead detective on all open RUV investigations. You could have given the warden attitude and a sub-atomic wedgie; neither would have changed a thing. Is there a *different* reason you and the warden didn't hit it off?" She studied him for a bit. "You okay?"

His fingernails started digging trenches into his palms. For most of the day, he had kept the date buried, out of the reach of his conscious mind. But Frankie's question forced it to the surface like a hand bursting through the loose soil of a freshly-dug grave. An image flashed through his mind: a coffin, a bloodless face painted like a ceramic doll's, blonde hair fanned over a white pillow. He forced the image down, deeper and deeper until it was gone and his anger eased.

Frankie was studying him intensely, searching for a sign. His eyes glassing over, rapid blinking, flushed cheeks, anything she could interpret as an invitation to talk about "it." Instead, he offered her a soft-edged glare that stated: *I appreciate your concern, but I'm fine. Let's move on.*

"Look," she said, her playful tone making it clear she'd received his non-verbal communication loud and clear. "I've allowed you to work without adult supervision until your partner completes his quarantine. Don't make me regret that decision." A beat. "Or I'll stick you with Bonino."

A smile eased its way across Huffy's face.

"I read your prelim," she continued. "Let's keep this short. Spare me the game show narrative."

He chuckled. Years in the trenches together meant she knew every one of his theories and beliefs about every topic from abortion (pro-choice with the caveat: "But we should sterilize some people") to boxers or briefs (commando). As a result, she was *intimately* familiar with his theory that every investigation was a series of closed doors he was required to open. His *Let's Make a Deal* game show narrative. *Let's see what's behind door number two, Monty!*

"Behind door number one," he needled, "is Palette, with help from Bachman's unlicensed pharmacist, killed himself. Behind door—"

"Suicide?" She scratched at an ear. "You would have to have one *helluva* buzz going to munch on your nutsack."

"It's unlikely, I agree. But let's wait to see what the tox report shows."

They batted theories back and forth for a while, including Frankie's that the location of Palette's severed nutsack was classic Russian mob. Huffy informed her that he and Button had discussed the same possibility when Button had called him back into cell C-56 after finding Palette's missing nutsack.

But there were no Russians on C Block.

"How long before Triton Security sends us Bachman's surveillance footage?" Frankie asked.

"The w*ah*den says it'll take a couple of days."

Huffy loved mocking Frankie's New England heritage, working *Whea'd I pahk the fahkin cah?* into as many conversations as possible.

She tucked her shoulder-length black hair around her ears, revealing the remaining soft angles of her make-up-free face. "Maybe it will take a couple of days because an inmate or employee carving up Palette would be bad for business."

Huffy shrugged.

"Will the outage affect the footage?"

"Shouldn't. Bachman's cameras have a twelve-hour battery back-up."

"Your prelim mentioned that a family member of one of Palette's victims might be involved. What file are we putting that in?"

"Things easily checked," he said—another of his theories.

"Wasn't the aunt of one of his victims a senator?"

"Four-term."

"Senators tend to have low friends in high places. You think she had someone—"

They both cringed.

A piercing alarm wailed for several seconds.

"What the fuck?" he yelped.

"We've had a bunch of false alarms since the power outages this morning," she replied, screwing a pinky finger into her ear. "No reason to start eliminating possibilities until we get Bachman's footage."

"So put a tail on the Senator and waterboard the old man?"

A wink. "See if he knows where Hoffa's buried."

Both smiled.

"And all of these shenanigans *supposedly* happened during the seventy-nine seconds Bachman's power was out?"

"Yep," Huffy answered. "Maybe we should bring Criss Angel in for a chat."

"Funny," she said, offering no indication she found it so. "Four officers on duty on C Block?"

"Yeah. And if it wasn't suicide or Criss Angel, I cannot think of a scenario where all four didn't know what was happening. Or worse."

She shook her head, looking more disappointed than surprised. Corrupting DOC officers seemed to be one of Bachman's approved recreational activities.

"Any cameras in the electrical room?"

"Nope," Huffy said through a yawn.

"So someone could have simply flipped a breaker."

A nod. "The superintendent at Witten Power said she'd let me know if Bachman had an outage and what caused it."

"Any progress on how the old man knew Palette was dead before we did?"

"Not yet, but Abrams thinks he could have overheard the planning of Palette's murder."

"That does not explain the timing of his confession." She grabbed a file folder from a neat stack on her desk and read for a while. "Rolo has the old man entering the precinct at 4:06 a.m., which was three minutes after the DOC officer discovered Palette's body." She closed the file and set it back on the pile. "Could someone at Bachman have called the old man with a heads up?"

"No outgoing calls between 11:41 p.m. and 4:09 a.m.."

"Cell phones?"

He shook his head. "Bachman is cell phone and Wi-fi-free, they have signal jammers, and a cell phone detection system that can pinpoint a cell phone's location if it sends or receives."

Frankie thought for a bit. "Suicide's a stretch, but if Palette *did* kill himself, the only way the old man could have known in advance was through Palette. And if someone killed Palette, the only way the old man could have known in advance was through the killer or an accomplice." She leaned back and cupped her hands behind her head. "The timing of his confession cannot be a coincidence. We have to assume he is connected."

"Could be an abusive relative, maybe a grandson, at least according to Abrams. I have Jarvis checking for connections between the old man and anyone living or working at Bachman. Jarvis can—"

Frankie's phone rang. She held up a "hold that thought" finger and answered it. Within seconds, she had narrowed her eyes and clenched her jaw so tightly that he wondered if the roots of her molars had been pushed half an inch deeper into her gums. "Are you kidding me, Wayne?" She slammed the handset into the cradle and pressed a button on the phone's base, venting as she waited for the call to go through. "When did it become the media's God-given right to know *every* detail on *every* friggin' case no matter—"

"What's up, boss?" Murphy's voice crackled over the phone's speaker. She lifted the handset to her ear. "Stop putting Wayne Desmond through to me," she demanded. "I am sick—" She listened for a bit. "I don't care if he pretends to be the *Pope*; if you can't figure out who's calling, don't send *any* calls through." She slammed the handset down again.

Huffy glanced at his shoulder-holstered Glock. "You want me to encourage Desmond to fuck off?"

Still fuming, she barked, "If anyone gets to shoot that prick, it'll be me." The thought seemed to calm her down. "Where were we?"

"I was saying I would rather cut off and eat my testicles than investigate the death of garbage like Palette. Jarvis can handle things until we get Bachman's footage."

Frankie grumbled while sifting through a stack of files. "Every detail of every case *has* to be broadcast to the entire fucking world no matter how sensitive or…" She found the file and waved it at him. "As long as I have a dead eight-year-old courtesy of what is almost certainly a stray *RUV* bullet, *you're* working Palette's case."

"Nobody, especially me, gives a shit about Palette, so—"

Her phone rang again. Instead of answering it, she studied the phone and listened, looking as though she was trying to decipher the caller's identity by each ring's pitch and duration. She set the file on her desk and answered the call.

While he waited, his thoughts turned to one of his least favorite topics: the RUV. He had investigated countless RUV crimes and knew more about the *Reinheit und Vollkommenheit* —loosely translated as "Purity and Perfection"—than anyone in the department.

The group was founded and led by DaMarcus Kennedy, a wanna-be kingpin. Kennedy and his younger sister were abused as children, first by their parents, and then by their foster father--a Priest--who abused both of them in every way possible. Two days after his twelfth birthday, Kennedy ended the abuse with a shotgun. Released from Juvie on his eighteenth birthday, he obtained his GED and enrolled in night courses at a local college. His sister's suicide ended his academic endeavors and sent him on the path that ultimately led to the RUV.

The group funded itself by victimizing fellow scum, but Kennedy saw his RUV as more than a band of modern-day Merry Men and himself as more than a thug. A principled sociopath, he had a misguided but deep-seated desire to make the world a better place by eliminating those he considered an unnecessary drain on the planet's depleting resources. Kennedy didn't care about black lives; he cared about the *right* lives, at least those he considered right.

Unfortunately, people in Kennedy's world were reluctant

to run to the police crying, "Officer, that guy just stole all my drugs." The combination of reluctant victims, Kennedy's intelligence, his ability to sniff out disloyalty, and his propensity for violence ensured most RUV bad deeds ended up in cold case boxes. But things tended to change when RUV bullets started killing eight-year-olds.

"Sounds good." Frankie hung up and motioned with a hand for Huffy to continue.

"Nobody cares about a shit stain we would have executed anyway. Let Jarvis handle Bachman until we get the surveillance footage."

She fell back in her chair and exhaled a week's worth of frustration. "Wayne Desmond can make all the bullshit claims he wants about a police cover-up. But a child *was* shot—in front of his mom and sister, for Christ's sake. And you know as well as I do that if the bullet that killed Josh Cutter came from an RUV gun, nobody will tell us shit, and ballistics will be useless. Palette was RUV, so maybe Kennedy was involved. If he was, maybe we get lucky with the old man or Bachman's footage. Maybe we get *really* lucky and Kennedy recruited a guard, who we flip when he's facing twenty years of alone time with people who aren't exactly fond of law enforcement." She dry washed her face and exhaled again. "I realize the chances are slim to none, but for now, the old man and Palette are our best shot at Kennedy."

Huffy didn't object; she was right. They'd been trying for nearly a decade to lock up Kennedy. The only time they'd come close, he managed to wriggle free thanks to a questionable alibi provided by his lawyer.

"What about Benny Carpenter?" Frankie asked. "What if Palette is related to a regime change at the RUV?"

"I never bought the regime change theory. Kennedy's loyalty radar is too strong; he would have sniffed it out. Carpenter is stupid, but he isn't *that* stupid."

A sly grin. "I like to think of every investigation as a series of closed doors."

He flipped her the bird. "How's life at home?" She ignored his question, grabbed a folder from her pile, and started to read. "Burying yourself in your work won't solve your marital problems," he added. She responded with a middle finger of her own. He snorted a laugh. His comment was a bit of good-natured payback for her offering him the same sage advice. Although, in his defense, he'd been burying himself in his work long before his marriage started falling apart. "We're both single," he continued. "Maybe you and I would make a great power cou—"

She snapped her head up, a ruthless stink-eye fully formed. "You're not my type."

He flashed both palms. *"Woah!* No need to make this a black-white thing."

She returned to reading the file and instructed him to "Piss off." He informed her of his schedule, including visits he had planned with DaMarcus Kennedy and a DOC officer, Derek Samuels, who'd called in sick for his night shift on C Block. At the door, he turned. "If you need one, I know a guy with a shoulder."

In the underground garage, he received a text.

Shoulder might b nice. Pig 9? PS dont see Kennedy w/out back up.

Life had taught him the best place to store his emotions was in a lockbox buried in a dark hole far below his surface. Frankie was the only person in his life who knew that lockbox's location and combination.

He replied with: Whea'd I pahk my fahkin cah?

He couldn't see it, but Frankie smiled.

9

Seated at one end of a small kitchen table, Huffy heard a familiar song playing in another room—a duck and wascally wabbit singing and dancing in unison.

"... we'll hit the heights, and oh, what heights we'll hit, on with the show, this is it."

A wrinkled tank top and boxer shorts, a wicked case of bedhead, and the fact it was well past noon made it easy for Huffy to deduce Derek Samuels was not a morning person. Waiting for Samuels to mix himself a cup of coffee-flavored rum, Huffy scanned a cluster of items in the center of the kitchen table. The items included a sugar container—"IHOP" engraved in the glass—two pill bottles, a jar filled with plastic utensils, and a single shaker containing salt and pepper. The shaker had him debating whether Samuels was a genius or just too poor to afford a second shaker.

Shit pay and shittier benefits meant inmates were always encouraging Bachman's COs to supplement their income. The size and condition of Samuels's apartment meant one of two things: he was poor and honest, or he was vastly undercharging for his services.

A baby began to cry somewhere in the apartment.

Samuels sat at the opposite end of the table, and Huffy started the interview, a nebulous thought hovering in the back of his mind. The thoughts, not uncommon, were similar to having a name on the tip of your tongue. He would hear or see something, intuit that it had value, then let the Scrabble tiles in his head rearrange themselves and reveal a message.

The process could take seconds, days, or months, but regularly ended with a piece of relevant information.

The baby's crying eased enough for Huffy to hear gunfire and a two-foot-tall, red-bearded desperado hollering: "I'm no Doc, ya flea-bitten varmint! I'm Riff-Raff Sam, the riffinest riff that ever riffed a raft!"

Ten minutes later, Huffy had made a few notes.

PTSD/Afghanistan. Called in sick drunk? Home alone all night. No calls/visitorsno alibi. GF (Molly Barnes) spent night at mom's (Theresa Adler 1385 Bridgeport Ave) Why?

During that ten minutes, he had also concluded that, in addition to not being a morning person, Samuels wasn't exactly a doting father, twice saying, "Girlfriend'll take care of it," when offered a break to soothe his disgruntled child.

Yet to see or hear that girlfriend, Huffy stood and thanked Samuels for his time just as the Scrabble tiles fell into place. He grabbed a pill bottle from the cluster of items on the table, the label confirming the detail his subconscious had caught earlier.

"Allan Abrams prescribed these?"

Samuels nodded.

"Scopolamine," Huffy stated, the name triggering a memory from an old case. "For your PTSD?"

"IBS. I'm allergic to everything else."

"Why would a psychiatrist prescribe you medication for an irritable bowel?"

"I see Doc Abrams twice a month." He sucked back the last of his coffee. "When I mentioned my IBS prescription was giving me the shits, Doc checked my history and wrote me a prescription. I'm glad he did cause now I can eat," lifting his empty mug, "and *drink* pretty much anything."

Huffy made a mental note, set the bottle back on the table, and followed Samuels to the apartment's front door. A homely woman (the kind of homely that made twenty-something look forty-something) had just entered carrying a bag from Walgreen's and another from Buck's Liquor. Huffy had an exceptional radar for abused women. When the woman padded past Samuels without lifting her eyes off the floor, Huffy's radar pinged like the sonar of a battleship passing over a fleet of submarines. He glared at Samuels, who was watching the woman walk toward the kitchen. The baby was crying again.

"Guess the girlfriend'll take care of that, hey Derek?"

Samuels said nothing.

Huffy, fighting an urge to provide a free lesson in *How do you like it?*, held the door open with his foot. "I know what you are."

Likely due to his daily dealings with short-fused inmates, Samuels seemed to sense danger. "Not sure what you mean?" he responded in a cautious tone.

"Women find ways to hit back, Derek. And sometimes," he leaned forward, forcing Samuels to step back, "PTSD or no PTSD, somebody hits back for them."

Before Samuels finished saying, "I have no idea what you're talking about," Huffy was headed to his car, his previously steady pulse rising in anticipation of his next appointment.

—

HUFFY CRUISED PASSED a wooden billboard he'd seen at least a dozen times, laughing uncontrollably the first time he had read its bold, black lettering. **NEIGHBORHOOD REJUVENATION PROJECT! COMING SOON: PLAYGROUND, SPRAY PARK, OFFLEASH DOG PARK AND MORE!** None of that was particularly chuckle-worthy, but the last statement was. **FUNDED BY: THE DAMARCUS KENNEDY FOUNDATION.**

Kennedy was a thug, not a kingpin, so the idea that he saw himself in the same light as mass-murdering "philanthropists" like Pablo Escobar was laughable. At least until Huffy realized that the backstories of Escobar, Mob Bosses, and even some of history's most brutal dictators all contained the same element: they started near the bottom and used street-smarts, ambition, and a lack of conscience to rise to the top. In that respect, Kennedy was every bit their equal.

His phone rang, Bluetooth routing the call through the car's speakers. Uh oh, he thought, eyeing the phone's display. He knew why she was calling. He decided to let the call go to voicemail but quickly changed his mind; she would just keep calling.

"What's up, boss?"

"Why don't you have back-up?" Frankie blared, the speakers squeezing her voice into a harsh, scratchy howl. He lowered her volume.

"DaMarcus won't try—"

"He's dangerous!" she snapped. "And he wouldn't hesitate to take a shot at you if he thought he could get away with it."

A long silence.

Frankie ended it with a frustrated sigh. "I've contacted Kennedy's surveillance team. I swear to God, Liam, if they have to break cover to save your ass, Sedrick Palette won't be the only person who had his nutsack for breakfast."

He smiled, despite knowing her concern was not out of an abundance of caution; Kennedy *was* dangerous. He would never admit it, at least not to Frankie, but, at times, he put himself in Kennedy's line of fire, hoping Kennedy would take a shot. Huffy was confident Kennedy would miss, but more importantly, he knew *he* wouldn't.

"Kennedy considers himself too vital to the cause to do something stupid," he said, trying to ease her mind. "Tell the boys in the van to go back to sleep."

Another frustrated discharge of air crackled over the car's speakers. Thanks to his soon-to-be-ex-wife, he had a Ph.D. in non-verbal communication. Although, when every non-verbal message was: *You're an asshole!*, a Ph.D. wasn't exactly hard to obtain.

Frankie repeated her threat to feed him his balls for breakfast, and he thanked her for the appetizing imagery and hung up. About a minute later, he pulled to a stop in front of Kennedy's dilapidated Victorian Gothic two-story.

In a similar state of disrepair as its neighbors, the "RUV Compound" still managed to stick out like a dislocated pinky finger. With one exception, every house in the area was covered in graffiti. It was a sign of respect. Opposites in the real world, fear and respect were synonyms in Kennedy's.

Why monsters became monsters did not change the fact they were monsters. Not being held enough as a baby, abuse, or having an uncle or priest prematurely introduce you to the art of fellatio weren't justifiable reasons for becoming homicidal; they were just convenient ones. Shit Kennedy had no control over had traumatized him; boo fucking hoo. Huffy knew better than most that childhood could be a dangerous time. But Kennedy's beliefs, including that people *he* deemed imperfect were societal limbs in need of amputation, were not born of horrific circumstances, they were the spawn of hate and willful ignorance. No matter how bad life got, hate was always a choice.

Huffy exited the car, but, with Frankie's warning still echoing in his mind, left his suit jacket crumpled on the passenger seat. What could it hurt to have his shoulder-holstered Glock in plain view?

In his usual attire (Chuck Taylor low-top sneakers, black jeans, a jean jacket, and a black T-shirt with *I Can't Breathe* across the chest), Kennedy was seated on the top step of a medium-length staircase. Behind him, a porch wrapped the entire house, its rotting, paint-chip-coated wood a perfect match for the home's *Norman-Bates-Buys-Big-City-Crack-House* retro vibe. The stairs stretched from the porch to the sidewalk where Huffy stood; *Black Lives Matter* painted in yellow on the freshly shoveled concrete to his left.

In addition to Kennedy, Huffy counted six RUV members

but knew more were inside the house. He also knew that, regardless of location, all would be armed. Two of the six were in chairs, and the other four were leaning against the house or the porch rail. Huffy wasn't surprised to see everyone with bandanas under their chins. Some people believed a recent rise in violent crime was due to stress or locked-down criminals going stir crazy, but Huffy had a simpler theory. Before the pandemic, if someone walked into a 7-11 with a bandana covering their face, the clerk would have pressed the silent alarm.

"I hear congratulations are in order."

Kennedy thanked Huffy with a tip-of-the-hat gesture. In addition to dreadlocks and a fondness for Bob Marley, Kennedy embraced his Jamaican heritage by zealously supporting Colorado's decision to legalize weed.

"Merry Christmas to you and yours, Huff." He extended his hand and offered Huffy a joint. "Ganja?"

Kennedy's crew found that funny.

"Should we have your old room in Juvie painted pink or blue?"

Kennedy beamed and spread his arms wide. "I prayed, Huff, and the Lord, He answered. Beautiful blue."

As clapping and whistling rose and fell, Huffy spied Chris Tam and Benny Carpenter leaning against the house behind Kennedy. Tam and Kennedy were the brains behind the RUV. And thanks to his size, demeanor, and a genetic resistance to knowledge, Carpenter was the RUV's primary slab of mindless muscle. Recent events and street-level rumblings had some in Witten PD convinced that regime change was afoot at the RUV. If true, the smart money was on Carpenter. Some were speculating the recent death of Josh Cutter was Carpenter's doing; a "stray" bullet his way of having the police get rid of Kennedy for him. A pending ballistics report was likely to nix that weak theory, but if accurate, it showed a surprising degree of intelligence. Carpenter was a mountain of a man and extraordinarily violent. But neither would help him if Kennedy found out he was secretly jonesing for the RUV crown.

"A boy," Huffy said approvingly. "Someone to carry on your good name."

Kennedy swiveled and spoke under his breath to Carpenter and Tam. Both men chuckled, Carpenter doing so while fondling a diamond-studded, cross-shaped earring. Huffy found the underworld's ironic symbolism amusing. Apparently, society's worst believed that Saint Peter was obligated to crank open the Pearly Gates to anyone wearing gold-plated religious memorabilia or sporting a cool Jesus tat.

"I was curious," Huffy continued, "if you asked Leo Hutchins to pass on a message to Sedrick?" Around-the-clock surveillance (a noose Kennedy was adept at slipping) had identified a new Bachman resident, Leo Hutchins, as RUV. Based on records provided by the warden, an assault on a guard had landed Hutchins in C Block three days before Palette's death. Coordinating the assault and transfer were well within Kennedy's wheelhouse.

His elbows on his knees, Kennedy discharged a puff of smoke. "Why would I send a message to a dead man?" His calm response meant he was aware of Palette's early passing. "Besides," he added, "I'm a man of peace."

Kennedy's crew found that funny, too.

Anger fueled by everything Kennedy did or said filled the space around Huffy's head with a vision. In it, Kennedy lurched backward, two 9mm bullet holes in his chest. Huffy then dispatched the rest of Kennedy's minions, blew a curl of smoke away from the gun barrel's tip, twirled it around his trigger finger, and slid it back into its holster.

"Your boy Sedrick wasn't a man of peace."

Kennedy finished a toke and held his breath. "Rotten apples in every pie, Huff." He exhaled. "Nine out of ten cops are trigger-happy racists. Don't mean the whole lot' a ya are bad."

More laughter.

Huffy had learned that it was pointless to play nice wit criminals of Kennedy's ilk. They understood that no matter how soft and caring, every word out of a cop's mouth had a single purpose. Without *real* leverage, Kennedy would never give up anyone or anything. But he did have a flaw shared by most criminals. Once you stripped away the bullshit, Kennedy was a hothead with a vendetta and a crawlspace full of guns. Over the years, Huffy had had moderate success with people like Kennedy by pushing their buttons until they uncorked and made a mistake. But in this setting, that strategy wouldn't work. Still, Huffy viewed his encounters with Kennedy the same way a boxer viewed trash talk; over time, the pressure would build and, hopefully, lead to an explosion. Huffy also loved trying to burrow under Kennedy's skin.

"You're full of shit, DaMarcus. You won't stop preaching your insane bullshit about it being a wolf's natural place to slaughter the lamb, yet you expect me to believe you disapprove of Palette raping and killing a disabled girl? I take it back; you're *worse* than a liar, you are a hypocrite."

At the mention of rape, Kennedy's head had shot up. Calm again, he said, "Sedrick got what he deserved." He toked. "About the other stuff?" He blew a THC-infused smoke ring. "The importance of a destination warrants forgiveness of those who sin while on the journey."

Huffy frowned. "Does it, though? For every lost soul saved, does a pedophile priest get one free altar boy? Or is it a two-fer? Is there a formula based on how far gone the saved-soul was?" Kennedy didn't respond. "I don't know, DaMarcus. I guess some would share your perspective. El Chapo, Bin Laden…Scar from *The Lion King*."

"At least people see me coming, Huff."

Wanting to keep Kennedy preaching, Huffy spread his arms and said, "Enlighten me."

"Some eat, some get eaten. Circle' a life shit. You know, like

VOICES

..." Kennedy toked until the glowing end of the ...is fingertips. "You and me ain't so different." He ...nt stub toward Huffy. "We both want a better ...e shithole we got."

Huffy smirked. "If you stopped smoking so much weed, you would realize the world is a shithole *because* of people like you."

Amused, Kennedy shook his head. "We're both scratching the same names off different lists, Huff. I just scratch a little harder. You should thank me."

Huffy laughed sharply. "Sure, and after that, I'll help organize an edibles bake sale to raise money for the RUV cause, or man the phones during a telethon meant to raise awareness for the plight—"

He froze, and his heart rate ticked up as he watched Kennedy reach into the pocket of his jean jacket. Instead of a gun, he pulled out another joint and a pack of matches.

"You're getting jumpy in your old age, Huff."

"A bit, I guess," he acknowledged. "But it isn't exactly the best time to be a cop." He glanced at his Glock. "Justifiable homicide isn't what it used to be."

Kennedy spewed a loud, genuine laugh. "Yeah, times certainly are a-changing, my brother. But it ain't all bad. Nowadays, all you need to burn down a forest," he lit the joint and tossed the burning match into the snow beside the stairs, "is one little match. Now..." he toked, "what the fuck you want?"

"I told you, I'm curious about Leo Hutchins."

Kennedy pointed at a van parked a half-block away, DIY RESCUE painted on its side. "Why don't you tell me? Your boys are always watching me. I bet they know what time I shit." A grin. "Every morning at eight, Huff. I'm a shittin', Rasta, *motherfuckin' robot*."

The crew roared at that.

"Speakin' a shit," Kennedy continued. "I know you guys

don't make much. A thankless job, for sure, especially with all the murders you gotta cover-up. On that subject, I saw on the news that one of *your* boys shot Josh Cutter, and y'all are covering it up. That true?" Huffy stayed silent, a rising tide of anger threatening to swamp him and knock him off his feet. Kennedy tisked. "Anyway, as I was saying, I know you guys don't make a lot, so if any of your DIY crew need a bit of extra scratch, send 'em over." He took another toke and again spoke while holding his breath. "My crapper ain't been flushing right."

Laughter chased Huffy to his car.

Speeding past the surveillance van, he cranked the radio and listened to part of "The Closer You Get" by Alabama and all of Kenny and Dolly's "I'll Be Home For Christmas," before clicking the radio off.

Music was an insufficient tool, nowhere near strong enough to distract him from his hatred of Kennedy—hatred made worse by a fact he refused to accept; he respected Kennedy. Not the man, but his conviction. Kennedy had amounted to far more than the sum of his parts. His passion, will, and a warped vision of the future had inspired blind loyalty from a small group of like-minded psychopaths. Huffy both admired and despised Kennedy's ability to inspire that level of ferocious loyalty. Occasionally, he grudgingly acknowledged the role envy played in that visceral hatred. Unencumbered by a badge, the law, or morals, and with no fear of the consequences, Kennedy could scratch his itches as hard and as often as he liked. It was like a brother tormenting his sister under threat of grounding or the loss of "computer privileges." Being fine with those consequences freed him to torment his sister at will.

And although it produced anxiety, not hatred, Huffy's lack of knowledge about the RUV's activities kept him up nights. Passion, charisma, determination, and a scapegoat for all of society's ills was a repeatable formula used to start world, race, culture, and other wars. Hell, the KKK began as a social club in Tennessee and, at its peak, had millions of members, not to mention a presidential candidate. Could anyone predict with any degree of certainty how big Kennedy's group of fanatical followers might one day be, or how many "cleansings" they would ultimately perform. And despite bad guys killing bad guys not being all that offensive a concept, Huffy knew collateral damage—like Josh Cutter—was impossible to avoid. And just as concerning as the inevitability of collateral damage was the knowledge that people like Kennedy had malleable definitions of what it meant to be a "bad guy."

10

Allan watched Frankie Bryant, motionless behind her desk, catching tears with a tissue before they had a chance to fall. He had seen so many good officers break when the stress at home mixed with the pressure at work, one fueling the other like gas on a flame until the fire was unmanageable. Affairs, divorce, alcohol, drugs, and suicide awaited many. In the new normal, all of those stressors were being compounded by an issue police officers, particularly good ones, were unaccustomed to dealing with: being seen as the enemy. For most, absorbing a bullet while protecting strangers was a risk taken, not for the prestige or forty thousand a year or the adrenaline rush, but because they cared. They wanted to make a difference. Bad people permeated every profession, but the vast majority of police officers, at least those Allan knew, were good people trying hard to keep others safe.

He had been counseling Frankie for several months, and "gut-wrenching" did not scratch the surface of what she faced. The recent shooting of an eight-year-old boy was a perfect example. Securing justice was an immense burden, a burden that exponentially increased when justice was owed to the family of a dead child. But in the new normal, the pressure to deliver justice for an eight-year-old *African American* boy was unbearable. The pressure she put on herself was enough to break most people, but as the SIU's first *black* Commander, she faced immense pressure from all sides—superiors, the public, and victims' families. She accepted that; it was part of her job. And she had no intention of "unburdening herself" by shitting on those she managed. She was not a cliché. Being a lousy manager slash asshole was not in her DNA.

Her only job-related complaint was the media, or, more precisely, specific media members. In the new normal, it was easy—irresponsible and dangerous, but easy—to use a lack of progress as the basis for suggesting police killed Josh Cutter and that Frankie was helping to cover it up. In their first session, she had tearfully admitted that it was easier to tell a parent their child was dead than it was to deal with certain media members. She despised that "People have a right to know!" was so often misused as justification for crossing lines that should never be crossed. "People," she had said, "have no such right. But victims and their families *do* have a right to privacy and don't deserve to have their pain exploited for ratings or a penny a click."

There was never a *good* time for someone to learn of a spouse's affair, but with all the pressure Frankie was under, he knew she would have preferred that Beth's infidelity had remained a secret a while longer.

"Sorry." Frankie dabbed at the corner of her eye with the tissue. "We are supposed to be discussing a case."

"It's okay," Allan said, the warm smile hidden beneath his mask conveyed through his soft, caring tone. "The case can wait."

"I just don't understand," she continued, her voice cracking slightly. "If life with me was so bad, why didn't Beth tell me? Why did she leave an adolescent trail of breadcrumbs that, *if* seen, *might* lead me to understand how she felt? If she had told me how she felt, maybe we could have repaired whatever she felt was broken."

"Sometimes, the anger that stems from betrayal worsens when we convince ourselves we should have seen and stopped that betrayal."

"I *was* a detective," she replied, straining for a smile that wasn't there. "On some level, I guess I knew how she felt. Or suspected, anyway." A beat. "At times, I wonder if my refusal to accept our marriage was in trouble is the main reason it is about to fail."

Her words hit him so hard that, for a moment, he assumed God had used her like a pull-string puppet to say: *You are doing the same thing with Clara!*

"I mean—"

She looked past him. He turned. Huffy, talking quietly on his cell, stepped in and closed the door. She wiped all emotion from her face and immediately picked up where they had left off before their meeting veered into her personal life.

"Wilhelm claiming he could have stopped the Holocaust by killing Hitler is consistent with Grandiose Delusions?"

"Yes," Allan answered, concerned by how quickly she had shut off her emotions. A cop thing. Can't show weakness. Terribly unhealthy, but he understood why she had developed the skill. He made a mental note to try and help her learn not to lock herself down.

His call finished, Huffy flopped into the chair beside Allan. "Did gramps happen to mention who shot JFK?"

Other than her half-hearted glare, she ignored Huffy's comment and asked Allan, "Is it all fantasy?"

"The split varies by case, but delusions are always a mix of fact and fantasy."

"So, there *could* be a grandson, who *could* be relevant?"

"And the old man *could* have killed 308 people," Huffy chided. "And he *could* have stopped the Holocaust." He responded to Frankie's harsh glare with a smirk and a shrug.

"I am convinced someone is abusing him," Allan said. "And based on the timing of his confession and what he knows about Palette's death, it is hard to imagine Wilhelm's abuser is not relevant to your investigation."

"What about Bradley Cross?" Frankie asked.

"Who?" Allan replied.

"The substitute teacher from Seattle," she clarified, exchanging a quizzical look with Huffy. "Wilhelm told you he killed Bradley Cross."

"Oh, right," Allan said. "What about him?"

"I called Seattle PD. Cross hung himself in his shower two years ago. No signs of forced entry or anyone but Cross having been in the apartment, all windows were locked from the inside, and the door was locked and chained." A beat. "You said Wilhelm told you he'd killed Cross because Cross was *going to* kill forty-one kids?"

Allan nodded. "Wilhelm believes he has stopped, in his words, *'the monsters society is lucky enough never to have seen on the news.'*"

"Cross," Frankie continued, "had thousands of child porn images and videos on his computer and was chatting with five boys under the age of twelve. He had made arrangements to meet one, a nine-year-old. SPD found a rape kit, a large roll of plastic, and a new, oversized suitcase in the trunk of Cross's car."

He understood how cops could be so matter-of-fact with the most horrific details. It was a necessary skill honed over time. Still, the skill never ceased to amaze him. Bradley Cross had clearly intended to rape and murder that nine-year-old boy. In a movie, Frankie would have taken a dramatic pause before delivering the information, and her voice would have been "heavy" or "sullen," or she would have "choked off her words." Instead, she had delivered the brutal facts as though dictating a grocery list.

"As with Palette's nutsack," she continued, "Wilhelm knew a detail he couldn't have. A few days before SPD found his body, Cross had chaperoned a Halloween party at the elementary school he subbed at. Wilhelm told you Cross died wearing a Batman costume?"

He nodded.

"SPD has never released that detail."

He thought for a moment. "He might have seen or read a news story about Cross. Maybe that story mentioned the Halloween party, and Wilhelm made a lucky guess."

"Maybe," she said. "But it is more likely he knows someone with access to our databases."

"Or," Huffy interjected, "the neighbor's dog told the old man the kid was going to be the first of forty-one kills and ordered him to proactively stop the carnage."

She fired a 'knock it off' scowl that nailed Huffy right between the eyes. "Regardless, a hundred-year-old man did not break *into* Bachman and overpower a serial killer four times his size. Until we have something better to go on, Doc, you may as well continue with the abusive grandson angle. Can you meet with him again tomorrow?"

Allan agreed then left after claiming he was late for a Christmas-tree hunt.

"What were you two chatting about when I came in?" Huffy asked Frankie.

"The old man," she answered, staring absently at her desk phone. "And some other stuff."

"Beth?"

She continued watching the phone as though willing it to ring, preferring to answer it instead of his question. Eventually, she offered a distracted nod.

"How can you work with him and talk to him about your private life?"

"Like I do with you?"

"That's different. We're besties."

"You know all my secrets." She sarcastically clicked her tongue. "I would still shoot you if you deserved it."

Her expression dulled, and he instantly knew why. She had been making the trip to *It's My Fault Lane* more frequently lately, blaming herself for Beth's indiscretion. Every time her mind went there, he wanted to shake her out of her daze and yell: *Smarten up!* Beth cheated. Period. End of story. No excuse could justify it. She had multiple options, and cheating should not have been one of them. Cheating is for the selfish and the weak. Still, it broke his heart to see Frankie like this. She was strong and held it in—at least at work—but she was hurting. Luckily, he knew how to snap her from her self-loathing. She had no problem blaming herself for Beth's mistakes, but she refused to allow him to do the same.

"I wish I had never told you about Beth's—"

"Don't start," she ordered, the 'Google Emotional Maps' voice in her head already rerouting her back to the here and now. "You didn't hear a rumor; you *saw* her. And you saw enough to know she'd cheated. When you confronted her, she denied it. When you forced her to tell me, she lied about the extent of what you had seen." A beat. "If I had found out about her affair only to learn you had known all along but never told me, I'd have shot you...*twice!* And you aren't exactly the kind of friend who could sit beside Beth at our dinner table and pretend nothing had happened. Besides, staying quiet would have allowed her to keep cheating. What if she hooked up with a diseased troll or a jealous psychopath? Or worse?"

"A Republican?"

Her subtle smile told him she had returned from *It's My Fault Lane*. "There's plenty of blame to go around, but you sure as hell don't deserve any."

A beat. "I just miss our group."

"So do I, but that's on Beth. We all have the right to draw lines people can't cross, no matter who they are. Regardless of what choice I make related to Beth, you and I are good."

He smiled as warmly as he could. He was happy he had brought her back from *It's My Fault Lane,* but he was also sad because he knew it would not be her last trip. She was in so much pain, and he wanted to help her end it. But he felt powerless. 'Listening' seemed like such a ridiculously inadequate option. Someone you love is hurting, and you help them by listening? That is bullshit. You don't deal with pain by suffering through it; you end it. You do what you have to do to make a clean, surgical break—an ice-pick through the eye and into the brain.

"Want some good news?" he asked.

"You've found the courage to accept you are a horribly flawed human being?"

"Almost."

She smiled. "Baby steps."

He smiled back. "Earlier today, I interviewed a CO from Bachman, Derek Samuels. When Palette died, Samuels was supposed to be on shift, but he called in sick. I had Rolo do some digging. Samuels's girlfriend, Molly Barnes, has an interesting connection."

He let the information hang in the air, staring at her like he had a juicy bit of gossip but was going to make her beg for it.

Frankie tired of the game almost instantly. *"And?"* she growled.

Pleased with himself, he said, "Molly Barnes is Benny Carpenter's cousin."

EVENING. DECEMBER 18.

Allan spat a mouthful of minty foam into the sink and reinserted his buzzing toothbrush. Through the mirror, he spotted Clara standing in the en suite's doorway, a basket of unfolded laundry held against her hip, and Hiccup tethered to her ankle by the unbreakable chains of puppy love.

On a scale of ten, Clara woke up a nine and, with minimal effort, spent the rest of the day a twelve. But an insemination-based metamorphosis always pushed her to a fifteen. Pregnancy transformed her shoulder-length, reddish-brown hair to shimmering auburn, her brown eyes to sparkling hazel, her slim body to slender, and it caused her bronze-colored skin to glow as if the sun had followed her from conception. She was five years his junior, looked ten years younger than that, and the effects of pregnancy seemed to double that gap. However, there were a couple of less-desirable effects: unpredictable and extreme mood swings and *Pregnancy Brain*. This pregnancy had spawned a nasty case of both.

In keeping with that behavioral volatility, Clara was glaring at him with a harshness he found confusing. The day had gone well, the Christmas-tree hunt ending with the capture of a full-figured, straight-spined, ten-foot spruce. While decorating it, they had even managed to have a normal conversation. Recently, a "normal" conversation was any conversation where neither got upset after finding hurtful meaning *between the lines* or in the speaker's *tone of voice*. When his eyes drifted to a rolled-up poster on top of the basket of unfolded laundry, Clara's scowl made perfect sense.

The poster, he knew, featured Peyton Manning—the corners of his mouth hiked into a confident smile, and his arm cocked and ready to deliver another game-winning touchdown. He knew that because less than an hour ago, he had hung the legendary quarterback in the nursery.

Peyton was décor, but his true purpose was to distract. He was their flea-flicker, their fake punt, their go-to razzle-dazzle on fourth and inches. Peyton was a Four-Star General in a battle over nursery décor. A good-natured back and forth meant to distract from the constant whispers of, "What if?" *What if the twins don't make it to full term? What if they are stillborn or die soon after birth like Khloe or Isaac? What if? What if? What if?*

That battle was fairly straightforward: everything Broncos and Manning that he managed to hang, pin, or glue on the nursery's walls, Clara would remove and relocate—usually to the den, which now looked more like a shrine than a home office.

As acknowledging the poster might land them on *Dateline Mysteries*, he returned to brushing his teeth while imagining Keith Morrison introducing the final segment of the Abrams's *Dateline Mysteries* episode.

> "But instead of happily ever after, the Abrams's Fairy Tale marriage would end in tragedy. And now, back to Josh Mankiewicz with the conclusion of Mile High Murder."

Clara flicked the poster off the basket and onto the floor, declared he was fighting a war he could not win, and waddled away as he finished up.

Peyton leaned against the bedside table, Allan started folding the still-warm laundry Clara had dumped on his side of the bed. Clara was under the covers with "her" dog on her lap. Hic was using everything in his puppy arsenal—tail wagging, soft whimpering, pleading puppy eyes, fractional head-tilts—to sway his favorite human while she channel-surfed and tried to ignore him.

"And *I am* the one fighting a war I can't win?" He dropped

a pair of balled socks into the basket. "I read somewhere that dogs have 100 expressions: one for 'walk,' one for 'pee,' and ninety-eight for 'Are you going to eat that?'" He chuckled. "I think Hic has 101."

Clara, as she always did, relented and tented the covers. Hic dove underneath, found *his* spot between her legs, circled until satisfied, flopped down, and capped the nightly ritual with a protracted "Do Not Disturb" puppy-sigh.

"And in one of nature's rarely seen moments," Clara narrated, "the reclusive Oreo-colored Shih Tzu settles into its natural habitat for a long night sleep." She pat Hic's duvet-covered head, settled on Jimmy Kimmel, and set the remote beside her leg. "I picked up your suit."

He turned sharply to her, brief eye contact enough for both to know what the other was thinking: she didn't want to hear it; he was sick of saying it. He was beyond angry. Her OBGYN's order had been crystal clear: "Other than for medical appointments, you need to stay home." She had never qualified that order with anything remotely close to: "Unless you want to do a little shopping or run some errands." Going stir crazy was not a valid reason to jeopardize the twins' health. More confusing was the fact he knew she was as concerned for the twins as he was.

"Chill," she said coldly, no doubt responding to his clear, albeit unspoken anger. "I wore a mask and picked it up after my doctor's appointment." She turned back to the TV.

Why start a fight? he thought, knowing that is precisely what would happen if he did not '*chill*.'

"I left it in your back seat."

"*Left* it?" he said, hoping a little sarcasm would ease the tension.

"Left, forgot…potato, potawto. I also *forgot* to return the Volvo's hide-a-key to its top-secret location. It's hanging in the entry."

Akin to the Bible's *Seven Signs of the Apocalypse*, owning a minivan was, to Clara, one of the *Three Signs of Unconditional Surrender to Parenthood*—the other two being the enjoyment of Pixar movies and a belief that "cute" was an acceptable adjective to describe human poop. Unwilling to surrender, she bought a "cool mom's" car. But as her pregnancy progressed—and extricating herself from her emerald-green Mini Cooper became harder than summiting Everest—she had adopted his Volvo. He added the wheel-well-mounted hide-a-key after her worsening case of *pregnancy brain* left him keyless for the *third* time.

The poorly folded laundry set aside, he crawled into bed just as Clara grabbed her belly and released a moan worthy of a panicked 911 call. But he was no longer terrified by the intensity with which she could verbally express her pain. "More cramps, or are they moving?"

"Moving," she answered, her breath shallow and quick.

A flash of worry flushed his skin. "You sure?"

A nod.

Relieved, he placed a hand on her stomach and, as usual, felt nothing. "They hate me," he moaned.

"They *don't* hate you," she rebuffed. A quick puff from her inhaler helped her breathing return to normal.

The twins were due in February, and he had yet to feel as much as a stretching finger or wriggling toe. A prenatal cold shoulder. Twins, he had read, often shared a supernatural-like connection—a spiritual bond that allowed them to sense each other's feelings regardless of geography. He had no way of knowing if his twins shared that transcendent bond, but they *clearly* shared the power of precognition. Both had no doubt seen some future punishment dad had doled out and were non-violently protesting from the womb. Sadly, he knew the prenatal snub was merely an amuse-bouche. Holding still when daddy's hand was on mommy's belly was a prequel to the bone-melting pain he would feel during the many *post-*

natal cold shoulders he would experience as a father. Many preceded by slamming bedroom doors and soul-crushing cries of: "I HATE you!"

He would give anything to hear those cries and feel that pain.

He placed his mouth against Clara's belly and bellowed, "As long as you live under my roof, you'll show me respect. We clear?"

"Technically," she tapped her belly, "they're under *my* roof."

He propped himself against the headboard, put on his reading glasses, grabbed his beeping cell phone off the bedside table, and read the text.

"Girlfriend?"

He swapped the phone for *Shutter Island* and started skimming pages, trying to remember where he had left off. "My old cadet."

"Right," Clara responded, watching Kimmel. "The *big* case. What is his name? Liam?"

"Yeah." He chuckled. "I called him *Ian*."

"What case?"

"Do you remember Sedrick Palette?"

Clara answered with an arched '*How could I forget?*' eyebrow.

"Well, *Liam*," he continued, "asked me to meet with an elderly man who'd confessed to killing Sedrick before prison staff even knew he was dead."

"Uh, huh," she mumbled, scrolling channels.

"He claims he could have stopped the Holocaust by killing Hitler as a child."

She settled on a *Seinfeld* rerun. "Killing Hitler when the old man was a child or when Hitler was a child? If you are ever going to get your novel published, you will need to improve your clarity."

Hatred of weak writing and poor grammar aside, the response was proof that after twenty-plus years of falling asleep to *Real-Life Tales of the Disturbed Mind,* nothing surprised her anymore. And following up with, "What is curious about an old man with a delusional disorder?" proved that *Real-Life Tales of the Disturbed Mind* also functioned as a quasi-training manual.

"Nothing," he answered. "He also told me that he had killed hundreds of people before they had the chance to unleash whatever evil they had planned."

"I guess that would make Hitler a pretty big miss."

A grin. "Yeah."

"He was a tad late on Sedrick Palette, as well."

He found his spot in *Shutter Island* and crooked the page's corner. "I couldn't put my finger on it, but there was something off about him. I got a migraine just talking to him."

Clara tisked. "Maybe crazy is contagious."

"He is not—"

"*Complicated*, not crazy. I *know*."

Her *enough already* tone was all it took to erect a wall of tension between them. It infuriated him that tension could so easily shut them down; he was a psychiatrist, for Christ's sake. According to Clara, that was a big part of the problem. She felt "analyzed." He knew he wasn't analyzing her. Although he *had* spent two decades digging inside people's heads. It wasn't inconceivable, he supposed, that he had lost the ability to communicate without unconsciously poking and prodding.

He read for a while, stopping twice to laugh at the *Seinfeld* episode Clara was watching: once when George got upset about the cold water causing "shrinkage," and again when he demanded to see Jerry's girlfriend naked. Fair is fair.

"Do you have an alibi?"

"Huh?" he grunted.

"You disappeared last night."

"Oh, right. I went downstairs and wrote for a while. Couldn't sleep."

"A while? I woke up to pee *thirty-five* times and didn't see you once." He replied with a scrunched nose and a shrug. "How *is* the world's greatest novel coming?" she added.

"Ready for my grammar-Nazi wife to check my work."

She was channel surfing again. "Do you think Hitler had proofreaders?"

"*What?*" he yelped, confused by the question.

A shrug. "Maybe there were grammar Nazis."

That's funny, he thought. Clara was funny in general, but her star shined brightest in the niche market of grammar humor. His favorite zinger to date? *You wouldn't know a dangling participle if it tea-bagged you.* His gut had hurt after hearing his usually restrained wife make a scrotum on the face joke. Laughter used to come easy for them, appearing randomly and with little provocation. Now? Not so much. *Thinking* something was funny was often the best he could do.

"Oh, change that back," he said, pointing to the TV. She handed him the remote, and he flipped back to a news broadcast where a portly man with a bad comb-over was speaking into a jumble of cell phones and micro-recorders. An on-screen graphic identified him as the warden of Bachman Correctional Facility. A second graphic was scrolling across the bottom of the screen.

...Palette found dead hours before his scheduled execution. Sedrick...

The warden's press conference soon ended, and Allan clicked the TV off. "The pictures Liam showed me were horrific." He set his book, glasses, and the remote on the bedside table. "Someone sure did a number on Sedrick."

"Blood and guts," she hissed. "It won't be long before we are feeding people to the lions again."

He turned to her. She immediately turned away, struggling

from her back onto her side. He stretched out a hand, intending to set it gently on her shoulder. Instead, he let it fall between them. He knew what he wanted to say. He had said the words countless times in his head. He was a psychiatrist with a Ph. D., and they had been together for over two decades; how could it be so difficult to talk to her? Time and time again, the words would rally in his brain. *Honey, ignoring our problems won't work. We need to talk about how we feel and why.* Then, full of purpose and resolve, they would march toward his mouth only to rearrange themselves along the way and exit as a comment on the weather or traffic or the outrageous cost of pistachios.

He recalled Frankie Bryant wondering if her reluctance to admit her marriage was in trouble was a key reason it was close to failing. Am I doing the same thing? Is our marriage barreling toward a cliff, but instead of pounding the brakes, I am closing my eyes and shouting, "There is no cliff!"

—

CLARA SNORING SOFTLY beside him, Allan, his hands cupped behind his head, was mapping the topography of the ceiling's stipple while pondering the words the warden used to end his press conference. *I have the utmost confidence in the SIU to confirm suicide and bring closure for the families of Sedrick Palette's victims.* That makes no sense, he thought. Palette's victims are long dead, and he was hours from execution; how would a finding of suicide bring closure to anyone? He soon concluded that the *only* thing a finding of suicide would bring was an end to any uncomfortable questions the warden might have to answer.

His eyes drifted around the room, stopping randomly on dressers and doorknobs and light fixtures. He studied every detail, and wondered about their manufacturing process, the materials used to make them, and the people who assembled them. When the distraction lost steam, he gazed out the bedroom window at the flickering pinholes of light in the endless black sky. He identified new constellations with names like "stick" and "crooked stick" and "odd-shaped rock." Again, the distraction worked, but only for a while. As they always did, the whispers of *What if?* eventually broke through. *What if? What if? What if?* No threat to the twins' well-being ever left unexplored. In addition to those endless whispers, his migraines—an affliction he had suffered with since childhood—were increasing in strength and frequency and now regularly shook his brain like a possessed mechanical bull.

Over the last several months, all of it had combined to make sleep elusive. And when his body and mind finally succumbed to exhaustion, the same terrifying dream would claw at the soft tissue of his brain. Every morning he would wake raw and fuzzy and feeling as though he had not slept at all. Everyone had bad dreams, but this dream was different. Repetitive and beyond vivid. While dreaming, he somehow remained aware of the real world around him. He could *see* himself sleeping beside Clara; he could *feel* her get up to go to the bathroom; he could hear Hiccup whimper and feel him kick as he chased dream-world rabbits or escaped nightmarish beasts.

He'd had the same dream every night for months, but the detail evaporated the moment he opened his eyes. Each time it wrenched him from sleep—his heart whirring in his chest, his skin doused in sweat—he would wonder the same thing: Why am I so scared?

The dream ran uninterrupted, start to finish, every detail always the same. It began atop a hill, a warm sun pinned high in a cloudless summer sky, the hill sliding lazily into a wide valley carpeted in broadleaf grass and perfectly placed random patches of wildflowers: Scarlet Gilia, Wild Blue Flax, Colorado Blue Columbine, and Pink Mountain Heather. Perfectly postured, towering evergreens guarded the valley on all sides, their pine scent triggering the childhood memory of his mom singing "Under the Boardwalk" as she spread Vicks VapoRub on his chest. Sometimes to ease a stuffy nose or head cold, sometimes simply to comfort him.

On the hill, a tree—naked and deformed, its scarred and knotted trunk bent at a ninety-degree angle. Its top two-thirds stretching toward the valley, as were its hundreds of skeletal arms and scores of broken and dislocated fingers, all burdened by swollen, arthritic knuckles. The tree, pathetic and desperate, seemed to be reaching with all its might for something beyond its grasp.

A general stood under the tree, a boy, not a man. Only his profile was visible: his soft jawline, smooth olive-colored skin, and a pyramid of freckles below his right ear.

The blue sky and glowing sun now smothered by thick, black clouds, the boy general surveyed the valley, its wildflowers dead, and its grass now stained by the blood of thousands of corpses. Floating more than walking, he descended toward the valley, stopping when a woman—her white nightgown glowing amidst the backdrop of mangled corpses and decaying flesh—clawed at his pant leg. "Only you can save us, Allan." Her eyes were dark and begging, her voice familiar but foreign; he recognized her but had no idea who she was.

Every night, Allan would watch the boy general place a gun to her temple and pull the trigger, the blast shattering the dream. He would wake, terrified but unsure why, his eyes as big as golf balls, and the sound of a gunshot reverberating in his throbbing head.

But tonight would be different. Tonight, he would remember the dream for the first time. In a few hours, he would wake, trembling and drenched in sweat, certain his subconscious had alerted him to an intruder. He would hold still and listen, hearing only the sound of blood pulsing furiously against his eardrums. He would search the pitch-black bedroom for uninvited shadows or shapes but find none. He would see Hiccup standing on the foot of the bed, rigid and alert, focused on the window. His low, extended growl would cause Clara to stir and grumble, "What the hell?" The clock radio would read 2:22. He would flip back the covers, trudge to the bathroom, take a second migraine pill and a third Ambien, and crawl back into bed. Twenty minutes later, the details of the dream would flood his mind.

At 3:12 a.m., unable to sleep, he would throw on a robe, leave Clara and Hiccup alone in bed, and set off to work on his novel. Hours later, he would wake on the den couch, fully dressed, and with no memory of how or when he'd got there.

MORNING. DECEMBER 19.

Six Days until Christmas.

Where is he? Allan wondered. He was fuzzy from a lack of sleep, but he wasn't *that* fuzzy. Sergeant Murphy had said Wilhelm was in the fifth-floor counseling office, but the office was empty.

Allan heel-kicked the door closed while balancing two coffee mugs precariously on his briefcase. The early morning sun, barely able to penetrate the room's glass-block window, had eased the gloom enough to forego flicking on the light. For that, he was grateful. Artificial light would only increase the pain in his throbbing head.

A grumbled, "Hello," floated from a dark corner and startled him. He managed to steady his wobbling hands and avoid catastrophe. He should know better. His six-year-old shell cordovan leather briefcase was a $3,000 Christmas present from Clara. If he stained it with two full cups of coffee, telling her would not have been an option; he would have had to buy an exact replica. Or leave the country.

Wilhelm was wrapped in the folds of an enormous, tan-colored leather chair. For a moment, Allan wondered if he had passed through a breach in Space-Time. Instead of the counseling office, he was now on the set of a cheesy 60's horror film: *Chairs!* In this scene, the killer had nearly devoured a frail old man. The next scene, he figured, would be a series of spinning FrontPage headlines.

CHAIR CLAIMS ANOTHER!
FEAR GRIPS CITY!

FURNITURE SALES PLUMMET!

Wilhelm's untouched breakfast sat on a small glass-top table between the two identical leather chairs. Allan set the coffee cups beside the plate of food and sat in the empty chair. "Black with half a teaspoon of sugar."

As if held by a 700-pound Sumo wrestler, Wilhelm struggled to wriggle free, then inhaled coffee fumes. A frown creased his forehead. "Sweetener," he said dejectedly, falling back into the chair's clutches.

Having retrieved a pad and pen from his briefcase, Allan stowed it beside his chair. "Sorry." He winked. "The only sugar I could find was the icing sugar on a half-eaten jelly donut." He eyed Wilhelm's scrambled eggs, toast, and bacon. "Not hungry?"

"Trying to maintain my girlish figure."

"How'd you sleep?" he asked through a sleepy grin.

"Better than I have in years."

His heart sank at the thought that Wilhelm's best night sleep in years had come on a concrete bed inside a holding cell. He wondered if it was because Wilhelm, out of his abuser's reach, now felt safe.

He sipped some coffee, slid on his mask, and asked Wilhelm for his full name, home address, and an emergency contact. Knowing patients, particularly involuntary ones, rarely opened up to strangers, Allan had spent their time together yesterday building trust. That investment, he hoped, would have Wilhelm feeling comfortable enough to provide the name of a friend or relative. Huffy could use the name to continue his investigation, and he could use it to ensure Wilhelm was released into caring arms.

"What kind of emergency are you expecting?" Wilhelm asked. "A heart attack when I see your bill?"

A chuckle. "With my skills as a conversationalist, you

should be more concerned about slipping into a coma."

Despite thinking the joke was pretty damn good, he wasn't offended when Wilhelm simply said, "Vilhelm N. Weissand." He noted the name. "And who can I contact if I need to?"

Wilhelm did not answer.

"Do you have any friends or family in the area?"

"No."

"In another State?"

"No."

"What about your grandson?" he asked. If Wilhelm reacted as he had yesterday, it would create an opening to dig deeper into his personal life. But Wilhelm didn't react at all. Sensing resistance on the topic of family, Allan decided to let Wilhelm take the lead and see where they ended up. "Would you like to talk about anything in particular?"

"The voices."

Wilhelm answered so quickly, Allan couldn't help but wonder if he'd been eagerly awaiting the question. The answer also had him wondering if Wilhelm might have a file with a mental health professional. He made a note to check the databases that would contain that information.

"You hear voices?"

Wilhelm sunk deeper into his chair and watched his thumbs tumble over one another.

"Internal monologue is common and nothing to be ashamed of," Allan reassured. "We use it to weigh the pros and cons of choices we are facing, or sometimes just as a coping mechanism. My wife and I have had our share of difficulties trying to start a family, and we are now expecting twins, so I often use an internal monologue to work through my fears and anxieties. Is an internal monologue what you mean when you say *the voices*?" Wilhelm shook his head. "Are they background noise?" he asked, thinking schizophrenia might be a possibility. "Like a radio playing in another room?" Wilhelm shook his head again. "Do you have conversations with them?"

That got Wilhelm's attention. "I am not crazy," he stated, steadying his anxious thumbs.

"I apologize. What I meant was, do you interact with the voices?"

"In many ways."

"Have you talked to someone about them? Someone I could speak with? Your family doctor…or someone like me?"

"You mean a shrink?"

"Yes," he answered, amused by the question. "Have you talked to a *shrink* like me about the voices?"

"I doubt there are many shrinks like you, Doc."

Speaking cryptically seemed to be an element of Wilhelm's delusion. Perhaps "knowing" things other people did not helped enhance the voices' mystique. Allan hadn't encountered the idiosyncrasy before, but mental illness was like that, each manifestation similar but not identical.

"Wilhelm—"

Allan's phone dinged with a message alert. He checked it—an order from Huffy to come to the lunchroom to review Sedrick Palette's tox report. He told Wilhelm he would be back and left.

On his way to meet Huffy, he debated a shortlist of potential afflictions, with dementia, schizophrenia, and Grandiose Delusions topping the list; all fit in one way or another. But he was now skeptical of the theory that Wilhelm had overheard the planning of Sedrick Palette's murder. How would that scenario result in a confession moments after Palette's death? Did the killers discuss the exact time they planned to kill him? And did they also throw in a random reference to the teacher from Seattle and his Batman costume?

He pressed the elevator's call button, a new theory starting to form.

—

FRANKIE HANDED THE tox report back to Huffy. "Is that enough PCP for Palette to Swiss cheese himself without a peep?"

"Doc's on his way—"

Huffy paused long enough to check and ignore his buzzing cell phone.

"You can't ignore her forever."

He stuffed the phone into his pants pocket. "Challenge accepted."

Frankie rolled her eyes. "How long has Abrams been up there with Grapplin' Gramps?"

"Not sure."

"Any reason for someone to sit in?"

He shook his head. "Abrams says he prefers to be alone with the old man. Doesn't want to spook him."

She shrugged a *Whatever*. "Thanks for last night, by the way. Nothing like a keg of red wine and karaoke to cheer a girl up."

People escaped life in a variety of ways. Huffy eased his burdened mind by working to turn his Brazilian jiu-jitsu brown belt into a black belt and singing karaoke. How a six-six ginger could flawlessly belt out Waylon Jennings and Merle Haggard was a mystery. Not that it mattered, but Frankie had lost the vocal lottery. She was a good sport about it, though, once joking she had been booted from the church choir because of a mass case of stigmata. *Only, instead of bleeding from their palms,* she'd said, smiling, *the parishioners bled from their ears.*

"Doc," Huffy said, looking behind Frankie. She turned as Allan reached them.

"How's it going?" she asked.

"A lot to unpack," Allan answered. "He is not volunteering much, but he is talking. I sense he has a lot to say. I just need to get him to trust me enough to open up. That probably means

I will have to allow him to guide me through his delusion. Its origin, its evolution. Maybe even what he believes is the end game."

"Sounds like a real hoot," Huffy said.

Allan smiled. "I'll take the safe stuff over the gun stuff every day."

Huffy handed Allan the tox report.

"Hard to say," Allan said after reading the report. "It isn't a high dose, and reactions to PCP vary based on several factors. The best I can do is a maybe."

"Maybe?" Frankie and Huffy said simultaneously, Huffy sounding annoyed, Frankie curious.

A nod.

"What good does *maybe* do us?" Huffy barked.

"I'm sorry," Allan said. "We all agreed suicide was unlikely. If the probability was twenty percent, that tox report likely lowers it to ten. Maybe even five. I may have a more plausible theory if you are—"

Huffy snatched the report from Allan's hand. "Leave the police work to me. That's why I have the gun, remember?"

He stormed out.

Allan turned to Frankie, who asked, "Is your theory fact or conjecture?"

"The latter, I guess."

"Let me know if it becomes more than that."

She walked away, leaving him alone.

"I can think of better ways to spend my Christmas vacation," he grumbled under his breath.

—

Allan returned to the fifth-floor counseling office only to find it empty. Confident Wilhelm had not escaped and was probably in the bathroom across the hall, he sat in one of the matching leather chairs and transcribed onto his notepad the theory he'd been mulling.

Instead of Wilhelm overhearing the planning of Palette's murder, what if someone fed him the details?

Wilhelm's mental illness, he thought, combined with something as simple as his abuser speaking to him through a wall or door, could have led to his belief in what he calls *the voices*. It was also a reasonable explanation for his knowledge of the teacher from Seattle. Regardless of how plausible that theory, one thing is clear: the most direct path to the person or persons responsible for Wilhelm knowing what he does is to explore *the voice—*

The sound of the counseling office door opening snapped him out of his head.

"Well, Doc," Wilhelm said, shuffling toward him. "Am I crazy?" He grunted stiffly as he eased into his chair. "Or just complicated?"

"Pardon?" Allan said, despite hearing the question clearly. Other than Clara and the odd cadet, he had never heard anyone use that phrase before. He scanned his memory, trying to recall if he had used it around Wilhelm. He hadn't, he was sure of it. Did I say it to Liam, and then he used it in front of Wilh—

"I asked if, like everyone else around here, you think I am crazy?"

Wilhelm's question and almost child-like tone had opened a door Allan needed to walk through. Doing so would help him gain Wilhelm's trust and, hopefully, start them on a path that would lead to his abuser's identity. He dismissed the crazy versus complicated statement as coincidence and replied, "Of course not."

Wilhelm appeared pleased with that answer.

How do I ask this question, Allan wondered, without contradicting what I just told him?

"Wilhelm, do you remember killing Sedrick Palette? Or did the voices *tell* you that you had killed him and provide you with the details of his death?"

All expression drained from Wilhelm's face. "You think I am making it up." His voice was void of energy and barely above a whisper.

Before leaving private practice, Allan had counseled a man who'd been a POW near the end of the Vietnam War. The cruelty and humiliation the man had endured should have killed him. In a way, it had. He was an empty shell—weary bones wrapped in a weathered sheet of wrinkled flesh. The loss of dignity could destroy a soul far faster than physical torture. Watching Wilhelm deflate and transform into that same empty shell, he decided Huffy's needs had to be secondary to easing Wilhelm's pain.

"When was the last time you felt at peace?"

"July 13, 1888." Wilhelm's voice had turned dreary and wet as though he was reading aloud from the operating manual of a medieval torture device.

Wilhelm was not pushing 130 years old, but there was nothing to gain by challenging his delusion. "Why is that date significant?"

Falling tears exposed vertical lines in Wilhelm's cheeks. The lines were so deep, Allan wondered if a lifetime of tears had followed the same path and eroded trenches in Wilhelm's pallid, wrinkled skin. "The next day, I heard the voices for the first time."

The weight of Wilhelm's reality seemed almost too much for his frail bones to support. *Should I stop?* he wondered. He wanted to. *Huffy could find another way. But he needs your help,* Allan thought, the voice oddly unfamiliar. *Whether you find out who is abusing him or not, you need to ease his pain.*

"Never having felt peace must be a terrible burden."

Wilhelm's pain and emptiness disappeared behind an inscrutable mask. "I enjoyed thirty-two years of relative peace before I heard the voices."

"In July of 1888, you were *thirty-two*?" Allan heard his voice pitch up slightly as if Wilhelm being 130 was plausible, but 160 was ludicrous.

A somber nod. "My wife and I owned what would now be called a Bed and Breakfast on the Inn River in Passau, Germany." For the first time, Allan detected a faint German accent. "Our two children passed young from Diphtheria, and my son was killed soon after the end of the Second World War.

"A man and woman who often spent time at our Inn had also lost young children. Our shared tragedies bonded us, and we became close. Although I did not recognize it at the time, the voices began exerting their influence over me on July 14, 1888. Soon after, the woman gave birth to a child that the voices took a strong interest in. For two years, the voices were relentless, their influence unlike anything I had ever experienced. I was convinced I had gone mad as only madness could explain my thoughts—thoughts I found increasingly difficult to disregard. In 1891, I heard about a man with an excellent understanding of the mind and traveled to Vienna to meet with him. Do you know the name Sigismund Schlomo?"

Allan did, and he mentally dusted off the only biography he had retained from university. Although no longer publicly using the name, the man *was* in private practice in Vienna around that time.

"Sigmund Freud."

Wilhelm nodded. "So, to answer one of your previous questions, *yes*, I *have* seen a shrink about the voices."

He swallowed a grin but couldn't help but enjoy the detail. He had read dozens of case studies on delusion and counseled people with a variety of delusional disorders. But until now, not one had incorporated the father of modern psychology. He began to find it challenging to subdue his fascination with the power and depth of Wilhelm's delusion. Instead of an experienced psychiatrist with a Ph.D., he was starting to feel like a Boy Scout nibbling on a smore while listening to a campfire ghost story.

"In January of 1894, no longer able to resist the voices, I did their bidding and sent that woman's four-year-old son into the river. Knowing what I was capable of but not understanding why, I fled to protect those I loved from whatever had broken inside me. I never returned." Wilhelm took a deep breath and exhaled slowly. "Some years later, I read that a passing priest had rescued the boy."

A beat.

"The voices convinced you to kill him; they had in*fluenced* you. How?"

"They make their wishes known in many ways," Wilhelm said dejectedly. Before Allan could decide if he should question the esoteric statement, Wilhelm continued. "I traveled, finding work where I could. Occasionally, an odd pain would run through me like an electric current." He slowly closed his eyes; he looked exhausted. "At that time, I did not understand its purpose, not as I…"

Allan waited several seconds for Wilhelm to continue. "Would you like to stop? We can take a break if you are tired?"

His eyes still closed, Wilhelm shook his head deliberately, seemingly saying: *Yes, I want desperately to stop, but I have no choice. I must continue.*

"In 1920," he went on, his eyes easing open, "while on my way to Belgium to find work during the Summer Olympics, I stopped in Munich and visited the Hofbräuhaus to inquire about lodging. When I left, a man robbed me. I had no money to continue my journey, so I took a job at the Hofbräuhaus.

"The next day, a man gave a speech there. He was an excellent orator, easily hiding his anger beneath his immense passion. The crowd loved him and cheered incessantly. I did not.

"Before I saw his face, I felt the same pain I had felt so often before. That pain drew me to him, increasing as I neared the room where he was speaking. When I entered the room and saw him and heard his voice, I knew who he was. Based on how often I had experienced that same pain, I knew we had crossed paths dozens of times. But I had never realized the encounter had taken place. I left Munich that night.

"Over the years, we continued to cross paths. I would not always see him, but I always knew he was close. No matter how often I moved on, I could not outrun that odd pain, experiencing it over and over again. Every step I took to distance myself from him only led us closer together."

The weight of Wilhelm's memories seemed to crush him, his body sinking deep into his chair. His delusion was the most detailed Allan had ever come across. Wilhelm was not telling a story; he was narrating his autobiography. In his mind, he *had* killed 308 people. And the voices *were* real, as were their supernatural powers, and, most importantly, the power they wielded over him. One way or another, he would confirm every whisper as fact and execute every order without regard for his own well-being or the well-being of others. Whatever mystical methods the voices used to influence him, Wilhelm felt powerless to disregard their wishes.

His head threatening to explode, Allan excused himself after making a quick note.

Wilhelm believes he kills monsters before they become monsters and that the voices have sent him to Witten. To do what?

13

The nurse dropped the blood pressure cuff into its wire basket. "I'm serious!" he croaked. "The Shining is the only parenting book you will ever need." Clara could not stop laughing. She had been laughing for the entire examination, so hard at times, that she had worried the nurse's stand-up routine would induce labor. "Trust me," he continued. "Start chasing those little shits around with an ax, and you just watch how fast chores get done. My son cleans his room until it's practically invisible." The nurse, his smile widening with every stride, dropped his disposable mask in the garbage as he left the exam room.

Alone, Clara felt good for the first time in weeks. Laughter, indeed, was good medicine. Sadly, she knew the feeling would pass. Her professed love of Stephen King was what led to the nurse's bit on *The Shining*, and one of her favorite King stories was *The Body*—a short story that became the movie *Stand By Me*. In a great scene, the coming-of-agers were short-cutting across a trestle bridge, each pretending not to be terrified by the prospect of an unexpected train. Sure enough, half-way across the bridge and two-hundred feet above the Royal river, Gordie Lachance spotted a trail of smoke rising above the distant tree line and shouted: "*Train!*"

Clara's fleeting moments of happiness always passed because, even if she couldn't see it, an approaching plume of thick, black, smothering smoke was always rising above a distant tree line. The cargo of the relentlessly chugging train could be any number of things, including a fight with Allan (usually over her "unauthorized absences" from her 3,000 square foot prison) or more bad news about the pandemic or escalating violence across the country. But the thickest and blackest smoke came from the stack of an unstoppable train pulling an endless line of cars overloaded with nightmarish scenarios related to the twins' well-being. That train followed her everywhere, its black smoke starving her of oxygen as it puffed and snorted like a rabid, charging bull. Staying ahead of it took every ounce of her energy. Occasionally, she contemplated letting the train roll over her.

The exam room door opened, and a petite, pony-tailed blonde skipped in carrying a wide smile. "Hey, girl."

"Hi," Clara responded.

She and the ultrasound tech, Marissa, worked in different departments and on different floors, so they had not met until after Clara started maternity leave. Not wanting to take any chances during another high-risk pregnancy, her OBGYN had insisted on regular ultrasounds, and Marissa was usually the tech.

"How are you feeling?" Marissa asked, efficiently prepping for the exam.

"I'm all..."

She hissed and winced when two globs of cold gel splatted onto her stretch-marked tummy.

"... right," she finished.

"Sorry," Marissa said through a sympathy-wince. Clara hissed again when Marissa used the transducer probe to spread the gel. "Picked any names yet?"

"Allan has, but I am not naming my kids after football players."

Marissa moved the probe, adjusted knobs, and twisted dials. "Levi is cool."

She considered the suggestion. "I don't know," she gently objected. "Although it works for a boy or a girl."

"Plus," Marissa chirped, "you can go Hollywood and name the other twin Lucky or Diesel."

"Or True Religion."

They giggled.

She watched Marissa work. Everything about the energetic twenty-six-year-old was bright and bubbly; she was the human equivalent of a flute of chilled champagne on a hot summer day. Her youth and energy had Clara contemplating her own age. For her, Time was a sadistic taskmaster running a deathly efficient factory specializing in the conversion of energy and muscle mass into wrinkles, age spots, crow's feet, and hair-dye-resistant gray roots. For Marissa, Time was a joke-telling-time-off-for-no-good-reason boss continually shutting down the factory for parties and team-building events.

Her thoughts turned to her twins and their futures. Maybe they'll be doctors? Or musicians? Or bubbly ultrasound technicians? *Who* will they be? she wondered. Will they change the world? Will one discover a cure for cancer, the other a free and endless source of clean energy?

Marissa pressed a button, and the room filled with the sound of life, the frenetic heartbeats instantly fueling a warmth inside Clara. The warmth strengthened quickly and erupted as a bright, spontaneous smile.

"Are you coming back to work after these miracles arrive?"

The question hit surprisingly hard. She had not realized until now just how distant life before the twins felt. Like the residue of a faded memory. "I haven't given it much thought. I guess it depends on what happens with COVID. And I would need to find a good daycare."

"Isn't that what grannies and grandpas are for?"

"I suppose," Clara said listlessly, choosing not to delve any further into her personal life with Marissa. The truth was, she had not spoken to her father since her mother's funeral ten years ago and had no desire to do so, especially to ask him to help raise her kids. A philandering bigot was not exactly a good role model.

When one heartbeat disappeared, Clara, picturing thick, black smoke rising above a distant tree line, eyed Marissa nervously. She felt mild relief when the energetic tech appeared unfazed by the change.

Marissa slid the probe to Clara's side-belly. "Any discomfort since your last ultrasound?"

Clara shook her head, then changed her mind. "Actually, over the last few days, my stomach has been…I don't know, *tight?*"

"Painful?"

"Kinda."

"Pain is for suckers," Marissa declared. "I'm getting an epidural the moment my pregnancy test comes back positive."

Clara giggled. "I thought it was cramps, but I'm not sure anymore. It feels different." A sigh. "I'm probably just getting fat. I've lost all willpower when it comes to anything choco—"

The word stuck in her throat.

Marissa's eyes were locked on the ultrasound monitor, her face twisted like she was watching a gory scene from a horror movie.

"What's wrong?" Clara asked, her panic unmistakable.

Marissa dropped the probe on the bed and raced from the room, ignoring Clara's repeated cries of: "What's wrong?"

—

WILHELM CONTORTED HIS face as though he had just heard Heisenberg's Uncertainty Principle explained in Klingon. "Is the coma you mentioned yesterday still an option?"

Funny, Allan thought, unable to muster even half a grin. His mind was on tilt, overloaded with useless information about Hitler and the Nazis, subjects that were clearly the core of Wilhelm's delusion. At times, his head had been pounding so hard and spinning so fast he had been unable to distinguish his thoughts from Wilhelm's ramblings. *Did you know that due mainly to increasing social, political, and racial unrest, it took Hitler only twelve years to rise from anonymity to Germany's unquestioned leader?* "No," Allan had responded. *Were you aware that Hitler replaced experts with loyalists in all key government agencies? Did you know many Germans believed God had sent Hitler to save Germany? Would it surprise you to learn the Nazis used propaganda to turn Hitler's every failure into a triumph and every loss into a win?*

No, no, no, no, no, and no. And no.

Wilhelm excused himself to go to the bathroom just as Allan's phone started to buzz. Clara was calling, probably to ask him to pick up whatever food item she was craving after her ultrasound appointment. He ignored the call but made a mental note to call her back.

During a recent break, he had completed a fruitless search of all relevant databases for any record of "Wilhelm Weissand" or "*Vilhelm* Weissand." He was tired and a little frustrated at the lack of progress. His phone beeped. He checked it. Clara had left a voicemail.

He grabbed his pad and scanned some of his notes.

> Wilhelm claims the fouryearold boy was Hitler. Who was he? Did Wilhelm lose a son? Trauma too much? Are the voices his con science? Did he hurt his son?
>
> Voices "saw darkness" pumping through boy's heart. Projecting? Sees/thinks there is darkness inside him? Sees in others?
>
> Quote: "The consequences of my failure are a constant reminder never again to fail to do what must be done." Blames himself for the Holocaust. Could he have lost his son (family?) in the holocaust?
>
> Has he eaten? Arrange for a physical.

"Oh!" Allan said, startled. Wilhelm was seated in his chair. "I didn't notice you had come back. You scared me."

"My bad," Wilhelm said, smiling a little.

Allan forced a chuckle. "I—"

His phone buzzed.

It was Clara again. This time, he decided to answer it. The marathon session had left him feeling like his brain stem had disconnected from his spinal cord, and his brain was now floating aimlessly inside his skull. Regardless of why she was calling, he would use it as an excuse to wrap for the day.

"Hi, sweet—"

Her panicked voice was so loud he had to hold the phone away from his ear to understand what she was saying. The moment he did, he sprinted from the room.

14

Frankie had caught Huffy's eye and waved him over. She was now watching him work his way through the busy IHOP while sipping her coffee, its satisfying aroma competing with others she found just as appealing: crisp bacon, sweet batter, gluey syrup, cinnamon, buttered toast. She listened to plates clank, cups rattle, silverware jingle, and people talk—each group seemingly trying to out-loud their physically distanced neighbors.

Huffy slid into the opposite side of the booth and immediately gulped from the black coffee she had ordered him twenty minutes ago. "This is freezing," he complained. He set the cup on the table and flagged a nearby waitress.

"*I* was here on time," Frankie countered sarcastically. She forked listlessly at her stack of half-eaten pancakes as Huffy asked the waitress for a black coffee in a clean cup.

"You ain't got the plague, do ya?" He snatched her fork and sawed-off a three-layered bite of syrup-soaked pancakes. "Wasn't this supposed to be a threesome?" He shoveled the bite into his mouth.

Frankie used a napkin to dab at a smear of syrup on her black blazer. "Abrams can't make it. Something came up."

Still chewing, he eyed her pancakes until she pushed the plate across the table. He smiled and dug in. "What came up?"

She dropped the napkin on the table, the white residue stuck to her blazer much more noticeable, and annoying, than the syrup. "He didn't say, but he did send me an email earlier this morning. He wants to transfer Wilhelm to Rodin."

He washed down his mouthful with a swig of cold coffee.

"Not sure why it is taking so long to unlock whatever information is in the old man's head, but as long as they aren't wasting my time, I don't care where gramps sleeps. A psychiatric hospital makes a lot of sense considering the fairy tales he's been telling."

The waitress returned with his cup of fresh coffee, topped off Frankie's, and ambled away like a battery-depleted Roomba carrying a near-empty pot of coffee.

"Any more on the grandson?"

He swallowed a gulp of hot coffee. "Ahhh…that is more like it." Another bite. "If there *is* a grandson, and he isn't a resident at Bachman, he will likely be looking for gramps, even if only to keep him quiet. Rolo's calling shelters and soup kitchens in case anyone's asking about a lost old man." He slurped more coffee. "Anything from Bachman?"

"If anyone knows anything, they aren't talking. What about Kennedy and Carpenter?"

"For now, Derek Samuels is the most likely connection to either. He's on shift at Bachman. I'm gonna swing by his place and try talking to his girlfriend, Molly Barnes. I've called her a couple of times. She keeps hanging up on me."

"Have we received their surveillance footage?"

"Nope."

She rolled her eyes. "How the hell are we supposed to conduct a proper investigation without it?"

"Maybe you were right about the footage being bad for business? Or at least bad for the warden."

She shrugged. "Still leaning toward regime change."

"Carpenter going after Palette makes no sense."

"Maybe it is a one-up for ten years ago."

She knew it was a giant leap. Ten years ago, an inmate had beat Palette to within an inch of his worthless life. The offending inmate claimed the fight was over a pack of cigarettes, but she and Huffy knew Kennedy had orchestrated the attack.

A fourteen-year-old girl with Down's syndrome certainly fit Kennedy's definition of "expendable for the greater good," but Palette had made the unforgivable mistake of raping the girl before killing her. There was no room in Kennedy's RUV for rapists.

He scrunched his face, looking like he had just caught the scent of rotting meat. "Your theory is that Carpenter killed Palette to show the RUV's rank and file that he could do what Kennedy couldn't?"

"It's a door we need to open, even if only to close it."

He shook his head. "That is a massive leap."

She shrugged. "Who knows why psychopaths do what they do?"

He drained the last of his coffee. "I buy Kennedy trying to finish what he started ten years ago. Hell, I buy Kennedy finding a way into Bachman to do it himself. But I'm confident a guy who uses the bunny ears rhyme to tie his shoes did not mastermind a murder on the most secure block of a maximum-security prison."

"Maybe Carpenter had help from someone smarter," she suggested, watching him check then disregard his buzzing cell phone. She always knew when the call he was ignoring was from Alex; he had a tell—a slow-motion blink with a subtle head shake; a *Please, God, not again!* mixed with a *What the hell have I done?*

"Alex deserves—"

"Stop," he ordered.

"But you—"

He dropped a ten-dollar bill on the table and left.

She instinctively rose off her seat only to slump back down. She *should have* chased him down and kicked his ass until it glowed through his grey suit pants. But it would not have made an iota of difference; he was acting like a child. And worse, he knew it.

If you did nothing with it, self-awareness was a curse, not a blessing.

Like every other marriage, Liam's had been far from perfect. But he and Alex had loved each other. It had been heartbreaking to watch him cut Alex out of his life with such surgical precision. He refused to talk about it, but to her, it looked like he'd come to the conclusion that pain would inevitably destroy their marriage, so he decided to condense that long and drawn-out process into a single weekend.

Last December eighteenth had changed everything for Liam and Alex. Hannah's death had not merely broken Liam's heart, it had ripped it out and run it through an industrial-strength organ shredder while it was still beating.

It hurt Frankie that she could not help him deal with the loss of his daughter, but you can't help someone who refuses to acknowledge there is a problem. She could not imagine the pain he was feeling or how it was affecting him, but she could and did understand why he was trying so hard to avoid it.

15

Allan had no memory of sprinting from the counseling office to the underground garage, weaving through traffic, leaving the Volvo idling in front of the Hospital's Emergency entrance, or berating the admitting clerk for taking more than two seconds to figure out where Clara was. And other than the burning in his chest, he had no memory of bypassing the elevator, racing up six flights of stairs, and frantically searching the third floor.

He finally spotted Clara, on a stretcher, being wheeled through two silver doors, AUTHORIZED PERSONNEL ONLY spread across both. He tried to follow her and her team of orderlies, nurses, and doctors, but a palm pressed firmly into his chest stopped him in his tracks.

"Mr. Abrams, *please!*"

He swallowed the vomit creeping into his throat. "What's wrong with my wife?"

The doctor removed his hand from Allan's chest, gripped him firmly by an elbow, and led him into a nearby waiting room.

"TTTS is a risk with MCDA twins, one we monitor closely. The Doppler showed..."

He stared at the doctor, seeing only a faceless blur and hearing an inaudible hum of sound. Words with no form, all structure and meaning lost in transit between his inner ear and brain. He knew everything about MCDA twins, including that they would be identical in every possible way: the same sex, same looks, same blood-type, same hair and eye color, even the same birthmarks. He also knew every risk they faced, *including* twin-to-twin transfusion syndrome, which was both rare *and* dangerous.

"What are they doing?" he eventually asked.

"Doctor Williams is going to determine if Fetoscopic Laser Ablation is an option."

"*If?*"

"If FLA is not an option, you will need to decide if you want us to perform Selective Cord Coagulation, which will stop the cord from providing to the least healthy twin. Without—"

"You want me to *kill* one of my babies!" Allan's tone was as venomous as his expression.

"If the donor twin is no longer—"

"The *what?*" he demanded, tears streaking his cheeks.

"Without Selective Cord Coagulation, you could lose the healthy and donor twin, and Clar—"

"Stop calling my baby that!"

A sigh. "I will update you when I can."

The lives of his twins reduced to a choice of one or the other, he watched the faceless blur walk away. But instead of a white lab coat, he imagined him in a plaid suit. And instead of disappearing behind the silver doors, he had ducked into the Used Car Manager's office, and reappeared a few minutes later. "Great news! My manager agreed to the stow-and-go seats and the video system, but you *must* choose between Peyton and Eli. You can't keep both."

Allan slumped into a chair, buried his face in his palms, and wept.

AFTERNOON. DECEMBER 19.

The last several minutes were a hole in Huffy's memory, not an uncommon occurrence; his mind tended to drift, particularly while driving. It was a miracle he had not yet plowed through a crowded intersection or crashed into the living room of a grandmother ogling Pat Sajak while scolding an accountant from Ohio for buying a vowel to solve:

Name this Pulitzer Prize-winning novel and Eminem song lyric.

TO K_LL A MOCK_NG B_RD _'MA G_VE YOU THE WORLD.

But regardless of his level of distraction, a part of Huffy's mind always remained focused on the road, at least enough to steer him safely through traffic. Either that or his brown Ford sedan was guided by the same do-good spirit that helped the blind-as-a-bat Mr. Magoo avoid all manner of gruesome deaths.

As the sedan continued mindlessly toward its destination, Huffy remained lost in thought. Other than his rantings, what proof do we have that gramps even has a grandson? If he does, it is a stretch to assume he's connected to Kennedy or the RUV. It's far more likely that the old man knows someone with access to our databases or who is connected to—

His phone rang.

He answered without checking the display.

"Liam, I don't want to—"

"What do you want, Alex?"

"I don't want to—"

"What. Do. You—"

"You wanted the goddamn divorce, remember?!"

A beat.

"Liam," she continued, her voice weighted down with sadness and disappointment. "I don't want to fight. I just want…" He heard her voice waver. She cleared her throat. "My lawyer sent you the documents over a month ago. Why haven't you sign—"

"I've got another call."

"Liam, don't—"

He hung up.

FUCK YOU! he wanted to scream. But he didn't. *He* was responsible for the state of their marriage, not Alex. At least she had tried. *Why* had she tried? Great question. He certainly had not made it easy for her, hiding his pain and anger and heartache from strangers and friends only to unleash it on Alex. That's the nature of marriage, he had tried to convince himself. Shitting on each other was covered by "For better or for worse," or "In sickness and in health." He couldn't remember which statute applied but was sure one did.

All bullshit, of course. Alex deserved his admiration, not his wrath; she had stuck around far longer than he would have had the situation been reversed. To some people, "Til death us do part" meant precisely that.

At times, he admired people with the capacity to love someone who did not deserve it, but mostly, he didn't understand them. It didn't require strength to stay in a dysfunctional relationship, forgive an abusive partner, or love a spouse who abused your child. Strength, he knew, often meant leaving, not staying.

Alex had tried so hard to make things work. He had not. He might have forgiven himself for that lack of effort had he not understood the selfish reason for it.

His phone rang again. This time, he checked the display.

"Miss me already?"

"Where are you?" Frankie asked.

"I'm leaving Molly Barnes's apartment. Her fresh bruises said a lot; she didn't say anything. Why?"

"We found the old man's grandson."

17

Allan's stomach was regularly threatening to empty. He felt as though the hospital's entire inventory of sedatives was airborne, and he had been inhaling from the toxic cloud for hours. His body was numb, and his mind a murky bog of unintelligible thought.

His elbows digging holes into his thighs, and the heels of his palms jamming his eyeballs deep into their sockets, he listened to the second hand of his watch, hours passing between each deafening tick. Never had the passage of time been so slow. So meaningful. So dreadful.

For as long as he could remember, he'd wanted to be a father, promising God countless times that he would sacrifice *everything* for the chance. God, it appeared, had finally decided to accept that offer.

After his mom died, his Bubby would often reassure him by saying, "God works in mysterious ways, but He is compassionate, and He will never give you more than you can handle."

Fuck you, God, he thought. Is it *mysterious* to bless those consumed by hate and selfishness with child after child, and deny good people even one? Is it *compassionate* to force me to watch my child grow up knowing he is alive because I sacrificed his brother or sister? And who are You asking me to sacrifice? The next Martin Luther King? Mother Theresa?

In the weeks after Isaac's death, Allan had rarely left his bed. Clara would bring him his meals; most he never ate. Food could not fill that kind of emptiness. Now, sitting in the hospital, time crawling like a mortally wounded animal toward an inevitable end, he knew the death of a fourth child would curse him to a life void of all things that made life worth living.

A metallic clang lifted his head.

The kaleidoscope of static created by the pressure of his palms against his eyes dissipated slowly. The approaching silhouette of a blurred, white lab coat forced him to his feet, his trembling legs struggling to support his weight.

Please, God. Please don't make me do this.

–

EVERY TIME THE silver doors clanged open, Allan thought: Here we go, decision time. But each time, a nurse or doctor would exit and hustle past him without a word.

Until the last time.

On that occasion, the white-smocked blur headed straight for him. Seconds from having to answer the question: "Is it okay if we kill one of your twins?" he felt his legs nearly give out, his insides turn to concrete, and his heart refuse to beat. His breath remained locked in his lungs, and his vision remained blurred by tears as his mind boarded itself up against the hurricane of pain striding toward him. Here we go, decision time.

But when his eyes cleared, he burst into happy sobs; the approaching, white-smocked blur was a doctor...a *smiling* doctor! The good news sent him sprinting to Clara's room, where he wrapped her in his arms. He held her for fifteen minutes, occasionally communicating via a garbled mix of weeping and talking that she somehow understood. He finally composed himself and released her.

"I can't imagine what that was like for you," Clara said. "But if one baby wouldn't survive, it would make sense for..."

She didn't finish. But she didn't need to. Would you sacrifice one of your children to save the other child *and* your wife? The answer was obvious, at least now that the question was hypothetical.

He used a fingertip to catch a tear sliding down her cheek. "I know. And maybe—" He sucked in a choppy breath and palmed tears off both his cheeks. "Maybe if I had been *forced* to make that choice, I could have—"

An irrational fear closed his throat. Suddenly, saying, "I could have killed one of our children to save the other," seemed to have the power to bring that choice closer to reality.

His eyes drifted down, stopping at his hand—a hand he had not consciously moved to Clara's belly. Suddenly, the amorphous entities growing inside her were more real than anything he had ever seen or touched. Trillions of replicating cells he would now, without hesitation, suffer the worst death imaginable for as long as it meant they would live for even one second longer than he. *Self*-sacrifice would be the *only* sacrifice permitted. In the imponderable flash of time it took for an autonomous part of his brain to direct his hand to Clara's belly, Allan Abrams transformed from everything he had ever been into the only thing he would ever be: a father.

Doctor Williams strode into the room.

"How are the Abramses?"

Maskless and forgetting all pandemic protocol, Allan rushed forward, shook Doctor Williams's hand, and thanked him profusely. Doctor Williams pulled a disposable mask from a nearby box and handed it to Allan. "Don't thank me," he said. "With Clara's strength and a little help…" he pointed up, "from you know Who, everything worked out wonderfully."

Masked and back at Clara's side, Allan again thanked Doctor Williams, as did Clara.

"I am going to prescribe something to lower your blood pressure," Doctor Williams told Clara. "And I have scheduled bi-weekly ultrasounds starting 8:00 a.m. on the twenty-fourth. You must make every appointment *and* avoid stress until the twins arrive."

"But I'm married," she quipped.

Immense and palpable relief ensured the laughter was more vigorous than the joke warranted.

"Is this something we still need to worry about?" Allan asked.

Doctor Williams shook his head. "With proper medication and more frequent ultrasounds, your biggest concern will be choosing colors for the twins' nursery." At the door, and unaware of the inside-joke looks that had been exchanged behind his back, he spun around. "On that note, would anyone like to know what colors you—"

"*No!*" Clara shrieked playfully as Allan pressed a finger-phone to his ear and mouthed *Call me*.

Amused by their reactions, Doctor Williams eyed Allan. "Clara needs rest." He pitched a thumb toward the door, and Allan acknowledged the order with a nod. "Oh, and Clara," Doctor Williams added.

"Yes."

"To save you a trip tomorrow, we completed a COVID test. I should have the results within a few hours."

"Thanks," she said.

They watched Doctor Williams leave.

"I don't mind waiting until you are dis—"

"*Home!*" she demanded, pointing at the door.

"But—"

"Save your buts. If there are no complications in the next few hours, you can come back and pick me up. You need the rest as much as I do. The last thing we need is for you to have anoth—" She cut herself off, an unspoken apology flashing across her face. He knew what she had almost said. But they were both emotionally exhausted. He gripped her hand and squeezed it gently. Apology accepted.

"*Promise* me you will go home and rest."

"Promise." He kissed her on the forehead and left.

Near the elevator, he passed a directory and noticed: MRI/RADIOLOGY/DIAGNOSTIC IMAGING 1.C.3.

Shit, he thought. He had missed his appointment to review his MRI results. He stupidly checked his watch, knowing the appointment was several hours earlier. He thought for a moment, then wondered if Doctor Williams could help. He found him at the unit's nursing station. Doctor Williams agreed to obtain the MRI and call with the results.

18

Everyone now present, Frankie used a remote control to lower the conference room's blinds and dim the lights. She scanned the group of assembled detectives and uniformed officers, then glanced at the image projected on the large whiteboard behind her.

"Meet Rien Gerhard." She thumbed at the mugshot of a clean-shaven, displeased man with steel-blue eyes, a scalp covered in tattoos, a cleft-pallet scar, and muscles where his neck should have been. "Rien enjoys working out, lifting weights, and exercising. He is one man-bun short of seven feet tall, and a protein shake shy of 300 pounds." A few "Ooohs" and "Ouches" were followed by a well-received impression of James Tiberius Kirk, Captain of the Starship Enterprise, ordering all phasers to be switched from *Stun* to *Kill*.

Frankie, briefly raising a manila file folder, quieted the room with her firm tone. "This contains everything we have on Gerhard." She looked toward a stack of identical folders on a table beside the door. "Grab one on your way out if you don't have one already." A click from her hand-held remote replaced Gerhard's mugshot with the picture of an elderly man blowing out candles on a large birthday cake, a semi-circle of smiling friends and family behind him.

"Rien's a POI in the disappearance of Henry James Talbot." She thumbed at the new picture. "Talbot was 72 at the time, and he is presumed dead. For obvious reasons, Gerhard is hard to forget, and several neighbors recalled seeing him in the weeks leading up to Talbot's disappearance."

"What did Gerhard have to say about that?" Huffy asked.

"As a platinum member of Witten PD's frequent flyer club, he lawyered up. Neither he nor his lawyer said much of anything. We had no evidence linking him to Talbot's disappearance and too few resources to keep an eye on him. He's been MIA since."

"Does he have a connection to the RUV?" he followed up.

"A presumed one."

"Meaning," Huffy said knowingly, "you believe Grapplin' Gramps's knowledge of Palette's death came from his connection to Gerhard and that Gerhard *and* Kennedy are involved in Palette's death."

Frankie nodded. "Like I said, a presumed one."

"And if you are wrong?"

"We have nothing."

"How'd we find him?" someone asked.

"Gerhard had called several shelters and soup kitchens claiming his 'grandfather' had Alzheimer's and had gone AWOL. The cell number he left led us to his apartment, which is now under surveillance. If the chance for collateral damage is low, the surveillance team will intercept him when he comes home. If not, those of you lucky enough to be chosen will join me and tactical for a little fun."

"Tactical and I," someone corrected.

A heated debate immediately broke out as to which was grammatically correct: "Tactical and I" or "Me and tactical." Those who didn't care—a large group that included Huffy and Frankie—left.

19

Allan continued past the line of identical, cell-like rooms in Rodin Psychiatric Hospital's North Wing, feeling more foolish with every step. He had just answered a question that had been picking at his brain since yesterday. If Wilhelm was a hero sent by "the voices" to vanquish monsters before they became monsters, why was he in Witten? What was his purpose? What was his "mission"? It should not have taken so long to find such an obvious answer; stress and a lack of sleep were beginning to affect his mental acuity. He was overthinking, looking too deeply, finding meaning in words and actions that held none. He should have listened to Clara and went home to sleep. Stress and exhaustion were a bad combination. Maybe it is all the Ambien? he joked. He didn't laugh. The joke contained a little too much truth to be funny.

Of course, Wilhelm's delusion meant the answer to the question was simple: Wilhelm was in Witten to kill a monster before that monster could unleash whatever evil he (it?) had planned. That delusion made him dangerous. An odd conclusion considering he tipped the scales at *maybe* one hundred pounds and walked with a cane. Laughable, actually. At least it was until Allan realized that in a gun-obsessed country, even an old man who needed a cane could be lethal.

Lethal to whom? he wondered, opening the door to room 8-F.

Unlike the South Wing, which was essentially a maximum-security prison, Rodin's North Wing accommodated people who, with only a few exceptions, could check themselves out at any time. Wilhelm's North Wing room, its pictureless walls painted prison-gray, was about the size of a small family room. Tucked into a corner was what could only be *generously* described as a "kitchen." Near the room's center was a small, glass-topped table book-ended by two red, plastic folding chairs, and beneath a barred window barely big enough to let in a few rays of afternoon sunlight was a single bed turned down with military precision.

Wilhelm, already seated at the table, was leaning forward, his nose just above a coffee cup. To Allan's surprise, a second cup sat on the table across from Wilhelm. Allan paused, wondering how Wilhelm had known he was coming. He'd made the decision to come thirty minutes ago and had not called ahead. Knock it off, he ordered. Stop overthinking things. It was good advice, and he took it. Besides, after a morning spent thinking one or both of his twins *and* Clara might die, then debating the pros and cons of sacrificing one twin to save the other, delving into the mystery of why Wilhelm made an extra cup of coffee seemed trivial.

Wilhelm leaned back in his chair. "No mask?"

Shit, Allan thought, realizing his N-95 was still in the Volvo's center console. He scanned the room for a box of disposables.

"I assure you," Wilhelm said, "I am contagion-free."

Less concerned with his forgotten mask than he was about settling his shaking hands with an injection of caffeine, Allan sat, then gulped greedily, making a sourpuss face the instant the coffee's bitter aftertaste registered.

Wilhelm winked. "Sorry. The only sugar I could find was on a half-eaten jelly donut."

Allan smiled, not caring if rat poison had caused the bitterness; it was afternoon, and, until now, his body had been caffeine-free. "You should be more comfortable here than in a holding cell." He sipped and grimaced again. "And as bad as this is, it beats the sludge at the station." He set the cup on the table. "I apologize for the unexpected drop-in, but I wanted to make sure you had settled in." A beat. "And I was hoping we could talk."

"About?"

Deciding Wilhelm might be dangerous, Allan came to Rodin instead of going home to rest. It seemed silly, as Wilhelm was unlikely to hurt anyone, but he felt obligated to at least try to identify "the voices" target, even if all it resulted in was a good story to add to *Real-life Tales of the Disturbed Mind*.

"I would like to talk about why you are here."

The meaning of Wilhelm's reaction—an exaggerated, almost comical frown—could not have been more apparent: *Because you sent me here!*

"Sorry," Allan said. "I meant, why have you come to our fine city?"

"Is it not obvious?"

Abrams smiled. "It may be, but my mind and body are a little under the weather, so you will have to help me out."

"I am here because of you," Wilhelm stated, watching Allan intensely. "We have much in common."

In no mood for riddles or games and confident he had established enough trust to start pulling at some loose threads, Allan moved on. "Why did the voices choose you to kill Hitler?"

"I am not privy to their motives." He inhaled coffee fumes. "But I am confident they had their reasons."

"When you failed, why didn't they send someone else?"

Wilhelm thought for a moment. "Hitler was a flatulent man." The statement nearly caused Allan to spit out a mouthful of coffee. Men, no matter how old, clearly never tired of fart humor. "And some of the medicine his doctor, Theodor Morell, prescribed for that condition contained high doses of strychnine."

Allan nodded. "I see; the voices sent Hitler's doctor to kill him."

Wilhelm again thought for a moment. "Did you know that of Hitler's six known lovers, three committed suicide, and a fourth died from complications related to an attempted suicide?"

Another nod. "The voices sent those women to kill Hitler, but they were foiled, murdered, and their deaths reported as suicides." He rubbed his temples to relieve the pressure from a brewing migraine. "If that is true, the voices must have sent Eva Braun."

"No."

"But she and Hitler committed suicide in his bunker."

"Adolf Hitler did not die in his bunker."

"Where did he die?"

"He was killed in Argentina on June 11, 1952."

"But everything I have ever seen says he died in his bunker."

"He died on June 11, 1952, in a heavily guarded jungle sanctuary in Misiones, Argentina," Wilhelm proclaimed confidently. "He was a shadow of the man he had once been. I could not tell if he was burdened by his actions or by his failures, but the Führer talked. I listened."

Delusional individuals were often as reliable as Google when it came to the subject of their delusion. And Wilhelm's confidence made Allan feel like a historian documenting a previously unknown version of history. Still, he was surprised by the detail. Someone suffering from Grandiose Delusions would be far more likely to say they were in the bunker with Hitler and Eva Braun than they would be to make a provably false claim.

Allan set aside the puzzling detail and continued. "You are saying you killed Hitler in 1952 in Argentina?"

A slow nod. "It took far too long for me to realize what the voices had been trying to show me." He closed his eyes. "Far too long."

Allan had stopped "doing the math" when it came to Wilhelm's delusion, but, according to Wilhelm's timeline, he had been walking the earth for almost 60,000 days. Every one of those days now showed on his face and in his movements. In his mind, the failure to kill a four-year-old Hitler was the reason millions of people died in the Holocaust, not to mention those killed during the Second World War. Pure fantasy... to everyone but Wilhelm.

"Why did it take the voices more than fifty years to kill Hitler?"

Hearing the answer left Allan slack-jawed at the power of Wilhelm's mind to protect his delusion. "The forces guiding me are not unopposed," he'd said. By pitting "bad" voices against "good" voices, Wilhelm could use inconvenient truths to *support* his delusion. The *good* voices failing to kill Hitler for over fifty years was not proof that they did not exist; it was proof that they were opposed by an equally powerful force intent on keeping Hitler alive. That single detail made Wilhelm's delusion bulletproof. He almost laughed out loud after thinking: Like labeling everything you don't like to hear as "fake news."

Allan wondered how well Wilhelm had protected his delusion? Untreated, potentially for decades, he likely had answers for even the most obscure questions. By now, he could have found and patched every hole in his narrative. Unsure if the question would help him better understand Wilhelm or merely satisfy a curiosity, Allan asked, "I'm not an expert on this topic, but I do know that many high-ranking Nazis evaded capture after the war, some for decades. Were you not able to hunt them down before authorities caught up with them?"

"My purpose is to prevent, not avenge."

Fascinating, he thought before asking, "Why was Hitler different?"

When Wilhelm spent several moments pawing at a scraggly patch of white hair on his chin, Allan wondered if he had found an unpatched hole.

"A new chapter," Wilhelm said, "cannot start until the previous chapter ends."

Allan decided now was as good a time as any to start digging into the vague statements Wilhelm was so fond of. "What do you mean?" Wilhelm would not elaborate, so Allan repeated the question. When Wilhelm again said nothing, Allan checked the time on his phone. If he delved into everything Wilhelm said that was either cryptic or made no sense, he wouldn't see the twins until their High School graduation.

"I have to leave but have a couple more questions if it is okay?"

Wilhelm nodded.

"You mentioned the voices *influence* you in ways other than speaking. How? Gut feelings? Intuition?"

"Those," he nodded again, "and others."

"How do you differentiate your gut feelings and intuitions from those of the voices?"

Wilhelm puzzled over the question for some time. "I believe they have a purpose for some of us and make that purpose known. Most people do not recognize their influence. And those who do..." Allan watched Wilhelm sweep his eyes over the small room as if to say, *We end up in tiny rooms in Psychiatric Hospitals*.

Wilhelm went on to say that the voices influence him, but his choices were ultimately his own. Why not ignore them? Allan asked. I did, Wilhelm responded before restating the consequences of that decision. When Allan asked about the possibility of misunderstanding what the voices wanted, Wilhelm dismissed the idea with a firm head shake and said, "On her way to work," he said, "a wife's intuition sends her back home, where she finds her husband with his lover. Her decision to return home will force her to make choices she might never have had to make. What impact will those choices have? Will she forgive her husband? Will they go on to have a child who murders the scientist who would have one day cured cancer? Or will she divorce her husband and save the world from that child? Are our detours always random, or can we be nudged toward a new destination for an unknown purpose?" He shook his head again. "If we listen, and if we see, there can be no misunderstanding. The voices are never wrong."

For reasons beyond his grasp, Allan disregarded several diagnostically relevant follow-up questions. "Do you ever have dreams that show you what might…" He hesitated, unsure from what part of his mind such nonsense had originated. "I mean, have you ever had a dream that foretold…" He couldn't finish. Dreams did not foretell the future; the question was idiotic. He was tired and stressed.

Wilhelm's ever-present emptiness resurfaced. "In 1888, before he was born, I began having dreams of a young boy and the unspeakable horrors he would one day commit. Each time I woke, I knew I had not dreamed of those horrors; I had witnessed them through a window—a window that allowed me to see what would happen if I did not act."

A flash of fear flushed Allan's skin, and a migraine that had been biding its time in the background suddenly hit with full force. He pulled two Thorazine from a bottle in his pants pocket and swallowed both along with the last drops of his cold, bitter coffee.

"Are you okay?" Wilhelm asked. "You look ill."

Allan fought to ignore the absurd questions clawing from his mind to his mouth.

"Just a headache."

"They will get better," Wilhelm said with fatherly tenderness.

How the hell could Wilhelm possibly know that my migraines will get better?

A wave of intense fear propelled him to his feet and out the door. He had to get away—away from Wilhelm. The feeling was as irrational as any he had ever experienced. Still, he raced to his car, locked himself inside, closed his eyes, and swallowed a scream. A long few minutes passed before he started the car and drove away, a question picking at his brain: What the hell is wrong with me?

On the drive back to Saint Pete's, he calmed after realizing a combination of Ambien, Thorazine, exhaustion, and stress had temporarily short-circuited a few wires. His weakening migraine and a radio ad for a psychic hotline then provided an answer to what Wilhelm had done.

He had stupidly asked Wilhelm if the voices could influence dreams. And Wilhelm, as adept at finding ways to support his delusion as hotline psychics are at flushing out information from naïve callers, jumped through that wide-open door with: *Of course, they can!* The same answer he would have provided if the question had been: "Can the voices see the future?" or "Can the voices influence people by rearranging the letters in their alphabet soup?"

Of course, they can!

Like a hotline psychic, Wilhelm had weaponized Allan's naivety and willingness to believe. And Allan, a psychiatrist with two decades of experience, had fallen for it—hook, line, and sinker. But by the time he had arrived at Saint Pete's to pick up Clara, his rational mind was once again flooded by irrational thoughts—thoughts he knew were ridiculous, but that he could still not stop himself from asking.

What if Wilhelm's presence in Witten wasn't random? What if he was here for a reason? What if he was more than just a strange old man? What if he wasn't delusional at all? Was he a threat? Could he actually hurt someone? Who?

20

The lukewarm cold pack on his forehead pinning him to the den's couch, Allan heard the faint click of the den door opening. He struggled to sit up, his head barking in protest. The cold pack fell into his lap. Clara had entered. A glass of water in one hand and a cell phone in the other, she whispered, "Doctor Williams," and handed him the cell. "About your MRI."

"Hi," he said in a hushed voice. "You tracked down my results?"

"Yes, but—"

Allan cringed. His brain shattering into a million pieces, he snapped the phone away from his ear, lowered the volume, and returned to the call.

"...did two COVID tests due to the high rate of false positives. The first test came back positive, so we—"

"Oh," he exclaimed. "Clara has asthma." A beat. "And what about the twins?"

"As I mentioned to Clara, there is no evidence mothers pass COVID to their fetuses. Clara's asthma is a concern, but the first thing we need to do is get the results from her second test and put a plan in place if it comes back positive."

"How long until you have the results?"

"The second test is more reliable but takes longer. Hopefully, we'll know today. In the meantime, Clara should stay home, as should you. If you must go out, wear a mask."

"I always do," Allan said, realizing immediately that the statement was untrue. He had forgotten to wear a mask a few times in the last couple of days. "Do I need to get tested?"

"If the second test is positive, yes."

"Just a second."

He started to explain the situation to Clara, but she cut him off with, "I know." He eyed her curiously. She seemed quite calm, knowing she had tested positive for a virus that had already killed 300,000 Americans.

He placed the phone back to his ear. "And my MRI?"

"All clear," Doctor Williams responded. "On that note, your doctor happened to mention your family history of hemiplegic migraines."

He was struggling to pay attention as a mass of COVID-related *What ifs* filled his head. "Yes." He tugged on Clara's thumb. She sat beside him on the couch. "I knew I had my mother to thank. I have had MRIs before, but with my migraines increasing in frequency and strength, I figured I would have another one, just to be safe."

"Have you had any memory loss or any other more severe issues?"

"No, thankfully. Not yet, anyway."

It was true that his migraines were worsening significantly. The timing suggested the reason was stress related to the pregnancy. Still, he had been fortunate compared to his mother. From her early twenties, she had experienced temporary paralysis, stroke-like symptoms, and severe seizures. During the last year of her life, seizures were a daily occurrence. She would reassure him after each one, saying it only *looked* scary and that she had not been in any *real* danger. But he was twelve. Every time she collapsed and spasmed like a suffocating fish, he thought he was watching her die.

And although she had experienced memory loss, he never believed she *accidentally* overdosed by forgetting (multiple times in a few hours) that she'd already taken her medication. It had always seemed more likely that she had decided a life spent in constant and crippling pain was not a life worth living. As his migraines worsened, he understood why she might have made that choice.

He thanked Doctor Williams for calling and hung up. He dug his fingers deep into his temples and sighed.

"It'll be fine," Clara reassured, using a finger to stir the sediment in the glass of water.

He looked at her like she was an alien, thinking: What the hell are you talking about? Don't you think we have been through enough? He studied the milky liquid. Am I mad at Clara for being so cavalier about contracting a deadly virus? Or at myself for possibly giving it to her? How hard is it to put on a fucking mask, Allan?

"You said swallowing pills hurt your head." She handed him the glass. "I dissolved them in water." She seemed pleased with herself, and he smiled a weak *thank you*. He took a sip and immediately made a *blech* face. "Finish it," she ordered, pushing the glass back to his lips. He did. She stood, took the glass, and lifted the cold pack off his lap. "Freezer?"

"No," he grunted. "It doesn't help."

"Maybe you deserve this."

"Huh?" he grunted, confused.

"Maybe it is payback for lying to your wife."

Her COVID diagnosis was preoccupying whatever mental acuity his migraine had not yet wiped out, so he couldn't tell if she was joking. For the third time, he apologized for breaking his promise to her to go home and sleep.

Squinting to try and stop the pressure in his skull from popping his eyeballs from their sockets, he scanned the den. "Where's my mask?"

She retrieved his mask off the desk and handed it to him. "Did you at least use your time wisely?"

"Huh?"

"Huh!" she mocked. "Did you figure out what Wilhelm is

suffering from?"

He slipped on his mask. "Grandiose Delusions. He believes he is a key figure in the Holocaust, and that, instead of in his bunker, Hitler died in Argentina after the war."

"Did you know," she started. Even in his weakened mental state, he recognized the tone. Before her stay-at-home order, she had filled her spare time with Hiccup, suspense and mystery novels, puzzles, and painting. An exceptional artist, she had, over the years, sold her work via consignment at three local galleries. Other than the twins' nursery, she had not painted anything since Isaac died. But recently, the combination of boredom, a lack of mobility, and a significantly increased channel package had made TV her go-to time-killer. The tone of her "Did you know" signaled she was about to educate him on something she had learned on TLC, CNN, or the inappropriately named "History" channel.

"That DNA testing," she continued, "proved the skull found in Hitler's bunker, supposedly *his* skull, was female?"

He nodded, vaguely recalling the documentary they had watched on the subject. "But didn't they find his teeth?"

Clara scowled. "Eighty-year-old *fragments* of *false* teeth."

"Hitler had false teeth?"

"Yep. He was a flatulent SOB, too."

Allan tried to smile, but it hurt too much to move the muscles in his face.

"No DNA testing done," she continued, "just comparisons to X-rays *supposedly* of Hitler's false teeth."

"Supposedly?"

She screwed her face into a *Seriously?* "Allan, if the most powerful man in Germany wanted to fake his death and hide from the world, I am pretty sure he could have had an X-ray or two re-labeled and a few tooth fragments planted in his bunker." She yawned. "Evidence supports the theories that he didn't die in his bunker, and he escaped Germany using a network of tunnels under Berlin."

"Really?"

A nod. "Dozens of high-ranking Nazis scattered around the globe, but the most powerful Nazi of all decided to accept his fate?" She yawned again. "You never thought it was out of character for history's worst narcissistic sociopath to commit suicide?"

The mention of suicide got him thinking about Wilhelm's stories. Without thinking, he asked, "Did Hitler nearly drown as a child?"

A quick nod. "Ironically, he was saved by a priest."

His migraine was turning his head inside out, so it took longer than it should have to realize why that was ironic.

Clara placed her hands in the small of her back, pushed her belly forward, and grunted stiffly. "The lucky bastard had a ton of near misses." She ambled to the door. "Near the end of the first World War, a British soldier had a wounded Hitler in his sights but chose not to kill him." She stretched and grunted again. "Too bad he didn't know the consequences of not pulling the trigger."

—

IN THE FETAL position on the den's couch, Allan was focusing on Channel Five's top-of-the-hour newsbreak as it played on the wall-mounted TV. Contrary to any conventional treatment of headaches, concentrating on white noise, like a radio or TV on at low volume, had proven effective as a pain reliever. The harder he concentrated, the further the needle dropped. Why? He had no clue.

Later, while he was hovering between consciousness and sleep, the boy general returned. As his consciousness dissolved away, he maintained an awareness of his real-world surroundings. The couch's suede pressed against his cheek as he watched the boy general survey the death and devastation.

A blur of images on the wall-mounted TV registered as he studied the scarred and knotted tree's arthritic fingers reaching for something beyond their grasp. He listened to the news broadcast as the woman clawed at the boy general's pant leg and whimpered: "Only you can save us, Allan!"

As his dream-world-self fought to hold him in sleep, his real-world-self pleaded: "Wake up! You don't have to watch this!"

He forced his eyes open.

A scrum of run-down industrial buildings had replaced the boy general and the valley.

Am I awake? he wondered. Or still dreaming?

The concrete and brick buildings leaned awkwardly next to each other, as unsteady on their feet as the addicts and drunks who used them for shelter. One building stood out from the rest and had sun-faded letters painted above its entrance. BROWN'S AUTOBODY REPAIR.

Where am I? he wondered, unsure whether his dream- or real-world self had posed the question.

He took a single step and found himself inside the repair shop. Beams of dust-filled sunlight entering through slits and holes in the windowless walls made it look like the building had been shot and stabbed and left to die.

In the distance, he saw a thin rectangle of sunlight.

It's a door! he thought.

A powerful desire to leave—to *escape*—forced a step. He slipped but righted himself. He looked down. He was standing in an oil slick; the slick was growing—alive beneath his feet.

He started to run.

Every frenzied step doubled the weight of his legs and cut his strength in half. The oil, now covering the entire floor, continued to rise. It reached his ankles, then his knees, then his waist. His pistoning arms smashed against the surface, spraying oil in every direction. He caught a mouthful, its taste familiar. It isn't oil, he thought. It is blood!

At his shoulders, the rising blood compressed his chest, pushing his internal organs through his ribs like Play-Doh through the fingers of a gripping fist. The blood breached the corners of his mouth and filled his lungs. Submerged, he spasmed and writhed, flailing against the sensation of drowning. A minute passed. Then two. Then five. Then, he felt his chest expand and contract.

I can breathe!

In an endless ocean of black, a woman floated up toward him, the fabric of her glowing, white nightgown rippling as she glided through the darkness. Face to face for a moment, she said, "Only you can save us, Allan." She sank slowly, the glow from her nightgown fading to a pin prick of light, then disappearing.

Floating below the surface of the blood, Allan looked up. A man was hanging by his ankles from the ceiling, a torrent of blood gushing from a trench cut into his neck. Like a tap being shut off, the blood slowed to a trickle and stopped. His head, tethered to his body by a strip of skin stretched as thin as dental floss, descended, stopping an inch above the surface. His eyes were cloudy and lifeless, his face like melted wax. His mouth repeatedly opened and closed. He made no sound, but Allan heard his words as guttural screams: "KILL ONE! SAVE MILLIONS! KILL ONE! SAVE MILLIONS!"

Allan floated in the darkness for what felt like hours. A beeping sound faded in and grew louder. He focused on it and followed it back to consciousness. A man in a white lab coat peered over the rims of his glasses. "You gave us quite a scare." His words were slow and garbled. To his left was a small, white box affixed to a metal stand. The box was beeping. Allan studied it for some time before realizing what it was.

Why am I connected to an IV?

21

Brown's Auto Repair was located in Camper's Village—an area infested with addicts, prostitutes, drunks, and other filth that lurked in Witten's darkest corner. The essence of that filth—depravity marinated in motor oil and seasoned with human waste and vomit—hung thickly in the air as Frankie navigated the pitch-black labyrinth of halls.

"Son of a *bitch!*" she hissed, buckling at the waist. "Ow-ow-ow. Fuck." she whined, rubbing her shin until the stabbing pain disappeared. Upright again, she repositioned her flashlight, its dusty beam revealing her attacker as a three-wheeled Walmart shopping cart.

By now, generator-powered lights should have been illuminating the path from the shop's lobby to its rear bays. But they weren't, so the shopping cart was only one of several hazards she had encountered: broken bottles, syringes, old tires, discarded clothing, several single shoes. The pair of blood-stained granny panties had been more of a curiosity than a hazard.

Frankie stepped over the corner of a soiled box-spring and followed the flashlight's chalky beam, random thoughts cluttering her mind. What's for dinner? Microwaved pepperoni pizza, again. Why won't Liam acknowledge his pain? Because he is a man, men are idiots. Why is this disintegrating shithole making me think of my marriage?

Most marriages, she assumed, weren't dissimilar: the monotony of everyday life occasionally spiced with a dash of good and a sprinkle of bad. Beth had needed more. For a while, Frankie managed to convince herself that she had forgiven

Beth. If you tried hard enough, she'd learned, you could fool yourself into believing that grudging acceptance was forgiveness.

She entered what was once Brown's repair bays. The sound of air compressors, glugging motor oil dispensers, and whizzing torque wrenches now replaced by the rumble of an unseen diesel-powered generator. Five spotlights—four pointed at the floor and one at the ceiling—combined to create the illusion that a large ray of sunlight had punched a perfect circle in the metal roof. Thanks to the upward-pointing spotlight, Frankie could see an inverted, headless body hanging from the rafters. Seeing no ladder or roof access, Frankie wondered how the body got up there.

Liam was inside the circle of light watching two CSIs and Dan Button work.

Huffy nodded toward the well-lit and *hazardless* path leading directly from a rear door to where he stood. "Why didn't you come through that door?" he asked Frankie over the generator's baritone hum.

Of course there's another way in, she thought, stopping at the edge of a large, irregular-shaped pool of blood. "Who's the Vic?" she asked Button.

Perhaps unsure which piece constituted *the Vic*, Button eyed the severed head at his feet, then glanced up at the suspended body. "Daniel Holmes."

"RUV for about a year," Huffy added. "Low level."

Frankie, eyeing the head, asked Huffy, "You hear about Grapplin' Gramps?"

"What about him?"

"He's AWOL." She read a text. "It's about goddamn time," she grumbled, pocketing her phone. "Let's go."

"Where?" Huffy asked.

Already halfway to the door, she said, "Wilhelm's grandson just came home."

22

Why am I in the hospital? Allan wondered, his gaze sliding from the beeping IV to Doctor Williams, who was at the foot of the bed peering over his glasses. "How long have you been taking Thorazine?"

Despite his mental haze, Allan recognized the condescending tone and resented the judgment. "I *know* it is an antipsychotic," he stated. "But I can't handle triptans. Thorazine is the only drug that makes a dent in my migraines." He ignored Doctor Williams's skeptical frown and turned to Clara, who was slumped in a chair beside his bed. The moment they made eye contact, her eyes sank to the floor. He watched her for a moment, curious about the reaction. He turned back to Doctor Williams. "Why am I here?"

"Clara gave you two Thorazine before the...*incident.* When she woke from a nap, she found you in your car in the garage. You were unconscious." Doctor Williams paused, his expression suddenly somber. "The car was idling."

"The garage?" Allan questioned. "In my car?"

"Migraines can cause memory loss, as can Thorazine." Doctor Williams turned to Clara. "What other medications are in the house?"

A beat.

"Clara?"

"Sorry." Her head snapped up.

"What other medications are in the house?"

"The blood pressure medication you prescribed." She thought for a moment. "Maybe a few morning sickness pills."

Curiosity creased her brow. "Why?"

"If mixed with Thorazine, certain medications—"

"I *didn't* mix any medications." Her tone indicated her displeasure at the insinuation.

Hours earlier, Doctor Williams had warned them that stress could be dangerous for Clara and the twins. Hearing the tension in her voice, Allan said, "I remember now. I had a migraine and took two Thorazine at Rodin—" His flitting glance offered Clara a fourth apology for lying to her about meeting with Wilhelm. "When I got home, I fell asleep in the den and…" His mind drifted, searching for details that weren't there. "I don't remember going to the garage or getting into my car. I suppose it is possible, particularly if I took the wrong med—"

"I did *not* mix any medications," Clara insisted.

"Sweetheart," he soothed. "It has been a crazy day. No one would blame you if you accidentally gave me—"

"I DIDN'T!"

Trying to calm her, Allan looked to Doctor Williams. "Everything's fine, right?" he asked hopefully. "It doesn't matter anymore."

"Your reaction was severe, not what I would expect from a few Thorazine. An unknown allergy is a possibility. We did some blood work, and I will let you know the results, but, yes, the danger has passed. When you feel up to it, you can go home."

Doctor Williams left.

Allan stretched a hand toward Clara. She hesitated but shuffled to the bed, her eyes on the floor. He took her hand and smiled. "So, you want me dead, huh? What gives? A lover? Life insurance?"

His attempt to ease her anxiety failed.

"*Honey,*" he pleaded, his thumb caressing the back of her hand. "It wasn't your fault. I could have taken too many

Thorazine on my own. Or, as Doctor Williams said, I could have an unknown allergy."

She sighed. "It isn't that, it…"

He waited for her to continue. When she didn't, he tugged her pinky finger. "*Tell* me."

Her eyes flitted around the room. "It was probably a reaction to the drugs, but you were mumbling in your sleep about 'killing one to save millions.' You have been acting…" Her eyes returned to his. "I'm worried."

"About what?" he asked stupidly.

"What do you think, Allan?" she snapped. "The twins. Me. Us. *You!* It isn't like you have a stellar track record with this type of stress."

The words hurt, but he refused to let his pain show. She had enough on her mind. "We have both been feeling—"

"Don't tell me how *I am* feeling." She ripped her hand from his. "You don't know *anything* about how *I am* feeling."

"I just meant—"

"I know what you meant, and I am sick of being analyzed. I am your wife, not your patient."

He fought the urge to challenge her. He hadn't analyzed her. But arguing the point would only make things worse. "I'm sorry. I'm not trying to analyze you. We are under a ton of stress. Whatever nonsense I mumbled while I was asleep was because I was stoned out of my mind." Hoping to change her mood, he rearranged his face into a forced smile. "We'll both feel better after we get some rest."

Hard edges instantly darkened her expression. *Get some rest?* the look seemed to say. *You mean like you promised to do earlier?* She fidgeted with the edge of his blanket. "My second test was negative. Doctor Williams tested you. You're negative."

"Well, that's good—"

She turned and walked away.

His relief at knowing COVID was, at least for now, not something they had to worry about had already been crushed by the guilt he felt for adding to her stress.

After a sufficient period of self-loathing, he noticed the wall-mounted TV was on. In need of a distraction, he increased the volume.

> "…to kill one in every hundred who contract it, so the drug has the potential to save millions of lives. Bill."

> "Thanks, Rona. Up next, we'll look at whether the recent string of deadly home invasions is related to escalating violence across the country. But first, here's Steve Noble with more on the gruesome discovery on the city's east side. Steve."

> "Thanks, Bill. As reported earlier, police found the decapitated body of Daniel Holmes hanging in an abandoned autobody repair shop. Allegedly a foot soldier in the RUV, Holmes was linked to—"

He shut the TV off, convinced, at least for a moment, that he had somehow seen the future in a dream. *You're losing it*, he thought, snorting a derisive laugh. *The TV was on while you were asleep. Come to think of it, so was the TV in the den.* He set the remote control on a tray beside his bed, grabbing his cell phone in the process. "Kill one, save millions," he muttered, realizing that snippets of multiple news stories had seeped into his semi-conscious mind. "You really are losing it," he grumbled.

Ten minutes later, while playing *Words Story,* he received a call from a staff member at Rodin Psychiatric Hospital. Wilhelm was missing, and they wanted to know if Allan knew where he was. He did not, stated so, hung up, and returned to his game. He needed to keep his mind active. He did not want to fall asleep. Sleep meant dreams.

Several games later, his eyelids were heavy. He fought hard, forcing them to open every time they eased shut. But exhaustion eventually won.

A terrifying new dream began the moment he fell asleep.

23

Huffy followed Frankie, who was struggling to keep pace with the tactical team's choreographed ascent of the Ritz's main stairwell—a synchronized, adrenaline-filled blur of weapons and body armor. All fire escapes, stairwells, and elevators were guarded, so unless Rien Gerhard could fly, he was trapped.

According to the surveillance team that spotted Gerhard about an hour ago, the sole X-factor was the elderly man he had hauled inside by the elbow. Huffy hated X-factors. They had a nasty habit of becoming lead stories on the nightly news.

The tactical team consisted of six officers plus the Breach —a beast of a man who would get the party started by using a three-foot steel battering ram to "pick the lock" on Gerhard's apartment door.

The team mustered in the third-floor stairwell. Huffy, his back against a wall, eyed Frankie. Late afternoon was urgently dissolving into evening, so he could barely make out the *God, I miss this shit!* sparkle in her eye.

The Ritz—a villainously misleading name considering the squalor—appeared empty. But rather than a low vacancy rate, Huffy knew the lack of visible activity was because most Ritz tenants responded to law enforcement the same way cockroaches responded to the flick of a light switch.

Tactical Team Leader, Sergeant Amil Baines, eased the door open, the sound of creaking hinges echoing through the stairwell. From Huffy's position, he could see into the hall. Half its lights were missing or did not work, and most of the rest were flickering as if undecided. The lack of light made the hall look more like a rectangular cave, its damp air wreaking of urine, and its floor littered with discarded clothes and garbage and, about halfway down, a child's tricycle. Probably stolen, Huffy thought.

Baines signaled for radio silence, then led the team swiftly through the hall, one team member stopping about halfway. His job, Huffy assumed, was to discourage curious onlookers from exiting their apartments. Although most Ritz residents avoided law enforcement, some would love to take a shot at an unsuspecting cop.

At the end of the hall, Baines's upright palm ordered a full stop. He crouched against the wall and cautiously peered around the corner. Huffy did the same. About a hundred feet from their position, a rail-thin, provocatively dressed woman was trying to push her way into an apartment. "Fuck off," an unseen man growled. A hand sent the woman hard against the opposite wall. A laugh was followed by the sound of a slamming door.

Sprawled awkwardly on the floor—only one high-heeled red shoe on—the woman struggled to her feet, retrieved her other shoe, and used its eight-inch heel to hammer on the door. "Gimme my money, you cocksucker!"

Huffy had to stop himself from laughing out loud. The woman's workplace hazards included regular beatings, rape, and, whether she realized it or not, occasional encounters with budding serial killers. The fact she was wearing a disposable mask was not only ironic, it was just plain funny.

Her efforts to secure payment ineffective, the hooker pulled off her mask and limped toward the tactical team's position. "The shitfuck in 339 has the tiniest dick I ever saw," she yelled over her shoulder. "And I got a five-year-old son!"

Another hand signal from Baines brought a team member to his side. One hand in the air with all five fingers spread wide and the other holding a small mirror Baines was using to see around the corner, he dropped one finger at a time as the hooker approached. A few feet from the team's position, she spun around, presumably to direct another round of obscenities at the man with the tiny dick. Baines dropped his last finger, and the team member pounced, clasped his hand over her mouth, and pulled her around the corner. Terrified and flailing, she froze at the sight of the heavily armed tactical squad. Baines raised a "Shhh" finger to his mouth. When the wide-eyed hooker nodded, the team member released her and directed her down the hall.

The team hustled around the corner and toward apartment 341. As they clustered at Gerhard's door, the hooker shouted, "You fucking cops have no right to be—"

Their backs against opposite walls, Huffy and Frankie exchanged concerned looks. Assuming Gerhard had heard the hooker, they had just lost the element of surprise, and a dangerous situation had just become a hell of a lot more dangerous.

His heart thumping, Huffy caught movement—a shadow—under the apartment door to Frankie's left. Someone was watching them through the peephole. Huffy tightened his grip on his gun, thinking: Don't you dare open that fuck—

The breach's battering ram sent splintering wood in every direction. Frankie and tactical stormed Gerhard's apartment. Huffy, wanting to make sure the shadow next door had no intention of getting involved, held back for a few moments. When the shadow disappeared, he started forward, then froze; a woman was screaming inside the apartment to the right of Gerhard's. When she stopped abruptly, Huffy started sideways. The adjacent apartment's door swung open, a huge man dashing out.

"Police!" Huffy shouted.

Three hard strides and the man was gone, diving into a stairwell. Huffy lunged across the hall, spun, and slammed his back against the wall. "Subject's in the west stairwell," he bellowed into his headset's microphone. "Red Adidas tracksuit, white sneakers."

Huffy had no idea if Gerhard was unarmed and long gone or if he was armed and crouched in the stairwell, waiting for a head to poke through the door. He kicked the door open and spun back against the wall. No shot. He rushed inside, thrusting his gun randomly at every vague shape and shadow.

"Clear?" Frankie called from the hall.

"Clear."

Frankie, followed by two tactical team members, entered the stairwell. Huffy directed them down the stairs; he charged up to the roof.

At the top of the stairwell (billowing puffs of icy breath leading Huffy to make an early New Year's resolution to do more cardio), he scanned what he could see of the rooftop through a six-inch gap between the open door and the frame. The sun had set, but a clear night sky, bright moon, and lights from other buildings were enough to make out two boots—toes up. He took a deep breath, kicked the door all the way open, and launched himself onto the roof, his gun held stiffly in front of him, its barrel in sync with his darting eyes as they jumped from point to point.

To his right, an unconscious uniformed officer lay on his back, the side of his face covered in blood. As if God was slowly increasing the volume, the sounds of the city began to register. Huffy scanned the area while feeling the officer's neck for a pulse. "10-999. Westside rooftop stair—"

He lurched forward, searing heat shooting through his body. He landed on his stomach and slid along the frozen gravel covering the roof, his cheek burning as the tiny rocks grated his flesh like cheese.

He pushed himself onto all fours. Where's my g—?

Another flash of pain exploded from his ribcage. He flipped and landed face down. He lay there, unable to move, his cheek alternating between icy-cold and searing heat. He again tried to move, but his muscles refused. Footsteps. His vision blurred, he forced himself to focus. Gerhard was about ten feet away. He bent over and picked something up.

My gun!

He strained, summoning just enough strength to pry his chest off the snow-covered roof. A shadow fell over him and blocked the stars dotting the night sky. He heard someone yelling but couldn't understand the words.

Then, he saw, heard, and felt nothing.

–

HER FRUSTRATION HAVING progressed to anger, Frankie repeated her order. "You need to go to the hospital."

Huffy heard her but was already off the roof and gingerly descending the stairs. Gerhard had ambushed him and used his ribs and face for field-goal practice. The last three-point attempt had knocked him unconscious. The sound of tactical team members running up the stairwell probably saved the city the cost of a line-of-duty funeral.

Gerhard not reaching the ground (alive or dead) meant he had successfully covered the short distance to one of two adjacent rooftops. Gerhard may have escaped, but Huffy's brain remained bulletless, so he'd decided the altercation was a draw.

Standing on what remained of Gerhard's door, Huffy surveyed the sparsely furnished apartment. It was about the size of a dorm room and as well-kept as a crack house.

"I didn't think you could get any uglier," Detective Paul Mendez croaked. "My money's on you in the rematch, though." Huffy didn't respond. "He caught our scent," Mendez continued, pointing to a window that opened onto a fire escape. "Climbed out the window and into his neighbor's unit. When she screamed, he coldcocked her, then…" He snickered.

"I guess you know the rest."

"What have you found?" Huffy asked, his swollen jaw strenuously objecting to the movement.

"Old man was hiding in the bathtub."

"Grapplin' Gramps?"

"No." Mendez chuckled. "Poor bastard shit himself when we breached. EMTs took him to Saint Pete's." Mendez eyed a small kitchen table covered with dirty dishes and scattered papers. "We've found check stubs in seven names, mostly Social Security and Veterans pensions. Five drivers' licenses, half a dozen credit cards, stuff like that."

"Anything in Wilhelm's name?"

Mendez shook his head. "But we aren't finished. You sure he gave us his real name?"

Huffy spent a minute walking through the apartment and ended up beside Mendez. "Gerhard may have more than one place. Make sure you look for mail with a different address."

"Will do."

"Anything connecting him to Kennedy or the RUV?"

A frown. "Like an Employee of the Month certificate or—"

"Liam!"

Sharp pain sliced through his ribcage as he turned. Frankie was in the doorway. "Hospital," she ordered.

"I'm fine," he responded as the room started to spin, and his body cried out: *Like hell you are!*

"Now!"

Unsure which of the three Frankie's he was seeing was the *real* Frankie, he decided to listen to all of them and head to the hospital.

EVENING. DECEMBER 19

The haze of sleep still fading, Allan lifted his head off the pillow and waited for the hospital room to come into focus. When it did, he quickly located the wall-mounted TV. "Shit," he groaned, his head falling back to the pillow.

The TV was off, which meant that a news story (or, in this case, scenes from a horror movie) slipping through the cracks in his unconsciousness were not plausible explanations for his new dream. A dream that had not featured a freckled boy general or decapitated man hanging from the ceiling of an autobody repair shop. The star of his new dream was a tattooed Asian man, his crumpled body forming an island of bones and burnt flesh near the center of a yellow-streaked pool of blood. A neon sign from the dream was still flickering in Allan's mind: **NO OXYCONTIN OR OXYCODONE. 24HOUR SURVEILLANCE.** And he could still hear the sound of—

A familiar voice turned his head.

Outside the door, Liam Huffy was talking to Clara, sadness enveloping her like thick, black smoke. His hand on her shoulder, he dropped it after noticing Allan was awake and watching. He said something to Clara, then, moving like a man in considerable pain, entered the room.

When Huffy reached the foot of the bed, Allan pointed to a COVID protocol sign on the wall. Huffy glanced at it. "I hear you're—"

"Please put a mask on," Allan insisted.

Huffy, looking displeased and offended, turned to the door

—a box of disposable masks clearly visible on a shelf just inside the room. Instead of walking over and grabbing one, he took two steps back and continued. "I hear you're still flying high from the drugs you took."

Why is it so fucking difficult to wear a mask? Allan wanted to shout. A mask stopped you from doing absolutely nothing, so it was a mystery to him why some people found it so hard to throw one on and help prevent people from dying. The only civil liberty wearing a mask infringed on was the right for the ignorant to be selfish. A mask was not a hazmat suit. The more time they spent together, the less he liked the man Huffy had become.

"Accidentally took," he clarified. "And it looks like I am doing better than you."

"A few bruised ribs." Huffy touched the blood-stained gauze on his cheek. "And a little extra *rugged* for my rugged good looks."

"What happened?"

"More like *who*," Huffy said, followed by, "Rien Gerhard."

"Who?"

"Grapplin' Gramps' grandson."

"*Jesus.*" Allan pushed himself to a seated position.

"We found drivers' licenses and credit cards in Gerhard's apartment." He spread the fingers of one hand. "Five missing old men. All open cases."

Relieved Wilhelm was now safe, Allan said, "Thank God you caught him."

"Almost," Huffy corrected. No doubt in response to Allan's immediate look of concern, he added, "*Relax.* We'll have his grandson in cuffs soon enough."

He pulled a crinkled, disposable mask from the inside pocket of his suit jacket, slipped it on, and exited the room.

Now you put on a mask? Are you kidding me?

Huffy spoke briefly to Clara and handed her what Allan

assumed was his card. Clara watched him walk away, glanced at the card, and stuffed it into her purse. Her eyes shifted hesitantly into the room, her sadness even more profound. She lowered her chin to her chest and walked away, returning a few hours later to pick him up.

–

EVERY TIME THE Volvo's suspension absorbed an imperfection in the road, Allan's head rapped against the passenger's window. He had spent most of the drive praying that, with two hospital visits in one day, there was no truth to the adage that bad things came in threes.

He lifted his head off the glass and looked at Clara. "Why are you going this way?"

She ignored the question and traffic and slid the car blindly into the slow lane. Panicked, he snapped his head to the right, relaxing after seeing the lane was clear.

For a while, he watched the world zip by, the blur of cars and buildings moving in and out of focus, his mind doing the same until a neon sign caught his eye.

What the...?

His heavy breath fogged the window until the sign: **NO OXY CONTIN OR OXYCODONE. 24HOUR SURVEILLANCE** faded into the distance.

Have I been there before? Did I see the sign on a previous trip to the hospital? He turned back to Clara, his confusion lingering for a fraction of a second too long.

"What's wrong?" she asked.

He didn't answer, but only because he had no clue what to say. "What's *wrong*?" she repeated, her tone and snarled lip suggesting anger, not concern. He desperately searched for an answer other than: *I didn't tell you? I see the future in my dreams. My last dream was about a tattooed Asian man being burned alive. I'm not sure how, but that dream is connected to the pharmacy we just drove by. Nothing to get stressed over, though.*

"Just a migraine," he lied, grimacing. He dug two fingers into his temple.

Clara locked her hands around the steering wheel—her fingers and knuckles bloodless and white—wrenched the wheel to the right, and brought the Volvo to a jarring stop on the road's shoulder.

"What the hell is wrong with you?"

"Everything is fine. It—"

"No, *Allan*, everything is *not*—"

She winced and cradled her stomach with a forearm. He reached for her, but she pushed his hand away. "Liam told me that the old man's grandson is a killer." She smashed a hand on the top of the steering wheel. "A *killer!*"

Unsure why Liam would choose to scare her, he again tried to lean in and comfort her; once again, she shoved his arm away.

"What if he comes after his grandfather when you're with him? Will everything be *fine* then? Will everything be *fine* if the twins grow up fatherless like…"

Her regretful expression acknowledged she had gone too far but stopped short of apologizing.

"Sweetheart, I—"

"I can't deal with all this bullshit *and* worry that the stress from…" Her face flushed as she strained for whatever word she'd wanted to say. She threw her arms in the air. "…*everything* that is causing you to have another breakdown," she finished.

"It *wasn't* a break—"

"I want you off this case!"

"You're overreact—"

"*Now!*" she demanded, her breathing fast and shallow. "If you care about our twins or me, you'll pass that crazy old man off to someone else."

Pregnancy had always intensified her emotions but never to this extent. Like him, she had to be dealing with the same endless barrage of *What ifs*, and those *What ifs* could generate powerful emotions. But that did not explain why she was acting so irrationally. Passing Wilhelm off would not change a thing. More frequently, her emotions were causing her to jump from zero to sixty in an instant and without provocation. Still, as unreasonable as she was acting, continuing with Wilhelm made no sense if it added to her stress, which, illogical or not, was dangerous.

He sighed. "I'll pass him off first thing tomorrow."

For a moment, he stared at her, and she ignored him.

As she accelerated into traffic, he leaned his head against the window and closed his eyes, unsure why promising to pass Wilhelm off felt like a lie.

—

HIS THUMB STILL crushing the TV remote's unresponsive buttons, Allan yelled, "Do we have any goddamn triple-A batteries?"

Clara, her eyes on the floor, exited the en suite and hustled from the room. He took two steps toward her but stopped. Fuck it, he thought. A minute later, he was on the bed and staring at the ceiling when his phone beeped. The garage's overhead door started to rise as he read Clara's all-caps text stating she was headed out to buy some **GODDAMN TRIPLE-A BATTERIES**. He swung his legs off the bed, intending to race to stop her and apologize for being an asshole. But his feet refused to move.

He listened to the garage door close. The house fell still and silent. He slumped onto the edge of the bed and closed his eyes. For the first time in their married life, he felt the raw emptiness of being alone. For the first time, a feeling he had kept at bay for months broke free and hit with full force. The sharp edge of that pain sliced him open like a Samurai's tanto and left a bloody mass of entrails at his feet. *What if this is it? What if our marriage is over? What if we are simply in the process of coming to that realization?*

They arrived home from the hospital about an hour ago. During the drive, he had promised to pass Wilhelm off first thing in the morning. Clara, dissatisfied with that time-frame, suppressed her building anger until the Volvo came to a stop in the garage. Once the engine was off, she had exploded, making it crystal clear that *"first thing in the morning"* was not soon enough. It did not help when he sarcastically offered to wake up a colleague and pass him off tonight. But by then, his concern for her stress had evaporated. How could she not see that everything that had happened to her had also happened to him? Like her, he was stressed and scared and not sleeping. Like her, he was terrified by what might await the twins. And like her, he deserved compassion and understanding. He may have promised to pass Wilhelm off, but they had *both* promised: "For better or for worse." And that promise meant they should face life's challenges as allies, not enemies. That their problems, no matter how big, should bring them together, not tear them apart.

An hour later—both still angry at each other and themselves and the world—an uncooperative TV remote had sent him into an irrational rage and sent her on a late-night quest for some "goddamn triple-A batteries."

He texted her an inadequate, one-word apology before trying one final time to crush the remote's power button into submission. When he failed, he hurled the remote across the room and watched it sail through the air and crash against the side of a dresser, its batteries exploding out of their compartment and scattering across the floor.

–

CLARA HAD LEFT intending to kill two birds with one stone: satisfy an intense craving for a gingerbread latte and give Allan time to calm down. But by the time she pulled into the Starbucks parking lot, she had changed her mind. Questioning the decision but trusting her instincts, she removed a card from her purse and called the number. After a brief conversation, she exited the parking lot and cautiously navigated the snowy streets toward downtown Witten, her mind on Allan's progressively erratic behavior.

They met over twenty years ago at Denver's Mercy General Hospital. Their first date was on that same day in one of the hospital's cafeterias; they shared a blueberry muffin and a can of Tahiti Treat. Even then, Allan had talked about kids. It was one of the reasons she had fallen in love with him. Young, handsome, intelligent, funny, loved kids—he was everything her father was not.

But that ardent desire to be a father only made his current behavior all the more puzzling. Why would he add to her stress knowing how dangerous it could be? Was a crazy old man worth jeopardizing hers and the twins' health? What power did the old man have over him? His grandson had murdered multiple people, and Allan *still* could not see the danger? *Really*? And did it even matter what Allan could or could not see? What he *refused* to see. No, it didn't. If he would not walk away from a situation that was putting her and the twins' health and safety at risk, if he refused to acknowledge the danger, then she had no choice but to take matters into her own hands. If Allan would not protect them, she'd find someone who would.

—

THE WAIT IN the station lobby had frayed Clara's nerves. Several times she had started for the door only to turn around and sit back down. She did not know why she had come or why she could not leave. A premature case of mother's intuition, maybe. Whatever it was, it had brought her here and wanted her to stay.

Liam led her to his office. She stuffed her mask in her coat pocket and sat in the chair in front of his desk. Her thumb ground at her purse's leather strap as Liam closed the blinds. They had seen each other at the hospital, making small talk until Allan woke up. She sensed Liam had forgotten that Allan introduced them at the city's Christmas party two years earlier. When Allan left to mingle, she and Liam talked. She remembered thinking he was nice. And handsome. Not George Clooney or Ryan Reynolds handsome, more subtle. The kind of handsome you missed until it jumped out and surprised you. She had glimpsed it in his smile and when he unexpectedly opened up about his marriage, confessing how challenging he found it to convert his feelings to words. "I know what I want to say," he'd said regretfully. "But I can't force the words out. Usually, I just say nothing." She noticed it again when he talked about how his wife wanted to start a family but how he was unsure. "I hate what this job has done to me. I doubt I will be a good dad. And why have kids if you are just going to mess them up by being a shitty parent? I see the results of that every day."

Liam closed the last blind and eased gingerly into his chair.

"How are you feeling?" she asked in a concerned tone.

He hovered a hand near his ribs. "A bit tender." He pointed to his bandaged cheek. "As for this?" He clicked his tongue. "Hard to believe I could get any uglier, but...."

She wanted to smile and, for a moment, thought she had.

"Don't take this the wrong way," he continued, "but when I gave you my card, I wasn't really expecting you to call." A flash of handsome. "How can I help?"

This is a mistake, she thought. I shouldn't be here.

"The case you are..." She paused for a long, slow breath, both thumbs now smoothing her purse's leather strap. "The case you are working on is creating stress. It's dangerous. The stress, I mean. For my twins and for—"

She felt her phone vibrating. Allan was calling again. As she had for the last hour, she ignored him.

"I know," he said tenderly. "Allan told me you have lost…"

She held eye contact for a moment but lowered her head when she felt a tear on her cheek. She discreetly wiped it away. She didn't want Liam to see her cry.

"Over the years, we have lost three—" She inhaled a choppy breath. Tears started falling from both eyes. Too many to catch. Liam dug in a drawer, stepped around his desk, and handed her a Denny's napkin. She thanked him and dabbed tears. "What if the man who hurt you, the grandson, what if he comes after Allan while he is with me? And what if…" Her voice fell away. Liam dropped to a knee and set a hand on her shoulder. She tilted her head and came within an inch of accepting his comfort with her cheek. She thought better of it. "I don't want Allan working with that old man. It sounds silly, but he—" Another choppy breath. "I'm afraid."

He lifted her chin with a curled finger. She could smell his cologne. It was sweet but masculine. He smelled safe. His eyes were searching hers so intently she was certain he would see her thoughts. A rush of tears welled in her eyes, but they were good tears—tears that meant someone felt safe enough to let down their guard. A part of her wanted to let go completely. To fall into his arms and bawl like a child. To be held and told everything was going to be fine. Not told what she was feeling was wrong or that she should look at things differently, from another perspective, not hers, someone else's.

Her head had fallen back toward her chest. His finger moved gently under her chin and raised her eyes to his. "I won't let anything happen to you," he comforted.

His words were tender but powerful. He did not make promises he could not keep.

"Besides," he continued reassuringly, "the case will be over in a day or—"

She heard the door open. Liam looked up and immediately retracted his hand. She turned. An attractive woman wearing a black pantsuit and red flats was in the doorway. She was questioning Liam without saying a word.

"DaMarcus Kennedy is here," she said. "Interview Room One."

"Thanks, Frankie," Liam responded.

The woman eyed him for a long moment before leaving without closing the door.

Suddenly, Clara felt extremely uncomfortable as all her doubts about coming to the station flooded back. She thanked Liam for listening and hurried to her car.

25

Through the one-way glass separating Observation and Interview Room One, Huffy watched DaMarcus Kennedy and his lawyer, Olivia Madson. Physically, they were nothing alike. Kennedy, his dreadlocks tucked under a white wool cap, was tall, thin, and muscular but multiple cosmetic surgeries from any definition of attractive. In contrast, Olivia Madson inhabited a stunning shell. Her shoulder-length blonde hair accentuated her hypnotic green eyes, and her soft, symmetrical facial features were the opposite of Kennedy's hard lines and rough edges. A smattering of freckles across the bridge of her narrow, slightly upturned nose gave her an undeserved air of innocence. And although professional, her navy-blue skirt and white blouse were tight enough to leave very little about her toned body to the imagination.

Physically, they were as different as two people could be. But where it mattered, Madson and Kennedy were matching hemorrhoids on society's asshole.

Madson's father was a Hells Angels Road Captain, and her mother an "Old Lady." Upon passing the bar, Madson's full-time job became defending Daddy and Co. Rather than part of her job description as Huffy had first suspected, dating some of daddy's friends turned out to be your standard dysfunctional attraction to bad boys. When a rival gang member killed daddy in prison, Madson expanded her clientele to any lowlife who could pay her rate. Olivia Madson's moral compass, if she'd ever had one, was shattered beyond repair.

Huffy sat across the stainless-steel table from Madson and a smirking Kennedy.

"You wanna reschedule, Huff? You look like shit."

"You know, DaMarcus, I don't recall ever having an innocent man bring his lawyer to a voluntary chit-chat with the police."

Madson said, "Questioning my client every time someone steals a chocolate bar is, by definition, harassment. I recommend you get to the point."

"I'm glad you clarified." Huffy flashed a smirk of his own. "I never know if you're here in your official capacity or your *other* capacity."

Madson was pulling double duty as Kennedy's fiancé, so the meaning of "other capacity" was unambiguous. She rose out of her chair, her bulging baby-belly disproportionate to the rest of her athletic frame. "If we are here as a test audience for your stand-up routine, this voluntary *chit-chat* is—"

"Save the D-list theatrics for court." Huffy signaled for her to sit by patting the air. She held her ground for a moment, then lowered herself stiffly back into her chair.

"Sometimes, Huff, you gotta foul mouth." Kennedy leaned forward. "In a different place, that mouth would land you in a world—"

Madson had dug her French-manicured nails into Kennedy's forearm. She was supremely clever but had he finished his sentence, even she would have struggled to frame the comment as anything other than threatening a cop.

Huffy nodded at Madson's massive, glittering engagement ring. "Nice rock, counselor. DaMarcus tells me you're expecting a boy. Congrats."

Madson glowered. "My client agreed to participate in yet another of your fishing expeditions because he wants to help find whoever killed his friend, Danny Holmes. I—"

"I bet he does," Huffy said.

"I suggest you ask your questions," she continued, checking her Gucci watch. "We have a gender-reveal party to get to."

Madson's arrogance was already pushing Huffy's switch, jabbing and slapping it like a spoiled toddler at elevator call buttons. Every time they played this game, she would, without asking for or needing permission, end it whenever she decided it was time to pick up her ball and go home. She had that power because an unseen force protected Kennedy—a psychotic, motherly spirit constantly nagging him. *Don't touch that door. Wipe your fingerprints off the knife. You missed a bullet casing under the dresser.*

Huffy had witnessed every conceivable way people inflicted pain on each other. Still, nothing pissed him off more than defense lawyers like Madson, who would not hesitate to do and say *anything* to free clients or mitigate their punishment. The unfortunate reality was good people would never be safe as long as the monsters living next door (and teaching their children, baptizing their babies, and coaching their kid's soccer teams) were protected by a system meant to protect victims.

True to form, fifteen minutes later—after Kennedy had answered every question that didn't matter and ignored every question that did—Olivia Madson, without asking for or needing permission, picked up her ball and went home.

26

Clara had not responded to any of his calls and texts. Allan's paranoia was constant, her and the twins dead in a ditch beside a deserted country road his most frequent visualization. But moments ago, the sound of the garage's rising overhead door had flooded him with relief and sent him racing to her.

They both entered the kitchen simultaneously, and he knew instantly that she had something to say. She didn't look angry; she looked determined. Like she had been rehearsing the words for hours and encouraging herself to say them: *You can do this, Clara!*

He tried to wrap his arms around her, but she refused, both hands placed against his chest. She pushed him back, her eyes distant and cold.

"I feel like my life before the twins never happened. Like I —"

"That is not true. You're—"

"It is how I *feel*. It..." She briefly dropped her eyes to the floor. "My feelings and emotions are..." Her shoulders sagged, a sigh expelling most of her determination. "I am all over the place right now. Some days I have no idea why I feel the way—"

"It is hormones, and—"

"Stop interrupting me!"

"Sorry. I'm only trying—"

"I *know* what you're trying to do." She locked her jaw and spoke through pursed lips. "I don't need to hear it. Okay?" Before he could respond, she added, "Can we please just forget today ever happened and go to bed? Is that okay? Do I have your permission to do that?"

Sadness and disbelief turned his stomach into a Roller Derby track. All he was *trying* to do was help her feel better. And she did not need his permission to do anything. But telling her that would only upset her more and add to her stress; they'd had enough stress for one day.

He again tried to hug her. She brushed by him and plodded up the stairs. He followed.

He climbed into bed as she took off her earrings, set them on the dresser, and started toward the en suite. She froze after a few steps.

"What?" he asked.

She struggled but managed to bend far enough to scoop the TV remote off the floor. She cradled it in her hand and stared at it like it was an injured bird.

"What?" he repeated.

She sighed. "I forgot the batteries."

After a half-second of silence, he erupted into convulsive laughter. She joined in.

Ten minutes later, they were in bed and watching TV.

"Where were you, by the way?" he asked.

"Huh?"

"While you were out *not* getting batteries. Where did you go?"

"Oh." She eyed him briefly. "I was at Starbucks. I needed to think…and a gingerbread latte."

They had been together for more than two decades and knew each other as well as they knew themselves. He knew she was lying.

—

WHETHER DRUG-INDUCED hallucinations or visions of the future, Allan's dreams now kept him awake as often as they wrenched him from sleep. Tonight, despite a double dose of Ambien, a lack of sleep was putting the power of his exhausted mind to terrible use. Every time he drifted toward unconsciousness, the same urge—an urge he did not understand and was losing the ability to resist—would jolt him wide awake. When he could fight the urge no longer, he peeled back the covers and dropped his feet to the bedroom floor. He padded around the foot of the bed and stood over Clara.

You don't have to do this.

He watched her chest rise and fall.

You are not thinking straight.

She stirred as though sensing someone was standing over her.

What the hell are you doing? This is crazy.

AFTER MIDNIGHT. DECEMBER 20.

Five Days until Christmas.

Several inches of fresh, mostly untouched snow covered the streets, which made perfect sense; no one in their right mind would be out for a midnight drive in the middle of a snowstorm.

No one, except him.

Its anti-lock brakes causing it to shudder, the Volvo stopped just beyond the deserted parking lot's entrance. Seeing no cars in either direction, Allan U-turned and parked a few feet from the building's entrance. For what felt like several minutes, he watched the wipers swipe furiously at the onslaught of kamikaze snowflakes. He wasn't dreaming, but nothing felt real. An urge to investigate a dream had brought him to a part of the city that even cops avoided. Why had he had the urge in the first place? Why had he been unable to resist it? Why was he *still* unable to resist it? Isn't it obvious? he thought. Because you are not *in* your right mind!

A minute later, standing and shivering under a snow-bloated store-front awning, he peered into the flurry of white darkness, dead silence amplifying his increasingly belligerent internal voice. You're losing your fucking mind, Allan. Before Clara realizes you are gone—or worse, you get murdered—get in your car and go home.

He took one tentative step, then another, but not toward the Volvo. A few strides from the brightly lit entrance to Ling's Pharmacy, he heard a distant scream. He stopped and turned toward the sound. A flash of light caught his eye—the flash so brief he wasn't sure he had seen anything at all. Then, a second flash confirmed there had been a first.

What the hell are you doing? he wondered, starting toward the light. His feet were not his own. Like a computer virus, a force had seized control of his Central Nervous System and was forcing him deeper into the most dangerous part of the city.

Exiting the parking lot, a chill, unrelated to the frigid temperature, spun him around. Even through the deluge of snow, the neon sign glowed brightly. **NO OXYCONTIN OR OXYCODONE. 24 HOUR SURVEILLANCE.** He had first seen the sign in a dream, then again on the drive home from Saint Pete's. He looked back in the direction of the light flashes, then to the neon sign. Soon, he was moving his head back and forth like he was seated center court at Wimbledon. His next step seemed immensely important. Should he go home? To Ling's? Should he head toward the light? Did it matter? Regardless of which direction he chose, would he end the night in bed beside Clara? Or was his life now like a Choose Your Own Adventure book? Would every new choice start him on a path with an entirely different ending? Maybe his adventure had started days, weeks, or even years ago? Rather than just starting, perhaps his story was nearing its end?

Surrendering to whatever force had brought him to this place, he hustled across Elm Street and into a vacant lot wedged between two run-down commercial buildings. Both appeared dark and lifeless, but at this time of night and in this part of town, he knew he was not alone. The thought of curious eyes following him sent his pulse racing and his feet *whishing* faster through the deep, wet snow.

Emerging in the parking lot of a Texaco, he could now tell that the light flashes had come from an adjacent alley. He tried to step toward it, but his feet remained frozen, the snow gripping his ankles like hardened concrete. His legs were making one last-ditch effort to regain control of his mind and body.

They failed.

Multi-story buildings sheltered the alley from the worst of the wind and snow. Despite having absolutely no clue what he was looking for, he wandered through the alley, eventually stopping in front of a prone refrigerator box wedged between a dumpster and a three-story brick building. Someone was sleeping inside the box, their large hiking boots protruding from its partially open bottom. Allan started when the boots suddenly retreated inside. He moved cautiously forward, a rustling sound conjuring the image of hundreds of rats swarming Box Man in search of food: a tasty eyeball or scrumptious testicle or deliciously seasoned anus.

A distant car alarm began to screech like a wounded animal.

Allan stuffed his leather gloves into a jacket pocket, pulled out his cell phone, and inched it toward the box, a bubble of blue light cutting weakly through the darkness. Two clasped hands were poking out from a tear near the box's bottom. Dark spots of varying sizes and shapes covered the hands—a mix of dirt, food, and whatever else might coat a homeless man's hands.

The howling car alarm was now competing with the distant wail of approaching police sirens, but Allan heard neither, his mind preoccupied with answering questions like: How could the desire to investigate a dream be strong enough to suppress every rational thought and instinct? And how could I be stupid enough to end up hunched over a homeless man in a dark alley in the worst part of the city?

One of Box Man's purplish fingers twitched. The mental image of a rat gnawing on one of Box Man's tendons caused Allan's skin to bristle as though crawling with thousands of industrious ants.

The wail of police sirens—moving closer fast—finally registered and spun him around. A few hundred feet away, four police cars flew past the intersection where the alley met Jackson Street. Moments later, the sirens stopped abruptly.

Allan turned back, his eyes drawn to a flickering reddish-orange glow in a window above a door in the building behind Box Man's home.

Is that a fire? he wondered.

–

THE SNOW-SLICKED roads were challenging to navigate. Huffy was also having trouble hearing Frankie's crackling radio commands over the blaring sirens and the sedan's furious wiper blades. But he understood enough of: "—ffy, wha— yo— ETA?" to reply with, "On site in less than a minute."

On site was The Last Drop—known locally as *The Drop*. The dive was in Camper's Village; thirty hell-on-earth blocks that had earned its moniker thanks to the significant number of people who "camped" within its boundaries. Some camped in boxes, others in dumpsters, and a few even hunkered down in abandoned vehicles—anywhere that offered protection from the elements and the area's other more substantial dangers. A disproportionate percentage of Witten's homicides occurred in Camper's Village or were linked to one or more of its residents. Even with a badge and gun, Huffy avoided the area like the plague that it was.

But tonight, he had no choice. An anonymous tip had led two undercovers to The Drop, where they spotted Rien Gerhard drinking by himself. Twenty minutes later, two tactical teams and a dozen cops had discreetly surrounded the bar. It was a lot of force but based on the evidence found in his apartment and a statement from the old man he'd had with him, Gerhard had murdered at least five elderly men. He would no doubt be armed, probably with Huffy's gun, so they weren't taking any chances. This time, if he ran, it would be into the barrel of an AR-15. And if he preferred a "You'll never take me alive" ending, tactical would happily oblige. Even a hostage wouldn't help him as "acceptable collateral damage" was a term created specifically for places like The Drop.

Huffy and his convoy arrived at The Drop as Frankie was finishing over the radio.

"...UCs are in the first booth to the right of the main entrance. In addition to Gerhard, there are six patrons, a bartender, and a server. Huffy and I will try to catch Gerhard by surprise. If we can't, I will call in his location, and tactical will come in hard. Everyone else is to remain in position and intercept *anyone* who comes out."

He reached Frankie as she closed her car door. "That's not business casual." She stuffed her gun into her purse.

"Master of disguise," Huffy replied, only *reasonably* confident gunfire would not erupt the moment Gerhard saw him. Their run-in at the Ritz had occurred in near-dark. Additionally, Huffy had taken two prescription-strength painkillers, replaced the gauze covering his cheek with two large, skin-colored bandages, slid into a pair of jeans (that luckily still fit), put on a Harley-Davidson leather jacket, and covered his red hair and the wound on his head with a Colorado Rockies ball cap. Still, they had to be careful. Criminals of Gerhard's ilk had highly developed warning systems, a sort of criminal sixth sense. Only, instead of dead people, they saw, smelled, and sensed law enforcement.

He held The Drop's main door open for Frankie, hoping he had done enough to circumvent Gerhard's warning system.

—

WHAT HARM COULD possibly come from one more stupid decision? Allan thought, curiously studying the lambent glow in the window above the door behind Box Man's cardboard home. Is that a fire? he wondered, unsure. He blew hot air into his cold, cupped hands, coating them with a thin film of moisture. What else could it be? He slid his hand to the door's handle and pushed. What a surprise, he thought sarcastically, finding the door locked.

He pulled his hand back, the frozen metal biting his flesh and ripping it from his palm. The pain was instant and agonizing. "Fuck," he whimpered, clapping his hands together and burying them between his legs, the sting bringing back the memory of a laughing, tenth-grade bully forcing Allan's fifth-grade tongue against an icy steel fence post.

He pulled his gloves from his pocket, hoping their warmth would ease the pain. Before he could slide them on, the box convulsed and spasmed, and a dark figure—Box Man—emerged. Allan instinctively backed away. When Box Man stood, Allan turned to run but tripped, falling on his back.

"Microsoft Motherfucker," Box Man yelled, starting forward.

Allan frantically crab-walked backward, a flash of bright light momentarily blinding him. He scrambled to his feet and sprinted toward Ling's. For a few hundred feet, he repeatedly shoulder-checked, each time expecting to see the psychotic, flashlight-wielding homeless man a half step behind and gaining, his dirt-encrusted hands inches from grasping Allan's jacket collar.

Safe inside the Volvo, Allan's chest heaved as he sucked in oxygen. The snow had stopped falling; he could see the beam from Box Man's flashlight, dim and vague and moving erratically.

The fire in his chest out and his heart returning to its normal rhythm, he cupped his hands around a blowing heat vent, one palm still stinging. He turned his hand over. He was bleeding; the door handle had taken a souvenir. He fished in the center console for a napkin, finding one under a blank prescription pad. As he pressed the napkin into his bleeding palm, panic caused him to freeze, then pat frantically at his jacket pockets. "*Fuuuck*," he moaned, realizing Box Man had also taken a souvenir. Should I get them? He checked the distant alley, where the flashlight was still bouncing and bobbing. No fucking way, he decided. I'll buy a new pair. A vision popped into his head and caused him to add: *Before* Clara finds out, of course. In the vision, Clara was chasing him with the baseball bat he kept in the bedroom closet. She was swinging for the fences, his head the ball, her voice bordering on satanic. "You march your ass back there and *get* them! Those were hand-sewn, cashmere-lined, Chester Jefferies gloves—a 400-dollar birthday present, you dumb shit."

Embarrassed by everything he had done over the last few hours, he dropped his forehead to the steering wheel and closed his eyes. What is wrong with you? he asked, only half-joking. He took a moment to try and come up with an answer, only to realize he had no idea what was wrong with him. His embarrassment shifted toward concern.

At some point, his beeping cell phone lifted his head off the steering wheel. Shit, he thought, reading the text. Where am I? Great question, Clara. I'm investigating a dream I had about an Asian guy being burned alive. I was nearly murdered by a homeless man with a grudge against the Microsoft Corporation. Nothing to worry about, though. Home soon. Hugs.

His phone beeped again; Clara had sent the same message, this time in all caps. He looked into the rearview mirror, barely recognizing his own reflection. "Now what?" he asked. The reflection did not answer.

—

A LONG CONTEMPLATION had led Allan to conclude that, regardless of the consequences, honesty was the best policy. He decided he would respond to Clara's texts with the truth (whatever the hell that truth was). That is, if he could figure out how to explain something to her that he himself did not understand. But then, he remembered the blank prescription pad in the Volvo's center console. He weighed both options, then changed his mind. Instead of the truth, he would tell a harmless lie. For the twins' sake. No reason to add to Clara's stress. He sent her a text: Out of migraine meds. Couldnt wait. Home soon. He then wrote himself a prescription.

Inside Ling's and unsure lying had been the right choice, Allan was waiting for the pharmacist to fill his prescription.

"No shit," he grumbled. Finished reading the instructions on a bottle of Head & Shoulders, he set the bottle back on the shelf. A flash of movement turned his head. About thirty feet away, he glimpsed what looked like an elderly man wearing dirty jeans and a white, long-sleeved shirt exiting the aisle. You can't be serious? he thought, his feet already walking him in that direction. More to prove he had not suffered a psychotic break and that the old man was *not* Wilhelm, Allan shuffled to the end of the aisle.

Fast old fella, he thought, surprised by how quickly the old man had traversed the length of the store. He increased his pace, watching the old man turn into the window aisle. Rabbits frequented their acreage, and whenever Hic saw one, he would tear after it, his brain shut off for the duration of the chase. That is how Allan felt now. His brain shut off, he was operating on instinct, chasing an old man around a pharmacy without any thought for how idiotic the exercise was.

He turned up the window aisle but saw no one.

"What the hell?"

He doubled his pace again, reaching the rear aisle in only a few seconds. Again, he saw no one.

Over the P.A., he heard, "Prescription pick-up for Abrams."

Ling's was small, the bulk of its merchandise spread over two dozen or so parallel aisles, each approximately thirty feet in length. Scrambling across Ling's back end, Allan checked each aisle like a frantic parent searching for a wandering toddler. Back where he'd started, he scanned what he could see of Ling's. Other than the staff, he was alone.

"Prescription pick-up for Abrams."

His Thorazine in hand, he exited Ling's and started toward

the Volvo, still searching for signs that anyone but him had been at Ling's. But the tracks in the snow were his own: one set leading across Elm Street toward the Texaco, another coming back, and a third set leading from Ling's front entrance to where he stood now.

Did I imagine him?

He climbed into the car and closed the door, his eyes sliding to the rear-view mirror. He started at the sight of the stranger. They looked the same, but the stranger was confused and embarrassed, and rightly so. He had just spent two hours investigating a dream, almost getting murdered, and chasing an imaginary man around an empty pharmacy. Allan continued to make eye contact with the stranger, wondering if he had any answers for his bizarre behavior. He did not.

—

BY ANY MEASURE, The Drop was a dive. Ripped and stained red-cloth-covered booths lined its outer walls, and a motley collection of tables and chairs, many held together with years of overlapping duct tape, filled most of the rest of the space. The aroma of stale beer and peanuts blended with body odor and depression to create the sour funk of despair. The only good thing about the bar, in Huffy's view, was the music. Trapped inside a refurbished jukebox, the boys from Nazareth were belting out the chorus of "Hair of the Dog."

Huffy and Frankie were seated at the bar, which was as nondescript as the stocky, balding, forty-to-sixty-something bartender dropping off, "A gin and tonic for the lady, Bud Light for the gentleman." Huffy thanked him and sucked a mouthful of beer. He ignored Frankie's discreet glare. Coming to a place like The Drop and not drinking, or worse, drinking anything non-alcoholic, was no different than walking in wearing a navy-blue windbreaker with *'POLICE'* printed across the back.

They were watching Gerhard through the large mirror behind the bar's wall of assorted alcohol bottles. Dressed in a white tracksuit and nursing a bottle of Sam Adams, he was about sixty feet away at a table adjacent to a hall leading to the bathrooms and an emergency exit. His warning system, at least so far, had not alerted him to their presence.

Three of the six customers were in the booth beside Gerhard, and he was almost certainly armed, so they had opted for Plan B. Huffy would watch Frankie's back while she went to the bathroom. From there, she would instruct tactical to enter through the Emergency Door, which she would open. If Gerhard got spooked and headed for the front door, Huffy and the UCs would take him down.

Frankie took a sip of her gin and tonic, grabbed her purse, pecked Huffy on the lips, and headed toward the bathroom.

Huffy, eyeing Gerhard through the mirror, was already concerned. Gerhard was watching Frankie approach and anxiously tapping the mouth of his beer bottle and pounding a furious beat with his foot. Nervous criminals were dangerous, particularly those who were armed and violent.

His eyes jumping between Frankie and Huffy, Gerhard suddenly stopped his finger-tapping and heel-thumping, and all expression drained from his face. Fuck, Huffy thought, realizing the big man's sixth sense had just whispered: "Those two look out of place."

Huffy slid off his stool and started toward Frankie, trying to reach her as quickly as he could without arousing suspicion. Halfway to her, he accidentally made eye contact with Gerhard. The change in Gerhard's expression made it clear that Huffy had made a mistake. Desperation, panic, and a massive spike of adrenaline contorted the faces of violent criminals in a very specific way.

"Frankie!" Huffy shouted, drawing his gun. But it was too late; Gerhard already had her in a choke hold with a gun pressed to her temple.

A moment of paralyzed silence was followed by shrieking and a flurry of activity as patrons and staff dove under booths and tables or dropped out of sight behind the bar.

Frankie's face was purple, Gerhard's choke hold having instantly cut off her air and blood supply. His eyes jumped between the three guns pointed at him.

"*Gerhard!*" Huffy patted the air behind his back, signaling for the UCs to drop their weapons. "On three, we are going to set our guns on the floor and let you walk."

Frankie's right arm was limp at her side, her left suspended in mid-air by muscles unable to communicate with her brain. Someone as powerful as Gerhard could quickly cause brain damage or a stroke, not long after, death.

Gerhard was backing slowly toward the hall, carrying Frankie with him, her shoes two feet off the floor. "Back the fuck off," he ordered, his gun now a few inches from Frankie's temple.

Huffy focused. He tuned out all distractions while thinking: Control your breathing…breathe in…hold…breathe out. He lifted his free hand and extended a finger. "One!"

Gerhard stopped, his eyes locked on Huffy's raised finger.

Huffy moved his hand to the right, hoping Gerhard's eyes would follow. They did. Laser-focused on Huffy's hand, Gerhard let his gun slip further from Frankie's temple. Instead of at her head, it was now pointed forward and aimed at the floor. Huffy knew he had no margin for error, but he also knew he had no choice.

Breathe in.

He steadied his gun.

Hold.

He raised a second finger.

Breathe out.

"Two!"

He pulled the trigger.

Terrified staff and patrons screamed as Huffy's bullet blew through Gerhard's hand. He dropped his gun and released

Frankie. By the time she hit the floor, Huffy had reached Gerhard and delivered a powerful kick to the side of his knee, bending it in a gruesome and unnatural inward direction. Gerhard yowled and crumpled to the floor, Huffy instantly on top of him. He drove his forearm into Gerhard's throat, his howls became airless gurgles. Huffy pressed his gun into Gerhard's forehead. Rage colored Huffy's face crimson and fused his upper and lower jaw. All he could hear was the voice shouting: *SHOOT HIM! HE WOULD HAVE KILLED FRANKIE! SHOOOOT!*

He drove his forearm harder against Gerhard's windpipe, trying to flatten it against the floor. Gerhard's eyelids fluttered, and his eyes rolled up. Huffy's switch wasn't just on, its handle had been wrenched so hard it had broken off. He felt, heard, smelled, and tasted only rage. In a flash, that rage became a need for vengeance. One bullet would punish every sick fuck who'd raped or murdered or molested or abused. One bullet would wipe away all the injustice and lenient sentences and legal loopholes. One worthless sub-human's death would wash away all the carnage Huffy had been helpless to stop.

Gerhard went limp.

Huffy was blind to everything except his finger pulling on the curved steel trigger, numb to everything except the release that pulling that trigger would bring, deaf to everything except the voice inside his head screaming: *SHOOOOT!*

28

The smell announced the story as accurately as a street-corner newsie: *"Extree! Extree! Read all about it! Man found burned to death in the Old Johnson Mill!"*

In this instance, the *"Old Johnson Mill"* was a warehouse a few blocks from The Drop, where, not long ago, two UCs had pulled Huffy off Rien Gerhard a microsecond before the contents of the Neanderthal's skull soiled a wrinkled gray suit and a perfectly good career. Despite a raw throat and grapefruit-sized bruise on her forehead, Frankie was fine. She didn't *look* tough, but in a fight with a speeding Mack truck, Huffy would have no problem putting a hundy on Frankie.

Rows of 400-watt LED lights hung from the warehouse's ceiling like inverted flower bulbs. Walking briskly, Huffy watched Dan Button use twelve-inch tweezers to fish in a reddish-brown pool of sludge. As he got closer and the smell began to overwhelm him, he slipped on his mask. The body was a gnarled mass of bones and burned muscle and flesh surrounded by a murky moat of liquefied human. He noticed several yellow streaks in the sludge. Years earlier, he had been testifying in court and missed the aftermath of the RUV's inaugural *going away* party. That party had introduced the group's unusual method of saying goodbye to hated friends and foes alike. But the next day, he reviewed the crime scene video with Button. Amidst a narrative on an array of topics, including the appropriate wine pairing for barbecued human, Button managed to slip in the odd bit of medically relevant information, which is how Huffy knew the yellow streaks were melted human fat.

In places, he could see bones, while in other areas, the tissue was relatively intact. On a patch of pristine skin, he recognized part of a tattoo he had seen several times over the years. The tattoo—a devil dragon with a claw cupped near its mouth as it whispered into the victim's ear—had been on the right shoulder. Somewhere in the remains was the devil dragon's left-shoulder nemesis—a whispering angel dragon. The victim, Huffy knew, had stopped listening to that dragon long ago.

Huffy crouched beside the pool of melted gangbanger. "So ends the life of Chris Tam."

Button dropped a piece of Tam into a plastic evidence bag, labeled it, and set it aside. "You got here fast."

Huffy slid his foot back, the sludge creeping outward as if Tam's life-force was trying to slink away and re-form as Chris Tam 2.0. "I was close by."

The sound of footsteps turned him around.

"Who's the goop?" Frankie asked, striding toward them. Gerhard's choke hold had given her voice a raspy, Rod Stewart-like quality.

"Tam," Huffy replied.

She leaned forward and sniffed the air. "Smells like a regime change to me."

Huffy didn't respond.

"Anything useful?" she asked Button, who was still digging in the sludge.

"I have no idea what most of it is," he answered.

Frankie took another whiff and grimaced. "He reeks. I'll be outside."

Huffy had a brief Q&A with Button and headed for the door. "Make sure to dust all points of entry," he called out over his shoulder.

It took him a little less than a second to realize that exhaustion had cut his IQ in half. The statement was as intelligent as Button telling him to check a suspect's alibi. The mental slip had him recalling the time he had worked a case for thirty-nine straight hours before face-planting into a bowl of clam chowder. Frankie, bless her heart, still found ways to weave the *Chowdah Incident* into their conversations. Not eager to add the *Tam Gumbo Affair* to her ammo belt, he decided that getting a few hours of sleep wasn't the worst idea.

–

FRANKIE'S OFFICE COUCH was much closer than his basement suite, so Huffy had driven to the station, hoping for a few hours of sleep before the sun came up. Whatever sleep he had managed to get had failed to revitalize him. Instead, it had drained the last of his energy and patience.

"What do you mean he isn't there?" he snapped. "He's a hundred fucking years old and locked in a psych ward during a pandemic. Where'd he go, bingo?"

Murphy sighed tiredly. "Rodin's North Wing isn't a prison, Huff."

Huffy, dredging a hand through his hair, watched Gerhard through the one-way glass. His hands and ankles cuffed and connected to a belly-chain, Gerhard had received just enough medical attention to ensure Witten PD avoided the wrath of Amnesty International. Or, in the case of an animal like Gerhard, the wrath of PETA.

"Tell Rodin's staff to find him and bring him *here!*"

Huffy followed Murphy out of the observation room and stepped into the attached interview room. He dropped a sheet of paper on the table and pointed to Gerhard's bandaged hand. "Hope I didn't get your whacking-off hand. Your cellmate in Bachman might like his balls tickled. You like to spit or swallow? I know you meatheads love protein."

"How's your ribs and head?" Gerhard fired back, his bruised neck and damaged throat causing his voice to sputter and lurch like a prepubescent teen.

Huffy sat. "Thanks for leaving all that evidence in your apartment. It was helpful."

A snigger. "*Fraud?* Really? I'll be out by Valentine's Day. I'll send you some chocolates."

Huffy pushed the paper containing five photocopied drivers' licenses across the table. "Five counts of first-degree murder, a half-dozen if you include Palette."

"Who?" Gerhard asked, ignoring the paper.

"Sedrick Palette is the last card you have to play. Why don't you prove you're smarter than you look and tell us who killed him and why?"

Gerhard eyed the paper long enough to look disinterested. "Don't you need evidence for a murder conviction? Maybe a body? Or a witness?"

"Who says we don't have a witness?"

Huffy nearly keeled over when dumbfounded blankness wiped out Gerhard's arrogant smirk. He had seen the same look many times, almost exclusively when guys like Gerhard learned the police had unearthed unexpected and case-closing evidence. Huffy listened closely, wondering if he might hear the gears inside Gerhard's thick skull grind to halt, then crunch and clang as they slowly reversed direction on their way to a high-speed review of the last five years, searching for someone who'd witnessed something they shouldn't have. But he heard nothing. Instead, he watched Gerhard relax. No one would ever mistake the juice-junkie for a theoretical physicist but understanding the workings of the universe was not the same as mastering the ins and outs of an interrogation.

"You ain't got shit."

Huffy explained how police had located Gerhard's 'lost grandfather,' then said, "And as it is somewhat unlikely he hopped over Bachman's walls and used an invisibility cloak to sneak past guards and cameras, we are hoping you'll tell us how he knows what he does about Sedrick Palette."

Gerhard glossed over the paper. Moments later, relief brightened his face. Huffy assumed the confident look was a bluff. But with Wilhelm missing, he could not disregard the possibility that Gerhard had crossed the old man off his to-do list.

Huffy's eyes sank to the paper, five elderly men staring back at him through the lens of a DMV camera, all delivering the same message from beyond the grave: "You royally screwed this one up, Einstein."

Huffy exited the interview room, preoccupied with a question for which he had no answer.

Why didn't I have someone protecting the old man?

MORNING. DECEMBER 20.

Allan trudged through the wet snow, his feet heavy and cold, every step requiring all his strength. He was mentally and physically exhausted. He had spent the night trying to will himself to sleep. The way he felt, he was certain he'd failed. Still, he must have fallen asleep at some point because snippets of last night's dreams were stuck in his head on repeat: a decapitated man hanging by his ankles from the roof of an industrial building, an Asian man being burned alive, and a slightly different version of the boy general dream: hundreds in the sea of dead had stood, resurrected.

He rounded the corner and was not surprised to see several news vans and a group of protesters in front of the downtown station's main entrance. Based on the signs and chants, the protesters supported a mix of causes, but most were demanding racial justice and wanted to ensure police understood that black lives mattered.

He and Clara supported most of what the nation's protesters were demanding, including calls to defund police, provided "defund" meant reallocating resources. Oddly enough, every officer Allan had talked to about the subject agreed. To them, it was common sense. Instead of four officers dealing with a situation that did not require a gun and that they weren't adequately trained to handle, why not send two officers and a social worker? Doing so would free up the other two officers to deal with situations that *did* require a gun and that they *were* trained to handle.

One aspect of the "police question" that Allan continued to struggle with was how entrenched each side was. It seemed impossible for people to agree that systemic racism could exist within a system where *most* police officers were good people trying to do the right thing under incredibly challenging circumstances. But like so many issues now, opinions were argued as facts and there was only one right set of facts.

His and Clara's circle of friends was small, mostly work friends who gathered socially as a group. Pandemic aside, that group rarely interacted anymore. Conversations would turn into debates, the debates into arguments, and the arguments into feuds. At times, the anger seemed sufficient to last generations; the Hatfields and McCoys 2.0.

Throughout history, the chain of events that led to mass death and destruction were easy to recognize, but only long after the damage was done. More frequently, Allan found himself worried that Pandora's Box had been opened, and whatever had been unleashed could no longer be stopped. He feared that in fifty years, people would look back and say: "The signs were so obvious. How could they have missed them?"

Shivering at the thought more than the temperature, he pulled on his mask and caught part of a live cut-in on his way to the lobby door.

> "... short for Reinheit und Vollkommenheit. The RUV's founder and leader, DaMarcus Kennedy—currently being questioned by police—has been the focus of several homicide investigations. Most recently, a jury acquitted Kennedy in the death of Joffrey Rothstein, a wealthy, local businessman who died under suspicious circumstances while awaiting trial on sex trafficking charges. An anonymous source inside Witten PD has confirmed that a power struggle within the RUV is responsible for the recent deaths within the group as well as the unsolved shooting death of eight-year-old Joshua Cutter. However, a lot of people are saying police killed Cutter and are covering..."

—

HUFFY AND FRANKIE were in front of the one-way glass. Both greeted Allan with a nod and returned to their discussion about the shooting death of Josh Cutter.

Standing beside Huffy and Frankie, Allan watched an attractive woman remove a pad and pen from her briefcase. She leaned the briefcase against the leg of her chair. He recognized the dreadlocked man seated next to her from the man's repeated cameos on nightly newscasts. One of those newscasts, one from several years earlier, had stuck with Allan. A husband and wife had been tortured and hung in their basement. But it was not the crime itself that was so memorable. The couple, both HIV-positive and heavy drug users, had passed their addiction and disease to their newborn son. If the speculation surrounding their deaths was correct, DaMarcus Kennedy had taken *extreme* offense to their parenting choices.

Allan also recalled the story's queer footnote. An anonymous tip had led police to the home several hours after the couple was killed. When police arrived, they found the infant asleep in his crib wearing a fresh diaper and with a half-empty bottle of baby formula beside him. Based on the formula's temperature, someone had fed the boy within minutes of the police arriving.

As Huffy and Frankie ended their conversation, Allan continued watching the woman on the other side of the glass, mesmerized by her piercing green eyes. "Lots of action around here."

"You think *this* is a zoo?" Huffy said. "Wait until we arrest Bill Gates."

"Huh?" Allan grunted.

Huffy snorted a laugh. "Early this morning, we found the body of the RUV's Second in Command burned to a crisp. One of our guys interviewed a drunk who claimed Bill Gates killed Tam. Told us the *Microsoft motherfucker* gave him a pair of leather gloves to keep him quiet." A beat. "If you own any Microsoft stock, you might want to sell."

Allan's head suddenly felt like a microwave after Huffy had pressed COOK BRAINS. "Where did they find him?" he asked, already knowing the answer.

"A warehouse in Camper's Village," Huffy answered, his

crooked brow asking his next question before he did. "Why?"

Because I was at that warehouse last night, Allan thought about saying, followed by, *I'm the Microsoft motherfucker who "gave" the drunk the gloves.* But admitting either suddenly felt like a terrible idea. "I was just curious."

Huffy pushed his chin toward the dreadlocked man. "DaMarcus Kennedy heads the RUV. One of his numbered companies owns the warehouse where we found Chris Tam. Kennedy's not stupid enough to kill Tam in his own building, but I like to haul him in every chance I get. Drives his lawyer crazy. She…"

Allan faded from the conversation, once again drawn in by the lawyer. Her flawless skin, pony-tailed blonde hair, and the scatter of freckles across the bridge of her nose came together in a stunning package. But her attractiveness was not what he found so intriguing; he *knew* her. How? he wondered. Have I seen her before? In court? On TV? Does she remind me of someone I know? Is she—

"*Hellooo…?*" Huffy waved a hand through Allan's line of sight. "You in there, Doc?"

"Sorry." Allan snapped out of his daze. "What?"

"Wilhelm is in the counseling office on the fifth floor. I need you to babysit him. When I finish with Kennedy, we'll reunite the old man with his favorite grandson."

"About that. It…" Allan hesitated, unsure how Huffy would respond to a request to pass Wilhelm off to someone else. "It is likely hormones, but Clara's upset at my involvement with Wilhelm. In the interest of keeping my clothes in the closet and off the front lawn, I think it is best that I no longer…" Allan watched Huffy's inquisitive expression transition toward a scowl. Based on their switch-flipping encounter at the Academy, he wasn't sure he should finish his sentence. Thankfully, his vibrating cell phone provided a stay of execution. He turned his back to Huffy and answered the call. Doctor Williams got straight to the point.

"I am calling to ask if you are going to accept my offer?"

"What offer?"

"Clara didn't tell you?"

"Tell me what?"

"When I called yesterday, you were asleep. I gave Clara your blood test results and offered to arrange for you to speak to a colleague of mine about how you are handling the stress of recent—"

"I appreciate your concern, but I'm—"

"Allan," Doctor Williams interrupted, his tone that of a father about to lecture a headstrong teenager. "Clara told me what happened after you lost your third child. Knowing that, and knowing how much blood pressure medication was in your system, I am concerned you are—"

"My mental health…" he lowered his voice to a whisper. "My mental health is none of your business."

He hung up.

"Everything okay, Doc?" Huffy asked, sounding more like a curious detective than a concerned associate. Allan, unsure how he had overdosed on Clara's blood pressure medication or why she failed to mention Doctor Williams's call, wiped the confusion from his face and turned around. "I'm fine," he answered.

After prolonged and uncomfortable eye contact, Huffy returned to their earlier conversation. "You were saying?" Allan, already at the door, said it wasn't important. "Talk to Murph before you head upstairs," Huffy added.

Allan did, then headed to the counseling office, calling Clara on the way but hanging up before she answered. Why add to her stress? So she had forgotten to mention the blood test results and Doctor Williams's call and his *offer.* Big deal. Pregnancy Brain was a real affliction. Besides, he was far more concerned about his own mental state.

30

Huffy had questioned DaMarcus Kennedy dozens of times, and not once had Kennedy ever lost his cool. On the rare occasions he strayed close to the line, Olivia Madson would pull him back with a look or touch. And if neither of those worked, she would end the interview.

But this time was different.

Huffy was under Kennedy's skin, deep enough that Kennedy was ranting about everything, and more passionately than usual. For the first time, Huffy *knew* he had Kennedy. All he had to do was keep pushing.

"You're a fucking hypocrite, DaMarcus. You—"

"The world's—"

For the second time, Madson declared the interview over. And for the second time, Kennedy ignored her.

"The world's run by hypocrites, Huff. Priests who scare sinners into filling the collection plate. Churches who use that money to buy the silence of diddled little boys. Politicians claiming to be patriots outta one side of their mouth, while—"

"Spare me the sermon; I've heard it before and from people a lot more qualified to deliver it than a wannabe gangster. Next, you'll be cursing the white man for rigging the system. I have news for you, bud, the system *is* rigged...against criminals. Just like the NBA is rigged against short, white guys and porn's rigged against guys with tiny dicks. Boo-fuckin-hoo."

Huffy watched Kennedy's demeanor subtly shift. He could almost hear Kennedy's psychotic motherly spirit whispering:

He is baiting you. Calm down.

Huffy had to step up the pressure.

"You're no black Robin Hood, DaMarcus. You are the same as every other sick fuck whose dick gets hard when they get to choose who lives and dies."

Expressionless, Kennedy said, "With millions dying from a lack of proper health care, who needs gas chambers?"

A beat.

"What the fuck are you talking about?"

"Someone's *always* deciding who lives and dies, Huff. Usually, it's rich white guys. They march us to the slaughterhouse after fattening us up with the same 'greater good' bullshit they've been feeding the tired, poor, homeless, wretched refuse, tempest-tossed, huddled masses screaming, *'I can't breathe!'* for centuries. Maybe all the shit happening now is the match that burns down the forest. Maybe the voices of George Floyd, Jacob Blake, Rayshard Brooks, Breonna Taylor, and thousands of others are finally being heard. Who knows?" He shrugged. "Maybe it's time for someone who ain't rich and white to decide which lives matter."

"You?" Huffy asked.

Kennedy didn't respond.

Huffy, feeling his opportunity slipping away, slid his eyes lewdly over Madson's body, letting his gaze linger on her breasts. "And if your baby boy is defective? Will you stand by your principles and sacrifice the future king for the *greater good* or just change your definition of pure and perfect?"

Judging by the rage erupting from every one of her delicate pores, it was Madson, not Kennedy, who was about to leap over the table and gouge Huffy's eyes out. He looked back at Kennedy. He was smiling.

Game over.

Madson, no doubt seeing the same thing, composed herself and moved on. "My client informs me you are surveilling him 24/7. Regardless of whether that surveillance violates my client's rights, if he *is* under surveillance, you already know he was home last night from approximately eleven o'clock until I picked him up this morning to come here. Furthermore—"

"Your client knows all about our surveillance and has no trouble eluding it. He also hangs with rapists and murderers who are more than willing to do his dirty work." He turned to Kennedy. "Speaking of rapists and murderers, now's your chance to prove you're not a hypocrite *or* a psychopath. Help me get justice for Josh Cutter's family. We both know it was an RUV bullet that killed him. Tell me who fired it, and I will put in a good word with the DA." A beat. "Or is that why you killed Chris? Did he shoot the kid? Did he break the RUV's first commandment? Thou shalt not kill anyone the great and powerful DaMarcus Kennedy hasn't deemed expendable."

"Chris was my friend," Kennedy said, the truth of the statement conveyed in his genuine tone. "Even if he wasn't, you think I'm stupid enough to do him in my building?"

A shrug. "Maybe your neighbor's chihuahua orders you to kill people; I've heard they're a nasty breed. I'm not privy to the inner workings of the minds of the criminally insane, DaMarcus, so how the fuck would I know how stupid you are?"

"Someone is trying to make it *look* like I killed Chris."

"A conspiracy? Really?"

"I—"

"*You* killed Chris. It's only a matter of time before I can prove it."

The message behind Kennedy's confident grin was unmistakable: *Good luck with that.*

Huffy had once again extracted precisely nothing from Kennedy and wanted to drive a fist through the animal's face. With cameras rolling and protesters all over the country out for blood—cop blood—he would lose his job and probably his freedom. But for a split-second, it seemed like a fair trade.

"Me and Chris had big plans," Kennedy said smugly. "One day, I'll show you those plans." He leaned forward. "Up close and personal."

"You'll see Chris again soon enough, DaMarcus. Up close and personal." Huffy leaned as close to Kennedy as he could. "And it'll be me you will have to thank for the reunion."

Madson's threats were unnecessary. Huffy knew his lapse in judgment was a mistake. And with every word recorded and cops being offered up as sacrificial lambs almost daily, the mistake would likely be a costly one.

—

AT HER DESK, Frankie had paid an irate Olivia Madson proper attention while occasionally leering at Huffy, *Thanks for this!* always her message.

Madson shot her arm out stiffly behind her, blindly pointing a poisonous French-manicured barb at Huffy. "And if you think I am going to let him get away with it," she whipped her barb around and aimed it at Frankie, "you are as delusional as he is. I will have his badge by the end of the day. I have him on tape threatening my—" Huffy's badge sailed over Madson's head and bounced across Frankie's desk and onto her lap. Madson's head completed a 180 before her body started to move. "You arrogant *sonofa*—"

Huffy launched himself out of his chair. On the job, Madson was the equivalent of a fishing lure—eye-catching but otherwise very unpleasant. In court, he had seen her show no weakness, countering arrogance with confidence, aggression with defiance, and intimidation with disdain. But as he momentarily towered over her, she retreated. He brushed past her on his way to Frankie's office door. "Four months ago, I sat in court and listened to you argue your client deserved a lesser sentence because he was caring enough to preserve a sixteen-year-old's virginity by raping her anal—"

"Who the hell—"

"Maybe when your client gets out, you and DaMarcus will have a precious little girl of your own and will help your client celebrate his early release with some alone time with *your* daughter. I'm sure he will appreciate the fruit basket you give him as a thank you for preserving her virginity by fucking her in the—"

"That's my job!" Madson blasted. "My clients des—"

"Fuck your job! And fuck your clients!" His nostrils flared, and his eyes bugged. "What they deserve and what they get are light-years apart. You pervert the law for money, period. You betray victims and their families by saying and doing *anything* to win. Every crime your piece of shit fiancé commits is on you, so spare me the self-righteous bullshit about *doing your job*. No offense, counselor, but no matter how much it cost and no matter how many expensive works of art adorn its walls, it is *still* a rock." Walking out, he added, "Go crawl under it."

Madson watched him leave and turned to Frankie. "How professional."

Frankie rubbed her bruised throat. "He did say 'no offense.'"

Unamused, Madson stated she would be filing complaints with OIM and the Sheriff's office and suggested Huffy start applying for security guard positions.

Frankie moved swiftly around her desk and interrupted Madson's dramatic exit with, "File complaints with whomever you wish. If anyone bothers to investigate, the *only* evidence against Liam will be the word of a cockroach and his attorney."

Five minutes later, Frankie, reviewing a file, was interrupted by Detective Pete Jarvis. He handed her a flash drive. "Merry Christmas."

"You shouldn't have," she said. "What the hell is it?"

"Bachman's surveillance footage."

31

Where were you before Rodin's staff found you in the basement? It was a simple question that, for some reason, Wilhelm had repeatedly refused to answer. Why? Allan did not know, and, truthfully, he did not care. He was more concerned about other questions scratching at the inside of his skull like snared wolverines. Questions so ludicrous that he was seriously considering the possibility that Clara was right, crazy really was contagious.

From the tan-leather chair opposite Wilhelm, Allan lifted his eyes off the identical coffee mugs on the glass-topped table and moved on. "Rodin's staff found you asleep in the basement, access to which requires a keycard. How—"

"Is that why I am here?" Wilhelm asked incredulously. "Because someone left a door unlocked?"

"You are here because we found your grandson, and—"

"My grandson?" Wilhelm's interest level suddenly spiked.

"Yes. Detective Huffy wants you to talk to your grandson or meet with him or…I'm not sure what he—"

"*Talk* to him?" Wilhelm's leather chair groaned as he slid forward. "*Meet* with him?"

Allan couldn't tell if Wilhelm was scared, surprised, or found the topic humorous because his brain was threatening to explode if he didn't relieve the pressure. "Forget about your grandson. I need to know why I am dreaming about a boy…" He stopped himself, fighting questions he felt compelled to ask. Questions almost as ludicrous as the belief that a delusional old man would somehow have answers. Why am I dreaming of a boy general? Who is he? How can my dreams show me the future? Why do they feel so real? How can I remain aware of the real world while dreaming? How can I overdose on pills I never took? Why—

The sound of the door opening severed his thoughts, and Sergeant Murphy waved him into the hall, where he explained he'd come to fetch Wilhelm, adding, "Huff doesn't want to scare him, thinks it will give Gerhard an advantage, so don't tell the old man about the family reunion."

Allan, re-entering the counseling office a few steps ahead of Murphy, stopped abruptly. Wilhelm had just set a cup back on the table. *Was that mine?* he wondered. His eyes remained glued to the cup as Murphy retrieved Wilhelm and led him out.

Allan followed, the kernel of a thought beginning to form.

The three men were walking single file through the station's front end when Wilhelm froze. Allan hesitated, then followed Wilhelm's line of sight to the hallway leading to the interview rooms. After a shoulder-check, Murphy stopped and impatiently waved Wilhelm forward. He refused to move. Seconds later, Olivia Madson and DaMarcus Kennedy exited the hall; Wilhelm was laser-focused on Madson. When she and Kennedy were a few feet away, Kennedy stopped.

"See something you like, old man?"

Wilhelm ignored him, his eyes trained on Olivia Madson, who, looking uncomfortable with the attention, cradled her swollen belly and turned her back to Wilhelm as she passed. Allan and Murphy watched with the same befuddled expression. *What the hell is going on?* When Madson exited the station, Wilhelm rejoined Murphy, who frowned, shook his head, and led Wilhelm toward the interview rooms. Kennedy shifted his focus to Allan and studied him for a long moment as if trying to burn his image into memory.

Allan, watching Kennedy trot to the lobby exit, wondered: Why would he care if an old man ogled his pregnant fiancé? And why was Wilhelm so fixated on her in the first place? That thought triggered another. And why the hell does she look so goddamn familiar?

—

THROUGH THE ONE-WAY glass, Huffy watched a relaxed Gerhard yawn, confident the shithead's mood was about to change.

"How long will it take Jarvis to review Bachman's footage?"

Frankie sipped some ice water. "A few hours."

Something in her tone caused him to turn. The thoughts behind her eyes were unmistakable. Shit, he thought. She rarely factored in where and when; if she wanted to talk, she would. In this case, though, the timing actually made sense, as Gerhard was probably the reason she wanted to talk. He'd no doubt choked her to the point that she'd floated toward *The Light*. When God informed her there were no rooms at the Inn, she'd returned with a new-found appreciation for living life to the fullest. The thoughts behind her eyes made it clear that her first order of business was to help her ex-partner do just that by casting out his demons.

"We need to talk." Her crisp tone left no doubt that avoiding the topic—something he had managed to do quite successfully since last December eighteenth—was no longer possible. To any detective, even a rusty one, evasion was the equivalent of a matador's cape. She had been nibbling at the edges of the topic for about a month; it was a scab she simply refused to stop picking. That picking had intensified as December eighteenth approached. He had hoped that she would let it go once the date passed. But hope, he'd learned, was a cruel emotion.

At this point, he had two options; three if shooting her was on the table. Although unless he killed her, shooting her would only make her more insistent that they talk. Option one was to let her pick gently at the scab, which would still hurt and only delay the inevitable. Option two was to let her rip it off in one swift, excruciating motion. Feeling her eyes burning holes in the side of his face, he chose option four: glare at her hard enough to say: "Back off," but softly enough to plead: "Please, don't go there."

It didn't work.

Without saying a word, she made it clear there had only ever been one option.

"Is this *really* the best time and place?" His defeated tone acknowledged the futility of the question. He braced himself; she was about to tear off his scab.

"Better now than never."

Never? he silently objected. The truth was, he *had* dealt with Hannah's death. And as he walked away from her freshly-covered grave, he'd locked the mental door to her death and swallowed its key. Although, he would occasionally mull the possibility that that key was the cause of the constant burning in his gut, tumbling and turning and slowly dissolving, poisoning him a little more every day.

"Fine," he snarled, his eyes locked on Gerhard. "Talk."

"If I am getting help with my disintegrating marriage, surely you could benefit from a session or two."

"With who? Abrams? Not a chance."

"With *anyone*." A sigh. "Our chats at the Pig aren't going to cut it. I'm not a mental health professional. You need—"

"Mental health?" he scoffed. "There's nothing wrong with my mental health."

"I have noticed things. I am worried that—"

"What *things?*"

Another sigh. "Getting help with trauma does not make you weak or—"

"I *have* dealt with it."

As he felt his switch start to flip, it hit him; his switch did not turn his anger on and off, his anger was *always* on—a constant, internal fire. His switch merely flooded that fire with fuel. He tried to hold it in the off position but was not sure he could.

"Maybe I didn't deal with her death the way you or Alex would have, but I *have* dealt with it, in *my* way."

"What way is that? Ignore the pain until you start drinking again or have another heart attack? That is bullshit. Hannah's death changed you." Her voice shed some of its sharp edges. "Her death hardened you, Liam. You are angry all the time. Losing Hannah and Alex are wounds that won't heal on their own. You need to deal with it, and not in your way, but in the *right* way."

Let it go! he wanted to yell. But he knew she couldn't. Like most men, when life knocked him down, his process was to stand, rub in some dirt, and start walking again. And if whatever had knocked him on his ass was intent on doing it again, he would run instead of walk. But Frankie had the same process as Alex. When life served you a sloppy-shit sandwich, you didn't plug your nose, swallow, and move on; you *talked* about it. About how it tasted and smelled and felt in your mouth. Then you talked about whether it made you vomit. And if it did, you talked about what tasted worse, the vomit or the shit sandwich. That process was *dealing with it*. And *dealing with it* was, somehow, supposed to make you feel better.

"I appreciate your concern, but I've dealt with my divorce and with Hannah's—"

"What divorce?" Frankie's frustration was starting to sound more like anger. "You won't even sign the papers." She wiped away a tear. "Alex called me last week and begged me to get you to sign off on a divorce *you* asked for. If you didn't want a div—"

"I've dealt with her death, *okay!*" He finally turned to her, pissed off that she would not just leave it the fuck alone. His emotions mixed like combustible chemicals—the resulting explosion of heat searing every inch of his skin from the inside out. "Every day, I see her in the faces of other babies. I don't go home anymore because, if I do, I sit in her rocking chair and *feel* her in my arms. I can still *smell* her, for Christ's sake. Some nights I want to scream until I can't scream anymore, then stick my gun in my..."

Hannah had died almost exactly a year ago. Realizing that he was speaking about her in the present tense caused tears to well in his eyes and a baseball-sized lump to form in his throat.

"Every day, I deal with people who, after being destroyed by garbage parents, grew up to be animals. Every day, I...see..." his words broke apart and fell away. He sucked in a choppy breath. "Every day, I see the pain and suffering those animals inflict, knowing that for some fucked-up cosmic reason, Hannah lived just long enough to ensure the pain of her death destroyed—"

Frankie, tears streaming down her face, wrapped her arms around his neck. His body locked, refusing to accept the embrace. Hannah was ash in an urn on a bedside table in a 300-square-foot basement suite. Tears and hugs and self-pity would not change that.

He pushed himself free. The pain on Frankie's face and the wet streaks lining her cheeks hit him like a sledgehammer to the gut. His anger instantly reversed and turned inward. He had been blind. And stupid. His wounds had not healed; he had not dealt with Hannah's death. His pain was as raw as the day he'd held her and watched her take her last breath. His pain had never left; his subconscious had merely numbed him to its presence.

My way? he thought. Funny. Bury what you can, convert the rest to anger, and then machine-gun it in every direction. Don't be so hard on yourself, he added derisively. Uncontrollable anger issues, a problem with alcohol, a mid-thirties heart attack, and you sabotaged your marriage to your high school sweetheart. It could have been worse.

This time, he hugged her. "Your timing is impeccable," he

whispered. She choked out a choppy laugh. "Maybe I'm not the rock I thought I was," he added, stepping back. "Thanks."

A smile threatened but never materialized. "All in a day's work."

He nodded at Gerhard through the glass. "Now, if it is okay with you, I'd like another go at this asshole."

–

ALLAN JOINED FRANKIE at the one-way glass.

"I heard what happened. You okay?" he asked, curious why she had yet to look at him.

A shallow nod.

Seeing Gerhard for the first time, he realized how lucky Frankie was to escape with a bruised neck and golf-ball-sized forehead contusion. He also understood why Wilhelm was so eager to avoid his abusive grandson. "Are you sure?" he followed up. "If you need to talk, I—"

She pressed a button on the wall, and speakers in the ceiling began broadcasting the sound from the attached interview room. "I need you to watch and listen for anything Liam can use."

"Sure," he agreed. "Has Gerhard said anything so far?"

She sipped ice water. "Says the old man's crazy. Sees and hears things." Another sip. "But he isn't stupid. He is probably laying the groundwork for his defense."

They watched and listened.

Huffy, ignoring the piss-colored teeth exposed by Rien Gerhard's shit-eating grin, started the interrogation. "When I'm done with you, your long-lost gramps will tell us everything we need to know. That, combined with the evidence from your apartment, will be enough to convict you on five counts of first-degree murder."

Gerhard remained straight-faced and silent.

"Good." Huffy leaned back in his chair. "I hope you don't

say a word. I hope you sit there with both thumbs up your ass because I really don't give a shit who killed Sedrick Palette." He sniggered. "But the DA is willing to give you one last chance. We know you and DaMarcus Kennedy were involved in Sedrick Palette's death. Give us enough to nail Kennedy, and the DA will recommend you serve your sentences concurrently. If you lawyer up or stay silent, no deals."

Gerhard leaned back in his chair. "No clue what you're talking about."

"That isn't what your gramps told us," Huffy lied.

"Nobody'll believe him. Dude's fucked in the head. You might wanna ask the DA if old men who see and hear shit make good witnesses for the prosecution."

Huffy clasped his hands behind his head. "My guess is Gramps overheard you and Kennedy planning Palette's murder. But it doesn't really matter. He has knowledge he could only get from you. Give us Kennedy or rot in Bachman, both work for me."

"Who's DaMarcus Kennedy?"

"Hilarious." Huffy folded his arms across his chest. "You know what else is funny? If you hadn't scared the piss out of your gramps, he never would have ended up here. And without him, we might never have connected the dots to you." He tisked. "You're a criminal fucking genius."

Gerhard pawed at his chin. "If you had anything, you wouldn't be trying to get me to talk about a crazier'n shit old man and a dead guy I never heard of. And if I *were* involved with Kennedy, I sure as hell ain't stupid enough to give him up."

His eyes still locked on Gerhard, Huffy waved at the door. Moments later, Sergeant Murphy ushered Wilhelm in.

Gerhard looked casually at Wilhelm and then at Huffy. "What? Is it bring Daddy to work day?"

Huffy turned to Wilhelm, who was studying Gerhard with curiosity, not fear. A realization slapped Huffy across the face:

not only were they not related, they had no idea who the other was.

No doubt responding to Huffy's confused expression, Gerhard's shoulders started to shake, and he slammed a palm on the table. "You dumb cunts got the *wrong* gramps."

Frankie, now alone on the other side of the one-way glass, watched Huffy leave as Gerhard continued. "Holy shit, that's fucking hilar—*wait!*" Gerhard's eyes bugged. "Am I being punked?" He pointed at his reflection in the glass. "Is Ashton Kutcher in there?"

32

Wilhelm and Gerhard regarding each other as strangers had reignited a curiosity and sent Allan back to the counseling office to retrieve his coffee cup. His cell phone pressed to his ear, and his other hand holding the cup, he used an elbow to select "1" on the elevator's keypad. "Hello again to you as well, Doctor Lam. I am calling you about Wilhelm Weissand."

"How can I help?"

"I'm hoping you will search Wilhelm's room and review your security video from yesterday to trace his steps."

"Search his room?" Doctor Lam questioned. "What is this about?"

Having anticipated the question and knowing the truth would require a lengthy and potentially embarrassing explanation, Allan said, "I'm worried he is suicidal and that—"

"Yes, I have seen the scar on his wrist, but it is an old wound. To be perfectly honest, physically he is healthier than most men half his age, and as *smelling* coffee and a suppressed appetite aren't signs of mental illness, I am starting to wonder why he is even—"

"I know," Allan said, realizing Wilhelm had not told anyone else about the voices. "But *I have* met with him multiple times, and I'm hoping you will give me the benefit of the doubt and search his room for anything he may use to hurt himself, particularly drugs." He exited the elevator and spotted Sergeant Murphy near the end of the hall. "Sergeant!" Allan called out. Murphy stopped. "Thank you, Doctor Lam. And please check if any drugs are missing from your pharmacy."

"How would he have gained access to our—"

Allan ended the call, jogged to Sergeant Murphy, and handed him the coffee cup. "Can you have this analyzed?"

Murphy glanced at the small amount of liquid in the cup. "It isn't a Fun-With-Science crime lab, Doc." Allan's dispirited sag changed Murphy's mind. He reluctantly took the cup. "Analyze it for what?"

"Drugs. Specifically, hallucinogens."

Sergeant Murphy sighed and strolled away.

Approaching his car in the underground garage, Allan checked his beeping phone. Huffy's text read: Frankie's office. Now.

—

THE IDEA WAS absurd, and Allan was appalled, not only by the thought itself but by the fact he had the capacity to generate it in the first place. Like so much recently, it made no sense. He shoved it aside and entered Frankie's office.

"I'll call you back." Before the phone's handset hit the cradle, Frankie had shot the seated Huffy a deterring glare as though he were a Rottweiler about to tear meaty chunks off an intruder's face.

It didn't work.

Huffy bolted to his feet. "Why the hell did you have the old man's room searched? Are you a fucking detective now?"

How does he know about the search? Allan wondered. "I was worried he was suicidal and might hurt himself," he replied, unsure why he had felt the need to lie.

"Do you know the time and resources we wasted on your wild goose chase for the old man's non-existent grandson? What the fuck is wrong—"

"Why wasn't someone protecting him?" Allan roared, finally tiring of Huffy's inability to control his emotions. "You *knew* Gerhard was a suspect in five murders." He spread the fingers of one hand. "*Five!* And no one, including you, knew Gerhard wasn't his grandson, so why didn't you have someone protecting Wilhelm?"

Huffy's stunned expression surprised Allan, whose stern challenge seemed to have drained every ounce of Huffy's fight.

Huffy held his ground but then slumped into his chair, the unexpected retreat ending the tension. "I apologize. I've slept for about an hour over the last three days. I also have to restart the Palette investigation because our lone suspect is a *generic* piece of shit, not the specific piece of shit we are after. I have no idea how the old man knows what he does about Palette *or* the teacher from Seattle. I have no clue *who* killed Palette, how they managed to do it, or whether I will be able to link his death to Kennedy. And on top of that giant pile of..." He blew out a loud sigh, closed his eyes, and sunk even deeper into his chair.

Defeat, Allan could see, fit Huffy as well as his wrinkled gray suit.

"Huff," Frankie said. "When we are done, I want you to go home and sleep. And Doc, I need you—"

Frankie's office door swung open. Allan knew the man rushing in. Detective Paul Bonino had been a cadet seven or eight years ago. Now, thanks to a run-in with armed looters, he was a patient.

"We got a call from Saint Pete's," Bonino said urgently, dropping a picture of an elderly man on Frankie's desk. "Stanley Bostwick, seventy-six. His description of the man forcing him to sign over his pension checks fits Gerhard to a tee. Bostwick also said that to discourage him from coming to us, Gerhard showed him cell pics of an elderly man in a shallow grave."

Frankie cracked her neck. "Alright," she sighed, "drop whatever's on your plate and take the lead on this. Pull Maria and Anderson off the McCulloch assault and ask Rolo to see what he can get from Bostwick's family."

"Will do." Bonino turned to Allan. "Gramps wants to see you, Doc. Something about his grandson."

Instantly ashamed, Allan dropped his eyes to the floor. Previously a critical player in a homicide investigation, he was now useless. And Wilhelm—a man whose rantings he had certified as authentic—may as well have been an Alzheimer's-stricken patient regularly coming to the station with a bus schedule and claiming it was a map to the lost city of Atlantis. Allan followed Bonino out of the office.

Frankie to Huffy: "Ballistics came up empty on the bullet we pulled from Josh Cutter's head."

"I know," he grunted.

"Which means both the Palette *and* Cutter investigations are back to square one." She shook her head. "What a shit-show."

Appearing too tired and frustrated to move, Huffy agreed with a single, slow blink.

"For argument's sake," she continued, "let's assume we are dealing with a regime change at the RUV. Is your money on Carpenter?"

"I guess," he groaned, his words barely energetic enough to drop off the end of his tongue.

"Jarvis can run with everything related to Bachman. I want you to stick with regime change."

"Speaking of Jarvis, anything new?"

"Maybe." She grabbed a file off a stack on her desk, removed a mugshot, and showed it to him. "Jerome Banks. Consecutive life sentences for a double homicide. Through his lawyer, Banks asked to meet."

"About?"

"Says he saw someone, possibly a guard, outside Palette's cell during the power outage."

"And he waited to mention this because?"

"Lawyer says he was scared."

"He isn't scared anymore?"

A shrug. "We don't have many doors left to open."

Huffy, moving like an eighty-year-old man, rose slowly from his chair and slogged toward the door. He stopped when Detective Pete Jarvis burst in holding a memory stick. "You guys need to see this."

After watching the video on Frankie's laptop, Huffy asked Jarvis, "What did the warden say?"

"He hasn't returned my calls."

"Bad for business," Frankie muttered.

"Bachman contracts with Triton Security for surveillance," Jarvis said. "Triton's tech says he has no idea how it happened."

She handed Jarvis the memory stick. "Interview anyone with access to this footage, have our techs check it for tampering, and find out if any employees at Triton have criminal records or connections to inmates or staff at Bachman."

Jarvis confirmed the order and left.

"Could anything else go wrong today?" Huffy asked.

Frankie glanced at her watch. "It's still early."

33

Allan again found himself struggling with the absurd thought as he stared at his reflection in the elevator's scuffed, gold-colored doors—a Fun House version of a man with a cell phone to his ear. Shit, he thought. He pulled his mask from his pocket, put it on, and returned to his reflection. The warped image fit his frame of mind perfectly. Still, he could not shake the possibility that the thought might not be so absurd. A part of him knew meeting Wilhelm was not the catalyst for all the recent strangeness. Bad dreams and coincidences and odd occurrences happened all the time and were as likely linked to meeting Wilhelm as to changing toothpaste brands. But wasn't it possible Wilhelm was a factor? The bitter-tasting coffee provided proof of that, didn't it? If Wilhelm was drugging him, then meeting him could be the cause of all the recent strangeness. Couldn't it? And wouldn't drug-induced psychosis or drug-related hallucinations explain everything?

But why would he drug me?

The idea, he again concluded, was absurd. *And* paranoid, he thought. No one, particularly a delusional old man, was drugging him. Nor was a supernatural force guiding that old man. Despite how it felt at times, Allan also knew he was not barreling towards Crazyville. His dreams and interpretations of those dreams, and all of the coincidences and odd occurrences had a *rational* explanation. Exhaustion, stress, and a lack of sleep were wreaking havoc with his mind.

"Sorry about that," Doctor Lam said. "I had to take that call." Allan did not respond. Distracted by his thoughts and reflection, he had forgotten he was on hold. "Doctor Abrams?"

"Oh," Allan said. "Sorry."

"As I was saying, unless you are worried about untouched food, we found nothing of concern in Wilhelm's room."

"And you searched *everywhere?*"

A beat. "You're welcome to swing by with a glove and have him drop his pants."

Allan ignored the sarcasm. "What about your pharmacy?"

"I am sure you can appreciate the need to secure the types of drugs we keep in our pharmacy. Wilhelm could not have gained access to—"

"But if he…"

But if he what? Allan thought. If he could get in and out of a maximum-security prison, a locked pharmacy would hardly present a problem?

"But *if he* what?" Doctor Lam asked.

"Never mind," Allan said, curious about something else. "Did you tell Detective Huffy that I requested you search Wilhelm's room?"

"He'd asked me to notify him if anyone inquired about Wilhelm. He was worried about the grandson, but he did say *anyone*."

"Alright." Allan stepped through the opening elevator doors and headed toward the fifth-floor counseling office. "Please let me know what you find on your security footage."

"About that," Doctor Lam said. "Our security staff had already reviewed the footage before you asked me about it. The North Wing's main doors are guarded and monitored 24/7, and all other doors are alarmed and monitored with security cameras. We had no alarms while Wilhelm was missing, so we are confident he never left the building, but what is odd—"

"A malfunction?"

"Our alarms are tested weekly."

"When were they last tested?"

"Two days ago." A beat. "What is odd is, after he entered the stairwell on his floor, Wilhelm disappeared."

Without thinking, Allan blurted, "He vanished?"

A chuckle. "No, he just didn't show up on any of our surveillance footage, at least not until we found him early this morning asleep in the basement."

"Are your cameras also tested weekly?"

"Yes."

"Who handles your security and surveillance?"

"Triton."

Allan paused, finding it an odd coincidence that Triton contracted with Rodin *and* Bachman. But after remembering Triton was one of the country's largest security companies, he realized a coincidence was precisely what it was and moved on. "How could Wilhelm avoid being caught on your cameras?"

"The stairwells aren't monitored as they offer no access to the basement or the grounds, but regardless of where he exited, he would have had to pass a minimum of four cameras to reach the basement. In addition to not knowing how he gained access to the basement without a keycard, we have no idea how he managed to avoid being recorded."

"Do the cameras have blind spots?"

"It is unlikely, but we are checking. That said, even if blind spots exist, how would Wilhelm have known where they were?"

Before Allan could respond, Clara called. He thanked Doctor Lam and answered her call. After a status and location update—his broken promise to go straight home forcing him to lie about both—he hung up.

In front of the counseling office door, he wondered if the strange old man on the other side was still relevant. How could he not be? He'd turned himself in within minutes of Palette's death; how could the source of that knowledge not be relevant? And what about the teacher from Seattle? How had Wilhelm known about the Batman costume? When Allan began contemplating the possibility that Wilhelm killed Cross days before the substitute teacher started a 41-child killing spree, he rubbed his hands hard into his face and thought: You're exhausted and stressed. Just get this over with, forget about Wilhelm and Huffy and all the other bullshit, then go home and spend the holidays drunk and watching Clark Griswold have the *hap-hap-happiest Christmas since Bing Crosby tap-danced with Danny fucking Kaye.*

He tried to smile. Unsure if he succeeded, he closed his eyes, inhaled a deep breath, and opened the door.

Wilhelm was leaning against the far wall. "That man killed a lot of people."

"What man?" Allan asked, despite knowing the answer.

"Why did you think he was my grandson?"

Allan closed the door. "Circumstances led us to believe he was your grandson and that he was hurting you. We thought he was involved in Sedrick Palette's death and that you had used overheard details in your confession."

Wilhelm sagged. "You still don't believe me."

"Don't believe what?" he snapped, tired of Wilhelm's fantasies. "That you snuck into a maximum-security prison and slaughtered a violent serial killer four times your size, then magically appeared thirty miles away two minutes later and confessed to his killing? Or are you asking if I don't believe that you are gainfully employed as a hitman for omnipotent voices and that you caused World War Two and the Holocaust because a hundred and thirty years ago you failed to kill four-year-old Adolf Hitler? Yes, you are right; I don't believe any of that. You have a delusional disorder, and—"

"A *disorder?*"

"*Yes,* a disorder. You have created a fantasy and supported it with information a ten-year-old could find online. There are no voices, and Rien Gerhard—"

He froze.

Until now, anger at being played for a fool had distracted him from an obvious question.

"Why did you say he killed a lot of people?"

Wilhelm's knowing expression seemed to say: *You know why I said it.*

Clueless as to how Wilhelm knew *anything* about Gerhard, Allan mentally replayed a portion of Huffy's interrogation. Did Huffy say something while Wilhelm was in the interview room? What about after I left? Did Sergeant Murphy say something to Wilhelm?

"Doc?" Wilhelm said. It took a moment for Allan to refocus. Wilhelm was standing in front of him. "He has killed more than five," he added.

Allan's jaw slacked then locked. It took him several seconds to work it loose and say, "How can you possibly know Gerhard is a suspect in five homicides?"

Wilhelm gently placed a hand on Allan's shoulder. "I think it is time you meet my family."

34

Frankie could see the pack of hyenas through the meeting room's glass walls—about a dozen of them, one flanked by a man with a shoulder-mounted TV camera. Having spotted her, all were out of their chairs and ready to pounce. Wayne Desmond was front and center. Desmond was the exception to the rule that bald and black were beautiful—a physical deficiency that, sadly, he did not overcome with a "great personality." He was grotesque through and through.

She checked her watch. "Jesus," she moaned. It wasn't even two o'clock, and her feet felt like they were about to fall off. For the briefest moment, Beth snuck into her mind. On days like this—days that took weeks to end—there was nothing she used to look forward to more than a bottle of Cab Sav and a deep-tissue foot massage. Wine and Beth's magic fingers had the power to make the worst the job could dish out float away.

The attack occurred the moment Frankie opened the meeting room door, everyone shouting a version of the same question.

"I am here," she stated, her strong voice quieting the pack, "because we have made an arrest in a string of missing person cases dating back—"

"Are there any developments in the Josh Cutter case?" someone shouted.

"I am not here to discuss—"

"Without a ballistics match, do you have any hope of finding Cutter's killer?"

She was not surprised someone had leaked the ballistics report, nor was she surprised it had been leaked to Wayne Desmond. She refused to look at him, speaking to the TV camera instead.

"We are working every possible—"

"You have no suspects, no evidence, and no witnesses," Desmond said. "Is it fair to say that if Josh Cutter had been white, you—"

"The entire Witten police force is committed to solving *every* crime. And it is insensitive to suggest that a*nyone's* loved one is not a priority. As I stated, I am here to—"

"We've heard," Desmond interrupted, "that you are withholding bodycam footage showing police shot—"

"Police did not kill Joshua—"

"Then why not release all the bodycam foot—"

"Joshua Cutter's family has seen all body camera footage, and, as I have informed you multiple times, they have asked us not to release it." Frankie turned from the TV camera and spoke directly to Desmond. "I pray no one here ever has to live through the nightmare that Joshua Cutter's family is living through now. But if you do, I hope no one uses your unimaginable pain to try and sell a few newspapers. Rather than further traumatize the family of a murdered eight-year-old boy by throwing as much horseshit against the barn as your tiny hands can manage, please at least *try* to be a human being."

Frankie glared at Desmond while a young woman said, "You recently questioned DaMarcus Kennedy. Was that related to the Cutter case?"

Her eyes lingered on Desmond as she slowly turned to the young woman. "We questioned—"

"Is it true some within Witten PD are questioning your ability to lead the SIU?" Desmond asked. "And you have been asked to step down if Cutter's killing remains unsolved?"

Frankie ignored Desmond and continued answering the young woman's question. "We questioned Mr. Kennedy about an entirely different—"

"Is your personal life affecting your ability to solve the Cutter case and lead the SIU?" Desmond followed up.

Most in the room reacted predictably; the question was insulting. And, had Frankie been straight and male, it would never have been asked.

Frankie relayed what she could about Rien Gerhard's arrest and his alleged crimes, spent a few minutes ignoring Wayne Desmond while answering legitimate questions—most about Joshua Cutter—and left.

35

The craving (much worse than pickles and ice cream) that had roused Clara from her nap was now trying to lure her from the den couch to the kitchen. She dropped her hot, swollen feet onto the cold hardwood and moaned as a soothing chill cascaded up her calves.

"No, I did not just orgasm!" Clara shrieked. Sue Gibson laughed at her own joke and continued talking a mile a minute. Sue was her best friend, but a huge gossip. In no mood to gossip, Clara had been trying to end the call, but Sue simply refused to take a hint. Before her nap, Clara had switched all the phone ringers off but somehow forgot about her cell.

"Yeah, raped and murdered, I know. It's the fourth woman in the last six weeks." Clara listened. "Fifth? *Really?* Jesus." She wriggled her feet to a fresh cold spot on the floor. Through a yawn, she added, "Hey, I'd love to keep—" She listened. "I know, I wish you could come for a visit, too, but my OBGYN barely lets Allan near me." They laughed. "Anyway, Sue, I—" She listened. "I know, but sooner or later, everything will be back to normal and—" She listened for a bit, pulled her cell phone from her ear, closed her eyes, cracked her neck, and returned to Sue. "Sorry to interrupt, Hun, but my phone is about —"

She hung up. "My God, woman!" Clara groused, immediately switching her phone to silent.

She looked around the den, which was now more of a Denver Bronco's shrine. She hated football but loved the den's suede couch and cold hardwood. If she could muster the energy, which was a big *if*, she would head to the kitchen, satisfy her most common and bizarre craving, and come back for another nap.

"Hic," she called. The dog followed her as if she were a crumbling cheese wheel, so having to call him at all was odd. *"Hic!"*

She started to stretch and yawn but cut both short when she caught movement through the den's picture window. Motionless, she searched the yard, her heart pattering until a gust of wind sent a branch from a pine tree into spasms. She sighed and fell back against the soft suede. "Silly girl."

Allan would be home soon—too soon. She would have preferred more time (maybe a year or two) to come up with a reason for what she had done. But there *was* no reason, at least not one she understood. You could always tell him the truth, she thought. *Um, Allan, sweetie, I didn't tell you about Doctor Williams's phone call because it turns out I* did *mix up your medications. I nearly killed you. Ha! Isn't that a hoot? Man, pregnancy brain is the worst.* She yawned again, thinking: Why stop there? Why not tell him everything?

She closed her eyes, her mind returning to Valentine's Day. She was in her lawyer's office. *Maybe this is what a twenty-two-year marriage looks like,* she had told herself, her shaking hand holding the tip of a pen above the signature line on her divorce petition. *Maybe give it three more months?* Three months was not going to make a difference; she knew that. Love was a living thing, and like all living things, it could die. Although she sometimes wondered if her love for Allan had died needlessly. Had she *allowed* it to die? Had she accepted their marriage would fail simply because it was easy to accept? Why stress yourself out when, after a reasonable period of mourning, you could just fill out an eHarmony questionnaire and wait for a new Prince Charming to ride his electronic white horse into your inbox? People changed marriages like shoes. She had once wondered if the love for a child might be more disposable if people could trade in kids as easily as spouses. Don't like Susie's attitude? Trade her in! Little Jack wants to be a Jacqueline? Move on and try again! Too many polished cat skulls under Timmy's bed? Return him and try for a less deviant model.

Several times since that Valentine's Day appointment, she had wondered if she would have signed the divorce paperwork had she known she would get pregnant? But how could she have predicted that? She had not had the heart to tell Allan that she had been using birth control since Isaac died. Hope had become too painful. But, God had other plans. So, sixteen days short of "three more months," she traded a divorce for stretch marks, mood swings, and twins.

Tell him everything. Brilliant idea, Clara.

"Where's my friggin' dog?" she grumbled, struggling to her feet. She stretched again, her silk robe falling open and exposing her naked front. She wrenched the robe closed after catching more movement outside the den window. From where she stood, she searched the yard, her heart again thumping. She and Sue had talked about the string of recent home invasions involving women alone in their homes; five in total, all raped and murdered. The story had obviously spooked her. She felt like a kid home alone after watching a horror movie; one moment, she was sure she had imagined the movement, the next, she had convinced herself someone *had* been outside the window, watching her.

She relaxed when, once again, wind wiggled a tree branch. Or perhaps this time, the tree was wagging a finger and saying, "Silly girl."

A restless tree branch? A deer bounding across the lawn? A serial killer casing the joint? It didn't matter; she could no longer deny the lure of microwaved bacon smothered in chocolate sauce.

–

NINETY MINUTES EARLIER, Allan had called Clara and lied

about meeting a U of D Alum for a late lunch in Denver. No one in the car had spoken since. Allan, appreciative of the silence, had spent the time listening to the radio (Sinatra currently finishing a live version of Under My Skin) and contemplating his sleeping passenger. Despite the certainty of his diagnosis, he could not shake a nagging doubt about Wilhelm. Like a sliver you feel but can't see.

"*Because I've got you under my skin,*" the Chairman of the Board crooned. "*Yes, I got you under my skin.*"

Floating down I-70 along the Northwest edge of Denver, he settled into the hypnotic rhythm of the world sliding by. Only during these random silences—silences that wiped all thought and distraction from his mind—did he come close to accepting the reason for his nagging doubt. In these hazy, free-flowing moments, his rational mind would step aside just long enough for his irrational mind to whisper, "What if the old man isn't delusional? What if he is telling the truth?"

During those *anything is possible* moments, lucky guesses and Google searches would make room for less rational possibilities like an omnipotent entity wielding Wilhelm like a magical sword. But even then, he never *completely* let go of the truth: Wilhelm had built his world with excerpts from history books and biographies, and, when required, fables conjured in the same part of the brain writers used to populate worlds with dragons, ghosts, and vampires.

Wilhelm's world *was* real but only to him.

Still, despite the absurdity, he could not rule out the existence of a mystical force capable of influencing thoughts and actions. What else could explain a respected psychiatrist dropping everything, lying to his wife, and driving to Denver to visit the "family" of a delusional old man?

—

ALLAN TIGHTENED HIS grip on the steering wheel as the Volvo passed under a large arch, *Holy Cross* woven into its wrought iron.

A few minutes later, Wilhelm, despite his cane, was moving effortlessly through the foot-high snow. A few steps behind, Allan could not shake the feeling that there was more to Wilhelm than met the eye. Something hidden or perhaps even dangerous. A sickly feeling in the pit of his stomach caused him to shoulder-check, half-expecting to spy a member of Wilhelm's "family" following at a distance for some prearranged, nefarious purpose. Rather than alleviating his anxiety, seeing no one only heightened it. Am I being led toward something? Or *away* from something else?

He followed Wilhelm, inhaling the frigid, pine-scented air as they passed through a wooden arbor set into a line of densely packed trees and entered an open space guarded on all sides by towering evergreens. The cemetery was small, the final resting place of perhaps a few thousand people. Starting down a hill that sloped gradually toward the cemetery, Allan could not help but think of the dead, countless stories untold by headstones rising randomly from the snow-covered ground. He suddenly became aware of the eerie silence; the city's busied impatience kept at bay by evergreen walls. From nowhere, the magnitude of the pandemic hit. The finality of it. So many dead, their voices lost forever. He shuddered, his knees almost giving out.

Without realizing it, he had stopped walking. He spotted Wilhelm about thirty feet ahead. He had veered from the main path and was walking through the deep, untouched snow. Why does this place look familiar? he wondered, picking up his pace.

Wilhelm was on a knee when Allan reached him, his gaze sliding to a black, heart-shaped marble headstone to Wilhelm's left. As he read the inscription, Allan felt a locked door in his heart being ripped from its hinges.

Some dream of angels. We held one in our arms.
Kaitlyn Jessica Davis.

Called to play in Heaven after four months and two days.
Always and forever.
Mommy and Daddy.

Wilhelm finished clearing snow from a grave marker and stood. Allan read the simple words etched in the small grey stone.

Werner Karl Marbach
February 22, 1935 - June 15, 2011

"My great-grandson," Wilhelm said, cold air wrapping his words.

Allan's rational and irrational minds started a familiar debate. His irrational mind wanted to believe Wilhelm, while his rational mind argued that a random grave marker in a random cemetery was proof only of Wilhelm's commitment to his delusion.

"This *is not* your great-grandson." Allan stuffed his hands into his jacket pockets. "You did not kill Sedrick Palette; you are not responsible for the Holocaust; you did not kill Hitler, in Argentina or anywhere else; you are not 160-years-old, and there are *no* voices. I…"

His gaze shifted back to the little girl's heart-shaped stone, his stomach again twisted by the feeling that instead of being led toward something, he had been led away from something else.

"I have not aged," Wilhelm said, "not in the *real* sense, since June 11, 1952. Everyone I have ever loved is dead. Upon Hitler's death, I received the full benefit of the voices' power. Why then? Like so much else, I do not know. But since Hitler's death, the voices have provided whatever help I required: strength, stealth, speed…" a knowing look, "a power outage at a maximum-security prison. Since 1952, I have killed 310 people, including Adolf Hitler and Sedrick Palette. There *are* voices. And I am not here by chance; I am here *with you,* and for a reason I think you know but will not accept." His tone darkened. "But you must. Time is running out."

Allan's mind was as barren as the acres of white surrounding them. He'd heard Wilhelm increase his death count from 308 to 310 but had yet to process the new detail. His eyes wandered from headstone to headstone. You need to get home. The thought hit with enough force to nearly knock him off his feet.

He started back to the car.

As he ascended the hill and approached the arbor set into the densely packed evergreens, he stopped, his eyes locked on a scarred and knotted tree he had not seen coming in. The trunk was bent at a right angle toward the cemetery, its deformed branches and arthritic fingers all pointing in the same direction. *Look!* they demanded. *SEE!*

His urgency to get home exploded. He had no idea what had caused the urgency or why he could not resist it. Was he tired and stressed? Was the tree the same tree from the dream of the boy general, or just a trick played by an exhausted mind? Was the urge a manifestation of the guilt he felt about lying to Clara about where he was going and who he would be with? Or had it come from a mysterious, unexplored part of his brain? The same part responsible for his mother driving to his summer camp *before* he had broken his leg.

"How did you know to come?" he'd asked her on the way to the hospital.

"I just knew," she'd answered.

I just knew, he thought, unaware he was now running toward the parking lot. I just knew.

36

Huffy, hearing no reply for the second time, unholstered his Glock. He could feel it; something was wrong. Normally, an open front door would not be concerning, especially in this neighborhood. But there had been several deadly home invasions over the last couple of months. And although all had occurred on the opposite side of the city, the killer had left no evidence, which meant he was meticulous *and* smart—smart enough to change locations. And a secluded acreage community would fit his needs perfectly.

He used his Glock to nudge the front door all the way open. "Clara?" he called out for the third time.

This time he heard a reply—a moan, one inspired by intense pain.

He charged up the stairs, broke hard left, and used his free hand to send a partially open door crashing against a wall.

Clara's short, piercing shriek stopped him cold.

Fighting temporary paralysis brought on by embarrassment, he holstered his gun and unconsciously retreated while offering an incoherent, stuttering apology.

"Don't go," Clara said, relaxed now that she knew the intruder's identity. She scooched against the headboard and encouraged him to sit by patting the duvet.

He sat on the edge of the bed. "I'm *so* sorry, Clara. I—" He shoulder-checked. "Your front door was open. I heard...I thought you were in pain, so I—"

"I *was*," she cooed, smiling and dropping a hand on her belly.

"Oh." Embarrassment gave way to mild panic, and he pulled his cell phone from a jacket pocket. "Do you need an ambulance?"

"I'm fine," she reassured, gently touching his upper arm. "I get a tad vocal when the twins are rambunctious."

He blew out a gust of air: one part relief, two parts embarrassment. "I'm such an idiot."

"You're not," she soothed. "Besides, what girl wouldn't want her very own Knight in shining armor?"

"Why is your front door open?"

She forced her sculptured eyebrows together for a moment, then tapped a temple. "Emotional, scatter-brained, *and* forgetful—the pregnancy brain trifecta. I must have left it open when I let Hiccup out for a pee." She tried to wedge a pillow behind her back but couldn't reach and asked him to help.

"Hiccup?" he questioned, maneuvering the pillow into the small of her back.

"Perfect," she said. "Thanks." His fingers grazed her shoulder as he pulled his hand back. "We'd named him Biskit," she continued, "but when we brought him home, he had the most adorable case of puppy hiccups."

"Ahh." He rose to his feet. "Do you want me to track him down?" He twisted his mouth into a slightly wicked smile. "Hunting animals is kind of my jam."

She giggled and shook her head. "He doesn't leave my side for long. He'll be back as—"

She cringed, rocked forward, and clutched her belly.

He placed a hand on her shoulder. "Are you okay?"

She relaxed after a long, slow exhale. "Uh, huh." She tapped her belly. "My *dome* is hosting Monday Night Football."

Clara's robe had opened enough to expose a thin strip of bronze-colored skin on her belly. He tried to look away but couldn't. She took his hand off her shoulder and guided it around her stomach. He felt himself becoming aroused.

They had met a couple of years ago at the city's Christmas party. He wasn't sure she remembered. At the time, he had told his old professor that he married *way* up.

She pressed his hand against her side-belly. "Did you feel that?"

It took a moment for the word to reach his mouth. "Yeah."

"Don't you *dare* tell Allan about this."

He snapped his hand back. "Sorry. I didn't mean to—"

"It isn't that." A smile played on her lips, and her hand once again found his upper arm. "The twins stop moving every time Allan comes near them. He thinks they hate him. He'll go crazy if he thinks they like you more than him."

He smiled. "Keeping secrets." A wink. "Also my jam."

He felt her hand on his arm and her warmth radiating through him. Hannah's death had turned his already hard outer crust into a block of impenetrable ice. It made no sense, at least not to him, but Clara's warmth was melting that ice. Drops became a trickle, the trickle a stream, and the stream a river. Soon, his pain was falling away like house-sized chunks from a melting glacier.

She's married, he warned himself, feeling his cell phone vibrate. *You're* still married! He checked to see who was calling.

"Kitty stuck in a tree?"

He laughed. "Actually, the city reallocated our budget, so cat psychologists respond to those calls now." She smiled, but he didn't see it; he was distracted. Allan was calling again. The odd voicemail he had left earlier was why Huffy was here. This call sparked a memory from the morning; Allan was concerned his involvement in the Gerhard case could lead to his clothes ending up on the front lawn.

"So," pocketing his cell, "when are Allan and Wilhelm back from Denver?"

—

ALLAN'S URGENCY TO get home had spiked every time one of his many calls to Clara had gone unanswered. He had also called three other people, hoping someone could check on her. His neighbor had answered, but he and his wife were in Arizona. His call to a colleague had gone to voicemail. Desperate and with no other options, he'd twice called Huffy. The first call he left a voicemail that, at best, would have sounded odd. At worst, Huffy would have wondered how an insane person got his cell number. Unable to reach anyone, his mind had split in two, one side rational, the other not. Were Clara and the twins in danger? Of course not. His gut feeling in the cemetery was the result of extreme stress and a lack of sleep. But what if it wasn't? What if it was more than a gut feeling? And what about the deformed tree in the cemetery? Was it the tree from his dream of the boy general? Of course not. His frazzled mind had turned a random tree into a familiar one.

He had tried listening to music for a while, hoping the distraction would ease his mind. When it didn't, he tried conversation. But instead of easing his mind, the conversation was making him more anxious and frustrated.

"I know this *feels* real, Wilhelm," he said, unable to stop his mind from continually returning to Clara and the twins. "But that is because we interpret information to support our beliefs. The stronger the belief, the easier we find support. Maybe you came to believe your internal voice—your conscience—was independent and omnipotent, or your choices during the war had terrible consequences for the people you loved. Maybe…" His mind returned to Clara. He pictured her lifeless body sprawled on their bed, her stomach torn open, the twins gone. He forced the image from his mind. "Maybe you found it easier to believe the voices had influenced those choices. I wish I could help you, but I have been out of private practice for fifteen years. The best I can do is refer you to someone."

Wilhelm stared out the passenger window. "Your training and experience provide *proof* I have created a fantasy and supported it with what I interpret as facts."

The words barely registering, Allan offered a distracted nod.

"And the world is flat," Wilhelm continued. "And the sun revolves around the earth."

"Huh?" Allan responded, missing Wilhelm's point.

"The world's greatest minds have been wrong countless times. How is it that a psychiatrist from Colorado is so certain he is right?"

Allan did not respond.

"The nature of faith makes its subject unverifiable," Wilhelm continued. "If you believe what I have told you is fantasy," he leaned his head against the window and closed his eyes, "there are many ways in this technologically advanced world to prove you are right."

Silence settled between them.

Each time another call to Clara went unanswered, Allan's mind generated more horrific images.

--

WITH RODIN ON the way, Allan had dropped Wilhelm off, not recalling if he had stopped the car or forced him out as he sped past the hospital's entrance.

His calls to Clara were now continuous.

He flew by a massive slab of polished granite set into the "Y" in the road. Engravings in the twenty-ton rock directed those headed to Lower Manor Estates to the right and those headed to Upper Manor Estates to the left. He veered left.

The two-mile stretch cut into the side of Sawback Mountain aided in the illusion that Upper Manor Estates—only thirty minutes from downtown—was an isolated mountainside retreat. He had driven the road countless times, its natural beauty never ceasing to amaze. But this time, the road's purpose had changed. Instead of showcasing some of God's best work, its lazy curves and gradual hills and valleys seemed hell-bent on slowing him down. Instead of coating the transcendent scenery with a white, Christmas-Card-frosting, the falling snow was forcing him to slow down by making every rise and fall and twist and turn slick and treacherous. And not to be left out, the narrow bridge spanning Angels Gorge—a deep gash in the mountain—caused the Volvo to shimmy and slide after its tires hit the bridge's raised front edge. Regaining control, he sped home and brought the Volvo to a fishtailing stop less than a foot from the garage's closed overhead door.

He raced through the front door, not questioning why it wasn't locked, his mind now rotating through all of the horrific scenes he'd imagined since leaving Denver. He sprinted up the stairs to the master bedroom. Finding it empty, he flew back downstairs, cast a hurried glance into the den, and stopped abruptly just inside the kitchen. Oh, dear God, he thought, his body deflating like a popped balloon.

Clara was at the table twirling fettuccine onto her fork.

His immense relief was instantly replaced by embarrassment.

He had worked himself into a frenzy based on what? A gut feeling? Unanswered phone calls? Why had his mind defaulted to Clara and the twins being in danger? Was it out of the realm of possibility that she failed to answer his calls because she was asleep? Or because her cell phone had died, or she had not heard it ring? Yes, he'd called the landline, but his increasingly frequent and powerful migraines meant the ringers on the house phones were rarely on.

What the hell is wrong with me?

"Hi, sweetheart," he said, praying she had not seen his frantic sprint through the house. He joined her at the table. "How was your day?"

Clara shoved a forkful of pasta into her mouth and chewed it slowly. Her eyes narrow slits, she watched him, the space around her dark and cold.

Unsure why she was upset, he set his hand on hers. "Sweet—"

"Don't *touch* me!" She wrenched her hand away and stood. Her eyes trained on his, she lifted her plate off the table. For a half-second, he thought she might launch it at his head. "How was *my* day?" He watched her walk stiffly to the sink and scrape pasta—and possibly shards of porcelain—into the garburator. "My day was *great!* How was lunch with your U of D buddy? What was his name again?"

Shit, he thought. She knows.

He did not want to fight, not about Wilhelm, or overdosing on her blood pressure medication. He did not want to fight about *anything.* But she knew. Somehow, she knew. His eyes, tone, and demeanor were instantly apologetic. "Sweetheart, I'm sorry. I—"

She slammed her plate into the dishwasher.

"See," he defended, grasping at anything to avoid a fight. "I knew this is how you would react. I didn't tell you because I didn't want to stress you—"

"You promised to pass him off to someone else," she cried, her face tense and narrow. "You lied." A beat. "*You LIED!*"

"But he isn't related to the man we thought was his grandson, so—"

She smashed the granite countertop with both palms. "And spare me the bullshit about not wanting to *stress* me out because we both know—"

"I'm sorry, okay?" He stood, unsure if he should go to her. "The truth is, I don't know why I went to Denver with Wilhelm or why I—"

"*Enough!*" she screamed. "I can't take this anymore. You promised you were done with him and—" Pain contorted her face and buckled her knees. She gripped her belly with one hand and the countertop with the other. He took a step toward her, but her upright palm ordered him to stop. "You *promised* me, Allan. You…" She sagged, her anger vanishing. "Maybe it is mother's intuition or hormones," she continued weakly. "Or maybe I am losing my friggin' mind." Her eyes filled with tears. "He scares me, okay. I can't explain why, but he scares me."

"There is no reason to worry," he said, unconvinced that was true. "I told you, he isn't related to the man we thought—"

"And I am scared that this time the stress is too much. I'm scared you are having another…"

Her sad, tear-filled eyes fell to the floor. He reached for her, but she turned and walked away.

He wanted to go to her and *make* her understand. But how? How could he explain something he did not understand himself? Why, with their marriage dangling from a thread, was he insisting on running around with butcher knives taped to his fingers? He would no more disregard her wishes to drop Wilhelm as a patient than she would have deliberately given him an overdose of blood pressure medication. But how could he convince her? How do you rationalize the irrational? How do you use logic to explain the illogical? He had no reason to feel the way he did about a mentally ill old man. Nor did he have a reason to continually disregard his education, experience, and instincts in pursuit of…what? What exactly was he pursuing?

An irrational switch seemed to be governing his choices related to Wilhelm. And no matter how hard his rational mind strained and stretched, the switch remained out of reach.

He sat at the kitchen table, a migraine that had faded into the background now back and pissed off that it had been ignored. But the migraine was not why his head felt like it might explode. On multiple occasions, he had faced the question: Is keeping your relationship with Wilhelm worth losing Clara and the twins? It terrified him that, on every one of those occasions, his answer had been yes.

Maybe stress *is* affecting my mental health? he thought. Am I having a breakdown?

An hour later, he took two Thorazine and an Ambien and slid into bed. He watched Clara sleep, at one point playing a stupid childhood game every time her chest rose and fell. She loves me…she loves me not. She loves me…she loves me not. He stopped after realizing she would have to die for him to get his answer.

As he drifted toward sleep, a memory spurred a feeling that was somewhere between an urge and a compulsion. He pulled a pen and a bookmark from the drawer in his bedside table, jotted down a name, and flopped back onto his pillow.

Sleep would prove elusive as he rolled the name over in his mind. Was it significant? Or did the name, the tree, and so many other odd occurrences and coincidences have a much simpler explanation?

Am I having a breakdown?

37

Huffy's prolonged admiration of the retreating waitress's short shorts had Frankie twisting for a quick peek.

"Her perfect ass was here two nights ago," she said over the Blind Pig's country music and minimal background noise. "Why didn't you top up the spank bank then?"

"I did." His eyes brightened and gave away the punch line. "I made a withdrawal."

"*Ugh*," she grunted. "You're such a pig."

He laughed. "I'm a guy. It's kind of our thing." He gulped from his bottle of non-alcoholic Bud.

"How's AA?"

"That's an abrupt change in the conversation's direction."

"That other stuff was boring."

He swirled the beer at the bottom of his bottle. "Stopped going. Religious Kooks."

"You have a disease," she admonished. "You can't—"

"We're in a *bar!* Your concern is ringing a little hollow." She acknowledged his well-made point with a tongue click and two taps on the table from the base of her empty wine glass. "And disease my ass," he continued. "People can't choose *not* to have cancer. Alcoholism is no more a disease than sex addiction."

"I guess you would know."

He cringed. "*Ouch*."

A grin. "Fly too close the sun..."

He dipped the bottle toward her. "Touche." He finished what was left and set the empty on the table. "Speaking of sex addiction therapy, did I ever tell you that's where I met David Duchovny?"

She rolled her eyes.

"True story!" he exclaimed. "He was a young, heartbroken student, and I, a handsome but lonely instructor. Together, we—"

"You're a funny guy," she said in a poorly executed wise-guy accent.

"What is that from?"

"Ray Liotta in *Goodfellas*."

"Terrible," he said. "And he wasn't in *Goodfellas*."

"What?" she croaked.

He shook his head. "You're thinking of Kevin Spacey. Liotta was Keyser Soze in *The Usual Suspects*. By the way, did you know—"

She balled a napkin and threw it at him. "Prick."

He caught it and threw it back. "It isn't my fault…it's a disease."

They both smiled.

"What is next on the docket?" she asked. "A discussion on why *all* lives matter? Religion? Name that Kevin Costner bomb?"

"He was a tad stiff in *The Ten Commandments*."

The waitress returned with a perspiring bottle of fake Bud and a fresh glass of red wine. They both smiled a thank you.

Frankie sipped her wine. "Maybe a little religion is all we need."

His cockled brow forced her to elaborate.

"If the Burning Bush dictated the Ten Commandments to Moses, and Joseph Smith created the Book of Mormon using Seer Stones and a hat, then maybe if you stare into an empty bottle of non-alcoholic Bud long enough, you'll figure out who killed Sedrick Palette."

"Maybe," he said distractedly. Something she said had caused the Scrabble tiles in his head to start to shift. He swallowed a mouthful of fake beer. "Any news from our techs?"

A nod. "Bachman's surveillance system is essentially tamper-proof, as is the footage. And we found no connections between Triton staff and anyone living or working at Bachman. Which, of course, leaves us with fifty-seven seconds of messed-up surveillance footage from a system that cannot be messed with and nobody with a motive to mess with it." Unfazed by the bad news, Huffy sifted through the scraps of the '*You Fat Pig*' nacho plate and helped George Strait praise his exes for choosing Texas. "Techs said a power surge might have caused the surveillance system malfunction."

"They give odds on that?"

She tilted her head in the general direction of the waitress Huffy had been admiring. "About the same as you hooking up with her."

He laughed.

"I think we can rule out a power surge," he stated confidently. "The storm as well." He popped a cheese-covered jalapeno into his mouth. "Hard to take advantage of a malfunction you didn't know would occur."

A nod. "The footage from outside C Block shows that after the shift change at ten o'clock, no one entered or exited the block until the guard found Palette's body six hours later."

He slugged more beer. "How'd Jarvis make out?"

"He met with Jerome Banks again. Banks now has amnesia. Claims he didn't see anyone outside Palette's cell before, during, or after the outage."

"I figured as much. He was probably trying to trade a bullshit story for some extra privileges."

"Or he is afraid to talk," Frankie speculated.

A shrug.

She lifted the red file folder off the table and read while Huffy excused himself for a bathroom break. When he returned, she set the folder on the table and asked, "Allan Abrams is Derek Samuels' shrink?" He nodded. "Small world," she commented. "And why did you flag Samuels' scopolamine prescription?"

"I was curious why a psychiatrist would prescribe IBS medication."

"And?"

"Samuels' regular doctor confirmed he is allergic to most IBS meds. She said scopolamine is an unusual option, but it is legit."

"Why does that drug sound familiar?"

"You remember Rick Cockerill?" He cradled an imaginary beer belly with one hand and swirled a finger from the other around the top of his head. "Fat. Bald. Quit about a month after you started." A grin. "Don't think the two were related."

She gave him the finger. "Doesn't ring a bell." They both reached for the same nacho shard. She slapped his hand away and inhaled her prize. "To the victor go the spoils." She wiped her fingers with a napkin.

"How about the Ute Indian reserve robberies?"

"Sort of. Refresh my memory."

"A hooker pumped a john full of scopolamine and had him empty his bank account. He woke up the next day on a park bench with no memory of what had happened."

"Right," she said, her memory now jogged. "When they busted the hooker, she copped to multiple robberies using scopolamine."

"Yep." He chuckled. "Did you know it is also known as the *Zombie* drug?"

"I did not know that."

"Google did. Social dilemma, my ass; it's an amazing resource."

"We should dissolve some in Kennedy's water during his next Q&A."

"Yeah," he agreed. "Then shoot him."

Frankie distractedly eyed her wine glass, looking like she might be considering the option.

"At this point," he said, "we are looking at one option: Palette's killer, or *killers,* work or live on C Block and knew they would have a fifty-seven-second window."

She continued staring mindlessly at her wine glass. "Fifty-seven seconds?" she said skeptically. "To create that mess and leave no trace?"

He shrugged.

She sighed. "I say we give Palette full marks for a creative suicide and call it a day. Nothing else makes sense."

"Or we pin it on old man Smithers."

Frankie laughed. "And he would have gotten away with it if it wasn't for those meddling kids."

The comment led to a brief debate over which was the better cartoon series, Scooby-Doo or Sponge Bob. The debate ended in a draw, and the conversation rambled aimlessly for two more non-alcoholic Buds and another twelve-ounce "Piggy-size" glass of Shiraz. They touched on various subjects, including whether Trump was considering a name change to Joseph R. Biden, and if the title of his next book would be *My Struggle*. But they mostly talked about what everyone else was talking about; COVID deaths had just eclipsed 300,000.

"So," Huffy said. "You and Beth gonna make it?"

"That's an abrupt change in direction."

"That other stuff was boring."

A glare. "And my failing marriage is exciting?"

He guzzled the last of his fake Bud. "I read—" he burped, "an article in Hustler that said red-haired kids with anger issues are all the rage." He burped again. "And the more I drink, the better looking you get. Play your cards right," he circled his bottle in front of him, "and all this could be yours."

"I'm not a homewrecker." Her question about his unsigned divorce paperwork evident via the subtext, she added, "And I certainly—"

Huffy's expression blanked as though a bite from a poisonous spider had liquified the muscles in his face. The Scrabble tiles set in motion by talk of Moses and Joseph Smith had fallen into place.

"What?" she asked.

He stared through her.

She waved a hand through his line of sight. "Hellooo? Earth to—"

"We've relied on everything he has told us."

"Who told us?"

"Abrams."

"What did he tell us?"

He thought for a bit. "How hard could it be for a psychiatrist to manipulate a mentally ill old man into a confession?"

She grimaced. "Wait—what? Abrams? Are you serious?"

"He told us the old man could have heard about the teacher from Seattle, researched the death, and incorporated it into his delusion. How do you research a detail that was never made public? Abrams, on the other hand, has access to our databases. He could have found out about the Batman costume and fed that detail to the old man. Hell, he didn't even have to do that. He is the only one who's met with the old man; all he had to do was *tell us* the old man mentioned the costume."

"You *are* serious."

"After the old man confessed, Abrams said he needed a day or two to figure things out. But what if he already knew everything and needed a day or two to work on the old man? He doesn't record his sessions. Why? So we can't hear what they are talking about. And remember, it was Abrams who sent us on the wild goose chase for an imaginary grandson."

Frankie looked stunned by the leap. "But we both know him," she objected. "Maybe not well, but well enough to know he isn't involved."

"You have met with him a few times about *your* personal life. You don't know anything about him. He could be Hannibal fucking Lecter for all you know."

An eye-roll. "That is beyond laughable. But for shits and giggles, let's assume Allan Abrams is a criminal mastermind who coordinated the killing of Sedrick Palette and is now executing a ridiculous plan to either frame a delusional old man or use him to create reasonable doubt for a future jury. That hot mess of a theory would mean they knew each other *before* Wilhelm confessed, Abrams manipulated him into confessing, and that Abrams has an accomplice at Bachman." A pause. "I have heard you float some strange theories, but this is some real Alex Jones, QAnon bull—"

"Your relationship with him is affecting your objectivity. You are interpreting information to fit a narrative you *want* to be true."

Frankie shook her head aggressively. "I have no problem with objectivity. I'd arrest anyone if they crossed the line, including you."

"What about Josh Cutter?"

"What about him?"

"You are so focused on nailing Kennedy that you have missed the obvious, which—"

"Your theory is supported by absolutely no evidence, and *my* objectivity is compromised? *I am* the one missing the obvious? Jesus. Do you hear your—"

"Shit," he mumbled.

"What?"

He hopped off his stool and slipped on his suit jacket.

"Where are you going?"

He said, "Things left unchecked," and hustled away.

"Don't worry." She watched him leave. "I'll get the check."

—

HAVING SPENT AN hour freezing his ass off searching alleys, side-streets, and stairwells in Camper's Village, Huffy could feel the blood slogging through his veins like cherry slushy through a juice-box straw. In his idling car in a Texaco parking lot, he pressed his hands to a heat vent, rubbed in the hot air, and wondered what was pissing him off more: not finding what he'd come for, or being stupid enough to think he would. Realizing the answer was both, he shifted into reverse, tapped the gas, felt a *thud*, and hit the brake. He checked the rearview mirror but saw nothing through the frost-covered rear window. "Goddamnit," he groaned. He shifted into park and grabbed the door handle.

BANG! Startled, he peered out the driver's side window as a gloved hand struck the frosted glass. BANG!

He pushed the door open and forced the gloved hand's homeless owner to take two steps back. "Ran me over," the man screeched. "My lawyer'll sue you for ev—"

The man fell silent as Huffy rose out of the car and towered over him. It was late; Huffy was frustrated and tired and in no mood to deal with a nutjob. He flashed his badge. The homeless man flung his hands into the air. *"Don't shoot!"*

Huffy dropped into the driver's seat and watched the man walk about ten feet, spin, and fire a double-fisted bird. Huffy chuckled but cut himself off almost instantly, finally clueing in to what should have been obvious. "I'll be damned."

He exited the car.

Seeing Huffy start toward him, the homeless man spun again and power-walked in the opposite direction.

A comical chase ensued.

Each time Huffy shouted, "Wait!" or "Stop!" the fleeing homeless man would shoulder-check, realize Huffy was gaining, and shift into a higher gear. Tired of the chase, Huffy changed his strategy. "I have money for you!" At that, the homeless man turned on a dime. "Time'ta pay the piper," he croaked, extending a gloved hand toward Huffy, who was now only a few feet away. "Good'ta meetcha." He offered a broad, toothless smile. "Name's Piper." He slapped his hand hard against his thigh and broke into a loud cackle, which deteriorated into a coughing attack that ended when he hawked an oyster-colored loogie into the snow.

"I didn't run you over," Huffy said curtly. "And I won't charge you with assaulting a police vehicle if I can buy your—"

"Huh?" The man leaned to the side and peered around Huffy at the idling sedan. "Can't damage that. It's a pile a shit." Huffy waited through another thigh slap, cackle, phlegm-filled hack, and loogie before commencing negotiations. Several minutes later, the negotiations had, for the third time, slid off the rails.

"Gates is the key," the homeless man rambled. "Him and the chinks started the plague. Microsoft motherfucker." He scrunched his face tightly and screwed two fingers into a temple. "Implants microtopes…so we can't live without a cell phone…or, uh…computer, or that feisty cunt, Siri. Everyone's got'em: vaccinations, transplants, tit jobs. Soon, Gates'll press the button and…" He kissed his pinched fingers and exploded them apart. "*Poof!* Sayonara. Toaster bath. All of us, *dead!*"

Based on how often the man had redirected the conversation to Bill Gates and his plan to use a pandemic and "microtopes" to take over the world, Huffy again altered his strategy. "I know," he said. "Gates sent me for the gloves and told me to thank you for holding them. I'm supposed to give you money for…" He looked skyward. "*Shit.* Gates told me what you drink. He's gonna *kill* me." He pressed a finger into his temple and cringed.

Perhaps worried that a displeased Gates—watching via Chinese satellite—was firing up Huffy's microtopes (which, if detonated, would result in the loss of payment), the homeless man began patting the air and pivoting erratically. "Old Crow!" he yelped. "Old Crow! I drink Old Crow bourbon."

Huffy shot him with a finger gun. *"That's it."*

No doubt motivated by the close call, the man reduced his asking price from four hundred dollars to forty. Huffy swapped two twenties for the gloves and double-timed it back to his car.

Unsure about the hunch when he abandoned Frankie at the Blind Pig, he was even less sure about it now. He assumed it would turn out to be one of the biggest brain farts of his career, one referenced any time a ball-busting colleague needed a story that started with: "Hey, do you guys remember the time Huff...." Still, insignificant details often helped solve cases. And details did not get any less significant than a homeless man claiming "Bill Gates" gave him leather gloves to keep quiet about a murder. It was also a detail that, provided the majority of Campers Village's homeless population didn't own expensive leather gloves, was easy to check.

If Satan could take the form of a dog and order Son of Sam to kill young lovers, a crazy homeless man could sure as hell think Allan Abrams was the Motherfuckin' founder of Microsoft.

At a red light a block north of the Texaco, Huffy spied a neon sign in the window of a pharmacy. Thinking he may have caught a break, he sent Murphy a text.

```
If we haven't yet, get security footage from Lings pharmacy on
Elm Street  6 hrs either side of Chris Tam homicide.
```

38

His head still throbbing, Allan labored to the en suite, popped another Thorazine, and eased back into bed. Clara stirred. Hoping not to wake her, he lowered the TV's volume. When she stirred again, he muted the volume. She struggled but managed to roll over, raising her head off the pillow and scanning the bed. She patted a Shih Tzu-sized air pocket in the duvet. "Where's Hic?" she asked sleepily.

He was not surprised to hear no trace of her earlier anger. Her mood swings were a given; the variables were when, why, and how long they would last. He raised the covers long enough to reveal an Oreo-colored ball of fur between his legs.

"Traitor," she complained.

During the silence that followed, he could feel her watching him. He eventually turned to her.

"What?"

She inhaled a quick breath and opened her mouth to speak but seemed to think better of it.

"What?" he repeated.

She again looked like she wanted to say something. Instead, she grabbed the TV remote off the duvet, rolled onto her back, and increased the volume.

He watched her for a bit, part of him wanting to talk, part of him thinking it was best they didn't. He was tired of talking about Wilhelm—if that is what had been on her mind. He had no clue why he could not stay away from the old man, so being unable to explain it to Clara would only make her angry again. And he did not want to talk about the twins. He spent enough time dwelling on the threats they faced: Clara's asthma, her age, a deadly pandemic that only seemed to be getting worse, and whatever other unknown risks and obstacles they would face before they were born. And he sure as hell did not want to talk about whether he was having a breakdown. But what other than a breakdown explained his increasingly bizarre decisions and behavior? A good old-fashioned drug addiction? Could people tell when taking medication had become something more? Would he know if he had crossed a line? Isn't that what drugs do; blind you to reality so you continue getting your fix? He had no idea. What he did know was that he wanted his head to stop hurting and to sleep. One good night's sleep would help so much; he was certain of it. He had to be. The alternatives scared him.

"Can I change it?"

"Huh?" he mumbled.

"The channel. Can I change it?"

"Oh, yeah, of course."

Clara flipped channels until she found a Julia Roberts and Hugh Grant movie, the name of which he could not remember. But it didn't matter; Hugh Grant movies were like AC/DC songs; the titles were interchangeable and, therefore, irrelevant.

"Besides taking naps and eating chocolate-covered bacon," he said, "what did you do all day?"

"That pretty much covers it."

"Nothing more exciting?"

"Liam stopped by."

"*What?*" Allan snapped, immediately upset by the information but with no idea why. "What did he want?"

"To talk to you, I guess."

Distracted, he didn't respond. Liam must have got my voicemail. But why didn't he tell me he had checked on Clara? Is that how she knew I was in Denver with Wilhelm?

"What did he want?" he repeated, forgetting he had already asked.

"To talk to *you*," she snarled.

Hiccup released a low, extended growl. He soothed him with a head scratch. "Right, sorry."

They watched TV without speaking, his mind on questions with concerning answers. Did Liam tell Clara about my trip to Denver with Wilhelm? Did he forget she was worried about my involvement in Wilhelm's case? Why didn't he tell me he checked on her? What time was he here? Was it around the time I left the cemetery in Denver?

Clara fell asleep, and, eventually, so did he.

—

AWARE HE WAS dreaming, Allan felt Clara shift positions, her warm leg brushing against his. In his dream, he could see a vertical marquee, its unlit "S" turning HOSTEL into HO TEL. The dream's marquee sparked a memory of one he had seen in real life while on vacation with his mom in New York. Is it normal to have a real-life memory during a dream? he wondered.

He remembered standing under the marquee—its blinking, dancing bulbs spelling out RADIO CITY MUSIC HALL— trying to distract himself from the bitter cold by puffing on imaginary Camels. His dad smoked Camels. *More Doctors smoke Camels than any other brand!* Waiting for the doors to open, he'd occupied himself by blowing "smoke" rings until his mom ordered him to stop by flicking his ear. He rubbed it and scowled a harsh *What the frick?*, while wondering if she was worried smoking imaginary Camels would lead to an addiction to imaginary nicotine and, inevitably, death from imaginary lung cancer.

Allan lowered his eyes from the marquee in his current dream just as DaMarcus Kennedy and his pregnant fiancé bypassed a line of waiting patrons. A muscular, Latino doorman fist-bumped Kennedy and let them into the bar, bass from the dance music thumping like a massive heart until muted by the closing door. A white van pulled forward and blocked his view. He stepped around it; the line of patrons was gone, and the marquee was dark. The only light was an orange-yellow flickering glow in the bar's windows—a jack-o-lantern carved out of a rectangular, brick pumpkin.

Allan took a single step and found himself inside an office at the rear of the bar, Bob Marley staring at him from the far wall, ONE LOVE printed above his head. DaMarcus Kennedy suddenly appeared; a gun pointed at Allan's head. A gunshot. Brains and blood and skull fragments coated the door and part of a wall. He hurdled Olivia Madson's crumpled body, landing in the alley outside the bar. Kennedy was there.

They talked. Kennedy spoke about his excitement at becoming a father but expressed concern over the world his son would inherit. He spoke of wanting to change that world and how change was inevitable and already underway, claiming, "The signs are obvious. None of this is by accident."

Allan closed his eyes and heard: Wake up! You are dreaming. Wake up!

He opened his eyes.

He was in bed, Clara next to him, naked and no longer pregnant. She was straddling Liam Huffy, her hips moving rhythmically as his hands caressed her breasts. She looked at a bassinet beside the bed, then at Allan. "Only you can save us," she said.

Wake up!

He started to run, his limbs silent blurs as he raced through miles of deserted, snow-covered streets. He watched his real-world self in bed beside Clara, his legs kicking like Hiccup's did when the pup would run from whatever creatures haunted his puppy dreams. The *Unseen.* A relentless, chasing creature, its hot breath heard and felt while the beast remained in the shadows, visible only when a flash of moonlight reflected off its razor-sharp teeth.

Allan felt cold metal against his temple. He stopped running. He was back in the alley behind The Hostel. Kennedy was standing a few feet away, a gun pressed to his own temple. "He's my only son," Kennedy said.

He pulled the trigger.

The sound of gunfire forced Allan upright. He pressed two fingers to his temple and felt for blood gushing from a bullet wound. There was no blood and no wound. He whipped his head to the left. Clara was asleep beside him. He stretched a hand and touched her shoulder, her soft, warm skin confirming the dream was over.

His panic ebbed, and his heart slowed as questions filled his head: *Is DaMarcus Kennedy's son the boy general? Does Olivia Madson look familiar because she is the boy's mother?*

He slipped out of bed, rubbed sleep from his eyes, and listened to the freezing rain *tap-tap-tap* at the bedroom window like skeletal fingers. Halfway to the en suite, a familiar sensation crawled over his skin. He froze.

As a boy, a vague awareness would occasionally rip him from sleep—a variance in the air pressure or breathing his unconscious mind recognized was not his. He would bolt upright; someone or some*thing* was in his room.

The *Unseen.*

His mom, who'd snuck in to watch him sleep, would see his terror and emerge from the darkness. She would lay with him until he fell asleep, tickling his back and singing "Under the Boardwalk." That same terrifying awareness was now holding him motionless.

Someone was in their bedroom.

Freezing rain had coated the window with a translucent, icy film, the moonlight providing a vague, tenebrous glow. A barely audible whine slithered from the closet. Metal scraping on metal? he wondered, forcing a step. Of course not. You're tired, and your mind is playing tricks. He took two more steps but stopped when the sound repeated.

All houses have a voice: the chatter of rattling pipes, the moans from creaking floorboards, the ghostly whispers created by the wind breaching minute gaps in the home's protective shell. But this sound, one he was now certain was wire hangers sliding slowly along the closet's metal support bar, didn't belong.

Someone was in the closet.

The low light and sinister *tap-tap-tapping* at the window were colluding with his stressed and tired mind to create thunder in his chest. The same thunder he had felt as a child hiding under his bedsheet—a thin cotton shield protecting him from the beast under his bed.

A bi-fold closet door was open enough to see a few inches inside. Moonlight was catching the toe of a black running shoe. The whining sound returned, then…the shoe moved.

His eyes fixed on the shoe, he jerked the door open. He lurched back; a dark shape—a man—was at the back of the closet holding a baseball bat.

The primal shriek racing from his diaphragm materialized as a choppy "*Uff*" when a whimpering Hiccup leaped from the closet.

Allan exhaled loudly and scooped the terrified pup into his arms.

"*Quiet!*" Clara yelped, half-asleep.

"Sorry," he whispered.

His breathing steadied now that he could see the "man" in the closet was Clara's black ski suit hanging against the wall, a baseball bat propped beside it. A trembling Hiccup barked shrilly, not at the shape in the closet but over Allan's shoulder at the ice-coated bedroom window.

Clara struggled to a seated position. "*Hiccup,*" she screeched, a hand under her belly. "*Come here!*" The terrified pup continued barking. Frustrated, Clara gave up and entombed herself under the covers.

He moved slowly toward the window, cradling Hiccup and soothing him like he would a distressed child. "It's okay, buddy." He kissed one ear and rubbed the other. "It's just a little rain." Every step caused Hiccup to struggle harder until he broke free, leaped from Allan's arms, jumped onto the bed, and whipped around to face the window. Standing rigid on the foot of the bed, he growled and barked.

"It's okay, Hic," Allan repeated, turning to the window. "It's just—"

His body locked.

Through the window's translucent icy coating, he saw Wilhelm hovering two-stories above the ground.

AFTER MIDNIGHT. DECEMBER 21.

Four Days until Christmas.

Why can't I move? Allan's body remained unresponsive, and sound continued to filter in and fade out. "For how long?" a man asked. The unfamiliar voice escalated Allan's panic. Still, he couldn't move. Am I restrained? "I don't know," an angry female answered. This voice Allan recognized but could not place. "An hour, maybe more," she added.

He strained until his eyelids snapped open, bright light flooding his optic nerves. Soon, the light softened, and vague shapes began to register. Someone was leaning over him, rubbery fingers grasping his cheek and chin.

"Welcome back," the man said.

The room was a mosaic of static and blurred shapes, but he could make out thick, black eyebrows, the color blue, and the smell of eucalyptus. Soon, his darting eyes had confirmed what his mind had figured out; the angry but familiar female voice was Clara's. He moved his head from side to side, taking in information. He was in bed, Clara seated in a chair a few feet away. The thick eyebrows belonged to a paramedic, his latex-gloved hand holding a penlight and moving its thin beam between Allan's eyes.

"What is happening?"

"You fell," the paramedic said, a lozenge clicking against his teeth. "Took a pretty good wallop to the head."

He looked at Clara. Her vacant nod confirmed the paramedic's story.

"You're lucky you made it back to the house and called 911," the paramedic added. "It doesn't take long in these temperatures. You could have lost a few fingers and toes." He clicked off his penlight and clipped it to his breast pocket. "Or worse."

Allan sat up. "Made it back the house?" He lifted a hand to his skull and felt gauze. "*I* called 911?"

"Dispatch info was an adult male in distress," the paramedic said. Allan again looked at Clara. This time, her eyes dropped to the floor. The paramedic lifted his jump-bag off the bed. "We've done all we can here. You're gonna have a doozy of a headache, but there are no signs of Cerebral Edema. We'd need a CT scan to know for sure. Do you want to come to the hospital as a precaution?"

Still wading through a thick fog, Allan shook his head weakly. The paramedic responded by listing symptoms that required an immediate 911 call and left.

Allan asked Clara to explain what had happened. Speaking without expression or emotion, she told him that he ran downstairs after claiming he'd seen Wilhelm "hovering" outside the bedroom window. She watched from the window as he ran through the backyard and into the shop. "I couldn't breathe," she'd said. "My chest tightened, and I nearly passed out before I found my inhaler. I had no idea what was happening and couldn't do anything about it anyway, so I climbed into bed and waited for you to come back. I guess I fell asleep because I woke up to the sound of a siren. I found you lying near the front door. Hiccup was licking the blood off your face." She paused, then, with the first sign of emotion on her face and in her words, added despondently, "He growled at me when I tried to help you."

At the mention of Hiccup's name, his memory of the events returned. He *had* seen Wilhelm outside the window and remembered sprinting downstairs. When he opened the front door, Hic raced outside and disappeared around the side of the house. He followed Hic, thinking: What am I doing? Wilhelm could not possibly have been outside our second-story bedroom window. He remembered a rush of embarrassment hitting him hard when he entered the backyard, not because he'd found it necessary to scan for a ladder and Wilhelm's tracks in the snow or because he'd found neither, but because he'd chased a hallucination into the backyard.

The only tracks he saw were Hic's, and he followed them into the pitch-black shop. He remembered calling Hic several times before hearing a low, guttural growl, the kind you hear from a dog that has seen or heard something you haven't. Something he considers a threat. "Hic, it's me," he'd called out. Hic then snapped a shrill and urgent bark and…

And what? He strained to squeeze out a memory that was not there. Why can't I remember what happened next?

With Clara's explanation of events and his incomplete recall of them creating more questions than answers, he stayed quiet for a while, trying to figure out why he had acted so irrationally. So foolishly. Why was a hallucination or a trick of the eye not the *only* explanations he'd considered?

"Did I say anything before the paramedics arrived?" he eventually asked.

"Nope."

A casual tone had replaced her previously dispassionate one. He wondered if the change was because she was dumbfounded by what had happened or because she didn't care.

She flicked off the TV. "You were just lying there, bleeding."

"You don't sound very—"

Shit, he thought, seeing her eyes narrow and anger flush her skin.

"I don't sound very *what?*" she demanded.

He couldn't speak. Instead, he watched Hiccup scamper off the bed and scurry back into the closet. For a moment, he considered joining him.

"I don't sound very *what*?" she repeated sharply. "Distraught? Sad? Upset?"

"I'm sorry," he said. "I'm not thinking straight. It—"

"On top of all the other Wilhelm shit," she thundered, "now he is *floating* outside our second-story window? Do you know how crazy you sound?" Her features continued to harden, and her words were stacked on top of one another, no room between them for air. "Then, like a friggin lunatic, you run through the yard in the middle of the night? Half-naked? When it is twenty below?" She hurled the remote at the window. "Are you fucking *kidding* me?"

He watched the remote crash against the wall and fall to the floor. What the hell is wrong with me? Why am I doing this to her? To us? To our babies?

For the first time, he noticed blood—*his* blood—on the sleeve of her nightshirt. Clara followed his line of sight; she had not seen the blood either.

"Jesus Christ!" She tore the covers away and climbed stiffly out of bed. "I just bought this nightshirt."

As she slammed the en suite door closed, an unfathomable reaction began to build inside him—laughter. The response was fueled by the overwhelming stress caused by the twins and their complications and by his dreams of a freckled boy general, a dreadlocked gangbanger, and people being burned alive. And by the stress caused by the coronavirus, escalating unrest, and an old man magically floating thirty feet above the ground. All of that and Clara's comical concern over a ten-dollar nightshirt.

The involuntary reaction reminded him of a previous bout of giggles. During his Bar Mitzvah ceremony, his Bubby and Papa (and forty-one other guests) were holding their jaws in their laps as the Guest of Honor made his way to the bimah, braying like a deranged donkey. It was in university that he learned the inappropriate outburst was caused by the stress of such an important day, his mother's death, and, despite promising he would come, his father having more important things to do. But as he walked toward the bimah, the voice in his head was a cackling Davey Berkman, who, ten minutes earlier, had been busting a gut after asking, "Hey, Allan, how do you know a creepy old man is Jewish?" Too excited to wait for a guess, Davey quickly blurted, "He says, 'Hey little boy, wanna *buy* some candy?'"

A loud, dense *thud* snapped him out of the flashback.

Clara's crumpled body was just inside the en suite door, blood hemorrhaging from between her legs was coating her thighs and pooling on the tiled floor.

EARLY MORNING. DECEMBER 21.

V omit continued to swirl in Allan's gut. But instead of suppressing it, he had repeatedly tried to force it out, thinking its smell had to be more tolerable than the waiting room's mix of ammonia and despair.

Nothing other than that smell had registered. Not the half dozen empty chairs, the matching faux-fiddleleaf fig trees, or the pamphlets on the small end table beside him. *Breast Cancer: What you need to know. How to thrive with Type 2 diabetes. What are the long haul symptoms of COVID-19, and can they be treated?* A picture was on the opposite wall. Despite staring at it for long stretches, he could not recall a single detail. Not its faded watercolors, consolatory blue sky, or its red-bucket-toting toddler, the foamy edge of a gentle ocean wave rolling over her sand-covered toes.

Four hours ago, a nurse had told him there was a problem with one of the twins, comforting him with: *The doctors are doing all they can.* The hospital waiting room equivalent of: "Please hold as your call is important to us." For four hours, his mind was an impenetrable wall of thought. Which of my children is lying dead on a stainless-steel tray in the operating room? Peyton? Eli? Are both of my baby's dead? Is Clara dead? For four hours, his only companions were the red-bucket-toting toddler and the morbid residue left by those who'd sat in the same waiting room reciting the same useless prayers.

A gentle touch on his shoulder startled him and propelled him to his feet. *Thank you for your patience. Your call* really was *important to us, and we* really did *do everything we could.*

The white lab coat wearing blur said, "Your wife and baby are fine."

The words vaporized the malignant mass of dread ravaging every one of his trillions of cells. The nurse was wrong! There wasn't a problem with one of the twins. She had made a mistake! A glorious, wonderful mistake! He fought the urge to wrap his arms around the white lab coat wearing blur and twirl her while shouting: "THANK YOU! THANK YOU! OH, DEAR GOD, THANK YOU!"

Her detached expression finally registered, and her previously reassuring words began blowing holes in his chest like hollow-point bullets.

Your wife and baby are fine.

Baby. Singular. One child, not two.

One of his babies was dead.

"Your son did not suffer." She delivered the news with stolid compassion, like she was sad for his loss but also trying to decide what to have for breakfast. *French toast? An omelet?*

Amidst everything he was feeling, he sensed compassion…for *her*. Like so many first responders he had counseled, her job had frayed the cable that allowed her to feel. If she had not already, she would soon lose the ability to feel *real* emotion, her mind locking out anything but watered-down versions of the real thing.

"I am sorry for your loss, Mr. Abrams." *What about pancakes?* She took a moment to explain how his son had died, then added, "The surviving twin should be fine and carried to full term." *Should be?* he wanted to scream. How comforting. She concluded with, "Your wife's in recovery," glanced at a waiting nurse, and walked away.

The nurse approached caringly, gently placed a hand in the small of his back, and led him through the silver doors. His feet unsteady and his legs feeling detached from the rest of his body, he numbly plodded beside her until a horrific thought appeared from nowhere and stopped him in his tracks: At least we know what color to paint the nursery.

At that, the previously elusive vomit found its way onto the spotless hospital floor.

41

The sound of hard-soled shoes clacking on concrete echoed through the hall as Huffy trotted toward his destination. Button had summoned him to the lab—the "Bat Cave" as it was affectionately known—for a "sort of" Christmas gift. He was hopeful that the video he had left with an A/V tech and or Button's "gift" would result in a break. He shifted the two-hundred-dollar bottle of scotch to his left hand and used his right to fish his keycard from his pocket and open the security door.

"The big three-four." He set a red-bowed bottle of Johnnie Walker Blue Label on one of the lab's glistening stainless-steel counters. "Congrats."

"Forty-one," Button corrected.

"Really?" He rubbed the sleep from his eyes and yawned. "What does that make you in real people years?"

On a stool in front of a large microscope mounted to a stainless-steel table, Button smiled. "Did you know," he said in a tone Huffy knew well, "that psychopaths rarely reciprocate when they see other people yawn?" He removed a slide from under the microscope's objective. "It is related to a lack of empathy."

"Isn't that how they caught Bundy?"

Button chuckled. "I haven't processed the gloves you dropped off, but your *'sort of'* gift is there." He pointed to the cadaver table beside Huffy.

Huffy inspected the contents of the small evidence bag. "Why sort of?"

"Cause I'm not sure if it will be useful."

"Where'd you find this?"

"In Tam's sludge. We also found prints and human skin on an exterior door."

Huffy understood the forensic language but appreciated Button's lay-speak. His physical stature and degrees in medicine and law from Stanford gave him every opportunity to overcompensate, but he never did. Instead of: "The victim ingested substantial quantities of cannabinoids over a prolonged period prior to his demise," Button would say: "Dude smoked a shitload of weed before biting it." The fact he was *not* a pretentious look-how-smart-I-am prick was, in Huffy's opinion, the little fella's best quality.

"It looks like Benny Carpenter's." Huffy set the evidence bag containing an earring—a cross made of diamonds and gold—back on the stainless-steel table. "DNA?"

"Yep. And if we get lucky, I will let you know whose in six to eight weeks." Huffy's disgruntled sigh prompted Button to add, "Sorry Horatio, but we simply don't have the budget for the magical, same-day DNA crime-fighting equipment your CSI Miami team has access to."

"No worries," Huffy responded, heading to the door. "I'll have my hands full over the next six to eight weeks arresting people who don't yawn when I do."

–

HUFFY WATCHED THE A/V tech work on the fuzzy image pulled from Ling's Pharmacy's security video. He was certain he had something; he just didn't know what. And if whatever he had was important, he'd have an old friend to thank. More often than most detectives cared to admit, Barney Fife'ish dumb luck played a significant role in the outcome of cases. Trace any case back far enough, and, for better or worse, luck will have influenced the outcome. Solving five murders after incorrectly assuming Rien Gerhard was a delusional old man's grandson was a perfect example. However, when it came to luck, one case still made Huffy shake his head in disbelief.

On an August afternoon, the sweltering heat rising in waves off the blacktop, Huffy was on his way back home from the middle of nowhere when one of his four new tires blew. Back then, long drives in his topless, doorless Jeep were his preferred method of cooling off after a fight with Alex. As luck would have it, his spare tire was in his garage on top of the Jeep's four old tires, so he test-drove his brand new Triple-A membership.

Twelve songs into *Garth Brooks, Double Live*, Huffy's savior arrived.

The tire too damaged to repair, the tow-truck driver secured the disabled Jeep, and they headed back to Witten.

The skinny, Peterbilt-cap-wearing driver with a smear of axle grease across his sweat-beaded forehead asked Huffy the same time-killing questions he had no doubt asked everyone who'd ever ridden shotgun in the dusty rescue vehicle. *Got a name? Got a Missus? Any rug rats?* But, as luck would have it, the driver failed to ask a question he'd likely asked a thousand times: *What is it y'all do to for a livin'?*

A few minutes into the trip, Huffy was distractedly watching a cluster of items dangling from the rear-view mirror when one of the items—a bracelet—snapped him out of his daze. The bracelet had a miniature red di as its centerpiece, and its beads formed a repetitive color pattern: red-yellow-black. He had seen the pattern three years earlier on a coral snake tattooed around a dead woman's calf. The next day, he saw the bracelet in a picture given to him by the woman's distraught sister. Handing him the photo, the sister tearfully recounted the pattern's meaning: *Red on yellow kills a fellow.* A year later, with all leads exhausted, Huffy sealed that unsolved homicide in a box and set it on a shelf in the downtown station's basement, where it remained until, as luck would have it, he was rescued from a blown tire by the only tow-truck driver on the planet with the power to crack the box's dusty seal.

The bracelet was a souvenir.

For the rest of the trip, Huffy made careful but casual conversation, making sure to ask about the unique bracelet and how the driver had come to possess it. "My daughter made me that bracelet in art class," the driver had said.

How touching, Huffy had thought.

A few blocks from Witten's West End Precinct, at a repair shop of Huffy's choosing, the whistling driver unlatched the Jeep while Huffy slipped into the manager's office and made a phone call.

Not long after, six police cars rolled up and emptied. With eight guns and two shotguns pointed at his center mass, the skinny, Peterbilt-cap-wearing driver with a smear of axle grease across his forehead realized what was happening. He turned to Huffy with a dumbfounded look on his face: How did you know?

Searches of his residence and vehicles turned up enough *souvenirs* and other evidence to convict Jerald Frederick Goddard on sixteen counts, including seven counts of first-degree murder.

Barney Fife'ish dumb luck.

"I'll be damned." Huffy pointed over the A/V tech's shoulder at the now cleaned up image on the monitor. "Time and date stamp that and print me four copies."

–

FRANKIE WAS LIVID. "How the hell does this bring us closer to justice for Josh Cutter and his family?"

Huffy dropped into one of the two empty chairs in front of her desk. "I don't know what, but there is something to this."

Frankie handed him the picture. "Stick to doors labeled regime change."

"I'll go where the investigation leads."

She shook her head and pointed to the picture. "*That* leads nowhere. And you are not spending a penny of our resources or a second of your time on it."

He could not remember the last time she had challenged him on the direction of a case; he wasn't sure she ever had. "I'm telling you—"

"And I am telling *you*," she snapped, "that I get ten calls a day from reporters, nine of those calls are from Wayne Desmond. Last night, that prick was waiting for me when I got home. He stuck a phone in my face and asked me if Josh Cutter would still be alive if he were white."

"Just because you're under pressure doesn't—"

"I don't give a shit about the pressure. A kid is dead, and Kennedy is involved." She again pointed at the picture in Huffy's hand. "Every second you spend chasing hunches is a second you are not trying to put Kennedy in a cell."

"But—"

"*Enough!*"

After a stare-down worthy of Iron Mike Tyson, she said, "Regime change," and pointed at her door.

Huffy left.

He spent thirty-nine of the following forty-eight hours searching for more proof of what he knew he had, stopping only after he was satisfied that he had found it.

MORNING. DECEMBER 23.

Two Days until Christmas.

Asleep in a chair beside Clara's hospital bed, Allan shifted positions to try and ease his cramped real-world legs. Unlike dreams of the boy general, which ran start to finish, this dream was more like a mini-series, each successive dream a new episode. This episode, like the previous ones, began with a recap of the story to date: his arrival at The Hostel; brains and blood and skull fragments against an office door and wall; leaping over Olivia Madson's body and landing in the alley; cold steel pressed to his temple; a single gunshot dropping himself and DaMarcus Kennedy.

Allan could feel warm blood draining from the bullet hole in his temple. At the alley's opposite end, a man holding an object about the size and shape of a pineapple exited a white minivan and started into the alley, each choppy stride bringing him ten feet closer.

A few feet away, his face hidden in the shadows, the man extended a hand. The pineapple-shaped object was DaMarcus Kennedy's head. The neck was jagged and torn as though he had been fed to a woodchipper, his head yanked back at the last second. His cloudy, dead eyes blinked.

The man dropped the head into Allan's outstretched hands and emerged from the shadows. The "man" was actually a woman. All that remained of her face were bits of flesh hanging off her bones like shards of meat on a discarded Christmas turkey.

A familiar voice drew Allan's attention to the severed head

in his hands—Clara's head. "Only you can save us, Allan," she whimpered.

"Clara!" he shrieked, jumping out of his chair.

His eyes darted around the hospital room, relaying images his brain was decoding on a delay. Clara was in her bed, eyeing him as she would a stranger at the door in the middle of the night asking to use the phone. His heart dropped into his stomach. She's afraid, he thought, easing back into his chair. Of me.

"Sorry," he said. "Bad dream."

Clara retrieved her cell and sent a text.

He had spent most of the last two days in the chair, leaving it once to take care of Hiccup and a few times a day to use the bathroom. He did not recall eating but must have because he wasn't hungry. They had hardly spoken the entire time. What could they talk about? The weather? The Broncos? What type of flowers should they have at Peyton's funeral?

"I checked Hic into a doggie spa," he said softly. "We can pick him up or leave him until after Christmas."

Clara took a puff from her inhaler and flicked on the wall-mounted TV. "I need to be alone."

He was at her side before she had finished speaking, ready with ways to "fix" her heartbreak. *You wanted the sex to be a surprise? Well, surprise! We're having a boy. Don't be sad. This is all part of God's plan. Don't cry. God works in mysterious ways.*

"Sweetheart, 'I'm—"

"*Please!*" she pleaded.

She turned further, trying to hide her tears. The immense weight of heartbreak nearly dropped him to the floor. The death of a fourth child was obliterating what remained of their relationship. The expanse between them was now a Black Hole sucking in and crushing everything around it. Soon, nothing would be left of him. Of her. Of them.

By the time he had reached Rodin Psychiatric Hospital,

guilt had shoved aside his heartbreak. Several times he had promised Clara he was done with Wilhelm, and he had meant it, *every* time. Still, here he was, standing outside Wilhelm's door. Multiple times he'd summoned whatever cowardice was required to lie to her. The first lie was the most challenging hurdle to leap, but each successive lie had lowered the bar until he could walk over it without breaking stride.

His hand on the door's handle, he promised Clara this was the last time. And this time, he meant it.

Wilhelm was seated on his cot. His worn and dirty canvas shoes, jeans, and long-sleeved white shirt replaced by black sneakers, tan khakis, and a navy-blue collared shirt he was just now putting on. His upper body had an underlying strength— a fit, younger man wearing a Wilhelm suit.

Wilhelm nimbly worked the shirt's buttons. "No mask today?"

Allan, unaware he had forgotten his mask, thought: Who cares? I took every precaution to protect my babies; what good did that do?

Wilhelm finished buttoning his shirt. "To what do I owe the pleasure?"

On the drive from Saint Pete's, questions had tumbled inside his skull like lotto balls. Serious and important questions that required serious and important answers. Now, those questions were as serious and important as ones asked by toddlers. "Mommy, when I grow up, should I be a Paleontologist or a butterfly?" "Daddy, why can't I see my eyeballs?"

Wilhelm, now in front of Allan, placed a hand on his shoulder. "Are you okay?"

Allan lowered himself onto the cot.

"They can be confusing," Wilhelm added in a comforting voice.

Allan stared at his feet, praying for the floor to open into a gaping, endless chasm and swallow him. "What can be confusing?" he grumbled.

"The dreams."

He sat silent and motionless, not surprised at all by Wilhelm's statement. "What is happening to me?" he asked as if they had switched roles.

Wilhelm sat beside him on the cot. "Every day, good people die. And every day, people unworthy of life find ways to cheat death. Is that fate? Luck?" He dismissed both with a single shake of his head. "There are powers no one understands. Powers that influence us. Powers that create checks and balances, counter evil with good, and misfortune with fortune." He set a hand on Allan's knee. "Sometimes, they need our help."

Allan clenched his fists, blood flooding the muscles in his arms. He wanted to shake Wilhelm and yell: "Can't you see you're crazy?" Instead, he listened to his heart, its rhythm out of sync with his pulse as though someone *else*'s heart—an infected heart—had been transplanted into his chest. And that heart's dormant virus, activated by a predetermined combination of words and actions by a delusional old man, was now shutting down his ability to reason.

"I don't understand what is happening." He pushed his elbows into his thighs and covered his ears with his hands as if trying to block out voices only he could hear. "Why am I having so many horrifying dreams? What do they mean?"

"You know what they mean."

He jumped to his feet and spun around. "Why do you talk in riddles?" He lunged forward until he and Wilhelm were almost nose to nose. "Why am I dreaming of massacres and murders and my wife's severed head?" For a moment, he turned his anger inward, berating himself for believing his dreams had meaning and for thinking a delusional old man could decipher it.

"Events occurring now," Wilhelm said somberly, "will not

be a footnote in history. They are seeds that will be fertilized by hatred and division and watered by tears and blood. Your dreams are not dreams; they are visions. And there will be unimaginable consequences if you do not act on what they are trying to show—"

"Spare me the Ghost of Christmas Future *bullshit!*" Allan's bloodless fists were like sledgehammers at his sides. "There are no voices!"

Wilhelm remained calm. "I saw the evil Hitler would unleash long before circumstances allowed him to do so. I am here to help you see what I did not."

Among his miles of misfiring synapses, connections started to form. *Nice to finally meet you.* That is what Wilhelm said when we first met. Is it possible? Could he have been expecting to meet me?

"In Denver," Allan said, thinking his voice sounded different. Still his own, but different. As if he were speaking words chosen by someone else. "You told me you weren't here *in Witten,* but you were here *with me.* Is that because…" He began frantically snipping mental wires, hoping to sever the connection between his brain and mouth before he spoke the next few words. Words no sane mind could formulate, let alone speak. "Is that because," he continued, "the voices sent you to me?"

Wilhelm's eyes glassed over, and, for a moment, he seemed to disappear. "You are fighting this because you cannot accept what *must* be done."

A desire exploded inside Allan. A desire to end Wilhelm's riddles and lies. To end *Wilhelm.* He wanted to wrap his hands around Wilhelm's throat and cut-off every breath trapped in his ancient lungs. He had never felt this out of control; the power of his emotions was terrifying.

As if observing events from above, he watched Wilhelm fall to the floor. He watched himself straddle Wilhelm's chest. He felt his hands around Wilhelm's throat, squeezing. He squeezed harder and harder until he cracked Wilhelm's windpipe like a hardboiled egg. A voice screamed: *Squeeze harder! Kill him!* while another tried to calm him. *This is not real. It is stress and fatigue and emotion.* The voices mixed and became indistinguishable. *Kill him! This is not real. It is real! Wilhelm is poison! Squeeze harder! It is stress and fatigue and emotion. Clara warned you about him, but you didn't listen! This is not real. Kill him! Your son is dead because you refused to listen! It is all your—*

"Doc?"

Allan remained nearly catatonic until the sensation of being shaken shattered his mental paralysis.

"Are you okay?" Wilhelm asked. "You are trembling."

What the hell is wrong with me? he thought, looking through Wilhelm. I'm a psychiatrist, for Christ's sake. Why don't I know what is wrong with me?

43

Huffy hesitated inside the door, still questioning his decision to come. He could have just called. Clara, asleep in her hospital bed, had sent him a text stating she needed to "talk about Allan." Why had he come to the hospital instead of calling? And why buy flowers? Obviously, flowers were appropriate in these circumstances, but he barely knew her. Thinking the dozen red roses had been a mistake, he scanned the area and spotted a food cart about ten feet away. He took a step toward it but stopped when Clara said, "They're beautiful." He turned to her. She yawned and scooched herself into a seated position.

His weak smile hidden behind his mask, he eyed the vase of roses in his hand, wishing he had never bought them. Rather than inappropriate, they now felt inadequate to the point of insulting. *I'm sorry your child died; here's forty dollars worth of flowers.*

"Come in," she added warmly.

He padded to her bedside, each hesitant step tightening the knots in his stomach. In his line of work, he offered condolences as often as a funeral director. But this felt different. This *was* different.

"I'm so sorry for your loss, Clara."

"Thank you," she said. "And thanks for coming."

"I..." He looked away, pretending to search for a place to put the vase. He wanted to tell her, but the words refused to come. They were simple words and should have been easy to say. *I lost my daughter. Hannah was two months, ten days, six hours, and thirty-one minutes old. She had her mother's eyes and my temper. She was perfect. I miss her so much.* But the words were packed so tightly into his throat that he could barely breathe.

He set the roses on a table beside the bed and stepped back to Clara. God, she was beautiful. He leaned toward her, clueless as to why he had feelings for her. Could it be the shared loss of a child? Without ever mentioning Hannah, had Clara sensed his pain and instinctively recognized its cause? But how could that be true? How could a loss that rips people apart—a loss that ended his marriage—*draw* him to her? It couldn't, he knew that. Still, he had to fight hard to stop himself from wrapping his arms around her. He wanted to absorb her pain, to take it from her and make it his. Not to ease her burden, but to end it. He watched his hand inching toward her's but thought better of it and dropped his hand onto the bed.

"Allan mentioned you were sick of the hospital." His eyes were glued to the thin strip of blanket between their fingertips. "I felt the same way when I was here with—"

Say it! he ordered. The words were fully formed and on the tip of his tongue but refused to come. *When I was here with my daughter.*

Say it!

"But I wasn't sick of the hospital, just the food. God help Saint Pete's kitchen staff if Gordon Ramsay ever ends up here." His hesitant tone reflected his uncertainty. Is it okay to joke at a time like this? When she pressed her lips into a thin smile, he relaxed. "You look good."

"You're sweet." She shifted positions, her leg sliding under his hand. He pretended not to notice, and she didn't seem to mind. "But you are a terrible liar."

He wondered if his eyes were giving away the smile behind his mask.

"You can take that off," she said. "I'm fine."

"Are you sure?"

She nodded, and he slipped his mask under his chin.

"My doctor says it is too soon for me to leave, but my body disagrees. I have been through a lot less and felt a lot worse. A little plague is the least of my worries."

He wasn't sure if he smiled. He was focused on his hand, her warmth passing through the blanket and into his bloodstream, reviving parts of him he had thought were long dead.

"Your text said you wanted to talk about Allan. Is everything okay?"

She glanced nervously at the open door and dropped her chin toward her chest. She looked scared and unsure like she was about to turn Allan in for murder.

"He saw Wilhelm outside our bedroom window."

He pulled his hand off her leg and set it in his lap. "It's dangerous for old men to be climbing ladders." He smiled, hoping she would do the same. She didn't.

"Allan said he was *floating* outside the window."

He frowned.

"And before you came, he was asleep." She motioned with her eyes to the chair Huffy now occupied. "He kept apologizing...as if he'd hurt me. He kept repeating, 'Clara, I'm sorry. Clara, I'm sorry.' He talks while he is dreaming. Sometimes he says things, *crazy* things."

"Crazy?"

A shallow nod. "Earlier, he kept repeating, 'Kill one. Save millions'." She again looked nervously toward the door as though expecting Allan to be eavesdropping on their conversation. "After our third child died, Allan suffered a..."

He could see her fear and understood why she was feeling it. Grief was powerful. It could cause even the most grounded person to lose it, at least for a while. After Hannah died, he had experienced his share of strangeness. For a few months, he had seen Hannah everywhere. Once, while walking in Hastings Park, he'd discreetly followed a woman for ten minutes before finally convincing himself the baby in her stroller wasn't Hannah. Grief, he knew, also possessed the power to cause Clara to see and hear meaning in words and actions. When Alex packed Hannah's clothes into boxes for the Salvation Army and Goodwill, he lost it, accusing her of *never* loving Hannah and claiming that she was *glad* Hannah had died. Ridiculous, of course. Reminders of Hannah had been too painful for Alex. For him, spending time in her room and holding and smelling her clothes was a way to be with her. He felt comfortable in that pain. He craved it. Feeling pain was better than feeling nothing.

"It's just stress." He knew she wasn't seeking his advice, but as a man, the instinct was impossible to suppress. Not dissimilar to wildebeest crossing crocodile-infested rivers. Thankfully, she seemed reassured. He winked. "I'll keep him out of trouble."

They talked, mostly about nothing, until a call from Frankie sent him on his way. As he left, he caught Clara's reflection in the window; her smiling eyes were following him out of the room. For a brief moment, he thought of his father and how, in a single, magical moment at a High School dance, he saw his future in someone else's eyes.

44

Driven by shame, not curiosity, Allan's eyes roamed the small office, eventually landing on a picture hanging on a wall: **Love is Love** spelled out in rainbow-colored letters. What the hell am I doing here? he wondered, his eyes briefly meeting hers before retreating, first to her desk, then back to the picture on the wall behind her.

"Doctor Lam said you wanted to speak with me about Mr. Weissand." Everything about Laurel Stevenson was pleasant and professional, including her office, lavender sweater-vest, and close-cropped grey-brown hair.

"Sorry," he said. "I apologize for the white lie. I was hoping to talk to you about a personal matter."

"Oh," she said, surprised. "You wouldn't prefer to speak to someone you know? Perhaps a colleague you have a relationship with."

Talk to someone I know about whether I am losing my mind? Um, I'll pass. "That's okay," he said, thinking: Last chance. Are you sure you want to do this? "It's nothing dramatic. Probably just exhaustion and stress."

"Alright." She dropped her elbows onto the desk and flared her long, delicate fingers. "I'm all ears."

He told her everything he felt was relevant, including the pain and stress caused by his children's deaths. He told her about his ability to maintain an awareness of the real-world while dreaming and how he would fall asleep in bed only to wake up somewhere else with no memory of how or when he had got there. He told her about Clara finding him in his car in the garage with the engine running and about his odd compulsions. And how he found it impossible to resist them, whether the compulsion was minor, like writing a name on a bookmark, or it put him in harm's way. He told her about his dreams that appeared to foretell real-world deaths, and she had agreed with his assessment that portions of TV or radio news reports had slipped through brief cracks in his unconsciousness. She went a step further and suggested hypnagogia and hypnopompia—states of mind experienced while falling asleep and waking, both could include hallucinations influenced, at least partially, by real-world surroundings and events. He was embarrassed that neither had come to mind. He finished by expressing his frustration at his inability to self-diagnose. He left out only those details he felt were either too "out there" to be useful or potentially drug-related, like hallucinating killing Wilhelm and seeing him hovering outside their second-story window.

"Do you take any medications?"

"Thorazine," he answered, followed immediately by, "I have severe migraines."

"Have you been tested for—"

"No tumors. They're hereditary."

"Hemiplegic?"

A nod

"Any family history of mental illness or suicide?"

He hesitated, briefly considering his mom's overdose. "No," he answered. "Neither."

"Are you concerned for your safety or the safety of others?"

He shook his head. "Absolutely not."

She checked her watch. "Vivid and disturbing dreams are common, particularly during periods of extreme stress, and this *definitely* qualifies as extreme stress. And, as I am sure you know, Thorazine's side effects can include memory loss, anxiety, and disrupted sleep; all could be contributing factors."

He felt himself nodding, but he was unsure if he agreed with her or just wanted her to be right. She stood. "And you may want to consider the possibility your inability to self-diagnose is because there is nothing to diagnose."

Relieved, he stood and thanked her for her time.

At the door, she said, "Try to relax and get some sleep. If you still want to talk in a few weeks, I will be happy to help."

–

ALLAN SPENT THE drive back to Saint Pete's questioning her opinion. She was undoubtedly qualified to offer it, but how could her opinion be valid if she did not have all the information? Before he'd knocked on her door, a part of him had decided what her conclusion would be: You? Crazy? Ha! No chance! He then provided her just enough information to ensure that conclusion. If he had wanted a *valid* appraisal of his mental state, why did he confide in someone he had never met? And why leave out "killing" Wilhelm or seeing him "floating" thirty feet above the ground? And why not mention the dream about the Asian man being burned alive? He failed to mention that dream, he knew, because it could not have seeped into his subconscious via a TV or radio news report. That dream did not fit the narrative, so he'd excluded it. The same way delusional individuals exclude inconvenient facts, he thought.

On the walk from Saint Pete's underground garage to Clara's room, he marveled at the mind's power to protect and compartmentalize. His mind was now two independent parts. One part had made "killing" Wilhelm real, while the other part concluded "killing" Wilhelm had been a momentary break from reality. Not caused by a mental illness or a mind in the process of fracturing, but by exhaustion and stress. That part appeared to be the more powerful of the two as it had already convinced him that Laurel Stevenson was right; regardless of what he had withheld, there was nothing to diagnose. Oddly, he had begun to sense a third part, one unbound by emotion or bias. That third part's sole job seemed to be to fire warning flares meant to alert him to the possibility that his mind *was* fracturing.

Clara was asleep. He noticed a vase of roses on a table beside her bed. He searched the flowers for a card. Not finding one, he leaned in and kissed her on the forehead.

She opened her eyes.

"Hey," he whispered. She stretched, her eyes moving around the room. He watched her face brighten when she spotted the roses. "Secret admirer?"

"Lisa and a few nurses from my team stopped by to offer their condolences."

"Lisa Bell? Your supervisor?"

A nod.

"She brought you roses?"

"They miss me. Can't wait for me to come back."

He wasn't sure but thought he'd heard a hint of enthusiasm in her voice. *How was your day, Allan? Other than the whole dead baby thing, mine was great!*

"Where were you?" she asked.

"At Rodin meeting with...a colleague."

She spoke through a yawn. "Who?"

"Laurel Stevenson."

"About?"

Having anticipated the question, he had come up with an answer he knew would not upset her. "I asked her to take over with Wilhelm."

She hopped out of bed. "I can leave in a few hours. Come back then." She disappeared into the bathroom.

Her voice had a lightness to it like a child hospitalized for a tonsillectomy and excited by the prospect of unlimited popsicles. Acute Stress Disorder, he thought. The condition, typically referred to as "shock," could cause people to remain unaware of the triggering trauma, sometimes for days or weeks. ASD explained her inappropriate demeanor. It also explained why she felt ready to go home so soon. Her body had been through a lot, and feeling physically well enough to go home so soon made no sense. Her mental state was a different story entirely.

Trauma affected people in different ways. The mind was most powerful when it was protecting from pain. Clara had always built walls, the by-product of a childhood spent with a father she believed did not love her. None of her walls had been torn down, at least not entirely. Some were tattered, others merely chipped, most were somewhere in between. She had built each new wall on top of a rising and weakening foundation. And despite constructing them for one purpose, her walls—like all walls—served two. One side shielded her from the pain continually trying to climb over, dig under, or bust through, while the other side imprisoned her *real* emotions behind a lifetime of *baggage*.

The wall constructed over the last two days, a wall built to protect her from the pain of losing another child, may have been too much. Its weight might have caused all her walls to crumble, burying her ability to feel under the rubble. Hopefully, the damage was temporary.

He stared at the red roses, wondering about *his* walls. He had lost four children, too. Had he buried those losses instead of dealing with them? Had they managed to claw out of their mental graves? Were they now scratching at the soft tissue of his brain? Would he know if they were?

Before leaving, he placed a single red rose on Clara's pillow, hoping she would think of him when she saw it.

45

Frankie eyed Huffy across her desk and signaled with a finger that her phone call was nearing an end. He nodded, a part of him hoping the call would last for hours. Thanks to the paper in his hand, this was the first time he felt nervous around Frankie.

About a minute later, Frankie, still on the call, placed a finger gun to her head and pulled the trigger. It was then he realized he wasn't nervous. He was friendly with many people but had only one friend, and the paper in his hand had the power to damage that friendship. Possibly even end it. He wasn't nervous; he was scared.

Before Hannah, he had last been scared when he was fourteen, his ear pressed to his parent's bedroom door. They were fighting. Not arguing like normal parents; his parents *fought*. When his mom's screaming and crying stopped abruptly, he pressed his ear tighter to the door. Taking a beating was easier than watching one, so, whenever possible, he would redirect his father's rage—a child matador. Sometimes by wedging himself between them, other times by "accidentally" breaking something; the more expensive the item, the more effective the redirect. And if all else failed, he would call his dad a cocksucker or a faggot; two words his dad seemed to take particular offense to.

But this time, nothing had worked.

In the eternity that passed between his mom falling silent and his dad opening the door and speeding off in his '64 GTO, he *knew* his mom was dead. During those eternal minutes, the immense pain of being truly alone had crushed him, stripping the flesh from his bones as if he had showered in acid.

The next day, his father's GTO was back in the driveway, and his father was back at the breakfast nook promising, as he always did, that he would never drink again. And, as she always did, his black and blue mom had believed him. Thankfully, the cocksucker finally kept his promise.

But the damage had been done. Huffy would never again allow himself to feel the pain of that kind of loneliness. When Hannah died, he knew what her death would do to their marriage. At the time, he had been unaware of what he was doing, or, more accurately, *why.* That awareness came weeks after he cut short his third counseling session with a shrink Frankie ordered him to see. During that session, the shrink suggested he had subconsciously decided his marriage would end. *Being in control of how and when your marriage failed*, she told him, *was a less painful option than helplessly waiting for Hannah's death to rip it apart.* He walked out of the session after hearing that, confident she had no clue what the hell she was talking about. Why would he sabotage his marriage? He loved Alex.

Over the following weeks, he came to accept that the shrink had been right. From that moment, he had carried the pain of knowing *he* was the reason his marriage had failed. He still redirected that blame, often to Alex. He knew he was doing it but could not stop. If he put the blame where it belonged, he would have to admit he had been wrong all along. Worse, he would have to admit he had caused Alex immeasurable pain at a time her heart could hold no more.

As Frankie ended her call, he studied the sheet of paper in his hand, terrified that he had made a mistake. He should have followed Frankie's order instead of some bullshit instinct. For the third time in his life, he felt his flesh being stripped from his bones.

"Sorry." Frankie tilted her head toward the desk phone. "That was Jarvis. He says—"

A piercing alarm blasted. They both cringed and covered

their ears.

"They still haven't fixed that?" Huffy croaked after the alarm stopped.

A head shake. "Second one today. I've lost the hearing in both of my—"

A shrill chirp had them cringing again, anticipating another blast. When the alarm stayed silent, Frankie continued. "Jarvis says Jerome Banks offered a new detail in exchange for a transfer off C Block."

"What now? He saw an old man playing shuffleboard with Palette before cutting him to pieces?"

"He's sticking to his story that he didn't see anyone outside Palette's cell. But he told Jarvis that Derek Samuels and Benny Carpenter are Bachman's primary pharmaceutical suppliers. Banks claims someone else is involved but doesn't know who." She nodded at the paper Huffy was fidgeting with. "What's that?"

Ignoring a powerful urge to forget about the paper, he handed it to her. She read for about ten seconds.

"What the fuck is this?" she demanded, glaring over the top of the paper.

"Finish read—"

"I told you to stick with regime change, and you bring me this? What the hell are you doing, Liam? Your—"

"There is something to this."

"Coincidences and weak circumstantial evidence won't help us catch a child killer or nail Kennedy. For Christ's sake, do I have to throw shit and threaten to suspend you?" She flung the paper toward him. It slid to a stop halfway across her desk." This isn't a fucking cop drama, Liam. Josh Cutter—"

"Frankie—"

She slammed both hands hard onto her desk, the wind lifting the paper and inching it toward Huffy. "Josh Cutter's mother watched her son's skull explode! She then had to go home and wash her son's blood and brains off her face and out of her four-year-old daughter's hair. When I—"

"Frank—"

"No!" She leaned forward, her eyes wild and angry, the carotid arteries in her neck pulsing. "When I tell you to investigate regime change at the RUV, you investigate fucking regime change at the RUV." She glared at him for several seconds, retrieved the paper off her desk, and finished reading it.

"This is about *him*, isn't it?"

She had never questioned his professionalism before. It hurt, but he understood. She had walked in on him comforting Clara Abrams, an easy situation to misinterpret.

"Of course."

She twisted her face into a disbelieving mash of skin. "You expect me to believe the department's most senior psychiatrist has a vendetta against the RUV?" A beat. "Why would Abrams give a shit about the RUV? And even if he did, how the hell would he get close to any of them, particularly Palette?"

"I know it is weak but—"

"*Weak?* Are you kidding?"

"I know you want the kid's killer. So do I. But you have ten detectives on the Cutter case. Let me question Abrams. If I find nothing, I'll drop him and work 24/7 to find a way to nail Kennedy for Palette or the kid." Her hard edges were fading. He felt a spike of relief; he had underestimated the strength of their friendship or overestimated the impact of his insubordination. He felt confident enough to offer half a grin and say, "I'm just gonna do it anyway."

He waited, hoping for any verbal or non-verbal version of "Fine." Frankie was not a made-for-TV movie boss who took every opportunity to offload pressure. Shit flowing downhill was not her style. Heat from the press or Dickson was her burden, and she accepted it. But that was not why she was angry. She was angry because he had betrayed her by going to Dickson. And worse, she saw no justification for that betrayal. Still, doing everything wrong did not mean his instincts weren't right. Frankie would forgive him once he questioned Abrams and exposed him for who he was.

She passed him the paper. "I have every reason to believe you are wrong." Her voice was calmer now but still tinged with disappointment and waning anger. "And I am *extremely* hesitant to let you question one of *our* people based on evidence even you would normally disregard as coincidence." She paused, then gave him the sign he had been hoping for— a reluctant, acquiescent sigh. "This is your last chance," she added. "You can question him but in a non-adversarial way. And if you are wrong, you're going to give him a giant, ass-kissing apology."

–

ALLAN WAS AT his desk, every muscle in his body frozen, his eyes locked on the image on his computer monitor.

This must be fake, he thought.

With time to kill before heading back to the hospital to pick up Clara, he had tried to distract himself by organizing his office, the attempt proving as effective as distracting a starving lion with a ham sandwich. But he'd managed to maintain rudimentary function via a grief-induced autopilot. An operational numbness caused by barricading his emotions deep beneath his surface and protecting the release valve with more warnings than the core of a nuclear reactor: **STAY BACK! DANGER! DO NOT OPEN! EXTREMELY VOLATILE.** The warnings necessary because if even a single molecule of sadness escaped, everything trapped inside would explode and turn him into a quivering, useless mass.

While transferring a stack of patient files from the top of his filing cabinet into their respective locations, he had received a call from a Rodin staff member. Upon learning Wilhelm had once again disappeared, Alan stated, "I don't care," hung up, and turned his attention to his unruly desk, mindlessly shuffling and sorting until spotting a bookmark under a pad of paper in a desk drawer. The hand-written name on the bookmark stirred an odd compulsion, which led to an online search. That search had returned the image currently on his computer monitor.

"This must be fake," he muttered.

The moment the words left his mouth, a memory provided proof he was right. During a New York vacation, he and his mom were on a bench in Central Park, resting their feet and warming their hands, when a man approached, snapped a picture, and scurried off. He returned a few minutes later with the FrontPage of that day's paper. The lead was a feel-good story about the Mayor giving an eight-year-old from Colorado a giant key that opened every door in the city.

His mom had framed the fake FrontPage and hung it in the living room, never missing an opportunity to tell guests how proud she was that her son had received such a prestigious honor. At her funeral, he placed the rolled-up FrontPage in her coffin—a souvenir of their time together.

"This is fake," Allan repeated, unsure if he was confirming a fact or trying to convince himself of one. The picture of an adult male and a young boy had been taken on a dock in front of a large passenger ship. According to the caption, the boy's name matched the one Allan had seen on a grave marker in a Denver cemetery, the same name he had noted on the bookmark. Werner Karl Marbach appeared no more than half of the ten years the caption claimed he was. His shaved head, protruding cheekbones, and lifeless eyes embedded deep inside dark circles made the rail-thin boy appear inhuman. Werner Karl Marbach was a shadow of a real boy.

U.S. forces from the Sixth Armored Division had rescued Marbach and the adult male—listed as Marbach's grandfather—during the Buchenwald Death Camp's liberation. Unlike Marbach, the adult male appeared to have recovered from his ordeal, at least physically. And despite the photo wearing every day of its seventy-plus years, the adult male's identity was unmistakable. If the picture was authentic, Wilhelm had not aged a day in over seventy years.

On the bookmark, underneath *Werner Karl Marbach*, Allan noted the photographer's name and where and when he had taken the picture. Less than a minute later, he was navigating the automated phone maze at the New York Times while wrestling with the knowledge that, even for someone suffering from Grandiose Delusions, faking the picture and story would be extreme behavior.

A nasally female voice with a thick New York accent responded to his button-pushing and proceeded to explain the convoluted process for authenticating the picture. "Do you know how I could contact the photographer?" he asked. If he were alive, the photographer would be over a hundred years old, so Allan was surprised he had asked such a foolish question. But not nearly as surprised as he was when the woman put him on hold and returned with the photographer's phone number.

Unsure what to expect but too curious not to find out, he dialed the number. After three rings, an elderly man requested a name, phone number, and reason for the call. Allan considered hanging up but decided to leave the requested information.

On his way to pick up Clara, he concluded whomever he had left the message for was *not* the photographer; the photographer was dead. The image was a fake or a trick of the light or camera. It was borderline delusional to believe Wilhelm had not aged since 1945.

46

After arriving home from the hospital, Allan had watched Clara trudge through the kitchen, praying she would offer a somber look back. *I'm hurting*, the look would say, *but I still love you*. Instead, she disappeared into the den and closed the door.

An hour later, he was seated on the floor of the nursery, his back pressed against the rainbow painted on a mint-green wall, his eyes glassy but trained on two identical convertible cribs. *Why buy two cribs and two beds when you can buy two cribs that convert into beds?* Clara had reasoned. *Can't argue with that logic*, he'd agreed.

He looked around the room, seeing double: Two pedestal bassinets, two car seats (still boxed), two mobiles—one above each crib—each with dangling puppies and kittens ready to capture the attention of cooing twins. His eyes passed over a sky-blue wall with fluffy white clouds in the shapes of farm animals: two sheep, two cows, two ducks, two chickens, and two horses.

On the shelf between the cribs was one of the few items without a twin—a "sleep training" alarm clock. The clock was a smiling, tuxedo-wearing penguin with a digital clock set into its belly. According to that clock, sixty-one minutes had passed since they returned from the hospital. Sixty-one minutes since Clara, offering no indication she loved or needed him at all, had disappeared into the den. He had spent those sixty-one minutes in the same spot he was now. Twice he had stood, intending to go to her, to comfort her, to "be there" for her. Both times the immeasurable weight of grief sent him back to the floor. He ached with a pain so intense he prayed his heart would stop.

He had suffered enough.

He stared at the clock's digits until they blurred into an unrecognizable red glow. He cursed the imprecise nature of Time. Sixty-one minutes could pass in the blink of an eye or unravel slower than the evolution of a species. Time, it seemed, preferred the latter when it came to life's most gut-wrenching experiences.

Time heals all wounds, except that it doesn't. Life had repeatedly taught him that time healed nothing. Time was, it turns out, as sadistic as a serial killer relishing in the suffering of his victims. Time did not heal; it covered. It heaped layers of moments and memories on top of a wound so that the wound could fester and slowly rot the soul.

Regardless of how it appeared at any given moment, he now knew he would never be a father. Fatherhood was not part of *God's plan*. God's plan for Allan Abrams was to punish him for crimes he had no memory of committing. And to ensure He made His point, God had recruited Father Time to stretch the seconds into millennia. And perhaps for no other reason other than He could, God had also decided that the pain in Allan Abrams's head would forever fluctuate between a low-grade growl, and, as was the case now, heat and pressure so intense that a guillotine would be welcomed as treatment.

He dug his elbows into his knees, clasped a hand on either side of his head, and watched his tears fall to the hardwood floor. Yes, somehow, he still had tears. He closed his eyes and softly hummed, "Under the Boardwalk."

At some point, he heard the phone ring and tried to stand. He couldn't. His legs were void of strength, their muscle tissue dissolved by grief. But he needed to get up off the floor and go to Clara. She was devastated, as was he, but they were stronger together; they would get through this *together*. He had to make her see that.

A loud crash shattered the silence.

He sprinted down the stairs and into the den, stopping abruptly just inside the door. Clara was behind his desk. She was vibrating, her arms stiff at her sides, her eyes thin slits —cobra's eyes—and locked on him. Other than the monitor, everything from his desk was scattered over the floor.

"You *son of a bitch!*"

"What is—"

"You selfish son of a *bitch!*" Her chest was heaving, her lips drawn back so thin they had all but disappeared. "Isn't one dead twin enough?"

He slowly moved toward her as though traversing a minefield. "Sweetheart, what is wr—"

"Someone from *New York* called about your *picture*," she seethed, a finger pointed harshly at the monitor. "You selfish —"

Her breathing suddenly became labored. He started toward her, but she stopped him with an upright palm. She shook her inhaler and took two deep puffs.

"Over and over, you *promised* you were done with him." Her voice had lost all its energy. "But even after our son died, you still…" She tried to point at the monitor again, but her arm barely moved before falling limply back to her side. "You aren't *you* anymore, Allan. *I* don't matter." Her hands and eyes found her belly. "*We* don't matter. All you care about is that crazy old man." As she passed him, her feet heavy, her eyes on the floor, she said, "I don't trust you. Not as a husband *or a* father."

The words ricocheted inside his skull like bullets running on perpetual energy.

When she took her car keys off the hook in the kitchen, he did nothing. When she started her car, he did nothing. When the garage's overhead door rose, he did nothing. Home for a little more than an hour after the death of their fourth child—a death caused by stress *he had* created—Clara was gone, and all he could do was stand there and do nothing.

—

THE DEN RESTORED, Allan was seated at his desk, trying to rationalize an irrational obsession with a mentally ill old man. His eyes moved around the room, everything they hit deflecting his gaze to something else until landing on the bookmark beside the cordless phone.

Don't even think about it, he warned. "Yes," he agreed, "that is a *terrible* idea." He threw the bookmark in the small, black garbage can beside his desk and tried to stand. He couldn't. Instead of his legs being too heavy, this time, his muscles had simply refused the order. What the hell is wrong with you? he wondered, fishing the bookmark from the garbage. You're an idiot, that's what's wrong with you.

He dialed the number.

While waiting for someone to answer, Allan contemplated the photographer's age. Even if he had snapped the picture in his mid-twenties, he would *still* be on the wrong side of a century. That thought reinforcing the futility of the call, he hung up only to redial seconds later. Based on the strangeness of the last several days, he prepared himself for the possibility that the photographer was not just alive, he was 130 years old and still bowling Tuesdays, golfing Thursdays, and killing it at Saturday night bingo.

"Hello," Allan heard, the voice that of an elderly man. You have got to be fucking kidding. "Hello?" the elderly man repeated. "Sorry," Allan answered, trying to convince himself to hang up and burn the bookmark. After a long silence, the elderly man repeated himself for the third time. *"Hellooo?"*

"Mr. Reynolds?"

"Uh-huh."

"Harold Reynolds?"

"That's what people keep calling me."

What the hell is happening?

"Um, Mr. Reynolds, I'm Allan Abrams. I'm a psychiatrist with the Witten police department."

"Yes, my daughter-in-law told me you had left a message. I just spoke to your wife. She sounds like a lovely lady."

"Uh, yeah," he stammered, "she mentioned you'd called. Mr. Reynolds, I'm..." He hesitated and fought the urge to hang up.

"You're what?"

"I'm sorry to call so late, but I was hoping you might remember a photograph you took in 1945?"

"On my seventh birthday, I had Angel Food cake with vanilla icing and blew out every candle on my first try. But son, if I climbed Everest last Tuesday, I wouldn't remember a lick about it. Drives my daughter-in-law crazy." He chuckled. "But I doubt you care about what I can't remember from 1945."

"I do, actually. It is why—"

"What I mean is, you are talking to Harold Reynolds Number Two. You want Harold Reynolds Number One."

"Oh, sorry. The lady from the Times gave me this phone number."

"My father worked for the Times for forty-three years. He published a few books of his photographs. People occasionally call the paper wanting this, that, or the other. I don't mind taking the calls and helping if I can. It gives me something to do besides watching Jeopardy and The Golf Channel. Do you golf?"

"Uh, no."

"Probably a good thing. Golf's a lot like a marriage; fun occasionally, but mostly you're frustrated and throwing stuff."

Allan forced a weak laugh. "Mr. Reynolds, I'm sorry I bothered you, but would it be possible for me to speak with your father?"

When Mr. Reynolds answered "Sure," Allan thought: why am I not surprised? "You might try that lady from Long Island," Mr. Reynolds continued. "You know, the one with the big hair who connects people with lost loved ones." Before Allan could respond to the suggestion that he contact TLC's Long Island Medium, Mr. Reynolds added, "I never understood why people say the dead are *lost.* They must think Heaven is a giant dryer, and the dead are God's socks."

"I'm so sorry for your loss. Was it COVID?"

Another chuckle. "Is that a serious question?"

Allan, realizing he sounded less like a psychiatrist and more like someone who might need one, didn't answer.

"My father left us over ten years ago. He had a good run, though. Not many make it to ninety-six."

Only ninety-six? Man, do I have a story for you.

"Um..." Allan had no idea why he was about to ask the question but could not stop himself. "Do you remember any of your father's photographs?"

"Like the one of the elderly man and his grandson at the New York Passenger Ship terminal in 1945?"

"Yes," Allan said, as excited as he was surprised.

A one-syllable grunt of laughter. "As I mentioned, my daughter-in-law told me you had called and filled me in on why. I am looking at the picture now. It is in one of dad's books. What would you like to know?"

The question caught him by surprise; until this moment, he had not considered what he wanted. A short deliberation provided the answer. "Do you know how to scan and email a picture?"

"No, but I can have my pterodactyl chisel a copy into a rock and fly it out to you."

"Sorry, I didn't mean to—"

"I am having fun with you, son. What is your email address?"

Several minutes later, the scanned image was still speeding through cyberspace—an electronic bullet screaming toward him. When it struck, it would kill one of two possibilities: his mind had fractured, or Wilhelm had not aged in over seven decades. Not surprisingly, neither option was comforting.

Continually clicking *send/receive*, Allan scolded himself for calling Harold Reynolds Number Two in the first place. Clara was ready to divorce him because of the borderline psychotic shit he was doing, and what was his response? Do more borderline psychotic shit. Brilliant plan, Allan. While you're at it, why not—

The *ding* from a "new message alert" startled him and temporarily knocked his heart out of rhythm.

Hovering the cursor over the message from Harold Reynolds, Allan could not bring himself to open the attachment. What if the picture is authentic? That thought triggered another: If Wilhelm hasn't aged since 1945, what does that mean about everything he has told me?

"Fuck," he groaned, scrubbing his face with his palms. The hard edges of anxiety stabbing at the lining of his stomach, he double-clicked on the attachment.

Having repeatedly compared every detail of the online image to the one Harold Reynolds had sent, Allan was now convinced the online image was authentic. He grabbed the cordless phone and punched in nine digits. His finger ready to press the tenth, he imagined his conversation with Huffy. *Hi Liam, it's Allan Abrams. I have proof that Wilhelm is 150-years-old. And if he can live to 150, I doubt he would have had a problem passing through concrete walls and steel bars and making himself invisible to security cameras. Obviously, he is now our prime suspect in the death of Sedrick—Why are you laughing? You don't understand, Wilhelm is a 150-year-old hitman working for mysterious voices with the power to influence our—Hello? Liam? Hello?*

He hung up, his head a hornet's nest of incoherent thoughts. His eyes drifted randomly until landing on a DNA strand icon at the bottom right corner of his monitor. He'd used the ancestry website to research his unfinished novel.

He clicked on the DNA strand.

After several searches returned no results, he changed the location and repeated the searches. Still nothing. "I knew he wasn't 150—*Oh*, right." Allan, remembering a detail from a session with Wilhelm, changed the spelling of his first name to Vilhelm and hit *enter*.

No matter how many times he refreshed the screen or re-entered the search criteria, the result remained the same. Unwilling to accept it, he re-opened Harold Reynolds' emailed photo, enlarged it, and examined a small, blurred section.

"Impossible." He stared slack-jawed at the monitor, the reality of what he was looking at finally sinking in. His cell phone buzzed. It took a while for his ears to relay the buzzing sound to his brain. He checked the display and immediately wondered: Why is he calling me so late?

On the drive to the downtown station, Allan ignored the voice asking why Liam had been so vague as to the reasons their meeting couldn't wait until the morning. Instead, he spent the entire drive contemplating two far more important mysteries. The adult male in the New York Times picture had a mark on his forearm. Although too small to see any detail, Allan knew the mark was a tattoo—a six-digit number in faded blue ink; the *same* number tattooed on Wilhelm's forearm.

The second mystery was the single search result from the ancestry website. The result showed four names. `Helena Weissand, wife. Jakob Weissand, son. Amelia Weissand, daughter.` All listed under the primary result: `Vilhelm N. Weissand. Born: Wolfsburg, Germany, June 13, 1857.`

47

With an eye on Clara, Huffy finished closing his office blinds. She had called and asked to meet. Twenty minutes later, she was seated in front of his desk, hands clasped in her lap, thumbs tumbling over one another. Her upper body was rocking back and forth, the movement so slight she likely didn't know she was doing it. He had seen women in a similar state of anxiety many times, usually while they debated whether to retract a false alibi and send their husband or boyfriend to jail.

A manila envelope from *Stuckey & Freemont Family Law* was on his desk. He stuffed it into a drawer and sat.

"How can I help, Clara?"

She took a deep, choppy breath. "After our third child died, Allan had a breakdown. The stress was too much. He was self-medicating. I think…" She hesitated, her eyes filling with tears. "It is happening again. I am worried Allan might hurt himself…or me."

Huffy shoved aside his initial surprise at Clara's openness, stiffened, and moved forward in his chair. "*Has* he hurt you?"

Her tears gave away what her forceful head shake had tried to deny. He had seen too many women like Clara, women too afraid to tell the truth. The subtle signs were easy to spot if you knew what to look for. He did.

He removed a tissue box from a drawer and handed it to Clara. As she took it with a shaking hand, it hit him. Exposed to abuse his entire life—at home as a child and on the job as an adult—he possessed an exceptional radar for abused women. His feelings for Clara now made sense. He had instinctively known she was in an abusive relationship and confused his instinct to protect her with attraction.

Clara set the box on the corner of the desk and used a tissue to dab tears. The muscles in his arms tightened, and his fingers dug into the armrests of his chair like a lion's claws into antelope flesh. He forced himself to stay seated. If he stood, he might walk out of his office. And if he did, he would end up in Interview Room Three with his fist in Allan Abrams's face.

"Allan's here," he said, still trying to calm himself. "Waiting to speak to me."

"Oh," she gasped, angst weakening her features to the point she appeared child-like. "Please, don't tell him I'm here."

He stepped around his desk, dropped to a knee, and placed his hand on her shoulder. "If he is hurting you, I can make him stop."

She made no reply, but a reply wasn't necessary. He knew what she was thinking. And feeling. She found strength in his words. She found strength in *him*. Somewhere in her hazel eyes, he saw the acceptance of his promise to protect her.

He slid his hand along her arm until his hand touched hers. A subconscious awareness of her abuse could not be why he felt the way he did; there had to be more to it. His feelings came from a deeper place. His eyes met hers, then dropped to her trembling lips—a voice warned him not to kiss another man's wife.

—

HUFFY LEFT CLARA in his office; she had wanted time to compose herself. He then spent the walk to Interview Room Three trying to determine whether Allan Abrams was abusing her, one moment believing he was, the next thinking he wasn't. For some reason, his normally reliable radar was malfunctioning.

He entered the interview room, set an unsealed manila envelope on the table, and sat opposite Abrams—his foot pounding an erratic beat against the floor.

"Nervous?" Huffy's ambiguous tone offered only the possibility he was joking. He couldn't help himself. Regardless of what evidence he had, or, in this case, did not have, his instincts kicked in the moment he'd entered the room. Fourteen years of muscle-memory was hard to turn off. Although, this would hardly qualify as an interrogation. He had agreed to go easy on Abrams, so this was more of a friendly Q&A, a testing of the waters, so to speak. It had to be. Frankie was right when she said his "evidence" was circumstantial at best and coincidental at worst. She had also implied his interest in Abrams was related to Clara. He had denied it. And, if asked again, he still would. But he was starting to wonder if Frankie had been right. He had strong feelings for Clara and no valid reason for those feelings. And, staring at Abrams now, he felt a growing animus. Why? He wasn't sure.

"No," Abrams answered, his anxious foot stopping in mid-beat. "Why would I be nervous?" Huffy stared but said nothing; silence was an exceptional interrogation tool.

"You said we needed to meet *right away*," Abrams eventually added.

Huffy removed a small slip of paper from the manila envelope and slid it across the table. "You wrote yourself a prescription for Thorazine and filled it at Ling's pharmacy?"

Abrams leaned forward and glanced at the paper. "Why do you have my prescription?"

"Thorazine is an anti-psychotic, correct?"

"I take it for migraines."

"Your prescription is for one hundred milligrams per day. Ling's pharmacist told me fifty is the maximum dose for any use other than as an anti-psychotic."

"I take it for migraines," he insisted. "What is going on? Why do you have my prescription?"

"Sorry." Huffy intuitively backed off. "My instincts tend to take over when I'm in here."

Abrams did not appear reassured.

"By the way," Huffy added, "did you know Ling's is a couple of blocks from the warehouse where we found Chris Tam?" He tapped the prescription. "This was filled around the time he was killed."

Huffy watched Abrams's eyes glass over; his mind was drifting. He was remembering something. Subconsciously, his thumb started rubbing a bandage on his palm.

"What's wrong?" Huffy asked.

A beat.

"Doc?"

Abrams snapped back to the moment. "What?"

Huffy pushed his chin toward Abrams's hands. "Something wrong with your hand?"

"Oh." He eyed his bandaged palm, then dropped both hands into his lap. "No."

We found fingerprints and human skin on an exterior door, Huffy recalled Dan Button telling him earlier.

"Did you see anything?" Huffy asked.

"What?"

"While you were at Ling's, did you happen to see Tam's killer," he trotted two fingers along the tabletop, "*running from the scene of the crime?*"

"N—" He cleared his throat. "No."

Huffy removed a sheet of paper from the manila envelope. "Thorazine has side effects, right?"

"Most drugs do. What does—"

"Constipation," Huffy said, reading from the paper, "insomnia, anxiety, changes in your menstrual cycle, breast swelling or discharge." Amused at Abrams's growing confusion, he set the paper on the table.

"Liam, what does this have to do—"

"Thorazine has some *serious* side effects as well, right? Like breaks from reality, hearing voices. Things of that nature?"

"On rare occasions, yes. But—"

"You are Derek Samuels' psychiatrist?"

Abrams's twisted expression was instant and predictable. Huffy often asked questions, not because their answers were important, but to show he had done his homework. It helped keep subjects on edge and wondering: What else does he know?

"And you prescribed him scopolamine?"

Abrams squirmed in his chair. Should I answer that? Huffy imagined him thinking.

"Privilege won't allow me to discuss my patients or any medication I *may* have prescribed them."

Huffy removed a pill bottle from the manila envelope and handed it to Abrams but said nothing. Abrams read the label.

"Fine," he conceded, handing Huffy the bottle. "I prescribed him scopolamine for his IBS. It can be effective for patients with sensitivities to other drugs."

"Are you aware scopolamine can cause memory loss? In fact, the internet is full of stories of people doing some pretty crazy shit on scopolamine and not remembering any of it?"

"Memory loss is a common side effect of many drugs, but I —"

"Like Thorazine."

"What is going on?" Abrams demanded, his anger now obvious. "Did you really have me come here to answer questions I could have answered over the phone?"

"I'm just trying to get a few things straight in my head. Unopened doors, remember?" Abrams stayed silent. "One thing I'm curious about is why, in the wee morning hours and during a snowstorm, you drove to Ling's to fill a prescription?"

"I ran out of medication and couldn't wait until morning."

"Fair enough," Huffy said. "But with three 24-hour pharmacies closer to your house, why drive to a shitty little pharmacy in Camper's Village?" He smiled. "Do you have a Ling's frequent shopper points card?"

Abrams stood. "Liam, I'm exhausted." He started to the door. "Next time, ask your questions over the phone instead of wasting my—"

"Don't you agree it is an odd coincidence you were filling your prescription at the same time Chris Tam was across the street being barbecued?"

At the door, Abrams stopped, paused, then turned, his face blank; he had just realized why Huffy had asked him to come.

"You think *I* was involved in that?" he screeched. "Because I took a drive to clear my head and filled a prescription? What the hell is—"

Huffy set a plastic evidence bag on the table; its contents grabbed Abrams by the throat and choked off his words.

"Early in my career," Huffy said smugly, "I saw cases go unsolved because someone ignored an insignificant detail or failed to check something that could easily have been checked." He eyed the evidence bag. "Call it an epiphany or instincts, or maybe it was all the non-alcoholic beer, but it finally hit me; what if the drunk was right? What if 'Bill Gates' *was* in the alley behind the warehouse where Tam was killed? And what if Gates gave the drunk a pair of gloves? Insignificant and easy to check, no?" Huffy let the information hang in the air for a few seconds. "After all, how many Camper's Village residents can afford a pair of *Chester Jefferies* leather gloves?" A pause. "Care to guess whose fingerprints and DNA we found inside these gloves?" Despite never having played the game, Huffy's poker face was as good as any in Vegas.

"This—" Abrams started before cutting himself off. He looked stunned. "You're interrogating me."

The question forced Huffy to retreat. "No, I'm just tidying up a few loose—"

Abrams stormed from the room.

Huffy, pleased with how the interview had gone, looked at his reflection in the one-way glass. "Yeah," he said to Frankie on the other side. "There is something to this."

—

ALLAN JAMMED THE stairwell door open and descended the stairs two at a time. His mind on fire, he wanted to leave the station as fast as possible, so he had not heard Sergeant Murphy calling him. Seconds later, Murphy forced the closing stairwell door back open. *"Doc!"* he called out, breathing heavily. "You want…these lab results…or not?"

He stopped and spun around, spotting Murphy through a gap between two flights of stairs. "What did you find?"

Murphy took a deep breath. "Your coffee had high levels of Ace K."

He knew the information was important, but it took a moment for the detail to penetrate his clogged synapses. *Finally!* he thought, the tension knotting his body erased by a huge exhale. An explanation that makes sense: someone is drugging me. "Is that a street drug? Can it cause auditory or visual hallucinations?"

"Not sure…but it is linked to strokes."

Murphy's puckish grin instantly restored Allan's lost focus. Ace K, he thought. Acesulfame K. Sweetener. Hilarious. He continued down the stairs, this time taking them three at a time.

"Just screwing with ya, Doc," Murphy called down. "It's sweetener." Allan was in the underground garage by the time Murphy added, "But it has been linked to strokes."

48

Clara, preoccupied with a memory, stared blurry-eyed at the word MINI embedded into the center of the steering wheel. She was watching herself in her divorce lawyer's conference room, her shaking hand holding a pen above the signature line. She wanted to reach back through time and slap herself across the face. "Sign it!"

Why was I so weak? She pressed the *Start* button on the Mini Cooper's dash. I haven't loved Allan for a long time. Has it been a long time? she questioned. Does it matter? I don't love him now. How could I? He—

A slamming car door freed her mind.

One turn from the exit, her heart skipped multiple beats; Allan was there, in his car, his forehead pressed against the steering wheel. Please, don't look up, she thought, unconsciously accelerating. The volume of the Mini's revving engine surprised her. "Please," she prayed. "Don't look up." If he saw her or beat her home, he would ask questions she didn't want to answer, mostly because she was so raw emotionally that she wasn't sure she had the strength to lie.

A block from the station, she pulled over and sent him a text.

—

ALLAN IGNORED THE sound of the revving engine and continued taking deep breaths to settle his frayed nerves. Why did Liam do that? Does he really believe I'm involved in the death of Chris Tam? What the fuck is going on? Is this even real? Is it a new dream?

He lifted his forehead off the steering wheel and scanned the garage, the cars and concrete registering as a multi-colored blur. His eyes found the rear-view mirror—a hideous version of himself staring back: Bloodshot eyes set deep in their sockets, cracked and dry lips drawn back to reveal bleeding gums and rotting teeth, and skin so pale it appeared transparent. He closed his eyes and squeezed the image from his mind. When he opened them, the gaunt, hollow-faced man was gone, another man in his place. The man's face, aged decades by fear and anxiety, was riddled with confusion.

What the hell is going on? Why am I—

His phone beeped.

He read Clara's text and typed a reply: *It's too late. I'm too tired. I'll get it tomorrow. On my way home.* He hesitated, then deleted it and replied with a *Thumbs Up* emoticon. He had no desire to find out if refusing to satisfy her late-night craving was on the ever-expanding list of things that set her off. He could also use the time to clear his head.

While waiting for the steel arm to rise and tiger teeth to retract, a question repeated in his mind: Why did Liam do that?

As the steel arm rose, a shudder rippled his flesh.

A series of unopened doors, he thought. Liam's found someone to hang.

A beat.

Me.

—

THE LAST TIME Clara sent him on a quest to satisfy the same craving, he discovered only one *24-hour-not-very-convenient* convenience store in the entire city stocked her canned treasure. "This was my first and *last* expedition," he had informed her at the time. But a little more than thirty minutes ago, her text sent him back to the same unsavory location.

"Are you *serious?*" Allan snarled. The teenage, mask-wearing Circle K clerk raised and lowered his boney, unconcerned shoulders. "Can you check if you have any in the back?" Allan added.

"Nope."

"*Nope,* you're not going to check, or *nope* there aren't any in the back?" Allan's tone was urgent as though a trapped and desperate bank robber was killing a hostage every ten minutes until police met his demand for a can of thirst-quenching Tahiti Treat. *People are dying, you snot-nosed shit! Check the back!*

The clerk adjusted the single earbud stuck in his ear. "Don't got none."

Disgruntled and empty-handed, Allan left the Circle-K and, a few minutes later, pulled to a stop at an intersection, the on-ramp blocked by a police car. An officer standing in the intersection signaled for Allan to U-turn. He pulled forward and lowered his window. He recognized the officer, having met with her a few times about a year ago. He couldn't remember why.

"Accident," the officer said. "Parkway's closed between Lincoln and Taylor."

Unable to remember her name and in no mood to reminisce, he nodded and U-turned. Ten minutes later, he was lost. At a stop sign in an area that resembled the "before" picture in a gentrification brochure, he plugged his address into Google maps, hit start, and followed the directions for about a minute before slowing the Volvo to a crawl.

"What the...?"

His mouth open, he gawked at the vertical marquee—its unlit "S" turning *HOSTEL* into *HO TEL.* He drove slowly past an idling white minivan, a line of freezing patrons, and a muscular, Latino doorman letting DaMarcus Kennedy and his fiancé into the bar.

How the hell is this possible?

The Volvo idling at a deserted intersection one block past the Hostel, Allan tried to convince himself he had not driven past a scene from one of his dreams. What happened, then? How could I have seen all of this? I have never been here before to—Did I come this way on my first Tahiti Treat expedition? I must have. But everything is *exactly* as it was then? he questioned. Maybe that wasn't Kennedy and his fiancé? The same white minivan was here last time?

He closed his eyes, his mind now a mess of frantic thought. Why so many odd coincidences? How can I see the future in my dreams? Why am I seeing deaths before they occur? Who is the boy—

A calm voice broke through. "You can stop it."

His head shot up, his eyes locking onto the rear-view mirror; Wilhelm was staring back. Allan snapped his head around but found only his plastic-wrapped, dry-cleaned suit spread across the back seat.

What the hell is wrong with me?

He watched the traffic light switch from green to yellow to red. Every time his eyes drifted toward the rear-view mirror, he forced them forward, unsure what virus had infected his mind. None of this is real, he thought. It is all in your head. None of this is real. It is—

"You can stop it," he heard again.

He strained every muscle in his neck, refusing to look in the mirror or turn around.

What if I do stop it?

The thought snuck up on him and caught his rational mind off guard. If I can change what happens in my dream, even a little, it would prove the dreams are just dreams, not visions of the future. And if I proved that, maybe it would allow me to reset mentally and return to who I was before. He clenched the steering wheel. Before what? he wondered. Before I met Wilhelm? Before the twins? Before what? He gripped the wheel tighter and locked his arms; he was not going to turn right. He was *not* going to try and change the events of a dream; the idea was insane. But what if my dreams *aren't* dreams? What if they are more than—

"No!" he screamed, pounding his temples with the heels of his hands. He was not going to do any of that. He was going home. But how could everything that has happened tonight lead you to this specific place at this exact time? How can you be here at the precise moment what you saw in your dream is unfolding in real life? How—

The traffic light turned green.

He touched the gas. The steering wheel started to swing right; he straightened it. This can't be a coincidence. Go home! You must be here for a reason.

—

PARKED IN THE alley behind the Hostel, Allan heard two distinct voices, one arguing that trying to change the events of a dream proved he was in the midst of a mental breakdown, and the other offering suggestions as to how he could change the dream. What if I convince Kennedy someone is killing RUV members and that he is in danger? Maybe I can get him to leave town with his pregnant fiancé and—

Oh my God, he thought. Kennedy's son is the boy general! That's why I am here. That has to be why I am here. The boy's olive skin is a blend of his parents'. His soft jawline and freckles inherited from his mother, and his psychopathy from his father.

You can't believe that?

Kennedy's son is the boy general.

There is no boy general.

Change the dream. Prove it is all in your head.

It *is* all in my head!

None of this is real!

49

Allan entered the Hostel through an unlocked rear door, loud music and light drawing him to a set of restaurant-style swinging doors at the end of the dark hall.

His hand on one of those doors, he hesitated. "Turn around and go home," he heard. "You are losing your fucking mind."

He pushed the door open, a wall of heat and humidity instantly coating his body with a thin layer of sweat. A sea of people bounced in unison to a song with a fast, heavy beat—blacklight causing everything light-colored to glow. He maneuvered along the edge of the writhing crowd.

At the bar, he ordered and gulped a double scotch, his hand trembling like a rookie gunslinger two minutes before his first high noon. He immediately felt dizzy. He set the empty glass on the bar, his vision narrowing until all he could see were objects in the center of his line of sight. He leaned against the bar to stop from crashing to the floor. When the sensation passed, he looked around; everyone seemed to be discreetly watching him.

"Your plan was idiotic and a colossal mistake," he heard. "Get out of here, NOW!"

He double-timed it back around the crowded dance floor, looking up only once—making eye contact with a huge man with a mohawk. The man, fingering his bandaged ear, the gauze glowing in the blacklight, watched Allan push the swinging doors open. Convinced the mohawked giant was following him, Allan, his pulse beating three times for every thud of the furious dance music, ducked into the men's bathroom and locked himself inside the only stall with a door. He dropped the toilet's lid and sat. Unaware he was holding his breath, he expelled a blast of air. His eyes jumped between lyrics and jokes and stick drawings penned and scratched on the stall's walls and door. What if Liam's right? He wondered. What if this is drug-related? Am I over-medicating?

Unsure how much time had passed, Allan found himself at the bathroom's rust-stained sink, the spider-web cracks in the only mirror splintering his face into a clichéd but apt Jekyll and Hyde visual. His face mangled and jagged, Hyde was screaming, desperately trying to convince Allan that stopping a dream from unfolding in real life was a logical course of action. His face intact but aged beyond recognition by fear and anxiety, Jekyll was arguing those actions were proof of a fractured mind.

He splashed cold water on his face, dried it with a paper towel, crept to the bathroom door, and pressed an ear to the cold wood. He heard nothing—no music or talking or chairs being stacked on top of tables.

Is the bar closed? How long have I been here?

He pushed the door open enough to see into the dark hall. To his left was the unlocked door he'd used to enter the Hostel. To his right, light from the bar was leaking through the silver doors' porthole windows.

"You are in danger," he heard. "You must leave."

He eased into the hall, freezing after a single step when the bar's lights went out. A brief silence was interrupted by the sound of the men's room door slamming shut. He stayed still, hoping whoever had shut the lights off had not heard the sound.

The lights came back on. "Go wait in the car," a man said.

Allan sprinted to the exit door and yanked its handle. It turned freely, but the door would not budge. With seconds until the man burst into the hall, Allan frantically twisted the handle and repeatedly threw his shoulder into the door. Still, it would not budge. Spotting light from under an adjacent door, he took two hard steps, slipped into the small room, and silently eased the door closed.

Boxes and chairs and tables were spread haphazardly around the small room. As though he had been expecting Allan, Bob Marley—ONE LOVE printed above his head—smiled hello from the far wall.

How the hell is this poss—

The swinging doors crashed open.

The light!

He slapped at the switch, barely catching it with a fingertip.

In the darkness, his heart thumping so loudly he was sure the man would hear it from the hall, Allan inched away from the door until he heard it swing open and crash against the wall.

He froze.

The light came on.

DaMarcus Kennedy raised his arm; he was holding a gun. He pointed it at Allan's head.

"Don't shoot!" Allan pleaded. "I'm here to help you."

Kennedy closed the door and moved to Allan, stopping with the gun a few inches from his head.

"Please," Allan whimpered, "I'm a psychiatrist. I'm here to—"

"Sit the fuck down," Kennedy ordered. Allan, his eyes locked on the gun, felt for the chair behind him, found it, and sat. Kennedy moved around the desk, opened a drawer, and pulled out a gun that looked big enough to shoot RPGs. He stuffed the smaller gun into a pocket in his black overcoat and aimed the larger gun at Allan's head. "You're here to *what*?"

Allan was no longer concerned about changing the outcome of a dream, and he no longer cared if Kennedy's son was the boy general, or if there even was a boy general; all he cared about was ensuring a large-caliber bullet did not make an enormous exit wound in the back of his skull. The mental image triggered a flashback to a dream—blood and brains coating an office wall.

My blood and brains? he wondered.

"One of my patients is delusional." Allan's voice was thin and panicked. "He has incorporated you, your fiancé, and your son into his del—"

Kennedy cocked the gun. "How do you know I'm having a son?"

Instantly realizing the best way to make his brain-splattering dream a reality was to offer an answer that included Liam Huffy, Witten PD, or dreams of Kennedy's unborn son as the architect of a future Apocalypse, Allan said, "You need to trust me and lay low for—"

Kennedy snorted a laugh and relaxed. He scratched his temple with the gun barrel's tip. *"Lay low?"*

"It will sound crazy, but I have seen—"

Seen what? All of this in a dream? Are you seriously going to tell him that? You really are losing your mind.

"Seen *what?*" Kennedy asked.

Allan could not stop shaking. Even if he knew what to say, he doubted he could force the words out.

"Do I know you?" Kennedy's crinkled brow indicated he was already searching his memory for Allan's image.

He saw me! Allan remembered. "My patient is dangerous," he blurted, now desperate to distract Kennedy before he recalled their short but intense interaction in the downtown station's lobby. "Your family is in danger. You—"

"Yeah." A look of recognition brightened Kennedy's face. "I know you."

The words activated Allan's flight instinct. Time slowed to quarter speed as he scrambled from the chair and sprinted toward the door. Olivia Madson suddenly appeared in the office. He lunged left as her head exploded, coating him and the door and wall with blood and brains. Time sped up and started running at four times normal speed. All sound disappeared. He hurdled Madson's crumpled body and raced to the rear exit. A single, powerful push sent the previously immovable door crashing open. A few hard strides into the alley, he stopped, thinking: Why is Wilhelm here?

Everything went dark.

–

ALLAN'S HEAD FELT like a shaken magic-eight-ball searching for answers to *Where the hell am I?* and *What the hell happened?* Seeing his hand resting on snow sent a shiver racing up his arm and splashing into his brain. He felt a sharp pain near the base of his skull. He touched the area, his finger finding what felt like a hole. He tried to stand but had no strength in his legs. In fact, he could not feel his legs at all.

He spotted the Volvo about fifteen feet away, its rear bumper peaking out from behind a brick building. He strummed his fingers over the building's coarse skin until realizing where he was. "Oh," he stated, unconcerned, as if waking in an alley propped against a dumpster was a regular occurrence.

Movement by his feet drew his attention. A rat scampered up his shin, dismounted, and scurried along the dumpster's edge. No mask? he thought. What a dick. The rat tugged on what looked like a thick, black rope. A dark object about the size and shape of a large pineapple lurched each time the rat tugged on the rope. Allan pulled the object to his leg; it felt like burlap coated in warm, sticky milk. The rat squeaked in protest and disappeared under the dumpster. Allan lifted DaMarcus Kennedy's severed head to eye-level. Blood dripped from the torn neck flesh and coated Allan's shirt and pants. The smell of wet pennies hovered in the cold air.

He dropped Kennedy's head onto his lap and stared into the milky, dead eyes. "I warned you," he whispered. He used a thumb to open and close the mouth. "I know," he made Kennedy say. "I should have *laid low*."

Allan smiled. This is a fucked-up dream.

He dug his fingers into Kennedy's rubbery flesh like a Sous Chef inspecting the evening's main course at a restaurant for cannibals: *Only the freshest heads will do*. A cockroach crawled over his hand and into Kennedy's ear. Allan hurled the head away. Severed heads were one thing, but cockroaches were creepy, even in a dream.

The head tumbled to an upright stop just beyond the dumpster, its position creating the illusion that Kennedy was planted in the alley, his neck and head sprouting from the concrete like a deadlocked flower.

"Get up," he heard. "You must leave."

When one side of Kennedy's face brightened, Allan mustered the strength to stand. He staggered on wobbly legs out from behind the dumpster. At the opposite end of the alley, he saw a white minivan wedged between two police cars—swirling light bars coloring everything in Christmas red and blue. A man wearing a flower-patterned cabana shirt had his flashlight pointed at Kennedy's head. He raised the beam and shone it into Allan's face. "Don't move!" Cabana-man ordered.

During the fraction of a second the beam of light held him motionless, Allan concluded he wasn't dreaming, he was covered in blood from a severed head, and Cabana-man was a cop. Instinct took over and sent him racing to the Volvo. He fired it up and sped away just as cabana-man exited the alley.

Ten minutes later, his pulse finally slowing, he merged into light traffic on Martin Luther King Parkway. Ten minutes after that, his pulse once again started to race when he thought: What if Cabana-man saw my license plate?

AFTER MIDNIGHT. DECEMBER 24.

One Day until Christmas.

The moment cabana-man had started running toward him, Allan's flight instinct overrode all higher brain functions. That instinct gone, he had completed a mental reboot.

That reboot had him terrified.

Everything had seemed real: the taste of his scotch, watching Olivia Madson's head explode and seeing Wilhelm in the alley, feeling Kennedy's severed head in his hands. But for part of it, he had thought he was dreaming. If his mind *were* fracturing, he would eventually lose the ability to discern reality from fantasy. What might he be capable of while *thinking* he was dreaming? Could he hurt someone? *Had* he hurt someone? Had he killed DaMarcus Kennedy and blocked the event from his mind?

By the time he had veered left toward Upper Manor Estates, his paranoia had disappeared. Not because he had found proof that the paranoia was irrational, but because he had lost the ability to process what had happened over the last hours and days. His mind was shutting down. Reality and fantasy were fighting to occupy the same mental space. Events were as likely to be real as imagined. One moment, his reflections, speculations, and deductions were valid; the next, they were toxic, dissolving his gray matter like green alien blood eating through the hull of a disabled spaceship.

Nearing Angels Gorge, his eyes drifted to the rear-view

mirror—a creature was staring back. Its eyes were *his* eyes but dead, its features *his* features but gaunt and angular. The creature had devolved from Allan Abrams into something unrecognizable. Something subhuman. A *thing*.

"This is what it is like to lose your mind," the thing said.

He thought about plunging the Volvo (and the creature driving it) into Angels Gorge. The road ahead blurred as he pictured jagged, snow-covered rocks tearing through the car's flesh, its mangled corpse toppling and rolling, exploding seconds after crashing hundreds of feet below.

The Volvo's tires hitting the bridge's front edge shocked him out of his vision in time to see Wilhelm standing in the middle of the bridge. Allan crushed the brake with both feet and wrenched the wheel hard to the left. A *thud* preceded the Volvo starting to spin. It stopped after completing most of a 360.

He flung the door open and scrambled around the front of the car, the headlights cutting through the darkness and falling snow. Where the hell is he? Allan wondered before noticing a dark streak a few feet past the bumper. Is that blood?

He stepped into the headlight's beam and followed the streak.

Just beyond the end of the bridge, two legs—one bent grotesquely back on itself—were sticking out of a large snowbank.

51

With Chris Tam and DaMarcus Kennedy dead, the DA had concluded Benny Carpenter was orchestrating a coup. And with Carpenter locked down inside the Hostel, the DA did not want to take another step without a judge's approval. Frankie and Button had joined Huffy inside his car to wait for that approval.

Frankie, in the passenger's seat, read a text and *hmphed*.

"What?" Button asked from somewhere in the dark ness of the back seat.

Huffy looked over his shoulder. "You want a booster seat?"

"No," Button replied. "I'm sitting on the stack of vintage Playgirl magazines I found back here."

"Is that even possible?" Frankie said, still looking at the text.

Huffy flipped on the radio. "Is what even possible?"

She *hmphed* again. "Madson's son might survive."

Button blew hot air into his hands. "I've seen stranger things."

"The Netflix series?" Huffy asked, notching up the radio's volume to better hear Toby Keith profess his love of a *Red Solo Cup*.

From the backseat: "What has 200 legs and 37 teeth?" With no response, Button volunteered the answer. "The front row of a Willie Nelson concert."

Huffy notched the volume up again and sang along. "Red solo cup...I fill you up...let's have a party...let's have a party."

It had been a great day on many fronts; everyone was in a

good mood.

"Would you rather...freeze to death or listen to country?" Button answered his own question by exiting the car.

After watching Button walk under the yellow crime scene tape and into the alley, Huffy used a knuckle to draw a spiky-haired happy face in the frost on the driver's side window.

Frankie eyed the drawing. "He our Perp?"

Huffy, using the same knuckle to tap along to the music, gave his happy face a mild case of acne. "Still doesn't feel right."

Frankie was playing Dots on her phone. "Let's not do this again."

Huffy killed the music. "Too many coincidences."

Frankie stuffed her phone between her legs. "Huff, I watched you interview Abrams. You may have seen something, but I didn't. This is regime change. Molly Barnes' statement confirmed it. And after what we saw ten minutes ago on Kennedy's—" She checked the display of her ringing cell phone. "DA," she said before answering the call.

The mention of Molly Barnes toggled Huffy's switch. Three times he had reached out to her while Derek Samuels was at work. After some version of "I'm fine," she had twice hung up on him and once shut the door in his face. But earlier today, hospitalized after a beating Frankie had described as "Not quite bad enough to kill her," Molly Barnes finally drew her line in the sand. Derek Samuels was promptly arrested on multiple domestic violence-related charges.

But Barnes's *other* allegations, if proven, were more problematic for Samuels and his accomplice, Benny Carpenter. Thanks to an automatic life-sentence under Denver's *Biggest Habitual Offenders Statute,* a conviction for Carpenter would end his time as a private citizen. And regardless of what came of his domestic violence charges, Samuels would have at least ten years to regret his choices. Although being locked up with people who weren't fond of ex-law enforcement meant it wasn't a lock that Samuels would make it to his parole hearing.

Frankie ended her call. "Good to go."

—

HUFFY AND FRANKIE, along with detective Jeff Strand, two uniformed officers, and Benny Carpenter, were inside the Hostel. The rest of Strand's surveillance team was outside, as were multiple detectives and Dan Button's CSI team. Several other officers were wrapping up an unsuccessful grid search for the man Strand saw take off in a "light-colored Volvo sedan." And except for Carpenter, the Hostel's staff and patrons had been interviewed and sent home—tagged and released, free to swim away until law enforcement hooked them again in the future. With one exception, every one of those staff and patrons had seen nothing. The lone exception being an intoxicated man wearing a Denver Bronco's jersey who was willing to testify "on a stack of bibles" that the killer was ex-New England Patriots' quarterback, Tom Brady.

"Are you sure?" Huffy asked Strand

"Of everything but the color," Strand answered.

"Huff," Frankie called, waving him over to the bar where she was standing a few feet in front of Benny Carpenter.

Huffy fingered the collar of Strand's flower-patterned Cabana shirt and said, "Aloha." They set off in opposite directions, Strand toward a set of swinging silver doors, and Huffy to the bar.

He pointed at Carpenter's bandaged ear. "You and DaMarcus have a spat?" He shadow-boxed an upper-cut and mimed a bite. "Tyson-Holyfield Three?" A shared look with Frankie confirmed she knew why he was curious about Carpenter's damaged ear. "Where's your earring?" Huffy restated.

"Got mugged." Carpenter leaned against a bar stool, folded

his arms across his chest, and observed Huffy casually but with significant disdain. "Never a cop around when you need one."

Huffy maintained eye contact with Carpenter while asking Frankie, "How long can we keep Benny locked up while we work 24/7 to clear his good name?"

"Couple weeks. A month if we bend the rules." She clicked her tongue. "Two or three if we break 'em."

Carpenter checked his watch. "Let's get this shit over with."

"How'd you lose your earring?" Huffy repeated.

"I told you, I got mugged."

"Did you get a good look at your assailant?" Huffy asked in a concerned voice. "Could you describe her to a sketch artist?"

"Funny," a straight-faced Carpenter said. "You do magic tricks, too?"

"I do," Huffy exclaimed. "Wanna see me make your missing earring appear in an evidence bag from a recent homicide?"

A beat.

"If you found it at a homicide, then find the guy who mugged me, and your case is solved." A smirk. "You're welcome."

"You told officer Strand you were here until sometime after midnight," Frankie stated. "And you returned after we'd arrived. Before you left, did you see anything unusual?"

"Yeah," Carpenter snapped. "A skinny, clean-shaven white dude ran into the bathroom. I didn't see him come out."

"A skinny, clean-shaven white dude?" Huffy repeated derisively. "Is that the gangster equivalent to a bushy-haired black guy?" Carpenter stayed silent. "How do you know he never came out of the bathroom?"

"Not what I said." Carpenter dropped a hand onto each thigh. "Shouldn't you be taking notes so you can pin me to a story? Or at least so you don't fuck up the one I tell you."

"What did this skinny, clean-shaven white dude look like?" Huffy asked, his mind straying to Allan Abrams.

"An accountant," Carpenter answered.

"Short? Tall? Bald?"

"Sure."

"Ever see him before?" Frankie asked.

"Every Tuesday at the Country Club." A wink. "Tuesday's are half-price bellini night." He stepped away from his stool. "This has been fun, but I need my beauty sleep. If you'll excuse —"

Huffy planted a hand into Carpenter's thick chest. "Sit," he ordered.

Carpenter eyeballed Huffy's hand, then slowly lifted his head. "Careful." He leaned back against the stool and mimicked Huffy's earlier mime. "I bite."

Huffy glanced at his shoulder-holstered Glock and extended a forearm toward Carpenter's mouth, inviting him to *chomp away*.

Finished speaking on her radio, Frankie moved into Carpenter's personal space. "Earlier today, your cousin told us an interesting story about you and her boyfriend, Derek Samuels. Molly's a sweet kid. Pretty beat up but sweet. You must really care about her."

Judging by how fast the arrogance evaporated from Carpenter's face, the information had caught him by surprise. "Her personal life ain't my business."

"I'm sure you've heard about Josh Cutter," Huffy stated, drawing Carpenter's attention. "The eight-year-old boy shot to death in front of his mom and sister?"

Carpenter stared vacuously at Huffy.

"Well," Huffy continued, "we've recently obtained evidence that leads us to believe Mark Cooke fired the bullet that killed Josh Cutter. We're hoping you can help us locate Cooke.

You and Mark are still tight, aren't you?" A glance from Huffy had Frankie inching back. "Fun fact," he continued, moving his hand to the butt of his gun, "even when you are in two pieces, your thumbprint can unlock your burner phone. We found a video on DaMarcus's cell phone. I—" He turned to the main doors; two uniformed officers had entered and were walking quickly toward the bar. "I gotta tell ya," Huffy continued, "Mark Cooke on fire sure brought out the black in your eye—"

A dramatic shift in Carpenter's expression caused Huffy and Frankie to draw their weapons. The two uniformed officers broke into a sprint.

"Turn around!" Frankie ordered. "Hands on the bar!"

Carpenter's eyes bounced between Huffy, Frankie, and the onrushing officers, no doubt calculating the odds of escape. Realizing those odds were zero, he reluctantly complied. The officers cuffed him and led him away.

Huffy, already around the bar, grabbed a whiskey bottle from the liquor wall. With Frankie scrutinizing his every move, he poured a shot into a beer mug and set the bottle and the glass on the bar in front of him.

"*Literally* cutting the head off the RUV snake is probably a blessing." She leaned over the bar and dumped the whiskey in the sink. They exchanged he-said-she-said looks. *That was unnecessary*, his said; *You're welcome,* hers replied. She dropped back into her chair. "The next guy can't be as bad as Kennedy."

Huffy shrugged, starting back around the bar. "A lot of people said that about Obama."

"Boss?"

Frankie, smiling, wheeled around.

A female officer pointed to a security camera mounted above the liquor wall. "Surveillance cameras are live. Still haven't found the footage, though."

"It'll be on a server at Madson's house," Huffy said.

"Attorney-client privilege?" the female officer queried.

"No shortage of defense lawyers in Hell," Huffy answered, now beside Frankie, "should Kennedy and Madson choose to challenge the search."

They watched the officer nod then walk away.

"This was a regime change," Frankie said, picking up where they left off in Huffy's car. "Molly Barnes told us that Carpenter stole drugs from the RUV's stockpile and gave them to Samuels to sell inside Bachman. Carpenter either figured he'd make a better boss than Kennedy, or he was worried Kennedy would discover his side-business. Either way, the story is regime change."

"Maybe."

"*Maybe?* It's a cliché, but Samuels and Carpenter had Palette's tongue cut off because he'd discovered the scheme and threatened to rat to Bachman staff or Kennedy." Huffy didn't respond. "It also explains why they had to kill him before he was executed; they needed to send a message to anyone else who might talk."

"Jerome Banks said a third person was involved with Carpenter and Samuels. Abrams counseled Palette and Samuels, and he could have met Carpenter through either. If Abrams is the third person, he'd have a motive to kill Palette and the other RUV members if they found about what was going on."

"Your theory is a psychiatrist, without as much as a speeding ticket, is a drug kingpin offing RUV members?" She shook her head. "I have never seen you take such unsubstantiated leaps. You are disregarding evidence because you have got it in your head that Abrams is involved. Even rookie detectives don't make that mistake. Aren't you supposed to *open—*"

"I *have* opened every door and—"

"You haven't even *knocked* on the door that leads to Carpenter and Sam—"

He tried to walk past her, but she caught him by the elbow. "*Please* tell me this isn't about his wife."

He considered her hand, then pulled free and walked away.

52

Naked, his bloody clothes stripped off and stuffed into the washing machine, Allan rinsed his hands and forearms, a mix of blood and soap suds swirling down the drain of the laundry room's stainless steel sink. That has to be it, he thought. Temporary Schizotypal Personality Disorder brought on by extreme stress, fatigue, and a lack of sleep. Paranoia, magical thinking, hearing voices, an inability to distinguish reality from fantasy; all were symptoms of TSPD. But what about the bridge? He dried his arms and hands, his mind trying to block the fact hallucinations weren't a symptom of TSPD. What other than a hallucination would explain what happened on the bridge? The legs sticking out of the snowbank were the rear legs of a deer. He'd hit a deer, not Wilhelm. He had halluc—

Swirling red and blue light caught his eye.

Through the open laundry room door, he could see out the kitchen's bay window. A police car was in the driveway.

It isn't TSPD! he thought, his heart instantly smashing against the back of his breastplate. Cabana man saw my license plate! I killed DaMarcus—

The doorbell rang.

Don't answer it! Hide your clothes! You didn't kill anyone. You hit a deer. You're para—

The doorbell rang again.

He searched a small pile of dirty clothes and put on the only item that fit, Clara's silk robe. Unaware of the blood smear on his cheek and on the sash of the robe, he composed himself on his way to the front door.

"Hello," he said, praying he sounded calm.

"Evening, sir. I'm officer Leslie Strange." The cold air wrapped her words and caused her heavy, black jacket to crackle with even the smallest movement. She glanced at his lower third, her expression causing him to wonder if the silk robe wasn't long enough to cover his man parts. "Sorry for the late-night house call," she continued, her left hand on the butt of her holstered gun. "Your lights were on, so we figured someone was still up."

The word *we* had Allan looking to the police car in the driveway. Seeing no one inside doubled his pulse. Where's her partner?

Officer Strange jerked a thumb to her right. "We're responding to your neighbor's monitored alarm. There is evidence of a break-in and some blood at the point of entry." She gazed past him and into the house. "Nobody answered, and the house is dark. Have you seen your neighbors recently?"

"They're in Arizona…since Thanksgiving."

"Any chance they came home?" She again looked past him into the house. Her fascination with whatever was behind him reignited his paranoia. "Sir?" he heard her say. He couldn't respond; his vocal cords had short-circuited. He fidgeted with the robe's sash. Her eyes dropped, then immediately popped back up, her expression more serious now. "Are you the homeowner, sir?"

"Yes, my wife and I are—"

"Where is your wife this eve—"

Officer Strange stopped talking and was now staring intently over his shoulder. He turned. Clara was at the foot of the stairs. "What's wrong?" she asked. "Who's in our backyard?"

"Someone is in our backyard?" Allan's imagination got the better of him, and he pictured a SWAT team rappelling from the roof and crashing through the windows to capture the murderous psychiatrist inside.

"Evening, ma'am," Officer Strange said. "My partner is doing a perimeter check. Nothing to worry about. Are you okay?"

"Yes," Clara grumbled tiredly.

"Sorry to bother you so late. There was a break-in next door. Did you happen to see or hear anything unusual tonight or over the last few days? Cars you didn't recognize, strangers in the area."

Clara hesitated as if she'd remembered something but then decided it wasn't important. "No."

"Thank you, ma'am." Officer Strange returned her attention to Allan and pointed to his face. "I noticed a bit of blood on your cheek." She lowered her eyes to his midsection. "And on *your* sash," she added playfully.

He checked the sash and noticed the blood. His mind raced, searching for an explanation. "A deer," he finally said. "I hit one…a deer…with my car. On the way home. The blood is from the deer."

Officer Strange's deepening dimples reassured him the explanation had been unnecessary. "With the blood next door, and the recent home invasions, I wanted to make sure you didn't have any unwanted house guests forcing you to," she fired a finger gun at his chest, "get rid of the cops." Allan tried to laugh but instead released an awkward blotch of sound. "Sorry for the late-night visit," she repeated. "Keep your doors and windows locked, and call 911 if you notice anything unusual."

Unusual? he wanted to say, watching her walk to her patrol car. *Where do you want me to start?*

"You hit a deer?" Clara asked.

"Yeah." He locked the door. "On the bridge."

She yawned and headed up the stairs. Shaken, he followed her to bed.

53

Allan's senses woke reluctantly and one at a time. His vision last to rise, he squinted at the clock radio; its red digits reading 8:32. For the first time in months, he had fallen asleep the moment his head hit the pillow. He did not recall waking even once. He did, however, recall parts of three dreams. In one, he delivered DaMarcus Kennedy's baby boy, commented on his adorable smattering of freckles, then snapped his neck and dumped him in a trash can. In another—a dream he'd had several times recently—the boy general surveyed the valley of the dead as thousands of resurrected corpses stood. The third dream was the most vivid. In it, Clara was on the backyard shop's floor holding their newborn son—someone pointing a gun at his blood-covered head.

He stretched, his movements against the comforter the only sound. The bed empty beside him, he listened for Clara in the bathroom or downstairs. Picturing her downstairs triggered a vague feeling that forced him out of bed, his foot landing on Clara's silk robe. It took him a moment to realize the robe's significance.

He raced to the laundry room.

The washer was empty. He checked the dryer, thinking Clara had noticed his clothes in the washing machine and run them through. The dryer was cold and empty. His panicked eyes moved in every direction at once until he noticed blood on the attached mudroom's doorknob. *Did I touch that door last night?* Above the knob was a partial bloody palm print, too small to be his. *Oh God,* he thought. *Clara.*

His knees almost buckled, dread hardening his insides like quick-drying cement.

Wilhelm has Clara…and my son.

—

THE ULTRASOUND TECH used the transducer probe to spread globs of gel over Clara's belly. He had tried a few times to make small talk; Clara wasn't sure she'd even acknowledged the attempts. She was tired, but the early hour was not why she looked and felt like she had been run over by a Monster Truck.

The reason was Allan.

Over the last few days, as his behavior had shifted from erratic to bizarre, her concern about his mental state had progressed from worry to fear. And this morning, that fear became terror when she found his bloody clothes in the washing machine. He had lied about hitting a deer. There was no damage to the Volvo. And other than a handprint on the driver-side door, the only blood she had found—and there was *a lot* of it—was *inside* the car.

Before coming to her ultrasound appointment, she had done what she had to do. Allan had left her no choice; he was a threat. She *had* to protect her child.

"Clara?"

"Sorry?" she said, barely aware of the tech.

"I asked if you had picked out any names for her yet?"

Clara opened her mouth to speak, but the first name on a shortlist of potential baby names was lodged in her throat. She eyed the tech in a state of suspended animation until finally forcing out a garbled, *"Her?"*

"Oh shit," the tech exclaimed, realizing his mistake. "You didn't know. *Shit-shit-shit*. Clara, I'm *so* sorry."

"But…" She looked to the monitor, her confusion evident. "We're having a boy."

The flustered tech shook his head. "Early in pregnancy, it can be harder to tell the sex. But at this stage and with the image's clarity, he is *definitely* a she."

"But with MCDA twins, both children are the same..." She again glanced at the monitor. "Is Doctor Williams here?"

The embarrassed tech apologized again and agreed to check.

The shock of learning she was having a girl passed before the tech had left the room. For the first time in twenty years, the voices of her dead children were silent. Memories of failed pregnancies and false alarms had vanished. Her fears related to her child's future—and whether she would even *have* a future—disappeared. Her daughter would thrive; Clara could feel it. Mother's intuition to the power of ten. She passed a hand over her belly. Every choice she made was now critical because it impacted someone of infinite importance. All that mattered was her daughter.

A female doctor entered the small exam room and closed the door. "Hi, Clara. Doctor Williams isn't here, but I would be happy to answer any questions you have about your ultrasound."

Clara shook her inhaler and puffed. She got nothing. She tried again, and again she got nothing.

"Empty?" the doctor asked.

Clara nodded.

"Are you okay?"

"Fine." Clara dropped the inhaler into her purse. Despite no longer caring how her male child was now female, she said, "We are—*were* having MCDA twins. The twin who died was a boy."

A nod acknowledged the doctor understood Clara's implied question. "It is rare, but early in development, one of two male MCDA twins can lose a Y Chromosome and become female. I assume the sex was to be a surprise?"

"Yes."

"When this happens, the female twin will be born with Turner Syndrome. TS has a wide range of side effects, most minor, but some can be serious, things like skeletal abnormalities and organ defects. Doctor Williams will want to meet with you and your husband regarding this development." Clara's silence prompted the doctor to ask, "Do you have any other questions?"

Clara shook her head, and the doctor left.

Most parents, Clara assumed, would already be on their cell phones Googling if what sounded like fiction was fact. And if a male embryo *could* become female, most parents would then Google the risks Turner Syndrome posed to their child. But Clara's phone remained in her purse, her panic unrelated to Turner Syndrome and how it might affect her daughter. Clara's panic was the same she had felt hours earlier when she found Allan's bloody clothes.

Allan was a threat to her daughter.

54

Police Chief Tom Dickson, seated in his high-backed leather chair, returned the folder to Huffy. "Why didn't Frankie come to me with this?"

Huffy, standing on the opposite side of Dickson's large desk, knew the end-a-round was a short-term fix; Frankie would find out, as would Dickson. But there was no turning back now. "She's busy," he said, his voice scarcely above a whisper as if a lie told at a lower volume lessened the betrayal.

"It is weak," Dickson said. "But if Frankie's on board, go ahead and ask the DA for a warrant."

Huffy could not leave Dickson's office fast enough. After a quick visit with the DA, he returned to his office to prepare his interrogation. He was hopeful the DA would get him the arrest warrant in time, but even without it, once he and Allan Abrams were locked in a room, Abrams was not leaving. Although getting him to the station might prove tricky. The thought made Huffy chuckle, knowing Abrams would not come voluntarily, not after their last Q&A. And handcuffs and a police escort would guarantee a lawyer, which Huffy preferred to avoid.

In the middle of his interrogation planning, Huffy checked the display on his ringing cell phone. "Holy shit," he blurted. Before he finished saying hello, a hysterical Allan Abrams cut him off.

"Liam, I found blood on our back door. Clara's blood! Wilhelm has her. He is dangerous and—"

"Doc, calm—"

"Wilhelm has Clara! He is delusional and capable of anything. You have to help me find her before he—"

"I can't help you if I don't understand what you are saying. Calm down and tell me what's happening."

Abrams did, then agreed to come to the station.

Instead of thanking Santa Claus or whatever magical force had dropped a frantic Allan Abrams into his lap, Huffy dialed Clara. As he waited for her to answer, words she had recently spoken reverberated in his skull. *I'm worried Allan might hurt himself...or me.*

55

Allan ended the call with Huffy, redialed Clara, and hammered the gas, the Volvo's roof almost clipping the garage's rising overhead door. He stashed his Luger under the driver's seat. Until a few minutes ago, the Luger, his grandfather's, had sat untouched for thirteen years in a shoebox in the closet. He doubted he would even remember how to load or fire it.

"*Fuck!*" He slammed a hand against the steering wheel. Once again, Clara had not answered her phone.

"*FUCK!*"

Competing voices were pulling his mind in opposite directions. In one moment, signs he had seen over the last several days would make perfect sense; they were messages from a powerful force meant to show him something. A moment later, those same signs were simply odd events and strange coincidences being warped by a mind stretched beyond its limit by exhaustion, stress, and grief. His fractured mind was finding proof of what it believed, even when no proof existed; it was feeding its own paranoia. Was the blood on the mudroom door meaningless, or did it mean Clara was hurt? Dead? Had he been at the Hostel by coincidence, or had a craving for a Tahiti Treat led him there? Had every step and misstep and every planned or unplanned turn ended with him there at the precise moment real-life was unfolding as it had in his dream? Or was his fractured mind twisting the timing of events so that his dreams merely *appeared* to have foretold the future?

Had he mentioned the boy general to Wilhelm? I must have, he thought. Wilhelm incorporated the boy general into his delusion and decided he was either my son or Kennedy's. Wilhelm's delusion made him extremely dangerous. When what is real seems imagined and what is imagined seems real, a broken mind was capable of anything. A delusional old man did not require supernatural powers to shoot or stab a defenseless woman and her unborn son. He would not listen to reason, and neither logic nor facts would convince him his delusion was not real.

He believes my son has to die and will stop at nothing to kill him. I no longer have a choice. No matter how crazy I sound, I have to tell Liam. He can help me find Clara and my son.

56

Things had not gone as planned, but he could not let that affect the outcome. He had watched Clara park down the street and wait. After Allan sped away in his car, she pulled into the garage and, soon after, appeared in the bedroom, where she threw four suitcases on the bed and filled them with armfuls of clothes.

The suitcases overflowing, she stopped, her anxiety visible even from his distant vantage point. She pulled her cell phone from her pocket, but instead of answering, she pressed it against her chest, afraid to look at the display.

He saw the immense relief when she finally checked. After a short conversation, she hung up and started to unpack.

The cop, he thought.

Time had run out. He could not fail again. He would try one last time. If it did not work, *he* would do what had to be done.

57

Huffy, reviewing his interrogation plan, had not heard his office door open, but the vibrations from the door slamming nearly shook him out of his chair. Activity around his office ceased, and heads snapped up like a colony of curious gophers. All eyes were on Frankie, her fists indenting the top of his desk.

"I spent the last twenty minutes convincing Dickson not to fire you! Not suspend; not send you on a forced vacation; *FIRE!*"

Perhaps in response to the glistening, apologetic sheen coating his face, or because her intense surge of anger had short-circuited her emotional fuse-box, her ferociousness fell away quickly. She slumped into a chair in front of his desk.

Activity around the office returned to normal.

"Why?" she asked, her voice listless. "Why did you go behind my back to..." She sighed.

He had known Dickson would find out Frankie had not requested Abrams's arrest warrant. He had assumed the lie would cost him a suspension or maybe a temporary demotion. But his job? He had not contemplated that possibility. Still, he was confident the ends would justify the means. With the right kind of pressure, Abrams would crack. Once he did, the dust would settle, the consequences of his end-around would run their course, and he would repair the damage he had done to their relationship.

He slid a file across his desk.

She glanced at it and shot him a look, her anger threatening to return.

"*Read* it," he pleaded.

Her eyes locked on his, she lifted the file off his desk. She read for about a minute. "Dickson signed off on the warrant *without* the lab work?" She slid the file back to him. "Or did you lie about that, too?"

"Button has it on a rush," he said somberly.

"Why the hell would Abrams want Palette or *any* RUV member dead?"

He hesitated, sensing that beneath her calm, embers still had enough heat to reignite her fire. "Does it matter?"

Her resigned expression answered for her: *I guess not.*

"Maybe there is no why," he added. "Maybe he is just crazy."

"Hard to hide that much crazy."

A shrug. "Not a stretch to assume a shrink could fool a few people. And it's possible he didn't hide anything. His wife says he has a history of breakdowns and self-medicating. Maybe the death of his son fried his last wire. All I know is too many coincidences means they are not coincidences. Everything he told us was bullshit or self-serving. If not through Abrams, how would the old man know what he does?"

Another sigh, this one deep and prolonged like she was trying to force out all remaining resistance to his argument. "Have you sent someone to pick him up?"

Huffy smiled. "He came here on his own. He is in Interview Room One."

She pushed herself to her feet. "And if you're wrong?"

He dismissed the possibility with a look.

"He's a psychiatrist who teaches interrogation techniques," she added. "You sure you're up to the challenge?"

"He was a mess when he called me. He's terrified, thinks the old man has his wife." A confident glow spread across his face. "I'll be done with him in under five minutes."

58

Alternating between pacing and sitting, Allan sat in one of the interview rooms two empty chairs, dropped his elbows onto the small, stainless-steel table, and squeezed a handful of hair in each hand. *Why the fuck am I in here? And what the hell is taking him so long? Clara is—What if I can't convince him? Or—Jesus! What if it is already too late? What if she—*

Huffy entered the interview room—a laptop pinned to his hip—followed by a uniformed officer carrying a file box.

Allan bolted to his feet. "Clara's missing! I need you to help me find her." Huffy calmly set the laptop on the table and sat. The officer dropped the file box beside the laptop. "I found her blood on our back door!" Allan continued, his frenzied mind missing the significance of the officer closing the door, turning, and crossing his muscular arms across his chest. "This will sound insane, but Wilhelm has her. He is dangerous. I need you to—"

"Calm—"

"Wilhelm is *dangerous!* He has incorporated my family into his delusion. I *need* you—"

"I need *you* to answer—"

He pounded the table with both palms. "My wife and son —"

"I'll come back in a few hours." Huffy closed the laptop.

"*Wait!*" Allan knew Huffy was his only chance to save Clara. "I'll answer your questions."

Huffy gestured with an upturned hand for Allan to sit. He

did. "Where did you go last night after you left here?"

"Wilhelm has my—"

"*Where* did you go?"

Allan jumped out of his chair, his feet almost leaving the ground. "My wife and son are going to die! I don't have time for games." He started for the door. The officer refused to let him leave. He spun around. "Liam, what the fuck is going on?"

Huffy answered by eyeing the empty chair across from him.

Allan, refusing to sit, tried to calm himself. He had to convince Huffy to help find Clara. "I know it sounds crazy, but Wilhelm is not who he seems to be, and his delusion makes him dangerous. He has Clara and my son. Please, help me find —"

Huffy held up a sheet of paper he'd removed from the file box. "Any idea what this is?"

"I don't *care!*" Allan blasted. "I need—"

"It is a warrant for your arrest for the murder of—"

"I haven't killed *anyone!* Listen to what I'm telling you! It's Wilhelm! He—"

"Allan Abrams, you have the right—"

He launched himself toward Huffy, smashing both palms against the table. Huffy did not flinch. "I know my rights. I work for the fucking DA, *remember?*" Huffy eyed the officer, who grabbed Allan by his elbows. Allan struggled, but the officer cuffed him and forcefully planted him back in his chair. Allan's chest was heaving, his face radiating enough heat to raise the room's temperature. "Wilhelm is going to kill my wife and son. What is wrong with you? Are you stupid or just dead inside?"

Straight-faced, Huffy said, "Answer my questions or spend the night in jail, and we'll try again in the morning."

Allan's energy drained away; Clara and his son would be dead in the morning. He had to convince Huffy they were in danger, and he had to convince him *now*. He acknowledged his rights and rejected an offer for a lawyer.

"For the last time, where did you go last night after you left here?"

"Home. An Officer Strange can verify that."

"Stop anywhere on the way?"

Beads of sweat streaking his face and neck, Allan flashed back to the Circle K and the Hostel.

"No."

"Didn't get gas or pick up cream for your morning coffee?"

"No."

Huffy opened the laptop and turned it so Allan could see the image of a silver Volvo parked in front of a Circle-K. "What do you see?"

Allan's eyes swept over the screen on their way to Huffy. "Wilhelm has incorporated my family into his delusion. He's dangerous. We are wasting time that Clara and my son don't have."

Huffy swapped the image for a video and started it. "How about now?"

"Liam," he whimpered, ignoring the video, "I need you to believe me. Clara—"

"*Riiiiiight*, there." Huffy paused the video and pressed a finger to the screen.

Allan relented and viewed the image. He shuddered, every drop of blood instantly draining from his face.

"This video is from early this morning outside a bar owned by DaMarcus Kennedy." He laced his fingers behind his head. "If you left here and drove straight home, how did your car show up on security video from a convenience store a few miles from the Hostel, and later," tilting his head toward the laptop, "on our surveillance footage?" He dropped his hands to his lap. "On that note, not long after *your* Volvo makes its appearance, someone separated Kennedy's head from his body and redecorated a back office with the contents of Olivia Madson's skull." He paused. "Lucky for you, her son survived, so I can't charge you with his murder."

"I haven't killed any—"

"One of our officers saw a man in the alley where we found both pieces of Kennedy." He glanced at the paused image on the laptop. "The man sped away in a light-colored Volvo sedan."

"That is not my..." his voice trailed off.

Huffy restarted the video and paused it after a few seconds. "How long do you think it'll take our techs to clean up the blurred license plate on this *light-colored* Volvo sedan?"

Allan tried to speak but couldn't.

"By the way," Huffy continued, "did you hear about the kerfuffle on the MLK Parkway last night?" He shook his head. "Last year, a traffic stop that ended with an officer-involved shooting wouldn't have caused such a fuss. But that's the new normal, I suppose." A smirk. "What I find fascinating in an unexplainable cosmic sense is that the MLK is sixteen miles long and has dozens of access points. But the shooting occurred at a location that caused us to close the three on-ramps nearest to the Hostel. Also, as luck would have it, an officer redirecting traffic at one of those three on-ramps happened to recognize the driver of a silver—"

"*Okay!* I was there! And, yes, I saw Kennedy. But I didn't kill him. *Wilhelm* did."

"So you *were* at the Hostel and in the alley?"

"*Yes*, but I don't remember what happened. I had a drink in the bar. Someone might have drugged me."

"Someone drugged you?"

"I don't *know*," Allan answered, growing angrier and more confused by the second. "I am simply saying it is *possible* because I don't remember everything."

"Really?" Huffy pulled out another evidence bag, this

one containing a scotch glass covered with fingerprint dust. "Maybe you shouldn't mix alcohol and prescription medication."

Allan could only stare at the glass, certain it was his from the Hostel.

"How about we start with what you *do* remember."

"I saw Wilhelm in the alley, but then everything went black. I must have passed out. When I woke up, Kennedy's head was..." He stopped. His words were those of a raving lunatic. Every word providing more proof that he deserved to be locked up until his delusion (assuming it was temporary) passed. "Look, Liam, I know this sounds crazy, but Wilhelm is not who appears to be. He is dangerous. That's why I had Sergeant Murphy test my coffee and why I had Wilhelm's room searched. I thought he was drugging me."

"The old man is *also* drugging you?" Huffy's tone was as skeptical as his twisted face. "Convenient considering the circumstances, no?"

"I'm *not* lying!" He felt his energy returning. "Ask Sergeant Murphy. He tested my coffee and—"

"Yeah, Rolo mentioned some psycho was slipping you sweetener." Huffy tisked. "Careful, Doc. That shit's linked to strokes—"

"Stop patronizing me! I know how this sounds. I was wrong about the coffee, but I told you about searching Wilhelm's room at Rod—"

"I *found out* about the search," Huffy corrected. "And if memory serves, you told me you were worried he might hurt himself."

"If I had told you I thought Wilhelm was drugging me, you would have thought I was..."

A short silence.

"Speaking of crazy," Huffy said. "You've had breakdowns before, right?"

Stunned, Allan took a second to respond. "What the hell are you talking about?"

"I heard you went," a so-so hand gesture, "*a little nuts* after one of your kids died."

Allan clenched his fists so tightly he could feel the tendons in his palms. "After my third child died, I spent a few weeks in bed. I was depressed. Who wouldn't be?"

A beat.

"When my daughter died, I went to her funeral in the morning and caught a rapist in the afternoon."

Allan felt his insides harden. He wanted to punch Huffy in the face and point out that alcoholic cops with anger issues weren't exactly shining examples of how to cope with anything, let alone the death of a child.

"According to Doctor Lam," Huffy continued, "everyone who has met with Wilhelm agrees that, other than a coffee-based idiosyncrasy and a lack of appetite, he is as sane as me or..." A snigger. "Well, as sane as me, anyway."

This is crazy, Allan thought. I haven't killed anyone. How can I prove—

"The picture!" He jumped to his feet. "I can prove Wilhelm hasn't aged since 1945!"

Huffy creased his brow and shook his head sympathetically. "*Jesus*, Doc."

"*It's true!* I'll show you a picture of Wilhelm and his great-grandson in New York after they were liberated from a Nazi Death Camp."

"He has a *great*-grandson, too? From the real or imaginary side of the fam—"

"Let me show you the goddamn picture!"

The officer forced Allan back into his chair as Huffy worked the keyboard. He turned the laptop around. Seeing the image, Allan felt all hope drain from his body; Clara and his son were going to die.

"This is a spider from Iraq with a three-foot leg span," Huffy crowed, thumbing at the monitor. "Do you want to see a picture of a fifty-foot shark eating a helicopter?" He snapped the laptop closed. "Your picture wouldn't prove shit. And even if there is a picture and it is authentic, how do you know the great-grandson isn't Wilhelm? An alternative theory to Wilhelm not aging for eighty years *might* be that he grew up to resemble his grandfather."

Allan had missed that possibility. It took him a moment to formulate a response. "But the grandfather's name was Vilhelm Weissand. The great-grandson was Marbach, Werner Carl Marbach. I saw his grave in Denver."

A shrug. "Maybe the trauma of losing his great-gramps fried Werner's wires, and he created a fantasy world where *he* was Grapplin gramps."

Allan had missed that possibility, as well.

"Liam, I—"

"When I brought you in to talk to the old man, you told me people with delusional disorders interpret information in ways that support their delusions and, when required, they turn to science fiction and the supernatural. You also said people with substance abuse disorders could be delusional. With your history of breakdowns and the fact you pop Thorazine—a drug with side effects that include psychotic breaks—like smarties, are you sure you want to stick with Wilhelm being 150 years old? And that he got the better of a murderous psychopath three times his size and a third his age? A psychopath who was always armed and surrounded by people willing to kill to protect him." Another scoffing head shake. "You might have a New York Times bestseller there, Doc."

"If Kennedy was so big and strong, and he was *always* armed and *always* surrounded by people willing to kill to protect him, how did I get to him?" Allan fired back. Instead of responding, Huffy dug in the file box. "Liam," Allan pleaded. "I wouldn't believe me if I were in your..."

Allan's jaw locked at the sight of the two plastic evidence bags Huffy had just set on the table.

"You've heard of Occam's Razor, Doc? The theory that when all things are equal, the simplest explanation is usually correct?" He patted the larger evidence bag. "Care to guess whose blood we found on these—sorry, on *your* clothes?"

Allan stared at the clothes inside the bag, the same clothes he had left in the washing machine. *Did Clara give you those? Was she the one who told you I went 'a little nuts'? Why would she—*

"Based on preliminary lab work," Huffy continued, "we are confident *your* clothes contain significant quantities of DaMarcus Kennedy's and Olivia Madson's blood." He shifted his hand to the smaller evidence bag. "A thumbprint from these Chester Jefferies leather gloves matched a print from your belt buckle, as well as prints we found at the Hostel. They also matched prints from an exterior door handle at the warehouse where someone barbecued Chris Tam. That door handle contained traces of human skin, which we've sent for analysis." A pause. "But we know whose DNA we'll find, don't we?" Huffy used a thumb from one hand to rub the palm of the other. "How's your hand?" The action and question had Allan recalling the flesh torn from his palm by an icy door handle behind Box Man's cardboard home.

"You remember that warehouse, don't you, Doc? The one across the street from the pharmacy you drove to during a blizzard—ignoring several closer all-night pharmacies—to fill a *self*-prescribed order for the anti-psychotic drug, Thorazine?" Huffy packed the bags back into the file box and stood. "The only delusional psycho Clara needs to worry about is you."

Allan leaped from his chair. *"Please!"* The handcuffs broke his skin and lubricated his wrists with blood. "Wilhelm is going to kill—" The officer forced him back into his seat. "If Wilhelm kills my wife and son, it's your fault! You are *killing* them, you pigheaded sonofa—"

Huffy turned at the door. "You convinced Palette to kill himself and gave him enough PCP to do it. You killed Chris Tam. Last night, you surprised Kennedy in the alley, and when Madson saw you, you killed her. I have no idea why you did any of it, but I have enough evidence to make *why* irrelevant."

Huffy had one foot out the door when Allan shrieked, "Wilhelm's shirt!" Huffy stopped. "The one he was wearing when he turned himself in. It had blood on the sleeve. You saw it. Test it! It is Sedrick Palette's blood."

Huffy tapped a temple. "No detail left unchecked, remember? I tested the old man's clothes. The 'blood' on his shirt was dirt and coffee."

Huffy left to the sound of Allan's incoherent screaming.

Later, Sergeant Murphy helped an exhausted and defeated Allan Abrams exchange his psychiatrist uniform for an orange DOC jumpsuit and locked him in a holding cell.

CHRISTMAS EVE

Seated on a sweat-stained, three-inch-thick mattress atop the holding cell's single bed, his elbows on his knees and fists pressed into his cheeks, Allan heard multiple clangs as the latches in the cell's eight-inch-thick steel door disengaged. Sergeant Murphy entered and set an Applebee's bag on a small counter in the corner. "Figured you would prefer Christmas dinner from Applebee's to whatever slop is on the menu tonight."

Allan eyed the open cell door, thoughts of racing out and saving his family overridden by legs that refused to move.

Murphy turned just outside the door. "You've always been nice to me, Doc. This whole mess is...well, it's..." His tender look reflected concern and pity. "You'll feel better if you eat." He pulled the door closed.

Allan listened to heavy steps on the concrete fade away.

The scent of stuffing and spiced gravy soon had him wondering when he had last eaten. He couldn't recall, but hunger was not the reason his intestines were tangled like a box of Christmas lights. Hours had passed since his arrest—hours spent trapped and helpless, unable to convince anyone his wife and son were in danger. He may as well have been chained to a chair five feet from Clara as Wilhelm plunged a knife into her belly or placed a gun to her temple and pulled the trigger.

The thought had him recalling a recent dream: Clara on the floor of the backyard shop holding his son—a gun, a Luger, pointed at his blood-coated head. He'd woke before he could see whose shaking hand was holding the gun. It must have been Wilhelm, he thought. Who else could it be?

Helplessness and fear combined like volatile chemicals and produced a violent and sudden explosion of rage. He rocketed to his feet. Releasing a series of unintelligible roars, he smashed his fists into the wall—one fist, then the other, over and over and over until concrete chips fell to the floor and blood streaked the wall.

Anger, hopelessness, and adrenaline masked the pain from the broken bones in his hands. He pressed his forehead against the wall, his arms dangling limply at his sides, a steady stream of tears falling to the floor.

He eased backward until the backs of his knees hit the bed. He sat. Tributaries of blood had merged at various points on the grey, concrete wall and formed a single stream pooling where the wall met the floor.

He examined his broken hands, flipping them over and back, repeatedly flaring his fingers and tightening his hands into fists. *Why don't I feel any pain?* He rose off the bed and returned to the wall. He fingered the damage. *I punched a hole in concrete?*

The surreal event should have resulted in a slap to the face to wake himself from the dream. But he was not dreaming; he knew that. And oddly, that made sense, as did his unbroken hands and the small hole in the concrete.

It all made sense.

"She is still alive," he heard.

He spun around, expecting to find a guard speaking through the door's service hatch. Seeing no one, he turned back to the red-streaked wall.

"You need to get home," the same voice said. "She is still alive."

Again, he spun around. Again, he saw no one.

He had spent his entire adult life helping people on every rung of the ladder between sanity to insanity. He was now free-falling down that ladder, snapping rung after rung as he gained speed. Although he still possessed an awareness that a border between those two worlds existed, he had no idea what that awareness meant. Did it mean his mind was salvageable? Could he still climb his way back to sanity? Or did even the most broken minds possess that knowledge? Did Charles Manson, Ted Bundy, and others like them occasionally think: Man, I am one fucked up individual, or were they oblivious to their mental illness?

He fell hard against the wall and closed his eyes, scouring his mind for markers of mental illness. If he found them, he was confident he could backtrack his way to sanity and, in the process, destroy the rapidly replicating cancer infecting his mind. But instead of searching for those markers, his mind returned to the moment he had realized Wilhelm was delusional. At that moment, Wilhelm's body language and expression had made it clear he had lost his will to go on, but, at the same time, he was terrified of the consequences of stopping. Allan then recalled words Wilhelm had spoken in the cemetery in Denver. *But since Hitler's death, the voices have provided whatever help I required: strength, stealth, speed...a power outage at a maximum-security prison.*

He opened his eyes and fixed them on the cell door—Don't be stupid. He stepped to it—You have lost your mind. He gripped the service hatch, blood surging to his muscles and filling him with immense strength. He pulled. The door did not budge. He increased his force, but the door refused to give. He pulled harder, and harder, and harder, until...a *click.*

The door separated from the frame...

This is impossible. I must be dreaming.

...and squeaked as he eased it open.

"You need to get home," he heard. "She is still alive."

–

REGARDLESS OF HOW he had got out of his cell—the most reasonable assumption being Sergeant Murphy had failed to close the door—Allan wasn't going to waste the opportunity. And he knew he was on borrowed time, a Christmas Eve skeleton staff likely the *only* reason no one had discovered his empty cell.

Miraculously, he had made it to the underground garage, where he realized his key fob was in a plastic bag on a shelf in the personal property division. Then, he remembered the hide-a-key.

The dry-cleaned suit he had forgotten in the backseat now covered all but the collar of his orange DOC jumpsuit. If the Volvo and his civilian clothes allowed him to slip past the lot attendant, he would head home, praying he was not somehow connected to the stream of consciousness of his future-self. It has to be a dream, he thought, visualizing Clara and his newborn son in the backyard shop—a gun pointed at his son. It cannot be real. How could it be real? For the first time, he realized the Luger was under his seat. In his dream, the gun pointed at his son was a Luger. Does that mean Clara is safe? he wondered. If Wilhelm doesn't have the Luger, is my family safe?

"Get moving," he whimpered to the driver of the Jeep Wrangler ahead of him. Instead of waving as he drove by the attendant booth, the wrangler's driver had stopped to chat.

What if this *is* a dream? he wondered. Dreams were short, but *within* a dream, a lifetime could pass. Was it possible that all the recent craziness was a dream? Was there no rational explanation for the previous week's unbelievable events (and those of the last five minutes) because he was dreaming?

"*Wake up!*" he shouted at his real-world self, oblivious to the station's now wailing escape alarm. If he could force his real-world eyes to open, he would wake Clara and tell her about his bizarre dream. "Can you believe it? Me? *A murderer?*" She would laugh. "And nobody believed me when I said an elderly, psychotic hitman with supernatural powers given to him by mysterious voices was going to kill my wife and son?" She would feign shock and say, "Those *bastards!*" He would finish by telling her that he had simply walked out of his unlocked cell, through the station's back end, and to the underground garage, where the hide-a-key and the suit she had left in the Volvo's backseat allowed him to drive past the lot attendant. "You're welcome," she would say.

The escape alarm finally registered.

Fuck, he thought.

There was no room to get past the Jeep. Still, he could not let anything stop him; he had to save his family. He reached under the seat, his fingers searching for and finding the Luger. He set it in his lap and waited, praying he would not have to use it. Praying the Jeep would pull away.

60

Huffy, avoiding a few scrambling officers as he sprinted through the front end, was on his way to the A/V room to meet Frankie. She was already there reviewing surveillance footage. The Christmas Eve skeleton crew assuming the escape alarm had malfunctioned again, allowed Abrams's empty cell to go unnoticed for nearly eight minutes. Adamant he had locked it, Murphy—the last person in the cell before Abrams escaped—had obviously failed to properly secure the door. But it didn't matter. There was no way Abrams would get out of the building.

Huffy rounded a corner and narrowly missed Frankie racing in the opposite direction. He caught her in a few hard strides. "What happened?" he yelled over the wailing alarm.

"After he enters the stairwell, multiple cameras cut out. He might have gotten out of the building."

"*Clara!*" Huffy cried, lengthening his stride and pulling away from Frankie.

"He is on foot," she yelled. "She's safe."

Huffy tore through the front end toward the lobby door, the alarm making it impossible to hear Frankie.

In his car, Huffy smashed a palm against the steering wheel. "*Sonofabitch!*" He twisted the key until he felt it start to warp. The car's starter whirred but still wouldn't catch. Abrams was on foot and wearing an orange DOC jumpsuit, so wouldn't get far, but Huffy was not going to take any chances. "C'mon, you piece of—" The engine finally turned over. He reversed, the car lurching as it crashed over a speed bump. He jammed it into drive, pinned the gas pedal to the mat only to immediately crush the brake. "What the...?" He concentrated hard, trying to determine if what he was seeing was real or a trick of the low light and heavy snowfall. He switched to low beam.

"Fuck," he groaned. He hadn't hit a speed bump.

—

ALLAN EASED TOWARD the attendant booth, the alarm filling the garage with an unbearable, hollow wail. The Jeep was gone, but the steel arm and tiger teeth were blocking his path. He would not make it twenty feet past the booth if he gunned it. He squeezed the Luger—What? Are you going to add cop killer to your rap sheet? He tucked the gun under his leg and slowed to a stop.

"Hey, Doc," the attendant said over the alarm. "Sorry about the racket." He swirled a finger in the air. "Alarm's been malfunctioning since the power outages a few days ago."

Allan stared blankly at the attendant—Rick Johnston—amazed he had not already drawn his weapon and ordered him out of the car. He had been counseling Rick for about a month; he was on non-active duty after being shot trying to stop looters. Allan eyed the steel arm and tiger teeth. "Bad night for a late shift," he said, hoping the alarm had masked the panic in his voice.

A "Tell me about it" eye roll. "You and Clara must be excited," Johnston said, unwilling to let the alarm interfere with a little pre-Christmas small talk. "I tell ya, kids make Christmas magical all over again. I remember—"

"Sorry, Rick," Allan said, assuming Johnston was seconds from realizing the significance of the alarm, the orange "shirt" under his suit, and the sweat pouring off his face. "I'm late for a date with Clara."

Johnston cupped a hand to his ear.

"I have to go."

"Oh." Johnston pressed a button. "No worries."

The steel arm had started to rise, and the tiger teeth were retracting when Johnston jumped out of the booth. Allan reached for the Luger under his leg as Johnston bent down and stuck a hand through the window. "Merry Christmas, Doc." Allan nodded. "You too, Rick." They shook hands; Allan's were clammy and wet.

Johnston retreated into the booth just as someone screamed: "Out of the car! *Now!*"

Allan turned in the direction of the voice. Frankie Bryant was in the middle of the exit ramp a few feet behind the raised steel arm, her legs bent and braced, her gun pointed at him.

He instinctively hammered the gas. The driver's side window exploded, filling his left ear with a deafening hiss. A second bullet punctured the windshield and entered his right shoulder, knocking him hard against the seatback. Frankie refused to give ground.

"She is still alive. You need to get home. Don't stop."

A third bullet grazed his cheek and forced his head back and up, a hand momentarily coming off the steering wheel. The Volvo raised and lowered twice in rapid succession.

Did I hit—

Three more shots, this time from behind, each bullet making a "popping" sound as it blew through the rear window.

Sparks lit the tunnel as the concrete wall shredded the Volvo's passenger side. Cresting the top of the exit ramp, the car caught air and landed hard, sparks as thick as flames exploding from the undercarriage. Allan's body buzzed as though 50,000 volts of electricity were surging through his body. Instead of killing him, the current was filling him with unlimited strength and energy.

—

IN THE ABOVE-GROUND parking lot, Huffy approached what

looked like the body of an elderly man, his grey hair matted with blood that appeared black. The faint but unmistakable *Pop-Pop-Pop* of gunfire turned him around and sent him charging back into the station.

Racing through the lobby, he shouted to Murphy, "Call an ambulance for the old man in the parking lot."

"Huff!" Murphy's volume and sharp tone slowed Huffy to a fast walk. It was Murphy's expression that stopped Huffy in his tracks. "She's in the garage," was all Murphy said.

The escape alarm now silent, Huffy entered the underground garage. Several uniformed officers were standing in a loose circle about twenty feet away. Two of those officers turned when they heard him approaching. When he saw their faces, he knew Frankie was dead.

He stepped inside the circle.

Frankie's left foot was bent in the wrong direction, and blood covered her face. Part of her brain was visible through a large crack in her skull.

Rick Johnston said, "There was an accident on the Parkway, Huff. I got here late and didn't go upstairs. I had no idea we'd arrested him. I thought the alarm was malfunctioning again." Huffy dropped to a knee beside Frankie. "She fired off a few shots before he hit her," Johnston continued, already depersonalizing—*she*, not Frankie. Soon it would be *the Vic*. "I don't know if he tried to hit her or lost control of his car. I got off three shots after he…" A long silence. "I didn't know, Huff. I didn't know."

Huffy took Frankie's still warm hand, his tears splashing on the back of her hand and mixing with her blood. He kissed her fingers. "Whea'd I p*ah*k the f*ah*kin cah?" he whispered, gently setting her hand on her stomach. His cell phone buzzed. His eyes clung to Frankie's shattered body for a long second. He stood and checked his phone. Clara was calling.

By the time he had reached the lobby, he had told her that

Allan had killed Frankie and was probably headed home. And she had told him that she was in labor and the contractions had intensified so rapidly she could no longer drive.

"It's okay," he said, sprinting toward the exit. "Lock everything, kill the power, and hide. Do you have a gun?"

"Why do I need a gun?" Panic had tightened her throat and was hurrying her words. "Can't you get here faster? I'm calling 911 in case he—"

"I can be there before anyone else—"

"But I—"

"I'll call 911!" He didn't realize he was shouting. "Do you have a gun?"

"Yes," she answered, her voice a frightened whisper.

"Do what I said, get the gun, and hide." He hung up and rushed out the door, never hearing Murphy shouting: "Huff! What old man?"

61

In the white-out of falling snow, Allan could barely see past the Volvo's hood. He accelerated, the speedometer closing in on 50 mph. The car seemed to be driving itself.

Approaching the bridge over Angels Gorge, a familiar sensation crawled over him. He checked the rear-view mirror.

"That cop will be here soon," Wilhelm said.

At first, he observed Wilhelm as though he had been in the backseat the entire time. Then, he smashed the brake. The Volvo slid, fishtailing to a shuddering stop near the center of the bridge. He snapped his head around but had trouble finding words.

"How the…" he stammered, staring at Wilhelm in disbelief. "How did…"

Wilhelm peered through the shattered rear window. "I have been watching your wife and that cop. He will protect the child. With his life."

He lifted the Luger off his lap, intending to push it into the center of Wilhelm's forehead and demand he reveal where he'd taken Clara. But a wave of intense pain forced his palms hard against his temples.

"They will get better."

"What will?"

"The headaches. Once you learn to channel their energy for its intended purpose." Wilhelm again checked the rear window. "We need to go."

"What energy? Go where?"

"To your home."

"Why?" Allan demanded.

"You know why."

He thrust the gun toward Wilhelm. "*WHY?*"

Wilhelm remained calm. "I remained in Germany until the war—"

"*Why* do I need to go home? And where's my wife?"

"I tried to find what family I had left," Wilhelm continued, unfazed by the gun inches from his face. "I survived beatings, hypothermia, gas chambers, medical experiments and..." He squeezed his eyes shut, trying to force out whatever memory was flashing through his mind. "My great-grandson was the only family I managed to save." He opened his eyes. "The forces that have helped me all these years are now helping you." His face darkened. "And the forces that have opposed me are working on Clara and the cop."

"I thought *I* was crazy." Allan's words were calm, but his thoughts were rabid: Kill him! Pull the trigger! Shoot him! "But I'm not crazy, you are."

"You must do what so long ago I could not. You cannot allow the death and devastation we have witnessed in our visions to—"

"What do you mean, *our* visions?"

"The child from your visions, your child, will lead a group that will unleash death and suffering on an unimaginable scale. Your child cannot be allowed to lead that group."

Kill him! Allan pulled on the Luger's trigger but stopped one foot-pound short of emptying Wilhelm's skull all over the backseat. I can't kill someone, he thought. You killed Frankie. That was an accident. Kill him! He pressed the gun's barrel into Wilhelm's temple. "Get out," he ordered, using the gun to push Wilhelm's head toward the door.

A howling wind used large snowflakes to batter Allan's eyes and face as he pressed the Luger into Wilhelm's back and forced him against the bridge's rail.

"Shooting me will change nothing. What must be done will be done. By you...or by me."

"*Shut up!*" Allan's legs almost gave out.

"The voices will gain strength. Soon, they will provide you with whatever help you—"

"*SHUT UP!*" He pressed his free hand to his temple. "I am not going to kill anyone. *You are* not going to kill anyone. There are no voices."

"I once faced the choice you face now." Wilhelm leaned over the rail and stared into the darkness below the bridge. "Millions died when I failed to kill my son."

In an unexpected moment of clarity, Allan understood what Wilhelm meant. And like so much else, it fit perfectly into his delusion, even explaining why he had become fixated on Allan's and Kennedy's unborn sons.

"Adolf Hitler was not your son," Allan said. "History books are full of pictures of Hitler's mother and..." The words triggered a memory from one of their first sessions. Wilhelm had said his two children had died young from polio but added that *his* eldest son was killed after the war. Was it possible Wilhelm had a third child? A son? Could that son have been Adolf Hitler? Perhaps a sign that the last of his sanity had slipped away, Allan imagined a young Wilhelm and six other men standing on a stage as the great-great-grandfather of Jerry Springer riled up his raucous nineteenth-century crowd with: "When we come back, I will reveal which of these seven men is Adolf Hitler's *real* father!"

Jerry! Jerry! Jerry!

"Maybe if I had been a better husband," Wilhelm stated regretfully, "a *faithful* husband, my son would not have been born." He sighed. "Even after my infidelity, I had the opportunity to save millions of lives. But I failed to act. I failed to *listen* and *see*. My failure allowed my son to murder millions of innocent people. I will not permit you to repeat that failure."

Icy tears streaked Allan's face. "I am not going to kill anyone." In his mind, he had screamed the words, but they had only enough energy to fall off the end of his tongue.

Wilhelm's face hardened. "Then I must do what you will not."

Wilhelm managed a single step forward before a bullet ripped through his left shoulder and dropped him. He rose to his feet. Allan fired two more shots, both striking the center of Wilhelm's chest and forcing him against the rail. A fourth shot entered his skull an inch above his right eye and sent him toppling off the bridge and into the gorge. Allan rushed to the rail, frozen clouds of air exiting his mouth and nose, the Luger aimed into the darkness as though Wilhelm might float up from the depths like an unkillable slasher from a horror movie.

Suddenly, the feeling he'd had in the Denver cemetery—the unexplainable urge to get home—returned.

62

"**M**ove!" Huffy pounded the car's horn, but the crowd of protesters were ignoring his horn, lights, and siren. He thought about forcing his way through the slow-moving crowd but knew if he tried, some of the protesters would block him in.

"Fuck you, pig!" a passing protester shouted, spitting on the driver's side window.

He'd thought about firing his gun in the air but decided against it. Not because he would get suspended, but because several of the protesters were probably armed and might fire back. He was stuck. Protesters marching for justice were ensuring Clara Abrams received none.

Justice, he thought. What a useless concept—a unicorn chased by fools. An imaginary band-aid slapped over massive, gaping wounds that never healed.

He watched helplessly as the crowd filtered by, the traffic light repeatedly moving from green to yellow to red. He grabbed his phone and punched in 911. Allan Abrams was a threat. Huffy had realized *how* much of a threat when Clara brought him Allan's blood-stained clothes. *I'm leaving him,* she had said. *I don't know what he is capable of.* Huffy had offered to be there when she confronted Allan, but Clara had refused, saying there would be no confrontation; she would wait for him to leave the house, then pack and drive to a hotel. Confident he could get Allan to the station and keep him there, Huffy had relented. It was a decision he regretted when Allan, hysterical, called and said Clara was missing and that he had found her blood on a door. After convincing Allan to come to the station, Huffy had immediately called Clara, praying he had not made a terrible mistake.

Thankfully, she was safe.

Later, after Allan had been arrested and locked in a cell, he called her again. He could hear the immense relief in her voice. But he had also heard something else, something he had heard before but had not recognized. He had questioned his attraction to her, blaming everything from unacknowledged loneliness to the shared loss of a child. Ultimately, he concluded the universe had connected them because it could. He had feelings for her; *why* he had those feelings was irrelevant. What he'd heard in her voice changed everything.

She had feelings for him.

Huffy had not called 911 for one reason: Allan was a threat to Clara, a threat he planned to eliminate.

About to hit send, he noticed a fight had broken out. The fight quickly escalated, and several people became involved. Protesters raced from the intersection. Recognizing the opportunity, he rolled down his window and fired two shots into the air. The remaining protesters scattered, no doubt believing the combatants were now shooting at each other.

Huffy accelerated through the intersection.

63

Another contraction hit; her daughter would be born soon. Clara gripped the handrail at the top of the stairs. My inhaler, she thought, feeling her chest tighten. Where's my inhaler?

The contraction weakening, she followed the flashlight's thin beam into the pitch-black master bedroom. And my phone? she thought. She opened the closet doors. There's no time to get your phone. Get the gun! She thrust the beam randomly around the closet until it landed on an empty shoebox on the floor. Her legs nearly buckled as she stared at the shoebox. Allan had the gun. He killed Liam's boss and was on his way home...to kill her.

Until now, she had been unable to accept he was a threat. She had been holding onto the possibility that her fear related to the twins and her feelings for Liam had tainted her ability to accurately interpret Allan's words and actions. That she was seeing and hearing, not what was real, but what she wanted to see and hear.

Those doubts were now gone.

She unconsciously switched to survival mode. Her body flooded with adrenaline, and time slowed. The flashlight's beam seemed to move itself to the baseball bat propped against the closet wall. That's Allan's blood, she thought, seeing a dark smudge on the bat's barrel. She grabbed the bat, raced into the en suite, and locked the door.

Seated on the toilet, she clutched the bat to her chest. Her skin coated in sweat, she listened to her heavy breathing and pounding heart. Her stomach was rock hard, her contractions continuous, but she felt strong and full of energy. Her asthma was no longer a concern. Perhaps it was because her child was in danger, not from the pregnancy, but from Allan. She had heard of parents gaining superhuman strength to save their children—lifting cars or leaping from burning buildings. Maybe that is what's happening now, she thought. Maybe I'm—

The sound of a car caused her to gasp. She held her breath and prayed it was Liam. She pushed herself to her feet, opened the window, and stuck her head outside. Large snowflakes hit her flushed, sweaty skin and melted instantly. Two-stories below, the ground was a massive white cushion, soft enough to save her if she had to jump. "You won't need to jump," she consoled. "It's Liam. Please, God, let it be—"

"Clara!" a distant voice called out.

Oh, God, she thought. It's Allan.

—

SEATED ON THE en suite floor, her back pressed against the tub, every muscle in Clara's body locked as the contraction peaked. Why isn't Allan calling for me? Did he get into the house? The contraction eased, and her thoughts turned to Liam. Unless a baseball bat could stop bullets, Liam was her only chance. He was her daughter's only chance.

Another contraction started just as the lights came on.

He's in the house!

"Clara!" she heard him call. She wasn't sure from where.

She struggled to stand, the contraction trying to rip a hole in her stomach. The bat in one hand, she crept to the bathroom door. *What if I surprise him?* She pressed her ear against it. *He has a gun!* She unlocked the door. *I could knock him out with the bat and take it.* She inched the door open. *He has a gun! He will kill you!*

Through an inch-wide opening, she saw Allan—the Luger

at his side—standing at the foot of the bed. He was staring at the partially unpacked suitcases like they were the bodies of their four dead children. Her near-breathless gasp snapped his head to the left.

"Clara!"

"Stop!" she shrieked. Panicked, she dropped the bat. He rushed forward. She repeatedly tried to close the bathroom door, but the bat was wedged between the door and the frame. Allan only steps away, she kicked the bat into the bedroom and thrust her shoulder into the door, locking it a split-second before he crashed hard against it.

"Stop!" She was crying now. "*Please*, stop."

"Clara, what's wrong?" The knob twisted and shook, and the door gave a little each time he tried to force it open.

She inched backward, her hand stretched out behind her, feeling for the wall, and her eyes fixed on the door. "The police will be here any second," she warned in a terrified voice.

"You called the police?" His voice sounded excited, scared, and angry all at once. He pounded on the door. "Clara, open the…"

Motionless, she listened. Why did he stop? What is he do—

She cringed at the thought of him backing up to get a run at the door. She stuck her head out the window and surveyed the snow-covered ground two-stories below.

I can't! We won't survive.

64

Allan's forehead remained pressed against the en suite door. The vortex of sound—whispers, guttural howls, groans, and voices—that moments earlier had been swirling around his head was gone. A soft touch had silenced the airy roar. He had rotated his head slowly, freezing at the site of the wrinkled, age-spotted hand on his shoulder. The hand of a man he had shot four times. A man who'd fallen hundreds of feet before being obliterated by jagged, snow-covered rocks.

He should be dead. How come he isn't...

He knew how Wilhelm had survived. It was the final piece of a puzzle he had refused to solve.

Until now.

—

EVERYTHING WILHELM HAD told him was true; he knew that now. The voices, their powers, the people he had killed—including Hitler. All of it was true. From the moment they had met, everything Wilhelm had told him was true.

Sitting on the bed beside Wilhelm and listening to him speak, Allan wondered why he had failed to see it until now. But now that he had, every word Wilhelm spoke was gospel. When he said, "Killing Sedrick Palette ensured you and I would meet," Allan knew it was true. In their first meeting, Wilhelm had said, *Nice to finally meet you.* He had come to Witten for a reason, and when they met, that reason became clear. Had they met under any other circumstances, Allan, no longer in private practice, would have simply referred Wilhelm to someone else.

The voices had helped Wilhelm target and kill Sedrick Palette. And, as Wilhelm had said, the voices were now helping him. His unlocked cell door, a malfunctioning escape alarm, and so much more.

The voices were real.

Allan eyed the locked en suite door. He knew what he had to do. He knew what Wilhelm and the voices had been trying to show him. So much had happened over the last week. Was it only a week? he wondered. Hadn't his dreams of the boy general started seven or eight months ago? Around the time the twins were conceived. And hadn't his migraines intensified around that same time? Had the voices been trying to show him who his son would become for months, not days? How long had Clara known? *Did* she know? His eyes filled with questions that Wilhelm intuitively knew were being asked.

"The dreadlocked man did not die because—"

"I saw you there," Allan interrupted. "In the alley behind the Hostel. *You* killed Kennedy. You saved me."

Wilhelm dropped his chin toward his chest. "I had to allow him to shoot you," he said apologetically. Allan touched the base of his skull and felt a bump. That night in the alley behind the Hostel the bump had been a hole—a wound from a bullet fired by DaMarcus Kennedy. "But you were not seeing what you needed to see," Wilhelm continued.

"Why kill Kennedy's fiancé? And the others?"

A shrug. "I am not sure. Perhaps they had the potential to lead the group in the future." He stood. "Evil does not require much soil to take root. Your child will be born full of hate. That hate will never stop growing. I believe the events occurring now will allow hate to flourish. As mine did, your child will use that hate to fuel a movement, and that movement will gain enough momentum to take control of the most powerful office on earth, and with it, the most powerful armed forces in history. The war will cause more death and destruction than all previous wars combined." A beat. "We cannot allow that to happen."

Allan knew that was true.

"Does Clara also have to…" He could not bring himself to say the words.

"The evil growing inside her and the force protecting that evil are too strong. Like you, she will not understand what is happening; her irrational actions are caused by forces beyond her grasp. She will convince herself that her actions and thoughts are justified. As you once told me, that is how our minds work. We find proof of what we believe."

Wilhelm said Clara had sensed the threat he posed to her child. Allan knew that was true and knew it was why she had wanted him to stop seeing Wilhelm. He didn't, so she sought out Huffy's protection.

"Forces neither understands are connecting them," Wilhelm said. "*Powerful* forces that will stop at nothing to protect the child."

"My overdose," Allan stated, not needing confirmation. "At some point, Clara sensed *I* was a threat."

A somber nod. "She may not have been aware of what she was doing. She may have even convinced herself that she had given you her blood pressure medication during a moment of distraction. But by the time she knocked you unconscious with the baseball bat—the night you saw me outside your bedroom window—she knew the threat you posed. She would have let you die. You would not have, but she could not have known that."

Words the paramedic had said that night suddenly came back to him. *Dispatch info was a male in distress.* I didn't call 911, he thought. Wilhelm did.

Allan again looked at the en suite door. "Why didn't the voices have you kill…" The words "my son" stuck in his throat.

Although he no longer doubted anything Wilhelm said, he was still struggling to accept Wilhelm's purpose for being in Witten. What if the visions, Wilhelm's words, and the odd events and coincidences weren't proof of anything, let alone that an unborn child would one day be responsible for millions of deaths? And if they were proof of what was to come, could that future be changed? Could a single action or a series of actions change that future? Or would every action be the exact action required to ensure that future occurred?

"Perhaps only a parent can unlock the power of such a sacrifice," Wilhelm answered. "Or maybe there is no more powerful test of faith than what you must do now." A long breath emptied him of two lifetimes of pain and left him floating in a sea of immeasurable relief. "However, the most truthful answer is, I do not know. What I do know is I have paid whatever debt I had owed. You must now continue in my—"

He turned abruptly to the window as though someone had called his name.

A question fought its way through Allan's unshakable belief in Wilhelm and the voices. "You told me you could not be *forced* to do anything, that your choices are your own. What if I help my son choose a different path?"

Instead of answering, Wilhelm made his way to the window. With every step, his movements weakened, and his body aged decades. "I understand little about the force that has guided my life's work." He cocked his head and looked high into the night sky. "Except that it is never wrong." He turned back, his expression both apologetic and grateful. He held eye contact for a long moment, then dissolved into an orb of brilliant, white light. Heat exploded from the light like the blast wave from a nuclear explosion. Flames engulfed the bedroom.

Unharmed, Allan watched the light pass through the window and hover briefly outside as if Wilhelm had paused to say goodbye.

He stood, his eyes closed, heat melting the flesh off his

bones.

"Kill one. Save millions."

He opened his eyes. Wilhelm was gone, as was the fire. The room was as it had been.

"You must not fail."

He turned to the locked en suite door…

"She is still alive."

…and charged.

AFTER MIDNIGHT. CHRISTMAS MORNING.

Clara heard a loud crash inside the house. Keep running. Get your keys and get to the Mini. You can make it. Keep running!

"Clara!" she heard Allan call out. She turned as his head disappeared through the en suite window. He would easily beat her to the front of the house. Getting to her car was no longer an option.

"Hide!" a voice screamed.

She took three hard strides toward the shop before a contraction sent her to her knees.

"He's coming! Get up! Hide!"

The voice was her own but also unfamiliar—her conscience seceding from her mind to guide her as an objective third party. That same voice had to be responsible for her overpowering instinct to protect her daughter, an instinct that, despite her attempts to oppose it, caused her to leap from the second-story bathroom window. That same voice, she sensed, was the reason she was not sprawled beneath that window with bones sticking out of her lower body like porcupine quills.

"HE'S COMING! GET UP!"

She pushed herself to her feet and sprinted into the shop, her stomach as tight as a fist, but her pain non-existent. Feeling her way through the darkness, she heard Allan calling her from the backyard. She crouched behind a stack of empty

Christmas decoration boxes. Another contraction hit.

She could feel her daughter's head crown.

—

THE BULB HANGING from a ceiling joist in the backyard shop had steadied; its anemic, yellow glow barely acknowledged by the darkness. He found her in the back corner, hidden among boxes of Christmas decorations. She was seated, shoulders pressed against the wall, knees bent, legs spread so wide he wondered if she had dislocated her hips jumping from the window. She was naked from the waist down, steam from the amniotic fluid rising off the frigid concrete, the air polluted by the coppery smell of blood.

"*NO!*" she cried, her chest heaving—every short, shallow breath freezing the moment it exited her mouth. She crossed her forearms in front of her swollen belly as if flesh and bone could stop a bullet. Light knifing through a gap between two stacks of boxes spotlighted the space between her legs.

He could see a tiny, protruding head.

Shoot! echoed in his skull, his trembling hand barely able to support the Luger's weight. Her crossed arms mirrored his movements as he moved the gun erratically between her head and belly.

"*Stop!*" she wailed, lips stretched and twisted, sweat-soaked hair clinging to her face, eyes wild with pain and anger and helplessness and fear.

Shoot!

Tears stained his cheeks as his finger reluctantly found the trigger. "Forgive me," he whispered, surrendering. He had no choice. He knew that.

SHOOOOT!

My dream! he thought, his finger sliding off the trigger. *I was the one pointing the gun at my son's head.*

Waves of tears were now burning his skin like Holy Water

during an exorcism. After all the failures and heartaches, he was seconds from becoming a father, but these were not the tears he imagined he would cry on this day.

The voices in his head started drowning out Clara and his son.

My son will kill millions of people! But what if I can change —The voices are never wrong! Shoot! But what if—Stop the death and the devastation! Pull the trigger! You must not fail! Kill one to save millions! But—

SHOOOOO—

"Liam!" Clara cried. "In here!"

He listened. In a split-second of silence, he made out the thin, distant voice of Liam Huffy. "Clara!" he was yelling. "Where are you?" He was in the house, too far away to intervene. Too late to stop what was about to happen.

Clara lifted their son like a sacrifice to the gods, his body cut in half by a shard of weak, yellow light—his lower half shrouded in darkness, his face compressed into a mass of wrinkled and bloody skin as his tiny chest heaved and sucked in more air.

"Allan!" Clara screamed.

His eyes met hers.

"Don't kill our—"

66

Don't kill our—

One word would forever haunt him. One word he had heard in time, but that had registered one second too late. Had that word registered a single second sooner, he may have questioned what he believed long enough to stop, or at least long enough for Liam Huffy to reach the shop and stop him.

But it hadn't.

From that day forward, that one word would cause the same recurring nightmare. A nightmare that played from the moment he fell asleep until he woke, trembling and sweating and crying after being transported back in time to relive the events. A nightmare that replayed those events precisely as they had unfolded in real life. The same word heard in time but always registering too late. Too late to stop him from pulling the trigger. Too late to stop the Luger's terrifying blast. And too late to stop its bullet from tearing through soft flesh and skull and brain tissue.

One word.

Don't kill our...*daughter.*

NEW YEAR'S DAY

The church could accommodate a little less than one thousand; more than double that number came. In these circumstances, even during a pandemic, large turnouts were the rule, not the exception. And although well-received, the service had provided little comfort.

The massive church now empty, Liam Huffy held out his hand. Clara Abrams took it. She forced herself to her feet, her glassy eyes settling on a statue of a crucified Christ on the main stage.

"You have closed the investigation?" she asked softly.

He let her fingers slip through his and shook his head. "It is technically still open, but there is plenty of evidence, including his DNA at several homicide locations." Clara's eyes remained on the statue of Christ. "It' isn't justice." He used a crooked finger to catch a tear trickling down her cheek. "But Allan is no longer a threat and will spend the rest of his life in jail."

He watched more tears fall. He wanted to hold her, to comfort her. In one week, he had gone from hardly knowing her to loving her. He signed his divorce papers the day after Christmas, confident the universe had a reason for binding him to Clara in a magical, unexplainable way.

Like father like son, he thought.

He looked around the massive church, then held out his hand.

Clara took it.

CHRISTMAS EVE. SIXTEEN YEARS LATER

In a small room in the south wing of Rodin Psychiatric Hospital, a psychiatrist finished typing a note on her laptop. "I am sure you are sick of the question, but it is on my list. Any head pain?"

Head pain? Allan thought. That is funny.

His terrible dreams and crippling migraines remained, but they had discussed *that* head pain earlier in the session. Her inquiry was about a different kind of head pain.

One day shy of sixteen years ago, he had not doubted the voices existence or their powers. Hunches, instincts, acts of conscience, random changes in direction or plans; all were among the tools the voices used to steer the "Chosen" in the right direction. Good and bad voices competing in a never-ending battle to manipulate free will without overriding it. Great stuff for a novel.

One day shy of sixteen years ago, he had not doubted Wilhelm's story or his purpose for being in Witten. No doubt whatsoever...in his *mind*; it was his heart he had been unable to convince. In the cold, dark shop—a Luger pointed at the "boy general" from his dreams—Allan's heart would not let go of the possibility that his mind had fractured and that that fracture was why he believed Wilhelm's story.

What else besides insanity could explain all that had occurred? Only a fractured mind would believe an innocent child needed to die because he would one day be responsible for the deaths of millions of people. No matter how powerful the proof, a *sane* parent would always have sufficient doubt to stop from doing the unthinkable.

So, no matter how convinced he had been that the voices were real and that he needed to sacrifice his child, Allan knew his mind had fractured. He also knew that fracture had made him a threat to his family—a threat he could not control. Rather than try, he decided to eliminate it, and placed the Luger to his temple and pulled the trigger. Eight days earlier, awake and in bed beside Clara, he had wondered if they had suffered enough.

Apparently, they had not.

A surgeon pointing at an X-ray of a deformed bullet near the center of Allan's brain explained how, after tearing through soft flesh and skull and brain matter, the bullet had lodged in a location that had made it too dangerous to remove. The surgeon then pointed to another bullet near the base of Allan's skull. "I *was* able to remove that bullet," the surgeon had told him, adding that the slug was big enough to drop an elephant. "You should be dead," the surgeon said, adding, "Twice," for good measure. Asked to explain how the large-caliber bullet had come to be there, Allan claimed not to remember, confident the surgeon would not believe what occurred in the alley behind the Hostel.

Any head pain? he thought. That really is funny.

"No," he said to the psychiatrist. It wasn't a lie, not really. The head pain he'd felt for the last sixteen years had nothing to do with the bullet lodged in his brain.

"Would you like to talk about today's visit?" the psychiatrist asked. "You must be a wreck, knowing you are about to meet your daughter for the first time?"

Second time, he silently corrected. He grabbed a pill bottle off a small table and fished out two pills.

"For your blood pressure?"

Other than a recent bout of low blood pressure—a diagnosis he was sure his doctor had fabricated to justify the quarterly check-ups—he was as healthy as he had ever been. His doctor liked to suggest the bullet was blocking an electrical pathway used by the brain to send signals to the internal organs to age. Allan usually chuckled and often said he wished the bullet would block whatever signals his brain was sending to his increasingly wrinkled and age-spotted skin.

"No," he responded, dry-swallowing both pills. "Risperdal." He pocketed the pill case. "I'm delusional, remember?"

"Let's hope the change in medication works." She clicked her tongue. "We are running out of options." She typed a note while asking, "Have you spent any time thinking about what you will say to Levi?"

"Sixteen years," he answered. "Give or take."

Her tender look acknowledged she understood how difficult this was for him.

"What did you tell *your* daughter when she asked about the time you tried to kill her?" He apologized. He stood and started to pace. "How do I explain I believed I had been tasked by omnipotent *voices* to stop my 'son' from killing millions of people? And how, as a psychiatrist, I failed to recognize what was happening?"

"We have talked about this before, Allan. Being a psychiatrist was irrelevant. What you experienced was real to *you*. Despite that, you managed to stop yourself from harming Clara and Levi. That level of awareness during a psychotic break is pretty much unheard of." She slid her laptop into its case. "It might be easier if you have an idea what Levi might ask. Any thoughts?"

He stopped pacing in front of a calendar hanging on the wall. In the picture, snow-covered trees sheltered a small cabin, its windows filled with a warm, yellow glow from a crackling fire, the chimney exhaling a wispy spiral of contented smoke. A single happy-face sticker occupied a single square on the calendar. December 24. Had he considered what questions Levi might ask? He had thought of nothing else since the day he affixed that sticker. And on every one of those thirty-three days, he had come close to canceling. If *thinking* about meeting his daughter could come close to destroying him, what would *actually* meeting her do?

Would seeing her through plexiglass and hearing her through a phone finish tearing him apart? Would knowing that would be as close as he would ever come to her kill what remained of his soul? No hugs and kisses. No holding hands while walking through the park or helping pick out a prom or wedding dress. Seeing her would only remind him of everything he had missed and everything he *would* miss. And for the rest of his life, that knowledge would twist the knife he had plunged into his own heart sixteen years earlier.

But he didn't cancel.

"I don't know what she might ask. But she needs something from me. The least I can do is give it to her."

She retrieved a sheet of paper from her laptop case and handed it to him. "Clara passed on information Levi wanted you to have."

He glanced at the paper but didn't read it; he didn't need to. Over the years, he'd kept tabs on Levi. It was a project he'd started the day he started his sentence at Rodin. Day one of eight thousand and thirty. The security footage from the Hostel and the Circle K was useless. His Volvo appeared on both, but images of him were from the wrong angle or blurred or obscured just enough to make him unrecognizable. But there was plenty of *other* evidence, including his DNA at or near several homicide locations. But none of that impacted his decision to forego a trial.

In the death of Sedrick Palette, he had pleaded guilty to manslaughter after accepting the DA's theory that he had manipulated Palette into killing himself and supplied him with the drugs and tools to do it. He had also pleaded guilty to the First-Degree murder of multiple RUV members, including

DaMarcus Kennedy, and Second-Degree murder in the cases of Olivia Madson and Frankie Bryant.

Forty-four years reduced by half in exchange for saving taxpayers the cost of a trial. Twenty-two years for murders he still had no memory of committing. Murders he was confident, both then and now, he had *not* committed. But what he *had* done was come close to killing his daughter. And for that, twenty-two years seemed a few lifetimes short of adequate. So, he pleaded guilty to protect Clara and Levi and atone for the one death he *was* responsible for.

Whether an accident or intentional (he still was not sure), Frankie Bryant's death had haunted him for sixteen years, his pain peaking every New Year's Day on the anniversary of her funeral.

Without a body (or any records to prove the "victim" even existed), he faced no charges related to Vilhelm N. Weissand.

He set the paper on the coffee table.

"Are you aware that Liam Huffy will be with Levi and Clara?"

He nodded.

Eleven years ago, he had asked a friend for an updated picture of Levi. The friend dropped off a photocopied Christmas card. Spelled out in blue Christmas lights across the top of the card was **MERRY CHRISTMAS FROM THE HUFFY'S**. Five years old at the time, Levi was wearing a red and white dress and had reindeer antlers protruding from under her strawberry-blonde hair. Liam was behind Clara and Levi, a hand resting gently on their shoulders.

He did not blame Clara for moving on. After all, their separation on the day Levi was born hadn't exactly been stolen from the pages of a Nicholas Sparks novel, so "I'll wait for you" were not words he'd expected to hear. And Clara and Levi looked happy. Based on how the world had changed over the years, how hate and violence had solidified the *new normal*, he felt better knowing Liam was there to protect them.

When asked about the family member missing from the Christmas card, Allan's friend said Hiccup had never accepted Levi, biting her on multiple occasions. "He is living in bliss at a home for the elderly," the friend had said.

The most recent news had come a few months ago when Levi became the first junior to make her High School's *senior* debate team. Smart, he remembered thinking, followed by: First woman POTUS?

An hour after the session ended, most of which Allan spent trying to stop anxiety from burning a hole in his stomach, a heavy-set orderly opened the room's steel-reinforced door and barked, "Let's go."

Allan followed the orderly through a series of halls, stopping when he saw the door to the visiting room.

"Move your ass," the orderly ordered, opening the door.

Allan wiped his hands across his chest; sweat stained his orange jumpsuit. Seeing his daughter for the second time in sixteen years, his tears were instant. Apart from her long, strawberry-blonde hair pulled into a braid, she was Clara's teenage twin. The thought of twins sparked a migraine. Despite its other magical qualities, the bullet lodged in his head had intensified his migraines and increased their frequency.

Clara and Liam, holding hands, were beside the door about twenty feet behind Levi. Clara, the effects of age largely absent, was looking randomly around the room, her eyes determined to avoid the man who'd come so close to killing her child. Liam's eyes were cold and unwavering and locked onto Allan—a silent but unmistakable warning.

Allan sat in the stall and lifted the phone to his ear. Levi, already seated with the phone at her ear, offered an uncertain smile.

"Hi." His tears continued to fall. "Happy birthday...and Merry Christmas, too, I guess."

"You too," she said. "Christmas, I mean."

Her voice was both confident and anxious. Knowing she was also nervous was oddly comforting. As she had likely done a thousand times, Levi asked her mom for support. In this case, the support solicited with an unsure glance over her shoulder. Her olive skin glowed like her mother's had whenever Clara was pregnant. She was beautiful. He could not stop his tears.

"It's okay," she said, consoling him.

He felt like a child being soothed by a parent. "N-n-no, it isn't," he sobbed. "I'm s-so sorry. I—" He took a moment and tried to compose himself. "I was sick. I was *so* sick. I th-thought I was pro-*tecting* you and k-keeping you safe from—"

"It's alright. I'm good."

He used his free hand to wipe tears from one cheek then the other. "I b-bet you c-can't tell this is the ha-happiest day of my life." Sharing a laugh helped settle him. "I'm surprised your mom let you come."

"It wasn't easy." She glanced over her shoulder at Clara. "But we compromised."

Your mom's good at that, he thought, hearing Clara in Levi's voice and wit. In her eyes, he saw questions. He knew she had come with a purpose. The possibilities were endless, but he would give her whatever she needed. He owed her that.

"Is there something you need from me?" he asked tenderly.

She bit her lip and lowered her chin to her chest. For the first time, she resembled the teenager she was, not the woman she had so far shown herself to be. "Yeah…but I don't know how to…I'm scared to…"

His stomach nearly emptied; the fear she felt was his fault.

"It's okay," he reassured. "You can ask me anything."

She blew out a slow breath. "Mom said you used to hear voices. Is that true?"

He had tried to anticipate and have an answer for every

question she might ask, but that question surprised him. It rumbled around his brain for a while.

"I—"

"And the voices told you, you know, to kill us?"

"I was sick, sweetheart." His migraine smashed his brain violently against the inside of his skull. He rubbed his temples. "I'm *still* sick. But I could never have hurt—"

"Mom said you also had bad dreams." Unable to focus, his eyes wandered around the room. Without realizing it, he answered her with a distracted nod. "Did the dreams feel real?" she continued.

His racing mind produced another distracted nod.

Tears rolled down her cheeks, each one dissolving a hole in his heart.

"Thanks for being honest." Relief brightened her face and peace settled in her eyes. "I was scared to come. I wanted to cancel, like, a *million* times. A part of me needed to talk to you, but another part warned me to stay away. Does that make any sense?" She continued before he could answer. "I've had a weird dream for as long as I can remember. I thought I was a real psycho until I overheard mom and dad talking about your…"

It took all his strength to conceal how crushed he was to hear her call Liam, *dad*.

"…and that's when I knew we had to talk." She lowered her voice as though wanting only him to hear. "It's always a version of the same dream. I'm some big military leader, and lots of people are dead. It's weird, but it feels like I'm watching news being broadcast from the future. Like it's real, not a dream." She remained oblivious to the astonishment spreading across his face. "Did you ever feel like you were meant to be just one thing?"

Yes, he thought. A father.

She smiled. An innocent smile. The smile of a sixteen-year-old unaware of what the world was capable of. "Maybe that's my destiny. Who knows, maybe one day I will be the first girl—sorry, *woman* President." Her smile widened. "I could pardon you." She giggled nervously and turned to Clara.

Suddenly, the image of the boy general rolled through his mind. He had seen his profile so many times—never his face, always his profile: high cheekbones, soft jawline, smooth, olive-colored skin. No, he thought, staring at the pyramid of freckles below Levi's right ear. No. It isn't possible. But he knew it was. The boy's jawline and features weren't soft because he was young; they were soft because the "boy" general was a girl. His daughter, not his son.

"You must not fail," he heard. "She is still alive."

She, he thought...

The thumping in his head began to ease.

...not Clara...

Then waned to a low hum.

...Levi.

ACKNOWLEDGEMENT

In addition to our families, we have so many to thank, including everyone who purchased a copy of Voices. Jason and I sincerely hope you enjoyed it. If not, feel free to contact us via our website. We are continually trying to improve our writing and storytelling.

www.jmspratnerauthor.com.

We would also like to thank Ted & Katy, Randall, and Sandy.

BOOKS BY THIS AUTHOR

Coming Soon...

Visit our website to sign up for special pricing on our next novel, Fortress.

Home sweet home?

www.jmspratnerauthor.com

CAUTION! HUGE SPOILERS AHEAD!

We thought it might be fun to share some thoughts on *Voices* and point out things you may not have noticed.

1. What is *Voices* about? Jason's original thought nugget was: *What if a street-corner preacher knew something we didn't?* I read his screenplay and said, "Wow! This really sucks. But given enough time and effort, we could turn it into a cool novel." So, we used the premise to explore the question: Could you kill your child to save the world? My answer has always been: No, I couldn't. IMHO, a parent who is not psychotic (which is probably why Jason and I disagree on this issue) would always find reasons to doubt the "proof." Jason, the cold-hearted bastard that he is--did I mention he's a lawyer?-- believes he could make that sacrifice. I suppose we agree, but only in theory. What proof could you see that you would not find a way to discredit/discount, at least enough to stop from offing your offspring? And would you also not believe you could change that future by changing your child?

2. What (who?) are *the voices*? Again, Jason and I disagree on this. (For those keeping score, I'm right again, and he is wrong: Mike - 2, Jason - 0.) Jason's theory is the voices are a random, vague force influencing people all willy-nilly (or something nonsensical like that. I'm not sure, I wasnt really listening to him). My theory is that *the voices* are more akin to our conscience. Deep down, most adults know whether their actions/words are right or wrong. We may justify them, or try to convince ourselves our niggling little voice is wrong, but deep down, we know. To me, that is the essence of *the voices*. They are that niggling voice constantly trying to manipulate our free will without overriding it.

3. Here are some anagrams we used. Levi=Evil; Rien Gerhard=Red herring; Vilhelm N. Weissand=Heaven's mind's will; J.M. Spratner =**"J"**ason + **"M"**ike + **"Partners."** I was pretty drunk for most of this, so I probably forgot quite a few.

4. Jason chose the surname "Abrams" to hint at the story of God asking Abraham to sacrifice his son, Isaac. We also used the name "Isaac" in the story. Jason chose "Clara" because Hitler's mother's name was Klara.

5. Many of the numbers in the story (i.e. digital clock readouts) correspond to bible verses. Example: At the end of chapter 11, the time 2:22 references Genesis 22:2, which is God telling Abraham to sacrifice his son, Isaac. And

3:12 references John 15:12, which tells us to love one another "as I have loved you." In Chapter 53, the time 8:32 references Romans 8:32, which talks of God sacrificing his son.

6. Was Allan crazy, or is Levi destined for some really bad shit? Our intent was to create the possibility that, yes, Allan lost his mind. Wouldn't any sane parent be more likely to think they'd lost their mind and not: *Well, I suppose Junior has got to go. Marge! Where's my dang hatchet?* In our view, the answer is no, Allan is not crazy, and, yes, Levi is destined for some really bad shit.

7. We wanted to put it out there that hindsight is clear re Hitler/The Holocaust/etc. There were signs people should have seen, and many did but ignored. We wanted to ask: What if that is occuring again now? What if the division, hate, partisanship, and other bullshit are seeds for the next great conflict?

8. Jason and I are huge Stephen King fans and both think he is one of the greatest storytellers of all time. I am also a huge *Seinfeld* fan. Hence the multiple references to *Seinfeld* and SK.

9. Yes, it is true that a male MCDA twin can lose a Y chromosome and become female (and that female child will have Turner Syndrome). On that note, we thought it cool/ironic that the RUV--an organization founded on the principal of "purity and perfection"--would end up with a leader, who, by their definition, would not be "Pure and Perfect." It was a shot at hate organizations, and people who hate. They are flawed/misguided/hypocritical, but they either can't see it, or they are willfully blind to it when it suits their cause. Is it wrong for me to say I hate people who hate?

10. Sorry we killed Frankie; we really liked her.

11. Our biggest struggle. Jason is an accomplished screenwriter but had never written a novel (they are vastly different animals), and I am still learning how to write well (it will be a *long* journey!!). We struggled with a lot of things (writing a novel is incredibly difficult, and writing a *good* novel is almost impossible), but our biggest struggle was convincing readers that Allan was a normal dude whose biggest wish was to be a father, then, a week later, he's "lost his mind" and might kill his child. If we failed to convince readers of that possibility, then we felt we could not place Allan's child in proper jeopardy and the last third of the story would not work as well as it could. We hope we succeeded.

*AND NOW FOR SOMETHING
COMPLETELY DIFFERENT.*

Got a book club? Want to Zoom chat with world famous authors about their book?

Well, we can't help you with the latter, but if you have a Book Club and want to read one of our books and review it with us during a 1-hour Zoom chat, we would be happy to oblige. Just contact us through our website for details. Also, if you have questions about *Voices* we would be happy to answer them.

www.jmspratnerauthor.com

ABOUT THE AUTHOR

Jason Mcculloch

Jason became the world's youngest billionaire after his parents were gunned down outside a local movie theater. His secret life as a vigilante crime fighter came to a crashing halt when he lost everything investing in Olivetti portable typewriters and some sort of robot butcher. Jason then parlayed a law degree into a Partnership at a 100-year-old law firm. Jason and his family live in Edmonton, Alberta. Jason is an award-winning screenwriter, and his screenplays have placed in the top half of one percent in the prestigious Nicholl Fellowship; an annual screenwriting competition organized and judged by the same folks who bring us the Oscars.

ABOUT THE AUTHOR

Mike Johnson

Mike lives in Edmonton, Alberta, with his wife, Molly, and their children. Chi-chi, the middle child, is a ferocious 6lb Mexican with no concept of size. Chloe, the youngest, is a rescue, and Boots, the oldest, is a needy Persian. M & M also own three real children; all are for sale. Mike has self-published 3 children's illustrated books centered around character development (topics like compassion, sharing, and honesty). The Barry & Friends series is available in 13 languages and 78 countries. Okay, that isn't true, but is it really a lie if it has the potential to be true? Mike also self-published a real estate investment book and guide, which is available in 13 languages and...er, never mind.

Manufactured by Amazon.ca
Bolton, ON